PARNO'S DESTINY
The Black Sheep of Soulan: Book 2

Creative Texts Publishers products are available at special discounts for bulk purchase for sale promotions, premiums, fund-raising, and educational needs. For details, write Creative Texts Publishers, PO Box 50, Barto, PA 19504, or visit www.creativetexts.com

PARNO'S DESTINY
The Black Sheep of Soulan: Book 2
by N.C. REED
Published by Creative Texts Publishers
PO Box 50
Barto, PA 19504
www.creativetexts.com

The following is a work of fiction. Any resemblance to actual names, persons, businesses, and incidents is strictly coincidental. Locations are used only in the general sense and do not represent the real place in actuality.

ISBN: 978-0692679685

PARNO'S DESTINY

N.C. Reed

TABLE OF CONTENTS

CHAPTER ONE

-

"I don't understand why you don't want me with you! You may need me!"

Parno McLeod, youngest son of Tammon McLeod, King of Soulan, and newly appointed Lord Marshal of the Army, rubbed the space between his eyes as he tried to reason with Doctor Stephanie Corsin-Freeman.

"I have explained this before," he said patiently. "It isn't that I don't want you with me. In fact, your absence may very well be the death of some of my own men. But I need you here, training new field surgeons, much more. The few lives you might save in the West may well pale in comparison with the lives your trainees save in the years ahead."

"Years?" Freeman was taken aback by that. "But. . .but I thought. . .I mean you completely destroyed the enemy at the Gap, Parno! How much longer can the war last, with that done?"

"Stephanie, we destroyed only a small part of the Army that the Nor have arrayed against us. That field army was a bold dash, at best. An attempt to end the war early by conquering the heartland of the Kingdom. There are two much larger armies attacking us in the West. And so far, they are prevailing. Slowly, yes, but they advance each day."

"The Nor Emperor has put too much into this effort to quit. He has devoted years to this one task; to enslave us, or destroy us. He will not stop until he has done that, or we have completely defeated him. There can be no peace between our peoples, so long as their Imperial line remains intact."

"All the more reason I should be with you, then!" Freeman rallied. "You *need* me. If something were to happen to you, then we might all suffer the consequences."

"You know that's not true," Parno replied, uncomfortable with the importance she placed on him. "There are many fine generals who can command at least as ably as I can. Certainly, some can command better, in fact."

"But *you* are the one who has produced a victory," Freeman snapped back. "None of them have."

Parno nodded in silent acknowledgment of that fact. His victory at the Gap, Pyrrhic though it was, had been a clear victory. But he knew that the war in the west would be different. Bloodier.

Much bloodier.

In the western lands he would have no natural barriers on which to base his defense. Wide open territory favored an aggressive attacker, with no cities to defend. He could move about at will, and not worry about what his enemy did.

"You aren't going," Parno said finally. "Period. You were at the Gap. Wasn't that enough combat for a lifetime?" *It was for me*, he didn't add.

Freeman sighed heavily, almost in defeat. She knew Parno was right. That didn't mean she had to like it.

"Very well, Parno McLeod," she said at last. "But if anything happens to you, if you die, I'll..." she trailed off, as if she had suddenly revealed more than she had meant to.

"I'll keep that in mind," he said seriously. In truth, he wished she were able to go. He would miss her, more than he wanted to admit. Despite their having gotten off to a rocky start, the two had settled into a fairly comfortable relationship. One that had grown considerably in the last few months.

"You had better," was all Freeman could muster.

"I appreciate the work you're doing," Parno offered an olive branch. "My men appreciate it too. If not for you, many of them would be lying at the Gap, instead of recovering in the hospital."

-

Parno McLeod looked at the assembled men before him. Where once there would have been an entire regiment of his now famed Black Sheep, there was barely a battalion remaining. Their losses at The Gap had been less than the other units involved, but they had been grievous none the less. After the hasty reorganization of the remaining forces, there were two battalions of men assembled before him.

The remaining Black Sheep would accompany him to the front where 2nd Corps was locked in combat with a large enemy force in the western part of the Kenty and Tinsee provinces. Just two days prior Parno's father, King Tammon of Soulan, had appointed Parno Lord Marshall of the Army of Soulan, commander of all military forces in the kingdom. A post once held by his brother, Therron.

But Therron would soon be relieved, by the Inspector General no less, for gross insubordination. He would be stripped of not only his duties and title, but also of his place as Heir Secondary to the throne of Soulan. Parno hoped that everything would be done by the time he reached the front.

The other battalion was an ad hoc formation consisting of the survivors of the other units involved at the battle of The Gap. Led by Colonel Bret Chad, these men would delve into the Kent province, hoping to retrieve their families from underneath the Norland forces now occupying most of their province. It was a dangerous mission, but one that Parno had promised them they could undertake as soon as possible. He owed them nothing less after their heroic efforts to prevent the large Norland army from invading the heartland of the Soulan Kingdom through the lightly guarded Gap. With that done, they would return their families to Cove Canton, and remain as a guard for the families and facilities there, while training, and refitting, as a battalion in Parno's own regiment.

"Morning, milord," Karls Willard, commander of Parno's Black Sheep, spoke as he rode up beside Parno.

"Good morning, Karls," Parno replied, broken from his reverie. "Are we ready?"

"That we are, milord," Karls' brother, Enri replied from beside him. Enri had been promoted from his position as Captain of the House Guard to Brigadier, and was now Parno's top military adviser.

"Captain Parsons has made arrangements for a squad of his Scouts, under Lieutenant James, to accompany Chad's men into Kent," Karls nodded. "They can depart at any time as well."

"Excellent," Parno nodded. He looked around for a moment, as if seeking comment from someone else, then caught himself. Darvo Nidiad wasn't there.

Not anymore, he thought sadly to himself. *I saw to that, didn't I?*

Darvo Nidiad had been Parno's retainer since the young prince had been out of diapers. Losing him at The Gap had struck Parno harder than anything else in his entire life had. But there was another presence now, as there had been then, to take up at least some of the enormous space left by the death of the wise old soldier.

"I believe we are in readiness, Parno," Cho Feng said softly. Feng had been a prisoner in the Jax Territorial Prison when Parno had started to recruit his new regiment, what seemed like so long ago. Impressed by the Oriental's demeanor, Parno had taken him from the prison that very day. Feng had been a fountain of military knowledge, having served as a training officer in his own nation's Imperial Army. His conditioning techniques and sword training had been invaluable to the men in Parno's regiment. His wealth of strategic knowledge has been even more valuable to the young Prince, who found himself thrust into a life and death struggle to defend his homeland.

Feng's presence did nothing to ease Nidiad's absence, but it was a comfort to Parno, none the less. He had learned not only to trust, but to depend upon Feng.

"Very well," Parno nodded, leaving his thoughts about his old friend behind. "Let's get under way." He spurred his horse over to where Colonel Chad sat, conferring with his new officers. The battalion he would lead was fragmented by the fact that the men under his command were from five different organizations. Organizations that had all but ceased to exist at the Gap.

"Bret," Parno spoke easily as he reined in by Chad's side.

"Milord," Chad smiled. Chad had once had the same opinion of Parno as most people in Soulan. The Prince was likable enough, but little more than a womanizing, brawling playboy. That attitude had changed forever during the battle. Chad and his surviving troopers owed Parno their lives and more.

"Any problems?"

"None but the normal, milord," Chad shrugged. "We'll have our organization difficulties squared away on the trail. We'll overnight at the Gap, then head on into Kent. My main concern is that some of the Nor army that hit us there will still be in the field. I don't expect any organized resistance, but I do expect to encounter bands of soldiers acting as brigands and the like. We'll avoid them where possible, until our mission is finished. After that, we'll do what we can to run them to heel."

"Do nothing to endanger your men, or your families," Parno ordered. "We'll repair whatever damage they can do. Once your men are refitted and retrained, you have my permission to take your unit back into Kent at your discretion and destroy any roaming bands you find." Chad's face split into a predatory grin at that.

"Aye, milord. It will be as you say."

"Godspeed then, Colonel," Parno extended his hand. Chad took it, nodding.

"Thank you, milord."

"Karls," Parno spoke as he reigned his horse around. "Let's be about it then."

"Column of fours, Major Seymour," the younger Willard ordered. The battalion snapped around at the order, and the troopers began filing out of Cove Canton, on their way west.

Toward the war.

-

Stephanie Corsin watched them go, a single tear trailing down her cheek. She cared very deeply for Parno McLeod. She acknowledged that only when she was alone in her thoughts, but recognized the truth of it none-the-less. She had come here only because Roda Finn had promised her she would be teaching real world medicine to field surgeons who would undoubtedly save many lives on future battlefields. It had been a challenge she could not turn down.

She hadn't thought much of Parno then. But seeing him in action, day after day, had slowly changed her opinion of him. Now, she truly didn't know what she would do if something were to happen to him.

And Parno seemed intent on ignoring her. Well, not ignoring, but. . .he seemed singularly uninterested in pursuing any sort of relationship with her. She knew the war and his new responsibilities weighed heavily on him, but still.

Suddenly inspiration struck her. There was one person she knew who held great sway over the Prince. And that someone was close by.

She would visit the Duchess of Cumberland.

-

"Milord, there's little doubt we're heading into a rare mess," Enri Willard commented as he rode beside the Prince.

"Do you mean the steadily advancing enemy, or the fact that my brother has been relieved of his post?" Parno asked, just short of being sarcastic.

"Either. Both."

"I know," Parno sighed. "But orders are orders. The King has decreed all this, Enri. And we have to stop the Nor advance. They are already too deeply into our territory. Every day they remain renders valuable crop land useless to us, and gives them time to establish themselves. Even if we drive them out right away, how many spies and saboteurs will they have left behind?"

"We'll root them out, Parno," Karls said grimly. Enri shot a warning glance at his brother, hearing him address the Lord Marshall so familiarly. Karls ignored him. He had earned his familiarity to Parno, and Parno encouraged it. Karls Willard was far more than the commander of Parno's personal regiment. He was the brother that Parno had always wanted but never had.

"I know, Karls," Parno nodded. "But what damage might they cause in the meantime? Meanwhile, there is a Nor army camped upon our land. One that outnumbers us greatly and is better trained than any we've ever faced. At the Gap, we had terrain on our side and Roda's wizardry. On the plains, we'll have neither. Not for a while, anyway."

Roda Finn, the cackling genius whose hard work had enabled the small force to hold the Gap against such overwhelming odds, was even now on his way to Nasil with a ten-man escort and a King's Writ to establish a larger, better equipped laboratory and factory with which to develop and produce his weaponry. If Soulan was to have any chance to win the war, they needed Finn's weapons.

There was more they needed, too. The physical training given the men in Parno's Black Sheep had proven its worth over and over during the four-day battle at The Gap. Their hellish training regimen had toughened the soldiers in Parno's regiment to the point that even on the fourth day, as they stood back to back being over-run, they were a match for any two or three Nor attackers.

That was toughness Parno intended to pass on to the rest of the Soulan Army. Parno had never imagined he would find himself in a position of authority in his father's government, let alone the Lord Marshall of the Army of Soulan. He had been the despised son for all his life and had expected that to remain the case. But in the space of week, that had all changed.

Parno intended to use his new authority over the Soulan Military to make the Army of Soulan the strongest, toughest and best equipped force on the continent if not the world. Never again so long as he could help it would his people suffer an invasion by the Nor. He would work to pass that ethic along to every soldier in the army, from the highest general to the rawest recruit.

First however, he had to ensure that there was a Soulan to defend. And at the moment that looked to be a daunting task. Soulan was under attack by forces that greatly outnumbered their own. To make matters worse, the Nor army was better trained and equipped than ever before.

And for the first time, the Nor had allied themselves with the Wild Tribes of the West. The Wildland folk were ferocious fighters, though they often lacked the discipline to fight as a cohesive unit. For generations parents had used the specter of the Wild Folk to frighten their children against bad behavior. Those threats were now a reality that no one wanted to think about.

So far, the Soulan Third Corps and its attached Militia units were holding the Nor on their own side of the Great River. Parno didn't know how long that would last, but he had to hope that General Raines could continue holding because he needed to concentrate on the more immediate threat.

A huge Nor army, numbering somewhere around two hundred thousand, was steadily pushing the First and Second Army Corps south. Already the Nor were into the Tinsee Valley, and they gained ground nearly every day. It was all General Davies could do to slow the advancing Nor juggernaut. Pushing them back seemed impossible, for now.

And the King, Parno's father, expected him to change that. The fact that for once he had Tammon McLeod's confidence did nothing to bolster Parno's own. Right now, he didn't see a way to make his father's wishes into a reality.

-

The Soulan Army Headquarters in the Field was a busy place, with couriers arriving and leaving almost constantly bearing dispatches, orders, and reports. The arrival of the Inspector General and his entourage was not unnoticed, but no one really thought much of it, either. Just another General.

But this was much more serious. The Inspector General's face was set in a grim frown as he and his personal aides approached the Headquarters tent of 2nd Corps. Davies looked up as the Inspector General entered, and stood, saluting.

"General Brock," Davies spoke. "We weren't expecting you, sir."

"I know," Brock returned the salute. "There's a reason for that. I have sealed orders for you from the King himself." He handed over a simple leather folder, which Davies took with some trepidation. He opened the folder, removing a single document sealed with the King's seal.

With trembling fingers, Davies opened the document. Was it his recall? He had lost the bridges at Lovil after all, and was currently losing ground almost daily against the Nor advance. Casualties had been very heavy as well.

He read the letter through, his face growing pale as the impact of the orders hit him. He looked up at Brock, who remained stone faced, then back to the letter, reading it again. Finally, with a long-held breath rushing out, he sat heavily in his chair.

"I. . .I don't. . . ." he trailed off, unable to find the words.

"I know," Brock nodded. "I was the same way. But the evidence is. . .well, it's true."

"What do you need from me?" Davies asked.

"The Prince's Own must be contained until this is over," Brock said simply. "I realize that your forces are strained, but I can't have them interfering. Understand?" Davies nodded.

"I have sufficient forces to. . .to ensure that they aren't an issue," he informed the Inspector. "I would never have imagined. . . ."

"None of us would have," Brock's face was hard. "But the facts are there, plain and simple."

"Who's to take command of the Army?" Davies asked.

"Parno McLeod," Brock said flatly. Davies' face flushed.

"You can't be serious!" His tone bordered on disbelief, if not outright derision.

"Watch how you say that, General," Brock warned. "And be aware that Prince Parno, with a command of less than five thousand men, most of them militia and prisoners, defeated a Nor army numbering at least fifty thousand strong just days ago at Cumberland Gap."

"He did?" Davies' face showed its shock. "I assumed that the forces from 1st Corp-"

"Arrived in time to clean up the field, nothing more," Brock said firmly. "It seems that the Black Sheep Prince is something of a lion on the battlefield," he almost grinned. Almost.

"When will he arrive?" Davies asked.

"He's on his way now I'm given to understand, but that's not my problem," Brock shrugged. "My problem is Therron McLeod. And his regiment. And his personality cult."

"This news will end his personality cult," Davies said grimly, holding the dispatch he'd been given in his hand. "No one will follow him now."

"Are you sure of that, General?" Brock asked. "I'm not. Nor is His Majesty. Hence the need for. . .discretion."

"What do I tell the others, then?" Davies asked.

"Prince Therron is ill," Brock shrugged. "He isn't aware of how ill just yet, but that's my concern. He'll be taken back to Nasil where the King will deal with him as is necessary. That's all I know. All I need to know." There was a finality in his tone that almost dared Davies to challenge him on that point.

"Very well," Davies refused the challenge. "Give me an hour and I'll have troops in place to deal with the Prince's Own. Will that be sufficient?"

"It will," Brock nodded. "I'll take care of the rest. Per the King's order, you're in command until Prince Parno arrives. You have his full confidence and support. His own words."

"Please extend my thanks to His Majesty," Davies bowed his head humbly. "Now, I have arrangements to make."

-

Therron McLeod looked up crossly from his desk as General Brock entered his tent without announcement or permission. He was followed by four of his own men,

"Even the Inspector General is required to observe protocol, Brock," Therron all but snarled.

"I'm about to," Brock said firmly. "Prince Therron McLeod, by order of the King, Tammon McLeod, you are relieved of your duties as Lord Marshall of the Armies of Soulan and will return with me at once to Nasil, where you will await the King's pleasure." Brock motioned his men forward without waiting for a reply.

"What is the meaning of this!" Therron shot to his feet. "Guards!"

"Save your breath, your treacherous swine," Brock snarled. "Your men are nowhere near, and in no shape to come to your assistance. Come quietly and leave with some dignity and respect intact, or you can allow the soldiers outside to see you drug from your quarters for treason."

"Treason!" Therron shouted. "On who's authority!"

"I may have mentioned the King, when I entered?" Brock replied. "Bring him," he ordered the quartet of men. Brock was in no mood for dallying with a man who would refuse his King's orders. Or place the entire kingdom in danger because of some kind of sibling rivalry.

The former Lord Marshall's ambulance, his personal transport, was already waiting outside. Therron noted that the driver was not his normal man. A glance around him confirmed that none of his men remained around him.

"I'll have your head on a mantel piece for this, Brock," Therron warned before he was shoved into the ambulance. The four guards followed him aboard.

"We shall see," Brock replied, his voice taunt with anger. He nodded to the driver who clucked the team into motion, headed south. The company of troops assigned to the General's command followed save for the squad that would accompany Brock.

"General, Godspeed," he turned to Davies. "Prince Parno should be here in a few days, a week at most."

"We'll await his arrival before making any large movements," Davies nodded.

"A word of advice, General," Brock decided to try and help Davies, if he could. "The boy will listen to you if you don't treat him like a simpleton. He's very bright and has an excellent mind for both tactical and strategic thinking. And despite his victory at the Gap you'll find that he is in no way arrogant or unapproachable."

"I'll remember," Davies promised.

"I must go," Brock motioned for his horse, and a trooper moved to bring the mount near. "God be with you and the Army, General Davies."

"Thank you, sir," Davies saluted. Brock sketched a return salute, and then was off at a gallop, trailing the ambulance.

"Well," Davies said, more to himself than anyone else. "I guess we'll see."

-

Memmnon McLeod walked the high walls of the palace grounds in Nasil, as he did each morning. It was his quiet time. The time he used to try and clear his mind for the day's duties ahead of him.

These days, he needed that.

The war was going badly and no amount of bravado, false cheer, or patriotic fervor could disguise that fact. It was doubtful that the people in the southern reaches of the kingdom knew the complete disaster that had befallen Soulan, but word was spreading. And all the provinces knew their militia units had been called to duty.

New units were even now being trained and Memmnon wished with all his might that Parno's instructors were able to be the training officers for these new units. What Parno and his men had done was nothing short of remarkable.

All the wishes in the world would not make it so, however. And some of the new units, as well as the old, were at Cove Canton undergoing the rugged individual training that Parno's own men had gone through.

If we had more time, we could field an entire corps of men so trained, he thought. *But time is the one commodity that we no longer have access to.*

He looked at the sun, estimating the time. By now, if things went according to schedule, Therron would be on his way back to Nasil, technically under arrest. Memmnon still had his doubts about how all that would play out in the end. It had been Tammon's decision not to mention the treason that both father and son suspected of the Lord Marshall. Former Lord Marshall, Memmnon corrected himself.

Which made him think of Parno, even now moving west with all that remained of his magnificent command that had served so well at the Gap. It was hoped that Parno would be able to turn things around in the west. If he could stop the Nor advance, let alone push it back, then it would buy precious time for other movements to be made.

But could he do it? There was no question that Tammon had laid a terrible burden upon the shoulders of his youngest son. A son that he had despised from the moment he was born. They all had. The entire royal family, and by extension the entire household, had ostracized Parno his entire life, blaming him for the death of their much-loved Queen who had died due to complications of childbirth minutes after Parno was born.

The only exception had been Darvo Nidiad, Parno's military retainer and trainer. The old soldier had served as Parno's surrogate father, giving him the love and attention that should have rightfully come from the rest of them.

And now Darvo was gone. Killed in action at the Gap.

Memmnon hoped that Parno would be able to cope without the steady influence of Nidiad's hand. True, he had other loyal retainers, including the foreigner Cho Feng and now both the Willard brothers. And his men, those who remained of Parno's own Black Sheep regiment, were loyal to the death. Memmnon was convinced that the entire group would charge the gates of Hell with nothing but a bucket of water if Parno commanded it.

At least partly because they knew Parno would lead the way.

And there was the difference, Memmnon nodded to himself, *between Parno and Therron*. Where Therron had led from the rear, traveling in a caravan of servants, escorts and hangers on, Parno rode with his men. One officer as an aide, one enlisted man as a runner and an escort of eighteen hand-picked men selected by Darvo Nidiad himself. When Parno's men slept on the ground, so did Parno.

That was the kind of leader that fighting men respected. The army was badly in need of such a leader and Memmnon hoped that Parno would have the time needed to gain the confidence of the two army corps now engaged in trying to hold against the Nor advance into the Tinsee valley.

Abruptly he stopped, drawing in a deep, cleansing breath. Today's walk hadn't worked. His head was still full of trials and troubles, but it was time for him to get to work. He paused for one more minute, looking north. North to where Parno would be approaching the army in the field.

"Good luck, brother."

CHAPTER TWO

-

It was the second morning after the departure of the Inspector General with Prince Therron that Parno arrived at Soulan Field Army Headquarters at the head of his column. By now word had spread that Therron had been taken back to Nasil in 'ill health'. Parno's arrival was expected by the army.

General Davies stepped outside his tent at the call of his sentry and snapped to a salute as the young prince stepped down from his mount.

"We can dispense with any amenities and niceties, General," Parno said at once, offering his hand. "I'm Parno McLeod."

A stunned Davies dropped his salute and shook the much younger man's hand.

"Welcome, sir," Davies said.

"Thank you. Do you have time to brief us on the current situation?" Parno asked as Enri and Karls Willard stepped to Parno's side, along with Cho Feng.

"O. . .of course, sir," Davies nodded, indicating the tent he'd just stepped out of. "Step inside if you will."

"Sergeant Berry, detail," Karls ordered and Berry nodded, posting his men around the tent.

"Major, have the men tend their horses and get them chow. Have fresh mounts saddled for the staff and the escort," Karls ordered Seymour, who nodded and set about carrying about his orders. Enri watched, proud of his younger brother though he would die on the end of a pike before admitting it. At least to Karls.

The four men entered the large tent and gathered around a large table where maps of the area were spread.

"At the moment, milord, the Nor lines stretch from the river east of Pari, to just west of Dreeden. Their line basically occupies an old trade route. We have managed to hold them there these last two days, but. . .I have to admit, sir, that's more their doing than ours."

"How so?" Parno asked, eyeing the map.

"The Nor haven't pushed very hard, sir, these last three, now four days,' Davies reported. "They don't seem to lack the manpower, so I have to believe that they've out run their supply train, at least for the moment. I can't think of any other reason for them to stay put when they know they have the advantage over us."

"Losing fifty thousand men in three days might make anyone stop and think," Enri Willard commented. "Perhaps they're being cautious now because without the army you destroyed at the Gap their flank may be exposed. They may be taking this time to re-orient for that possibility."

"Agreed," Feng nodded. "The loss of their eastern force has to come as a shock. They cannot take the chance that a similar action might turn their flank and expose their lines of communication."

"All speculation, gentlemen," Parno said. "Good speculation, but speculation none-the-less. General, have you any scouts in the areas to the Nor left? Are they using the river as an anchor for their lines?"

"They are, milord," Davies nodded, impressed already by the young man that was his new boss. "We've tried twice to turn them, but both times had to withdraw. The numbers are on their side, I'm afraid."

"Understood," Parno nodded. "Very well. I'll want to ride the front and see things for myself. What reserves do we have?"

"Ride the front?" Davies looked shocked. "Milord, sir, your brother, he never-"

"Never compare me to my brother, General," Parno said softly, but the coldness in his voice, his eyes, were loud and clear. "Reserves?" he asked again.

"Sir," Davies recovered. "Sir, we have the 5th Cavalry in reserve as well as the 4th Mounted Infantry. Both are positioned near the center, in order to respond to any breakthroughs."

"Very well. Tell me about the Nor right flank. Near Dreeden, you said?"

"Yes, sir. They've not occupied the town itself though I've no idea why. Their lines end about ten miles east of the town. I have scouts there watching for any movement but so far they have remained static."

"Are they entrenching?" Parno asked.

"No sir," Davies shook his head. "They are basically in camp mode."

"I see. Karls, collect Mister Parsons, will you please?"

"Milord," Karls nodded.

"General, have the 6th Cavalry and 5th Mounted returned from the Gap as yet?" Parno asked.

"Yes, milord," Davies nodded. "They have been off line two days, refitting and resting."

"Very well. Leave them out of the line, barring an overwhelming attack on our lines. What of the other cavalry divisions in 1st and 2nd Corps? Are they on the battle line?"

"Not exactly on the line, sir, but attached to our flanks in case the Nor try to get around us."

"How well are we anchored on the river?" Parno asked.

"Quite well, actually," Davies informed him. "The lull in the fighting has allowed us to fortify quite well in that area, as well as the rest of the line."

"How well is our artillery sited?"

"We're out of effective range of their lines at the moment, sir," Davies admitted. "We're established to interdict lines and lanes of approach to our own lines."

"Good enough," Parno nodded. "I want the. . .2nd Cavalry? Here at the eastern end of our line? I want them pulled off the line, as carefully and quietly as possible. If the line there is anchored well, then turning our flank there is unlikely. If you have infantry off line, or militia still reporting, you can use them to re-enforce the anchor points along the river, but I want the 2nd back here by tonight, ready for action on the day after morrow."

"Sir?" Davies looked puzzled.

"I'll explain tonight, depending on what I see today," Parno promised. Just then Karls returned with Doak Parsons.

"Mister Parsons, take a look at this," Parno pointed to the map, indicating the Nor right. "I'm told the Nor along this stretch of line are in camp, rather than entrenched. I want you to verify that and, as far as practicable, see how far that condition goes. Do not create an engagement. I'd prefer if the Nor never knew you were there."

"Yes, sir," Parsons nodded. "Take us a bit, milord. We'll need to swing around-"

"I'll expect a report from you sometime tomorrow, before noon, if possible, but early afternoon is acceptable. Is that doable?"

"Should be, milord," Parsons nodded after a minute.

"Then be about it, and Godspeed." Parsons sketched a salute and left the tent.

"Gentlemen, let's get mounted," Parno ordered. "We have a lot of ground to cover today. General," he turned to Davies, "you're in command. I have runners who will stay with you should you need me for any reason. We'll return before dark, I should imagine. If not, then I'll send a runner letting you know where we are."

"Yes, milord," Davies nodded, still stunned at the speed with which the young prince had taken charge. His brother would still have been 'resting'. The General left the tent behind them, and watched as the men mounted up, their saddlery and the escort's already having been placed on fresh mounts.

"We'll be back," Parno promised, and then set his heels to his mount. The small column darted away, Parno himself at the head.

Davies watched them until they were almost out of sight before remembering he had orders of his own to see to.

"Runner!"

-

Parno rode the lines, looking over the condition of the men, occasionally stopping to speak with individual soldiers and with line commanders. The morale of the army, overall, was still very good considering what they had been through. Parno inquired about supplies getting forward, medical treatment for the injured and general conditions along the entire front. The inspection served two primary purposes.

First, it allowed Parno to gauge the state of the troopers of the two army corps engaged on this front. He was satisfied that they were still combat capable, though tired. Their morale was suffering, but not broken. Overall, he liked what he saw.

Secondly, and perhaps more importantly, it allowed the men on the line to see their new Lord Marshall of the Army riding the lines on horseback and actually taking time to ask individual soldiers how they were faring. Were they eating well? Were they getting any rest? Was their equipment in good shape? Questions that Therron would never have bothered to ask even had he ever deigned to speak to the common soldiers in the field. Word spread through the ranks of Parno's visits almost as fast as he could ride the line.

His first look had been at the right flank, anchored on the Sand River Slough, near the Tinsee itself. The line was solid and artillery well sited. Newly promoted Major Lars inspected the pieces and the placement himself and assured Parno they were satisfactory.

By the time they had reached the middle of the lines, Parno realized he would never manage to ride the entire line before dark and decided to make camp. Sergeant Berry was almost apoplectic at the thought of Parno being encamped so close to the front but was accustomed to being overruled. Enri was more vocal in his objection but soon realized there was no sense in arguing.

The rest, far more accustomed to their Commander's habits, were already making plans for camp. The unit to their front was the 4th Brigade of the 3rd Infantry Division, part of Second Corps. The unit had suffered heavily in the fighting withdrawal down the valley and their morale was possibly lower than most. Word spread through the unit quickly that the Lord Marshall would be sharing their fires and their mess that evening.

This announcement served to incite a flurry of activity as armor was cleaned and campsites straightened. No one wanted the new Lord Marshall to find them lacking.

Parno and his staff scattered among the various campfires, each man eating in a different unit's area, listening to the men as they spoke of their actions so far. Parno himself dined with the Brigadier and his staff, but then walked the area, Sergeant Berry and his detail following dutifully.

Parno visited nearly two dozen different campfires, usually company-sized affairs, always to the hasty jumping to stand to which he always waved easily away. He sampled the fair at each fire despite not being over hungry and spoke casually to the troopers inquiring about families, home towns, almost any subject rather than the war and the Nor Army not more than a mile distant.

To say that the soldiers were surprised was to put it mildly. But they were also impressed. The same easygoing, casual manner than had allowed Parno to gradually win over the prisoners that had eventually became the Black Sheep worked its same magic here. Men who were professional soldiers, had served in the ranks for years and never been near the previous Lord Marshall were left with a very favorable impression of their new leader. Parno's only comment about the war itself was a simple one.

"We're about to start making them sorry they came here."

By the time a weary Prince of Soulan found his blankets the brigade, indeed the entire division, knew of his visit. Knew of it and found themselves taken with the quiet, unassuming prince and believing his simple statement. Victory would not be easy, nor without cost.

But there would be victory, never fear.

Before morning, the entire line would know that their Lord Marshall had slept on the open ground just as they had that night. Had eaten the same food they had eaten themselves and complained about it just as loudly.

-

Parno and his staff were in the saddle before dawn and he completed his turn of the battle line following the same pattern as the day before. By now soldiers were expecting him and received him happily, eager to get a glimpse of a member of the Royal Family that would share the same hardships they themselves endured.

Parno was for the most part pleased with what he had found and said so to Enri Willard as they returned to Davies' headquarters in the late afternoon.

"I agree, milord," Enri nodded. "I confess I expected things to be much worse. And I have to tell you milord that what you have done these past two days was a priceless gift to the men. Seeing you out along the line, sharing their hardship even for a night, was something special. Something that will be long spoke of in the Army or I am sadly fooled."

"They deserve to know that I'm willing to share the same hardships they are to defend our home," Parno shrugged. "And I am. The fact that my new position will prevent me from leading as I did at the Gap means that any chance I have to join them I have to take."

"True," Enri nodded. "Here, now, you will be directing, not leading. And there is a difference, to be sure. But, milord, word of how you defeated the Nor at the Gap has already spread throughout the Army. Thanks in part to my younger brother if I'm not mistaken," he added, smiling.

"What do you mean?" Parno asked, then turned in the saddle. "Karls, what have you done?"

"Me, milord?" Karls replied, far too innocently. "Why nothing."

"Then the Black Sheep circulating among the lines these past two days regaling the troops with word of Parno's leadership at the Gap was their own doing?" Enri asked, eyebrows raised.

"They are a talkative bunch," Karls shrugged but there was a light of devilry in his eyes.

"We don't need to give them false hope, Karls," Parno chided gently. "There were a great many factors working in our favor at the Gap that we will not have here."

"I know that, milord," Karls nodded. "But please consider. This army is about to go into battle under a new commander. One unknown to them other than, well, your ah, previous exploits, let's call it," he grinned. "They need to know that you've proven yourself on the battlefield. And there's no better way for that to spread through this army than from the mouths of the soldiers who followed you into battle."

"I know you don't like to speak of it, Parno," Karls rode closer, lowering his voice. "But your exploits at the Gap are the kind of thing that legends are made of. You fought shoulder-to-shoulder with common soldiers, in a desperate last stand where your death and theirs was averted only by the arrival of the King and his men literally at the last moment. That's the kind of thing they write poems, songs and books about, Parno."

"I just don't want them thinking that we'll be able to pull of something like that here," Parno sighed in acceptance. "We're not going to make a hash of this force like we did there. We don't have the terrain on our side and more importantly we don't have any of Roda Finn's gadgetry with us."

"We will soon," Karls spoke confidently. "He won't let us down."

"It's not him letting us down I worry about," Parno said softly. "It's us buying him the time to make his magic happen again."

The rest of the ride was silent.

-

"Billy, Carl, come here!" Roda shouted from the doorway of his new office.

"Yes, Master Roda," the two answered in unison, leaving the group of workers they had been supervising with strict instructions not to touch anything until they returned.

Roda surveyed the building they occupied, on the extreme outskirts of Nasil. The building was, or had been, a foundry, and its sturdy construction was considered ideal for the dangerous work Roda and his crews would be doing.

Raw materials were still arriving in bulk, and one of his new assistants, a very bright young military engineer by the name of Theodore Belkin was in charge of the unloading and storing of the supplies.

Roda tried not to show it, but he was feeling the strain of his new position as Master Ordnance Officer for the Soulan Army. It was in fact a new position entirely, based on his own work. It was not the position itself that worried Roda, but the fact that Parno was depending upon him to produce as much 'ordnance' as possible, in as short a time as possible.

Prince Memmnon had been true to his word however and no expense was being spared in equipping and manning the Foundry. The name had stuck fast and Roda saw no reason to change it. He would have preferred Arsenal, a term of the Ancients, but it was of no importance.

Prince Memmnon had provided Roda with an educated and skilled workforce, many of whom were women. Roda's conscience tinged at that, believing that women had no place in such danger, but they were strong, intelligent and willing to work in the dangerous environment for the opportunity to serve their kingdom. No one could fault their bravery or their patriotism.

Roda put those thoughts aside as his two principle assistants arrived.

"How is the training going?" he asked.

"Very well, sir," Carl answered for them both. "Everyone here is quite intelligent and when they don't understand have no qualms about asking for clarification. Everyone we've trained so far has both a steady hand and a keen eye. I don't think we could have asked for any better material."

"I agree, sir," Billy nodded. "They are eager and while afraid they are not handicapped by their fear."

"Good," Roda nodded. "Anyone who isn't afraid of just being in here is a fool and we don't need them within a mile of this building. Keep that in mind as you watch them. I hate the thought of women being involved in this kind of work," he spoke his own fear.

"I understand, sir," Carl nodded. "But they are doing quite well. And there is a shortage of able bodied men because of the war."

"I know," Roda sighed. Most of the men working at the Foundry at present were either too old to serve in the ranks or disqualified by some disability or other. "How long do you estimate before we can begin production?"

"Day after tomorrow, in limited quantities," Billy answered at once and Carl backed him up.

"Really?" Roda couldn't hide his surprise. They'd been at it less than two weeks after all.

"Yes, sir," Billy assured him. "We've reached a point in training where hands on work is soon to be required. Also, I believe that the bomb casings are already being poured as are the spikes for the Hubbel Arrows."

Roda nodded, knowing this was true. Other foundries were already tooling to pour the thousands of smaller iron balls needed for the mines and the arrows.

"We need to be producing quickly, but we can't afford any mistakes," Roda stressed.

"Any kind of accident here would not only set us back in supporting the Lord Marshall but also cost us trained workers. I cannot stress enough the importance of safety. Neither can you," he added.

"It's our first rule, sir," Carl promised. "And the people sent to us really are quite bright, Master Finn. We're very fortunate in that."

"Good," Roda nodded, his voice more confident. "Then we'll prepare to begin limited production day after morrow, correct?"

"Yes, sir," both assistants answered in unison.

"All right then, back to it," he shooed them away. "We've no time to waste."

He watched as the two hurried back to their prospective teams, already shouting for various workers to attend to them. Roda turned back to his own office, satisfied that things in the Foundry were well in hand. Despite his often-ill treatment of his chief assistants he trusted them to handle their work. Carl and Billy had been with him from the beginning, when they worked in cramped conditions at Cove Canton. They knew their business of building, or at least assembling, the 'ordnance' as well as he did.

Which left Roda free to do something no one was better at than he was. Design new weapons.

His ballista rounds had been a disappointment. When they worked, they worked quite well. When they didn't, the results were catastrophic. A round had exploded on its rail at the Gap, causing a rupture in the fortifications that nearly resulted in the loss of the entire line. As a result, the weapons were removed from use.

Since then, Roda had been trying to figure a way to make use of the weapons that would ensure the safety of the artillerymen and still be effective. Using them as direct fire weapons on the ballista was out. Nothing Roda could think of had made the weapons more reliable or safer to use.

He was still convinced however that the weapons could be used. Perhaps not in their current state, but in some way. A more or less directed weapon that, when fired, would fall among the enemy and cause maximum damage as well as shock value. The weapons worked, in so far as causing damage. It was the delivery system that was unreliable. Even dangerous.

A casual conversation with Cho Feng had given Roda an idea, one that he had shared with no one else as yet. Not because of any trust issues but because he simply wasn't sure it would work. And he had yet to develop a plan, or even an *idea* of a plan, to develop it.

Thus it was that Billy and Carl would supervise the work in the Foundry for now, while Roda went back to his design table. There had to be a way to make his idea work. Soulan needed every advantage it could get. *Parno McLeod* needed it. And Roda Finn promised *himself* if no one else that he would *not* fail Parno McLeod.

CHAPTER THREE

-

Stephanie Corsin-Freeman arrived at Cumberland House just before lunch. Edema Willows was sitting on the front porch with Dahlia Nidiad and both rose to wave at the carriage. Stephanie's escort, ten men from the Black Sheep who were well enough to work but not yet well enough to stand the rigors of combat, rode around to the corral where the Willows' servants waited to help care for the horses and see to lunch for the men.

"Hello, dear," Edema kissed Stephanie's cheek lightly. "How was the ride over?"

"Uneventful," Stephanie smiled. "Hello, Dahlia," Stephanie smiled.

"Hello, Doctor," Dahlia smiled slightly in return. The young woman was still suffering from the death of her father at the Gap. Add to that was the fact that Karls Willard, whom she had grown very fond of, was now far to the west with Parno and Dahlia had little to be happy about these days.

"Dahlia, please call me Stephanie," the doctor insisted. "We're practically the same age for goodness sake and it's not like we don't know each other!"

"Yes, Stephanie," Dahlia smiled again, perhaps a bit brighter this time.

"We'll be having lunch soon, dear," Edema told Stephanie. "I assume you'll be joining us? Perhaps stay the night?"

"Would it be an imposition if I did?" Stephanie asked. "I would like to talk to you about something rather. . .personal," he cheeks colored. Edema smiled.

"You are never an imposition, dear, you know that," the older woman assured her. There was little doubt in her mind what the young doctor wanted to talk about.

"Then, yes, I will. Will the escort be a problem?" She was not allowed to go anywhere off the Canton without an escort. By orders of Parno himself. While Stephanie wielded a good deal of power herself, no one would dare defy Parno McLeod. Especially not where Lady Corsin-Freeman's safety was concerned.

"Of course not," Edema assured her. "We were always accustomed to Parno's escort." Edema's face faltered for just a second at the thought of those happier times, but she recovered quickly. "I'll have Benson see to their quartering. And you shouldn't be so put out by them, dear. There is a possibility of marauders in this area after all."

Stephanie nodded, understanding Edema's meaning. It was possible that Nor troopers who had survived the battle at the Gap could be roaming the countryside, though no one had seen or heard of any so far.

Stephanie followed the other two women through the grand house out onto the veranda where lunch was waiting for them. The three of them talked pleasantly while consuming the light lunch, exchanging items of news and discussing recent events. Finally, with the meal finished, Edema leaned back in her seat and smiled at the young physician.

"So, you've set your cap for Parno, have you?" Her tone was conversational and it took Stephanie a minute to realize what the older woman had said.

"I beg your pardon?" was her instant reply, eyes darting toward Dahlia.

"Oh, please," the younger woman raised a hand to ward off objection. "Parno and I were raised together. It's not like I'd want him around all the time." A bright smile robbed her words of any sting and Stephanie found herself smiling in return.

"Am I so obvious?" she asked, hating the heat on her face.

"Well, perhaps not to strangers," Edema admitted. "However, let's be honest, dear. Your arguments are the stuff of legend among the people at Cove Canton." Stephanie's face grew even redder at that, realizing the truth of the statement.

"He is just so. . .so. . . ." she sputtered.

"Obstinate?" Dahlia supplied. "Pig-headed? Stubborn? Immovable? Stop me when I get warm," she laughed.

"So you *do* know him well," Stephanie sighed and Dahlia laughed out loud. Edema was secretly thrilled to hear the sound of the girl laughing. She had been through a great deal of late and this was the first time Edema had heard Dahlia laugh since the younger woman had come to stay at Cumberland House.

"I do, indeed," Dahlia nodded, unaware of Edema's scrutiny. "And I'm guessing you've got it pretty bad or you wouldn't be here."

"What makes you say that?" Stephanie asked.

"You're here to ask Edema what to do about him," Dahlia said, as if she was announcing some great state secret.

"I might as well be wearing a sign," Stephanie grumped, leaning back in her chair. "I tried to make him take me with him west, but he flatly refused."

"As well he should have," Edema said at once. "The campaign field is no place for a woman, Stephanie."

"I was with him at the Gap!" Stephanie complained. "How much worse could it be?"

"You were there for a few days of fighting, the rest was camp life," Edema reminded her. "The battle in the west is being fought daily. There will be no down time, no waiting, no privacy of any kind. You have no business being there." She leaned forward.

"And you would be a distraction that Parno does not need. Not now."

"What?" Stephanie spluttered.

"Oh, my dear girl," Edema leaned back again, fanning herself slightly. "It's obvious that he cares for you very much."

"It's not so obvious to me," she admitted.

"Yes, it is," Dahlia almost giggled. "Face it, Stephanie. You've met someone who is just as stubborn as you are and isn't cowed by your family's name or influence."

Stephanie's face clouded as she heard that, not wanting to admit that it might, *might* mind you, be true.

"I'm afraid Dahlia has you pegged, dear girl," Edema smiled gently. "She and I know Parno fairly well, she much better than I. If we can see his concern, his attraction to you, then I assure you it's there."

"Then why wouldn't he-" Stephanie began, but stopped as she realized the question had already been answered. Parno didn't need the distraction of her being with him in the field. Intellectually, she knew that to be true.

"Stephanie, the best way you can help Parno now is to finish the work you've started at Cove Canton," Edema interrupted her thoughts. "He needs, his *army* will need, the people you train to treat their sick and wounded. Without you, without your students, men who might otherwise live will almost certainly die. Men that Soulan needs right now more than ever." Edema paused, as if considering her next words carefully. Finally, she seemed to come to a decision of some kind.

"I have seen the Nor army, Stephanie," she said softly. "In my travels north to their lands with my husband, during out time of 'peace'. They are better equipped, better trained, than any Nor army in recent or ancient history. Their Emperor intends to *destroy* our kingdom and has poured vast resources into his attempt. And he has allied with the Wild Tribes of the west to do it," she finished, her voice taking on a new edge.

"What?" both younger women gasped. Tales of the Wildmen had been used to frighten Soulan children for generations.

"I have seen them," Edema nodded. "I have watched them training Nor cavalry. This war was not an accident, nor was it something that was started on the spur of the moment. Long and careful planning went into this attack. There have been many wars in the past between north and south, but this one. . .this one may well be the last," she declared.

"I believe that there will only be one surviving kingdom from this war," Edema told them. "May God be merciful to Soulan that it is we who survive."

-

"The Emperor wants to know why we are not attacking."

Lt. General Gerald Wilson, commander of Norland's 1st Field Army, looked up from his desk and the dispatched he had been studying. The house that he had commandeered for his headquarters was comfortable and he had taken one of the larger rooms for his office.

Standing just inside the door to his office leaning almost insolently against the door frame, General Charles Daly, his Chief of Staff, stood as if he was waiting for an answer. The fact that Daly was far and away his subordinate in rank was offset by Daly's kinship to the Emperor. Not for the first time, Wilson found himself wanting to arrange a battlefield death, meritorious of course, for Daly. But that would cause political complications Wilson could ill afford.

"We will be attacking again soon, Charles," Wilson settled for saying, forcing his voice to sound amiable. "Brasher's complete and total defeat, no, *destruction*, has forced us to re-evaluate our position and modify some of our plans. Once we've made sure our flank and our line of supply and communication are secure, we'll resume our march south."

"The Emperor doesn't like excuses," Daly replied. "He doesn't respond well to them. He wants action. He wants *results*."

"And he will get them," Wilson worked not to grate out. "But we must ensure our position and the safety of our army before we go any further into enemy territory. Prudence dictates these actions, lest disaster befall us."

"Prudence," Daly repeated slowly, as if testing the word. "I'm not sure the Emperor will understand the difference between prudence and reluctance. Or cowardice," he added, almost as an afterthought.

"Would he better understand our becoming stranded in enemy territory with our lines cut off and the army that he has worked so hard to train and equip be starved to death, destroyed in battle, or, at best, forced to withdraw if possible to avoid those things?" Wilson snapped. "Our rate of advance depended upon Brasher's success. That idiot walked right into a hornet's nest and kicked it over, leading to the destruction of his entire army! The remains of which are little better than rabble now and useless to us in any form. As a result, General, our flank is exposed. Unless we see to the security of that flank, which *was* to be provided by Brasher's forces, we risk a Soulan counterattack driving around us and disrupting out supply lines."

"Do I need remind you that this is spring time? There are no crops to forage on and little stores left in the areas we already occupy after the winter's end. We need those supplies to keep this army fed. Supplied with arrows, with medical supplies, with forage for our animals. Without those supplies, not only can we not advance we cannot win this war! Surely your education at the Imperial War Academy taught you such things." Daly's face flushed red at the jibe.

Wilson was gambling a bit, but only a bit he believed. The Emperor was a man of little understanding. He did not suffer fools, nor failure. But the current Emperor was also perhaps the smartest in recent generations. He had chosen his leaders, excepting Brasher perhaps, carefully. Men that knew what had to be done and knew how to do it. Wilson was convinced that Emperor Bane would recognize the intelligence of Wilson's caution and agree with it.

It was possible that Daly's reports would convince the Emperor that Wilson was slacking, but that was a chance that Wilson was forced to take. In either case, he had nothing to lose. If he attacked before securing his position, already so deep into enemy territory, lost the army and somehow survived, he and his entire family would be executed for his failure.

So, he was gambling on the best chance he had for success. That the Emperor would accept his own dispatches over those of Daly and be willing to give Wilson the time he needed to ensure not only the safety of his command but the success of the invasion as well.

"I'm sure the Emperor will have something to say about that," Daly's voice brought Wilson back to the current conversation.

"I'm sure he will, but until then I have work to do, Brigadier," Wilson emphasized Daly's rank. "You are dismissed." With that Wilson returned his attention to the dispatches on his desk, patently ignoring Daly's presence.

For his part, Daly's face flushed deeper still, his face contorting in anger. Still, he had little choice for the present but to observe the structure of command. Leaving the office in a snit, he prepared to return to his own quarters where he would prepare a new dispatch for the Emperor. A dispatch in which he would detail at length the failures of General Wilson to follow his guidance and resume the attack, as well as his casual disrespect for a member of the Imperial Family.

-

"Welcome back, milord," General Davies stood stiffly outside his own headquarters tent, watching Parno and his 'staff' dismount. Their horses were quickly taken away to be cared for by enlisted men.

"General, please relax," Parno said softly. "I'm not going to bite you, I promise." A slight grin robbed the words of any sting and Davies found himself letting out a long, slow breath.

"Sorry, milord," he said.

"Nothing to be sorry for," Parno assured him. "I know how Therron is. I really don't stand on pomp and circumstance, General. Let's step inside, shall we?" he suggested, looking around.

"Your man Parson has returned, milord," Davies informed him, guessing correctly at who Parno was looking for.

"Karls, please have someone find Doak and get him here," Parno ordered. Karls nodded, stepping back outside.

"How was your ride, milord?" Davies asked.

"Informative," Parno nodded. "I'm pleased, overall, with what I've seen. The men are in good shape, and still in relatively good spirits. I'm impressed, General. You and your officers are to be commended."

"Thank you, milord," Davies said simply. He wasn't the kind of man who preened. Before anything else could be said, Karls returned with Parsons trailing.

"Milord," Parsons nodded, moving to the map, taking out his notebook. "You were right, sir," he looked at Davies. "For whatever reason, the Nor right is not entrenched, not fortified in any way, and basically in camp mode." He used a pencil to trace a line along he enemy front.

"We followed their line back east for almost three miles, sir," he continued, this time to Parno. "We were careful, and I'm fair certain the Nor never knew we were about. They have pickets out, but only a little way from their main lines, usually no more than two hundred yards. There are huge gaps in the coverage of their pickets, milord, sometimes as much as a quarter mile." He paused, collecting his thoughts.

"Either the commander of that sector is an idiot, or he's lazy, or he just outright thinks there's no chance of an attack against his part of the line. His men are drilling, all infantry that we could see, but there's no real sense of urgency about them. Like they're going through the motions."

"Their discipline is lousy, sir, not only with their pickets and watches, but just overall. The men are not undisciplined, really, it's just the way the camp is being run. The officers appear to be taking their cues from their General and are not enforcing any kind of discipline among their men when it comes to noise, light, or movement. It's as if they don't care if we know where they are or what they're doing."

"Do they have any sentry posts or pickets covering their open flank?" Parno asked. "Out to the west of their position?"

"No sir," Parsons shook his head. "Just the same standard watches, two hundred or so yard out, give or take. We slipped around their flank for almost a mile, looking for just such a thing. Nothing."

Parno considered this, examining the information that Parsons had brought back for him. He made no mention of the absence of Parsons' normally thick accent. Doak Parsons was an enigma to most who knew him. Darvo had known something about his past, but had never shared that information with Parno. Parno wasn't going to ask.

"Milord, General Graham will be arriving soon," Davies interrupted

Parno's train of thought.

"Very well," Parno nodded. General Arnold Graham was the commander of 1st Corps, and a very close friend of Therron McLeod. Parno did not anticipate the meeting being a pleasant one, the war notwithstanding.

"Milord?" Parsons asked, clearly uncomfortable with so many high ranking individuals around him.

"Thank you, Mister Parsons," Parno grinned. Parsons shook his head at their private joke and left the tent to rejoin his own men.

"What are you thinking, milord?" Enri Willard asked, leaning on the map table, and studying the layout.

"I'm going to take three cavalry divisions and attack their right flank," Parno said calmly. So calmly, so matter-of-fact, that it took a moment for it to sink in.

"*You're* going to take?" Davies managed to speak first. "Milord, that's. . .surely you can't mean to lead the attack yourself?"

"Well, I won't be in the front, no," Parno shook his head. "But yes, I'll be in command. I want to take the-" he continued, about to lay out his plans.

"Sir, that's not. . .you can't just go about leading cavalry charges, milord," Enri Willard cut him off. "You're not a regimental commander anymore, sir. You're the Lord Marshall of the *entire Soulan Army*!"

"I seem to remember my father telling me that," Parno replied calmly. "I also seem to remember from my own education that the title of Lord Marshall means I'm in charge. I give the orders." His tone was light, but Parno's eyes were dark and serious.

"I'll have the Black Sheep there to keep him safe," Karls offered to the conversation. "We'll look after him right enough."

"I hadn't planned on them participating," Parno informed him.

"We won't be," Karls replied. "We'll be surrounding you." His statement was flat and simple.

"That won't be necessary, Karls," Parno shook his head. "I will-"

"If you're going, so are we," Karls cut him off. "Milord," he added, seeing the look of consternation on Davies' face as well as his own brother's. "I mean it Parno," he added, seeing the look on his commander's face. "You are *not* going without us and that *is* final."

Parno looked at Karls for a long moment, gauging his reply. Karls withstood the scrutiny without flinching. He had learned from Darvo Nidiad how to deal with Parno. Finally, Parno smiled slightly.

"Darvo would be proud of you, Karls," he said softly and Karls' stiffened in pride at the simple statement.

"Very well, Karls," Parno chuckled. "You and the Sheep will ride with me as my guard."

"I knew that," Karls nodded in satisfaction. Davies and Enri Willard exchanged a look but remained silent. Before anything else could be given into the conversation, the sound of several horses approaching could be heard.

"I imagine that will be General Graham," Parno said into the silence. Two minutes later Parno's guess proved correct as Graham stalked into the tent, glowering at everyone and everything around him. He eyed Parno almost caustically. Parno simply returned his gaze with a neutral expression.

"How is it that you are here and what has happened to Marshall Therron?" Graham demanded without so much as a hello.

"I'm here at the command of the King of Soulan," Parno replied gently, almost mockingly. "Therron is on his way back to Nasil, probably there by now, in the care of the Inspector General by order of the King. Would you like to join him?" Parno allowed an edge to creep into his voice as he spoke those last words, eyeing Graham steadily.

"Why has the King made this change?" Graham demanded.

"I asked you a question, General," Parno's voice was deadly soft and his eyes were shining brightly. Both Willard brothers recognized that look and stood a little straighter, cautious now.

"I expect an answer," Parno continued, never taking his eyes from Graham's. The staring contest lasted nearly a full minute but it was Graham who broke eye contact first.

"I have no way to answer since I am unaware of why Marshall Therron is gone," Graham said finally.

"He is *gone*, as you put it, because he refused a direct order from his Sovereign," Parno informed Graham calmly. Graham's eyebrows rose.

"Is this about what happened at the Gap?" he asked.

"I can't see how that concerns you, really," Parno said easily. "But since you asked, yes it is. Because of Therron's actions, or lack thereof, we nearly lost the war before it was truly underway. His planning ignored a dagger aimed right at the heart of Soulan itself. His insubordination could have sealed our doom, General. And that is why the King has acted as he has. Does that satisfy your need for information?" The question sounded innocent enough, but anyone listening would know better.

"I suppose it has to be, then," Graham said.

"Know this, General, right now," Parno's voice was like ice. "If you ever dare address me again as you just have, I'll kill you. If you ever question me again, except in the form of giving me advice, I'll kill you. And if you ever, just *once*, act in any way that is contrary to the well-being of the Kingdom of Soulan, I. Will. Kill. You. Do you understand me, General?"

A look of astonishment appeared on Graham's face as he listened, slowly being replaced with red faced anger. He actually took a step forward toward Parno until he noticed that the prince had his hand on his sword. Graham looked at Parno, perhaps *really* looked at him for the first time. While outwardly calm, the young Marshall's eyes were alight with violence. Graham realized for the first time that he might have made a mistake.

He had intended to confront the younger prince, intimidate him and perhaps even threaten to lead a revolt. He realized suddenly that he was as close to death as he had been in quite some time.

"General, I asked if you understood me," Parno's voice was almost a whisper. "I won't ask again."

"I understand, milord," Graham managed to choke out. Parno allowed his sword hand to relax.

"Now that we've established who is in command here," Parno said calmly, "you're just in time to be briefed on our first offensive action against the Nor."

"Offensive?" Graham almost stammered.

"Yes," Parno nodded, turning back to the map table. "We're going to attack the Nor right flank. They have left it open and basically unguarded. Up until now, they've had things pretty much their own way. Already they've pushed several hundred miles into our territory."

"There's a price to pay for that," the young Lord Marshall said softly. "And we start making them pay tomorrow morning."

-

Parno left the tent an hour later, leaving the movement of the units assigned to the attack to the Corp commanders and Enri Willard. The calm he'd felt when facing Graham was gone now, replaced with a cold fury at the insolence of the man.

Parno had expected trouble of course. Therron had made sure that he was popular with his top generals as well as many of the more socialite nobles in and around Nasil. In doing so, the middle McLeod brother had sought to secure himself in a position of power through sheer personality cult if nothing else.

His popularity among so many high-ranking officers would ensure his control of the army even in a coup or revolt. The support of petty nobles would help him politically when, and, or if such a move was made. Parno was fairly sure now that Graham was one of the men that Therron had depended on the most. As commander of 1st Corp, Graham had a powerful force at his command normally stationed in and around Nasil in a number of small cantons. With Graham's support, Therron would have found it very easy to secure the city and declare himself King, presenting a *fait accompli* to the kingdom at large.

But Graham's support alone would not have been enough. Parno frowned at that thought. One army corps, no matter how powerful, was not enough to ensure success of anything, not with four more equally powerful forces as part of Soulan's standing army, supported by the militia forces of the various provinces.

Parno didn't like his brother Therron but had to admit that the former Lord Marshall was in no way dumb. Foolish yes, but he was an intelligent man with a good education. He would know that 1st Corp would not be enough. He would have needed more.

Much more.

Another corps commander? Davies could be ruled out based on his friendship to Tammon McLeod. He would never have supported Therron's move against the King.

General Raines, the 3rd Corp commander could almost certainly be ruled out as well. His family had served in the Soulan Army for more generations than anyone could remember without resorting to records. His loyalty as well as that of his family were beyond question. Also, Raines and Memmnon had attended the Soulan Military school together and remained close friends to his day. No, Raines' loyalty was assured.

That left General Freeman's 4th Corp, and General Herrick's 5th Corps. Parno knew neither man personally and knew very little about them in general. It had never seemed needful to know anything about them, so he'd never bothered.

Obviously, it was time to change that.

Still, Parno was troubled. Even if both men had been willing to support Therron's claim to the throne, there were still the Provincial Militias to consider. Parno stopped short at that, his mind racing.

Except in time of war, like now, Provincial Militias were controlled and commanded by Provincial Governors. Men with extraordinary powers in time of peace to make decisions affecting their entire province and every citizen in it. True, their power was subject to the rule of the King and the Royal Decrees, a system of laws that applied to every corner of the Kingdom. Primarily however, the Decrees were instruments of protection of the rights of individual citizens of the realm. Not to limit or control the power of Provincial Governors.

What if Therron had convinced some of the governors to support his cause? How many might either refuse to send their troops to aid the King, or even lend them instead to Therron's power grab? If even half of them sat idle or threw their weight behind Therron, then. . . .

Parno felt his head swim. There had never been a coup in Soulan's long history. Never even a *hint* of one for that matter. Always, since the time of Tyree, the succession had been assured. A fact of life.

Parno was suddenly gripped by a wave of sadness that it would be someone of his family that had decided to break that long held tradition of stability. Truly, the family of Tammon McLeod was cursed.

Maybe it's time for another dynasty on the throne, he found himself thinking morosely. He wondered how deep the rot went in Soulan.

He needed to send a message to Memmnon before tomorrow anyway, so he decided to include these new thoughts in a separate letter. Sighing in disappointment, he headed for his own tent. He had a lot to do before morning.

Therron McLeod stood before his father insolently silent, fuming at his 'mistreatment'.

"Nothing to say, Therron?" Tammon asked, the edge in his voice the only indication of his anger.

"What is there to say?" Therron finally replied. "You've decided to favor Parno for whatever reason, and to do that, I had to be removed."

"Even now you don't see the danger, not to mention the disobedience in what you've done, do you?" Tammon spoke a bit more harshly this time.

"I am, or was, the Army Commander," Therron retorted. "I evaluated Parno's information as baseless and the panicky reaction of an untrained boy. The force I sent was more than sufficient, as you yourself proved, *Sire*." Therron managed to make the word sound like a slur.

"They were sufficient only because of the supreme sacrifice and tactical brilliance of the brother who's report you cast aside so readily!" Tammon's storm finally broke. "The only good thing that has come from your being Lord Marshall in this entire affair is that I acceded to your belief that he and his men would be useless in battle. Had I assigned him and his men somewhere else, then a Nor field army would like as not be occupying Nasil this very night!"

The King visibly calmed himself, resisting the urge to rub his chest. Damn his weak heart. It *would* betray him just when he was working up a good tantrum.

"So because he was in the right place, at the right time, he will make a more formidable Lord Marshall than the man who has trained and equipped the army that defends us?" Therron almost sneered.

"I hope he will make a better Lord Marshall," Tammon nodded, calmer now. "But he finds himself in that position because of *you*, not him. He did not desire command and refused at first to even consider it. In part I'm sure due to the death of Darvo Nidiad, leaving aside our treatment of him over the span of his life." He leaned forward.

"Make no mistake, son of mine. You stand here before me, defrocked and disowned because of *your own* arrogance and actions and nothing else. Leaving aside for the sake of the kingdom your plans to make sure it was you that sat upon the throne one day rather than your brother!"

Therron's eyes widened before he could stop them, giving himself away. He managed to get his surprise under control, but it was far too late.

"Surely you did not think you could engineer such subversion as you planned and I would take no notice, Therron," Tammon's voice was gentle this time. Mocking.

"I have no idea of what you speak," Therron managed to keep his voice steady. "The very idea is repugnant to me."

"I see," Tammon sat back, motioning to the Chamber Warden. The door behind him opened to admit Jon Keen, Provincial Governor of the Alma province.

"Former Governor Keen has a very different tale to tell than you, my son," Tammon managed not to gloat. "You see, after your brother's visit to that area, Memmnon dispatched a unit of King's Constables to check into the situation there. You might recall that? Yes?" Therron nodded, hesitantly.

"It seems that their investigation was. . .particularly successful," Tammon informed his middle son. "So much so that their investigation into corruption in the Provincial Government led them to former Governor Keen himself, who, thinking that being under your protection meant that he was untouchable, was somewhat more. . .talkative, that he should have been."

Therron shot a menacing glance at Keen, who returned the look stolidly. He was caught out, with no real option left to him. Therron McLeod had made him many promises and delivered on none of them. He owed the man no loyalty as he saw it.

"It saddens me that it would be my own family that would subvert the long and unbroken custom of peaceful ascension to the throne of Soulan." The sadness was evident in Tammon's eyes as well as his voice. "Somewhere, I went wrong in raising my offspring. Very wrong, apparently," he sighed.

"Whatever Keen has told you-" Therron began, but Tammon cut him off.

"Don't bother with any more lies, my son," he raised a hand, suddenly weary of this confrontation. "Therron McLeod, of the House McLeod, you have by your actions against Crown and Kingdom proved yourself unworthy of the title and responsibility you bear. In light of that fact and of the evidence already arrayed against you in my possession, coupled with your complete disregard for a direct order of your Sovereign, placing the entire kingdom in jeopardy in doing so, you are hereby stripped of all rights and privileges of the station of a member of the Ruling House. You are relieved of your post as Lord Marshall of the Army of Soulan and will no longer occupy the second seat in line of succession to the throne of Soulan." Tammon paused, taking a deep, troubled breath.

"Further, you will live out the remainder of your days in exile along the islands of the Key Horn, where you will bear no power, no authority, and no seat of any kind. Your name will be stricken from the histories of the Dynasty of Tyree, and you will be forgotten. As if you never were. This is my Decree, spoken this day, in the presence of these witnesses, to be recorded in the Royal Archives. Three days hence you will be escorted to your new home by members of the Inspector General's office, where you will remain under constant guard so long as you shall live. I have spoken."

The official words said, Tammon looked at his middle son, a single tear falling down his right cheek.

"It is better than you deserve," he said finally, before leaving the room accompanied by his personal aides.

Memmnon stayed a moment longer but had no words for his brother. He motioned for the Warden to remove Keen, waited for the Inspector General's men to remove Therron, and then walked slowly to his office.

He would sit there before his fire for long time that night, looking for peace that simply would not come.

CHAPTER FOUR

-

Parno stood before the assembled Generals, eyeing each on in turn. Division commanders, brigade commanders, their seconds, and Parno's staff occupied the command tent of General Davies. Parno's first major move had been to promote Davies to command of the Soulan First Field Army, consisting of both 1st and 2nd Corps along with all attached Provincial Militia. He had expected Graham to object, but apparently Parno had made his point to Therron's puppet for he had simply nodded.

The men assembled before him led the 2nd, 4th, and 6th Soulan Cavalry Divisions, along with the 21st Separate Horse Archer Brigade, a unit of horsemen specializing in archery from horseback.

"Gentlemen," he said finally. "You've been briefed on tomorrow's assignment; I assume?" Heads nodded around the room.

"Good. We attack at dawn tomorrow. Divisions will attack with two brigades abreast, the third in reserve, with all divisions abreast in that formation. As our line faces east, the 4th will occupy the center, with the 2nd to the north, and 6th to the south." He pointed to the map now hanging along the tent wall.

"Note carefully our avenue of attack, if you will," he continued. "This is not an all-out attack, but rather a limited action with set goals and objectives. We will advance no more than three miles before halting our attack, no matter how successful it seems to be moving. I want that clear from the start. Do all of you understand that order?" Again, all head nodded.

"Excellent. There are approximately three infantry divisions on the Nor right that are not fortified, not dug in, and posting only a token picket. Our goal is to destroy those divisions in their camp. We will attack with the light of day and we will press the advantage for three miles, if possible. Why three miles, I know you're wanting to ask." A few heads nodded this time, others simply waiting.

"At that point, you will encounter a unit that is in line, fortified, with artillery in support. While we could probably still take the fight to them, our mission tomorrow is simply to remind the Nor that they have bitten off more than they can possibly chew. And to start making them pay a price for invading our home," he added. Several low growls of approval ran through the assembled commanders.

"Understand something else. Our goal is to completely destroy these units and their ability to fight. We do that by attacking their morale, their safety, and their supplies." He turned to face them fully now.

"For that reason, the reserve brigades will be carrying torches. They will fire every wagon, every supply and sutler tent, every house and every grain storage building along those three miles. I know," he raised a hand. "I know that we'll be hurting our own people in doing this, but buildings can be rebuilt. Homes replaced. But *only* if we drive these invaders from our soil first. And I promise you with all that I have, we are going to do just that."

"It won't be easy, it won't be blood free and it won't be overnight, but when we're finished there won't be a Nor soldier left in Soulan." He paused, considering his next words.

"We will take no prisoners," he said simply. Heads all around the tent perked up at that.

"We don't have the resources to feed them, for one thing," he informed the men. "Second, they aren't interested in taking any prisoners, either. This is war to the knife, gentlemen. With the blade in to the hilt and twisted. I want the Nor soldiers facing us to know that only death is waiting for them from here on out. The only other option is to leave our soil."

For a second there was nothing. Parno waited, reminding himself that these men weren't Black Sheep. They were however veteran soldiers now. They had been engaged in a fighting withdrawal for weeks. He was offering them a chance to hit back and do it hard. Do it in a way that mattered.

Slowly, eyes hardening, the men nodded both their understanding, and their agreement.

"No prisoners," a large, beefy man in the front row agreed. "No mercy."

"None," Parno nodded. "I will be with you tomorrow gentlemen, along with what's left of my men from the battle of the Gap. We will carry the Black Flag from now on. There will be no mercy, no quarter of any kind for our invaders. If you cannot agree to that, I truly do understand and won't hold it against you. But you will not participate in tomorrow's attack, either."

"Atten-hut!" Davies bellowed and the men in the tent shot to their feet.

"Is there a man here that argues with the orders?" he demanded in a voice that made Parno think of Darvo Nidiad.

"*No Sir!*" over a dozen voices thundered together.

"Then say it with me!" Davies ordered. "No Mercy!"

"*No Mercy!*"

"No Quarter!" Davies continued.

"*No Quarter!*"

"No Prisoners!" Davies concluded.

"*No Prisoners, Sir!*"

Parno nodded, more than satisfied.

"Very well, gentlemen. Your orders are as simple as I can make them. Keep your formations together, keep your men in line. I don't want to leave a single man behind if we can help it. Not one. Listen for bugle orders, and be especially alert for the withdrawal horn. We will return to our line of demarcation, and from there to our own lines. Are there any questions?"

"Sir?" the beefy man in front called.

"Yes?" Parno looked at him. "General. . . ?"

"Brigadier Buford Beaumont, sir!" the man replied. "6th Division, 2nd Brigade, sir!"

"Your question, General Beaumont?" Parno asked, fighting a smile.

"If we encounter General Officers, are we to attempt their capture, sir?" Beaumont asked. "For interrogation purposes?"

"No," Parno shook his head. "Is that a problem?"

"Not in the least, sir!" Beaumont grinned wickedly. "Just wanted to make sure."

"Understood," Parno did smile, then. "Anything else?" No one spoke.

"Very well, gentlemen. Report to you posts. Men ready an hour before dawn. That's all."

The men all saluted, filing out of the tent on their way back to their respective commands. Several of them looked to Parno on the way out, nodding their approval. He returned the nod passively, allowing nothing to show on his face.

Once the last man had departed and he was sure they were away from the command tent, Parno let out a long, low breath and almost collapsed into a camp chair.

"Are you all right, milord?" Enri asked, frowning.

"That's the first time I've ever addressed a collection of officers like that," Parno admitted, slightly shame-faced. "I wasn't sure how I'd do."

"How you'd do?" Davies repeated, his own face still flushed from the energy Parno had unleashed in the departed commanders. "My God, sir, I. . .I have never in my career seen anything like it!"

"That bad?" Parno frowned.

"Bad?" Davies echoed again. "No milord, it was *incredible*! Did you *see* them? Those men walked in here beaten. We're outnumbered, facing better soldiers than we've ever faced before, and have been forced back day after day. You've sent them on their way tonight believing that starting tomorrow all of that is finished. It was well done, milord."

"Thank God," Parno slumped in his seat. "You do realize that tomorrow is just going to kick over a hornet's nest though, right?"

"I do," Davies nodded. "I only wish I was going with you to help with the kicking!"

"No, you're needed here, General," Parno shook his head. "You still know far better than I the shape of the Army and the disposition of both our own men and the enemy's. It's better for you to be here."

"I hope to gain a week, perhaps even a bit longer in this near stalemate with tomorrow's attack," Parno explained. "If we can forestall the Nor return to the offensive, then we may have some more help coming. We'll have to see. Until then however, we're on our own. First thing we have to do is show the Nor they don't get everything their own way."

"Good luck tomorrow, sir," Davies offered his hand. "And Godspeed."

"To us all, General," Parno accepted the offered hand. "To us all."

-

Parno rose early the next morning, before three. His aide, Captain Sprigs was waiting outside his tent fully dressed and ready when Parno walked outside.

"Good Lord, Harrel, did you sleep at all?" Parno asked, shocked to see the man.

"I did indeed, sir," Sprigs replied, bowing slightly. "Breakfast will be ready ten minutes from your say so," he added.

"Then say so," Parno nodded. "And join me," he added.

"Of course, milord," Sprigs nodded again, then left to see to preparations. Parno stood by the fire, warming himself. It was still early in the year and mornings were on the cool side. He had been there no more than five minutes when Karls Willard walked up to join him.

"Is everyone up before me?" Parno asked, causing Karls to smile.

"Big day the rumors are saying," he replied, holding his own hands out to the fire. "No one wants to miss out."

"We'll see how long that lasts," Parno snorted. "I really hope that everyone realizes this isn't going to be like the Gap. We're going into a real battle this morning, even if their right is unprepared. We're taking about twenty-five thousand men, leaving aside the Horse Archers, and attacking the flank of an army ten times that size. I don't even want to think of all the things that can go wrong. Horribly, terribly, ends badly for all concerned wrong."

"We'll be fine," Karls replied calmly, shrugging. "We'll take losses, I'm sure, but. . .we're hitting an unprepared force right at dawn. Their men will just be waking and prepared for another boring day in camp." He grinned at that, and the firelight dancing across his face made him look evil indeed. "Won't they be surprised!"

"They'd better be or we're done before we start," Parno told him shortly. "Confidence is all well and good, Karls, but let's not be cocky!"

"I'm not," Karls promised and wiped the smile from his face. "But I *am* confident. Parsons' men did an excellent job gathering intelligence. We know exactly where the enemy is weakest and where we can hurt them the most. All the commanders have their orders. I admit they aren't as good as the Sheep are, but they are good. Professionals. And they've been hit hard and pushed around. This is their chance to get some of their own back. Expect them to fight as hard as humanly possible."

"I do," Parno nodded as Sprigs returned followed by two cooks. Parno was not surprised to see a plate for Karls as well. There was also a fourth plate, and just as Parno was about to ask who it was for, Enri Willard materialized from the dark and took a seat.

"Morning, milord," he said softly, gratefully accepting the plate Sprigs offered. Parno looked accusingly at his aide.

"How did you know he'd be here?"

"I didn't," Sprigs replied. "I've learned to be prepared for any eventuality, milord. A job hazard when working for you, I'm afraid." The man said it with a completely straight face though Enri chuckled and Karls almost choked on his first bite of food.

"Everyone's in a jovial mood today, aren't they?" Parno didn't quite grouse. He wasn't in such a mood. He was worried and thought everyone else should be, too.

"Not too late to call it off, milord," Enri said, as if reading Parno's mind.

"It was too late the moment I issued the orders," Parno shook his head. "It's about more than what we'll accomplish in the attack, now. If I call off the attack after all that talk last evening, the men will have no confidence in me in the future. You know it's true," he added when Enri seemed about to object.

"He's right," Karls nodded, chewing wolfishly on his food. "Yesterday was something very special. If this attack today succeeds, then Parno's reputation is made among the army. No one will be looking over his shoulder wondering if Therron could have done any better." He paused to swallow. "If he calls it off, everyone will wonder if he lost his nerve. Not to mention compare him to his brother. And that's the last thing we need."

"We?" Enri raised his eyebrows at his younger brother.

"We," Karls nodded firmly. "Where Parno goes, all of us go." There was a grim finality in that statement that Enri chose not to explore. Not right now, anyway. And he would have to speak to Karls about addressing the Lord Marshall so. . .*casually*. It wasn't proper.

"Well, now that we've all analyzed it," Parno broke in before any other arguments could be raised, "let's hear your thoughts."

"We attack as planned and kick their ass," Karls shrugged. "They aren't prepared and they aren't expecting it. We'll do well, certainly at the first. The trick will be timing the withdrawal. We need to make sure that we're on the move back to our own lines before the Nor can organize any serious counter-attack." Parno looked to Enri. The older Willard was looking at his brother with something akin to respect, but nodded his own agreement.

"The timing is the key," he seconded. "We must be on our way out before the Nor generals can retaliate. We're taking a large part of our available forces into battle. We can't afford to have any of them cut off and destroyed in detail."

"The buglers will be important today," Parno agreed. "Anything else?"

"If the men sense a rout, they'll be hard to stop," Karls opined again. "Discipline is the key. I think you made that pretty clear yesterday, however. You have to trust the commanders to know and do their jobs now."

"I don't think they'll disappoint you, sir," Enri offered. "All of them want this to be successful, but they are as aware as you are of the force disparity. This attack can't be allowed to get out of control. Whatever damage we might do in an all-out attack will be countered by heavy losses of our own. Your plan is sound and your orders are clear."

Parno nodded, saying nothing else. He wished Darvo were here with him. As soon as the thought came to him, Cho Feng joined the group at the fire wearing his armor and carrying both swords. He looked as serene and fresh as ever.

"Good morning, gentlemen," he said calmly.

"Morning, Master Feng," Parno and the others replied in unison. Parno looked at Springs.

"Why don't you have a plate for him?" he asked.

"He's already eaten," Sprigs replied without a trace of smugness. Parno looked at Feng, who nodded.

"How did you know that?" Parno demanded.

"It's my job to know, sir," Sprigs answered simply. Parno shook his head at that and went back to his own unfinished breakfast. He wasn't hungry, or at least he didn't want to eat, but it would be a long time before he got the chance again today.

Sprigs was more than just an aide. He had been selected by Darvo, and trained by Cho, to be Parno's bodyguard. Parno was unaware of this even now though he did know that Sprigs had received more than the usual training at the hands of Cho Feng. Sprigs made sure that Parno went nowhere without him. Even if he had to disobey orders to do so.

"Well, I guess it's that time," Parno sighed, setting his plate aside. He'd managed to get most of the food down. As if they had heard him speak, Sergeant

Berry and his men walked into the firelight, leading their own horses as well as those of Parno and his staff.

"Now that's good timing," Karls said softly and Feng chuckled in the darkness.

"Let's mount up," Parno ordered. He still wasn't feeling the humor, but fought the urge to snap at his friends. There was no point in it. He hoped their confidence was well placed.

Once mounted, the small detail set out for where the bulk of the attack force was already waiting. In order to get into place and still achieve surprise, the attacking divisions had been forced to go over a mile distant from the western most Nor positions before going into line. The risk of even one awake and aware sentry spotting or hearing them was too great.

As they rode, more men took up positions around them. True to his word, Karls would have the Black Sheep riding as escorts for his General. Without orders being necessary, the Prince's Own broke into four companies. One fore, one aft, one to either flank. Parno was surrounded by his men. He shook his head at the fuss being made but said nothing. It would be pointless in any case.

The slightest slip of light was starting to show in the east when Parno made his way to the center of the line. Each division commander was there, waiting.

"Gentlemen," Parno nodded. "Are we ready?"

"We are, milord," all three assured him.

"Very well. Let's be about it then." It was a simple order. All that was required. The three men moved silently back to their own commands. Parno waited impatiently for the signals to pass. Finally, a runner approached Enri Willard.

"All in readiness, sir," the man reported.

"Fire the signal," Enri ordered the archer sitting next to him. The man nodded and nocked an already burning arrow. Bending his bow back, he aimed for a point far overhead and released it.

Within seconds similar arrows rose into the sky and the line of horsemen began to move forward.

To battle.

"Did you see that?"

Sergeant Joseph Ritter, Norland Army, looked up from his spot on the ground at the private.

"See what, Jenks?" he demanded. Jenks was always trying to make something out of nothing, Ritter groused to himself. There was nothing going on out here. So far as Ritter was concerned, that was something to be thankful for.

"Looked like. . .well, I don't know, really," Jenks replied, scratching his head. "Hey, there's another one!" he pointed suddenly. Ritter looked but saw nothing.

"You've been out here too long," Ritter told him grouchily. "There's nothing out there but fog!"

"I'm telling you I could see a light of some kind," Jenks insisted. "Like. . .like a flaming arrow. Yeah, just like that!" Jenks seized upon the idea.

"Yeah, shot from where?" Ritter demanded, now on his feet. Their relief should be here soon anyway, and he'd be glad to get rid of Jenks.

"Somewhere over there," Jenks pointed to the west. Ritter shook his head, sighing.

"Jenks, there ain't nothing over there but nothing!" he almost snarled. "The southerners are that way!" he pointed south-east. "We're outside their lines here by more than a mile, idiot."

Before Jenks could reply, both men felt a tremble run underneath them. Both moved slightly. This was quake country and this whole area was prone to large earthquakes with little or no warning.

But this was no earthquake. The tremor kept going, rumbling louder by the second. Through the noise Ritter heard something else. The whinny of a horse.

From the west.

Ritter had just enough time to realize that Jenks wasn't an idiot after all before a Soulan lancer ran him through. Jenks lasted another second before joining him on the ground.

The Soulan Army was coming to call.

-

"Bugler, sound advance, canter!" Parno ordered. The young man nodded, licked his lips nervously and lifted his horn. The tones of the bugle lifted over the noise of thousands of horses, picked up by other bugles along the entire line and echoed until the entire front was prepared. Training dictated that the line would wait for a count of fifteen from the bugle call's end, and then. . . .

The line broke into a canter almost as one. The Lancers among them lowered their weapons, prepared to take down the first enemy they encountered, while swordsmen drew their own weapons and prepared for battle. The reserves began passing the light from man to man, firing their torches for the day's work.

Behind them all Parno watched in grim silence as his plan unfolded. So far, so good. He looked to Enri and nodded.

"Bugler, Gallop!" the older Willard ordered. Again, the clear notes of the horn carried into the air, to be picked up and passed along by others. Seconds later the line increased its speed once more. The transition wasn't as smooth this time with gaps appearing in the line, but sergeants were quick to curse their men back into line.

It was a nearly solid wave of horsemen that hit the unprepared Nor right just at sun-up.

-

General Alfred Raymond had been awake for a half hour when the sun began to make its presence known over his camp. Commanding the 22nd Infantry Division of the Norland First Imperial Field Army, Raymond was holding the extreme right of line for the entire army. It was a boring and thankless job and his men hadn't so much as *seen* a Southron, let alone *engaged* one, since their arrival.

Raymond shared the opinion of many of the general officers in the Imperial army that the Soulan Army had been overrated for years and presented no serious threat to their forces. For this reason, he had not ordered his men entrenched, had erected no fortifications, and in general had ignored any kind of serious security provisions for his camp. His men were not exactly raw recruits but they were under trained and Raymond had been drilling them hard while his unit was in line unopposed by enemy troops. The Soulan line was at least three miles distant to the east and there were several other divisions between his and the enemy.

Raymond was eating his breakfast when he saw a man run past his tent, heading east. Another followed and then two more. Frowning, Raymond motioned for his aide to see what was happening. The young Captain, appointed for his family ties rather than his skills as a soldier, stepped to the open doorway of the wall tent and then outside beneath the fly over the field desks.

Raymond was looking right at him when an arrow pierced the young officer's eye. Without a sound the younger man collapsed to the ground, dead before his body settled. Raymond froze, cup half way to his mouth for a drink of coffee. He'd never seen a man killed in combat before.

Nor would he again after today.

-

Parno looked at the destruction around him as his group followed the first waves of Soulan cavalry through the Nor encampment. Dead Nor littered the ground all around them. Smoke from dozens of fires clouded the area around them though not to the point that visibility was a problem.

"All reports are that the Nor were caught completely by surprise, milord," Enri Willard reported, having been taking those reports from runners. "Our front lines are into the second camp area already. Our casualties so far are very light."

"Good," Parno nodded, and some of the tension that kept his stomach in knots relaxed ever so slightly. "Continue to press the attack as planned."

"We are, milord," Willard assured him. Parno glanced at Cho Feng.

"Your thoughts?" he asked simply. The Oriental sword master looked at him.

"Your men are performing very well," he said. "Keep to your original plan, for it is sound. You must preserve your own force while doing as much damage as possible."

Parno nodded in agreement. That had been his plan but it was comforting to get the same suggestion from someone more experienced.

"You may want to consider having your northern most units reduce their front and ensure they cannot be cut off from the main force," Cho added.

"Already done, Master Feng," Enri reported as he rode near. "The 2nd has one brigade front with the second holding along their left. The third is in support, able to assist either force as needed."

"Excellent," Parno nodded. "Maintain the pressure as long as we can up to our original line. Are the ambulances seeing to our dead and injured?" Parno had ordered a limited number of horse-drawn ambulances to follow the attack, supported by a brigade of mounted infantry. Their mission was to remove as many wounded as possible from the battlefield. It was risky, but Parno was counting on the force of the attack to prevent any organized attack on the medical train, and the escort to deal with any isolated pockets of enemy by-passed by the main assault.

"They are, milord," Enri nodded. Parno nodded, saying nothing else. There wasn't much for him to do at this point and he resisted the urge to either micromanage or ride to the front. That was not his place anymore. His subordinates knew their jobs and would do them without any elbow jogging from him. It was a difficult transition, but one he knew he must make.

Reports continued to come in from all over the front. By all accounts, the battle was going well so far.

-

Lt. General Gerald Wilson was having his own breakfast when a pasty-faced aide entered his quarters. Wilson looked up, frowning at both the interruption and the ill kept look of the runner.

"What is it?" he almost barked and the man flinched visibly.

"With respect, sir, but. . .the Soulanies are attacking our right!"

"What? Ridiculous!" Wilson stood, leaving his meal unfinished. "A raid of some sort?"

"We're receiving reports of a full-scale attack, General!" the young Captain stammered. "Large numbers of Soulan horsemen are hitting the right flank. The 22nd Infantry has been reported as overrun and routed from their camps and General Raymond is missing! General Hartley of the 29th Infantry reports that he is heavily engaged and that his men are being forced back steadily by the assault. There's also heavy smoke visible to the west in the vicinity of our lines."

For a very brief instant Wilson felt a tendril of fear running up his spine. This was the very thing he feared most though he never voiced that fear aloud. History had shown that the Soulan Army had a knack for flanking attacks and pincer warfare that Norland had never been able to withstand. He shook himself mentally.

This was what all their preparation was for, he reminded himself. Their men were trained to deal with this. He didn't know why the flank divisions were having so much difficulty, but he had cavalry of his own. Good cavalry.

"Send a runner to General Stone at once with orders for him to get his men mounted and prepared for battle. He is to report to me at once. GO!" The younger man ran from the tent as if he were pursued by a demon.

Wilson quickly donned his own sword and pulled on his boots. Already his personal servant was leading his horse forward. Wilson met the man at the entrance of the house he had made his quarters in and took the reins. His escort waited behind, already mounted. Wilson yelled for runners and dispatched several men in different directions with orders to get him information.

Stone rode up to him in less than ten minutes. A long time in battle, but not bad considering.

"My divisions will be mounted and formed in less than ten minutes," Stone reported without fanfare. "Do we have any idea of the size of the force or their current location?" Stone commanded the 1st Imperial Cavalry Corps, two entire divisions of expert horsemen levied with four battalions of the heathen from the Western lands.

"I'm waiting for that now," Wilson admitted. "I've got runners looking the situation over and gathering information. All I know for now is that Raymond is missing and his men have been routed. My last report from Hartley was that his men were hard pressed, but fighting. They are being forced back however, so I have to assume the enemy numbers are at least division strength."

"Likely more Corps level," Stone murmured. "I'd not attack a position as strong as ours with less than two divisions, no matter how well trained or experienced." A courier rode up at that point halting their conversation.

"Sir, General Raymond is dead and his men are in full flight, what's left of them," the man reported. "General Hartley is also in full retreat, unable to rally his men. They have taken heavy losses and the enemy is pressing their attack even now. General Taylor has his 16th Infantry on line and is preparing to receive the enemy, but none of his men are mounted and they have no pikes to counter a cavalry charge."

"Why are they so unprepared?" Stone demanded, drawing a scowl from Wilson.

"We'll deal with that later," he snapped. "For now, I want you to form your men and prepare to take the enemy in their left flank from our own lines. That will relieve the pressure on the right of the army, and prevent their getting into our rear areas. Hurry! I will ride to Taylor's position and try to rally those men from Raymond and Hartley's commands." He looked at the courier.

"Go directly to General Bagwell's headquarters and inform him of the situation. If he is not already marshaling his men, he is to do so at once and bring them to Taylor's relief. Ride!" The courier spurred his steed and took off at a gallop. Stone likewise went galloping back to his command.

Wilson set out to Taylor's position, his escort following. This was a disaster already, even if the enemy force was completely destroyed. The loss of so many men and so much in stores and equipment would not be looked upon with anything but scorn by the Emperor. Wilson needed to salvage what he could, while he could. He had no doubt that Daly would take full advantage of this attack to try and undermine his position.

He snorted in irony as he realized that this attack also validated every concern he had voiced to Daly about securing their flank before moving forward. The error was in worrying about the left. Apparently Therron McLeod had at least one competent commander in his retinue of boot licking nobles who knew his business. His spy network had missed that information and now Wilson and his men were paying for it.

CHAPTER FIVE

-

Parno felt uneasy for some reason. All the reports were good, the attack succeeding beyond his hopes so far. They had damaged the enemy severely while their own losses were all but negligible. For Parno there were no negligible losses, as each one represented a man lost to Soulan forever. But his losses when compared to the damage he could see in the Nor camps were almost non-existent.

So why did he feel so uneasy?

"Enri," he said, more calmly than he felt. "Sound the Recall and Reform," he ordered. "Now," he stressed when Enri looked at him.

"Sound Recall!" Enri shouted to the buglers nearby and both lifted their horns, one left and one right. As the call went out, Enri turned to Parno.

"Milord, we are not yet to the objective line," he said. "Why are we pulling back?"

"I don't. . .there's something wrong," Parno said, trying to find the words he needed. "I don't know what, but something is out of place. We need to call it a day, Enri. We've done well. Let's not endanger that by staying overlong."

"Milord, resistance is almost non-existent!" Enri pointed out. "We have them on the run! We should at least pursue to our original objective!"

"No," Parno shook his head. "There's something off kilter. I don't. . .I can't see what it is, but there's something wrong. I want our men reformed as soon as possible. Make it happen," he ordered more firmly. He was tired of arguing.

"Aye, milord," Enri's reluctance was clear but he followed his orders. As runners began to report units returning to the embarkation line, a galloping courier slid his horse to a stop before Parno's command group.

"Nor cavalry moving on our left in great numbers, milord!" one of Parsons' men reported breathlessly. "I can't tell how many, sire, there's too many to count effectively. My estimate is two divisions, based on pennant counts."

Parno felt his stomach knot. Two divisions of Nor cavalry on their flank and the balance of the Nor Army to their front. It was time to call this a day.

"How close?" Enri asked, a look of bewilderment on his face as he glanced at his Marshal.

"Less than a mile, sir!" the courier replied. "Moving parallel to our people for the moment. They have placed themselves between us and the Nor rear areas for now."

"All units are reformed, milord!" another rider called. "Awaiting orders."

"Sound the return to line," Parno ordered his buglers. Both began blowing the required call. Parno looked at Enri.

"We cannot let that force cut us off from our line of retreat," he said firmly. "Send a man to the commander of the 21st Archers, and have his men ready to screen out movements. A cloud or two of arrows might discourage all but the most hardy." He turned to Karls.

"How many men do we have mounted?" he asked.

"Just over five hundred, milord," Karls replied at once.

"Form the Sheep into line, then."

"Parno, our mission was to keep you safe," Karls half objected even as he sent runners to the separate companies to form on his location.

"I don't know how capable the others are," Parno said softly. "I do know how capable our men are. If the Archers need assistance, we'll provide it from the line. I want the Sheep to stand by to screen the medical train. Get them and the wounded back to our lines and do so right now! Go!"

Karls nodded and set his own horse in motion. Parno looked over at Berry, who looked distinctly uncomfortable.

"Don't worry," Parno half-smiled. "We're not going into the line today."

Berry might have sighed in relief. It was hard to tell with his usual stoicism in place.

"Archer Brigade in screening position, milord," Enri reported. "2nd Cavalry in support for the moment. How did you -"

"I don't know and that bothers me almost as much as knowing at all," Parno told him flatly. "For now let's just worry about getting our men out of here, all right?"

"Of course, milord," Enri nodded, and started yelling orders. Parno watched, hoping that he was in time to prevent a disaster.

-

"What do you mean, withdrawing?" Wilson demanded, looking at the courier.

"They have abandoned the attack, General," the runner repeated. "They are withdrawing back to the west at this time. General Stone and his men are approaching our own rear-right, but have had no contact with the enemy."

"My men report the same," Taylor added, receiving reports of his own at the same time. "The attack against our front has withdrawn. Not stalled, not halted, but withdrawn. I don't understand either," he shrugged. Where Raymond and Hartley had failed miserably, Taylor had done well and knew it. His men had held the line. Barely to be sure, but held they had. That gave him a certain confidence.

Wilson turned to a runner on a fresh mount.

"Inform General Stone he is to pursue the enemy and destroy them," he ordered grimly. "He is to press his attack to the fullest extent, halting before encountering the Soulan lines. Clear?"

"Yes, General!" the runner saluted and rode off at a gallop.

"Sir, that might not be the best idea," Taylor said hesitantly. "It's possible that is exactly the move the enemy hopes we will take."

"Therron McLeod isn't that smart," Wilson snorted. "He's a pompous, arrogant ass who is convinced of the superiority of himself and his army. He no doubt thinks he's won a great victory and now he's retiring to enjoy the laurels." Wilson looked grim as he gazed toward the west.

"He's about to learn that he isn't quite as smart as he may believe."

-

"How many?" Parno demanded as Doak Parsons and three of his men rode up, horses flecked with foam from exertion.

"Was I a bettin' man, which I'm not, I'd say there's a minimum of three divisions as we would count it. We've identified seven different brigades in the last twenty minutes. And they've formed up now and are moving through the wood line. It looks like they intend to try and pursue, or even ride us down."

Parno considered that. His men outnumbered the enemy, but the enemy was fresh. The deciding factor would be how well trained, disciplined and mounted the Nor cavalry were. He considered what his 'spy' network had learned.

"Do they look smart?" he asked. Parsons nodded.

"They do indeed, milord, bad as I hate to admit it. Dressed lines, flankers, van, and scouts. They know their business."

"Thank you," Parno murmured. "Please stay close by for the moment," he added absently. Parsons and his men moved just out of earshot.

He had the numbers, probably. His men had been in action for over two hours, however. They and their mounts were tired. While their losses had been light, there were still holes in their formations. The men would be flush with victory, eager to tangle with this Nor cavalry force, but that same eagerness could turn to ash if the battle was prolonged and the Nor infantry managed to get into the fight.

Still, he hated to simply turn and go when there was a chance to bloody the Nor again. Mind racing furiously, he turned to Enri Willard.

"How many archers do you think in the three divisions combined?" he asked. Willard blinked.

"I, ah, I don't know, sir," Willard admitted. "I'll find out."

"Quickly now," Parno nodded, waving for Parsons. The scout commander rode to his prince.

"Take as many of your men as you can lay hand to quickly and do two things. One, I need a screen to the east to warn me if the Nor infantry begin to come into play. Second, I need to know where that cavalry force is at all times and where they're heading. Understand?"

"Aye, milord," Parsons nodded. "We're on it." Parsons rode away with his subordinates running to gather their comrades. Parno waved a runner to him.

"I want you to find General Beaumont, 2nd Brigade, 6th Cavalry, and have him detach his unit and report to me personally. On the double, now!" The runner was gone at a gallop before Parno finished his last sentence. Enri Willard returned from where he'd been conferring with some of the staff officers.

"Milord, by most estimates there should be at least a full regiment of bowmen spread among each division. More in some places but at least that many, depending on today's losses."

"Have them pulled from the line and attached to the 21st Archer Brigade at once," Parno ordered quickly. "Then have all three division commanders reform line abreast in the same formation we used for the attack, but oriented east-west this time. Two up and one back as before. The center will be here," Parno stabbed a hand toward the ground beneath him. "I want it done now."

"Aye, milord!" Enri nodded and began dispatching runners with new orders. Parno sat his horse, absently chewing on his bottom lip. Was he missing something? And where had that uneasy feeling come from earlier? Had he ignored it his army would even now be hard pressed and in danger of losing a sizable number of its men and horses.

And we still might, he thought to himself. *This might not work.* He shook the thought away. It would work if everyone followed their orders and if orders arrived fast enough to make adjustments. And if the Nor were wanting a stand-up fight the way he thought they did.

It was too many ifs for comfort, but the truth was, the *fact* was, Parno needed a victory if he could get one. True he'd already led his men in a good effort and bloodied the enemy very well, but if they could engage and destroy, or at least defeat and drive off the Nor cavalry, that would help him at least two ways.

First, his men would have their confidence back. Winning on the field of battle was the best morale builder there was combat troops. Secondly, it would shake the Nor confidence in their new-found cavalry force. It might make them more timid the next time they met in battle.

And, I want to thrash them good just on general principles, he admitted to himself. This might be an opportunity to hand the Nor a good whipping and he couldn't afford to just toss that chance away. If it looked like he couldn't manage it, then he would order the withdrawal. Otherwise he would try and do as much damage as he could while conserving his own force.

It wasn't much of a plan in all honesty, but it was the best he could do on the fly.

"What are you planning, my Prince?" Cho Feng's voice broke into his thoughts. Startled, Parno whipped around to stare at his mentor. He hadn't even heard Cho ride up.

"I'm going to lure them forward into a trap, I hope," Parno told him, briefly outlining his idea. Feng listened without comment, then nodded slightly.

"A sound stratagem," was all he said. Parno fought the urge to curse. There were times when Feng could be infuriatingly quiet, and others when all Parno wanted for the man to stop talking. Feng always seemed to know which it was that Parno wanted and gave him the opposite just for spite. Or for fun, maybe.

"Archers are on the way, milord," Enri Willard arrived and reported. "Lines are reforming as well. We currently have one regiment spread across the front as a screen. So far only light skirmishing."

"Let's keep it that way," Parno ordered. "I do not want a major engagement except on our terms. Make sure all commanders know that." Willard turned and pointed to three runners who had heard the Prince's orders and they took off. Willard then turned back to Parno.

"What *are* our terms, exactly, milord?" he asked.

"Let them come," Parno told him. "I think they want a fight and we're going to give them one if we can do it in such a way that we have the advantage. I want to bloody this cavalry force, hard and fast, then we'll withdraw to our own lines."

"We'll clash if they offer battle here where we want them to and test their mettle. Before we can be hurt too badly however, we'll pull back. At that point the combined archer force will loose three flights as cover, then retreat with the rest of us."

Willard nodded as the plan played out in his mind's eye. It was a good tactic. It offered the most reward for the most reasonable risk.

"And if they refuse battle?" he asked.

"Then we'll let them," Parno replied at once. "I want a larger victory today if we can get it, but today has already been enough to help restore morale. And to let the Nor know that play time's over. From here on out, they pay for every inch of Soulan soil they walk on." The grim tone in his Prince's voice drew a nod of approval from all around him, though he didn't notice. His eyes were set ahead of him.

On the battlefield where his first large action was about to play out in front of him.

"How many?"

"We've identified at least a regiment of screen, General," the courier informed Wilson. "We've managed to get brief looks beyond at the main force and they may be reforming. They are continuing to retreat at the present, however."

Wilson nodded, considering. The Soulanies rarely formed unique Army Corps specializing in one branch as did his own army. That should mean that the two or three divisions of enemy cavalry facing him would not answer to an organized central command the way Stone's men answered to him directly.

But the fact that the Soulan Army didn't organize the same way meant that Wilson had no idea which southern General would be in command of this effort. Knowing who was in command might make the difference in battle. If Therron McLeod had organized this attack himself then it was also possible he was along and exercising command himself. That was highly unlikely given what Wilson knew of the Southron Prince. McLeod at his best was arrogant and over-confident.

"Inform General Stone that the enemy may be reforming to his front, and that I want him to engage the enemy as closely as possible. His orders are to do as much damage as possible to the southerners before they can reach their own lines. He is not, I repeat not, to engage the southern fortifications. Understood?"

"Yes sir!" The courier replied and spurred his horse away. Wilson sat for a moment, considering his next options. He motioned for another courier.

"Ride to General Taylor's headquarters. Inform him to take command of any stragglers from Raymond and Hartley's commands, incorporate them into his own force, and begin moving into a flanking position on the southerner's right flank." He looked to another runner.

"You will inform General Fairmount to form his entire corps behind Taylor and be prepared to press any advantage we can gain from this engagement. Go!" Both men tore away from him at high speed. Wilson watched them go, and his eye was drawn to movement. A look of disgust crossed his features as he recognized Daly and his retinue moving toward him.

For a moment he considered heading closer to the battle to avoid the man, but shook the thought away. Runners and commanders knew where he was for the moment. If he moved, they would waste valuable time relocating him.

"What has happened, General?" Daly asked as he approached. "I thought we were secure here." Sarcasm tinged the man's voice and Wilson was gripped with a near over-whelming urge to run Daly through with his sword.

"And I warned you that this was the very reason that we had halted our advance," Wilson shot back. "The Soulanies have attacked in force from our flank. They attempted to get into our rear areas but have been repulsed. We are now pushing forward in an attempt to engage them more closely before they can return to the safety of their own lines."

"I see," Daly replied. "Apparently our standing on the defensive was not effective."

"To the contrary," Wilson tried to sound friendly but it was a strain. "We were able to prevent the Soulan Army's favorite tactic from being used against us and thanks to General Taylor's efforts and General Stone's rapid response we still have the chance to do serious damage to the Soulan cavalry force." He turned away, looking toward the battlefield in the distance.

"They had to have stripped most of their active cavalry units from their lines to organize an attack on this scale. If we can cut them off, we stand an excellent chance of eliminating the most serious threat against our continued advance. With their cavalry force destroyed or even just damaged we will no longer have to be so concerned with flanking maneuvers such as this one in the future." He forced a smile as he looked back to Daly.

"This day may well be the beginning of the end, General."

-

"General Beaumont reporting, sir!"

Parno resisted the urge to smile. Beaumont clearly believed in leading from the front. The man's uniform was torn in two places, blood stained in one, and his sword was also bloody as it dangled in his hand, held down to his side. Three men rode with him and no more.

"How goes it, General?" Parno asked. Beaumont grinned at the Prince.

"We've given them a hot day indeed, milord!" he replied enthusiastically. "And I believe that we will soon have a chance to bloody them again, your orders permitting of course."

"Oh, my orders permit," Parno nodded firmly. "I want you to form your men right here, General," Parno motioned around him. "This is going to be the center of our line, and I want you right here. The others will form to your right and left of line. When the Nor come calling, we'll meet them with southern steel."

"Outstanding!" Beaumont positively beamed at the chance to be in the thick of the fight. He turned to his followers.

"Regimental commanders to meet here in five minutes. First and Second regiments to form front, Third in reserve. I want to see lines forming in no more than ten minutes from right now, so move!" All three galloped away, reins lashing their mounts to urge them onward.

"How are your men and horses, General?" Parno asked.

"Winded but able, milord," Beaumont replied at once. "We'll stand at least one good clash with no great difficulty. After that it will depend on how spirited the fight is."

Parno nodded. Beaumont's assessment agreed with his own. As he considered that he noted the Brigadier commanding the 21st Horse Archers approaching.

General Horace Whipple saluted smartly. His clean uniform was in stark contrast to Beaumont's, but Parno noted that the man carried a bow of his own already in hand.

"General, I am detaching all mounted archers from the three divisions and attaching them to your command for the rest of the engagement. You will form your men in three ranks behind the main lines, and stay out of the action unless and until you receive orders to the contrary."

"My plan for the moment is to engage the approaching Nor cavalry in open combat, bleeding them as heavily as possible before our mounts tire. As soon as you hear Recall sound, your men will ready their bows. If the Nor pursue, and I think they'll be mad enough to do so, you will launch three flights in rapid succession the minute they enter your range. The instant you loose the third flight your men will wheel and retreat along with the cavalry. Questions?"

"If the Nor begin to withdraw, may we pursue?" Whipple asked, eyes almost alight.

"Under no circumstances," Parno replied firmly. "You and your men are not expendable. I expect Nor infantry to approach our right within the hour. Our goal here is to bloody and demoralize the Nor cavalry force. To shake their confidence in themselves and their commanders. We will not seek a protracted engagement without our own infantry to support us." He paused, then grinned slightly.

"I only want to spank them today, General." Whipple threw his head back and laughed, Beaumont joining him.

"Then by the Crown, spank them we will, milord! With your permission?"

"Carry on," Parno nodded. Whipple and his runners turned to carry out their orders.

Parno returned his attention to the action around him. Regiments were already falling into line and Beaumont was riding to the front of his troops, screaming them into line and readiness. Parno caught sight of Enri Willard moving along the front and raised a hand to draw his Chief of Staff's attention. The former duelist reined his horse in beside the Prince.

"All commanders have their orders, milord," he reported. "I estimate we'll be prepared within ten minutes."

"Good, because I suspect that's about all the time we'll have," Parno replied, pointing to the front. Willard turned his mount, gaze following Parno's hand. Two of Parsons' men were riding toward them as fast as their horses would fly. A cloud of dust flew up around them as they reined their mounts to a halt.

"Milord, Cap'n Parsons' compliments, sir, and the Nor appear to be advancing in order. He estimates we're facing a full two divisions of cavalry, sir, with attachments also possible but unconfirmed. He further reports that a Nor infantry force is attempting to form on our right, but show no signs at present of advancing. He believes, milord, that force is the remnants of those units we attacked earlier trying to re-organize. We have men keeping an eye on them too, milord Parno."

"Very well," Parno nodded. "Please inform Captain Parsons that he is to take all precautions to preserve his force. You are to fall back under the Nor advance without engaging. In fact, I'd prefer it if they thought we were in full retreat. Please pass that along to the screen commander as well."

"Will do, milord!" the man nodded and he and his companion headed back for the approaching enemy.

Parno watched them go, trying to picture in his mind the way the battlefield was developing. He had studied maps of this area in detail before he had made the trip west, and had looked again last night to make sure he knew what he was getting his men into. In addition, he had the report of Parsons and his men from two days prior, so there shouldn't be any surprises in the geography.

The unknown factor here was in the abilities of his men and those of the Nor cavalry and their commander. Was he aggressive? Cautious? Would he attack them head on or try for subterfuge and hit them on an oblique? He turned to Enri.

"Make sure we have a few scouts along the western edge of our flank," he ordered his Chief of Staff. "We don't know who's in command of that cavalry force. I think he'll hit us head on trying to prove himself and his men, but that might just be wishful thinking."

"Already done, milord," Enri nodded, smiling slightly. "That's what you pay me for," he added before Parno could extend his thanks. "Let us deal with the straps and buckles, milord, while you watch over the wagon. We can't have you distracted by mundane tasks that any good commander knows to make."

"How many good commanders do we have, Enri?" Parno asked, surprising the older man. "How deep does my brother's rot go in this army?"

Willard's face showed his own discomfort at the question, having been one of those duped by the turncoat prince.

"That's not directed at you," Parno told him flatly. "You should know that, by now," he added. "You've earned my trust, Enri, and my respect. I'm speaking about those we don't know. Those who may have little or no respect for the authority of the King. Men led astray by promises my brother made when he assumed his ascension to the throne would actually happen."

"It seems that it almost *did* happen, milord," Enri was almost hesitant. "Milord, I want you to know that I had no ide -" He stopped at Parno's upraised hand.

"If I thought you had been, you would be dead already," Parno told him simply, and Enri blinked. He knew far better than most that the young Prince's words were not an idle threat. "Put that worry from your mind. We have plenty to worry over at the moment without you borrowing useless notions."

"Aye, milord," Enri nodded, inordinately pleased at Parno's assurance. It seemed wrong, somehow, that a veteran soldier should be reassured by a man who had fought only one battle so far and had not yet reached twenty-one full seasons of age, and yet. . .Enri Willard shrugged mentally. It was what it was. There was a quality about Parno McLeod that inspired men to follow him. To do more than they themselves thought possible.

And thank God we have him, Willard thought darkly, turning his attention back to the wood line ahead. In mere minutes thousands of Nor cavalry would come screaming out of those trees with blood in their eyes and a need to prove themselves. He and the rest of the army did indeed have plenty to worry about.

Unaware of Enri Willard's soul searching, Parno watched as Beaumont finished dressing his lines, cursing and kicking and even complimenting on occasion. Parno smiled at the memory of Darvo Nidiad that Beaumont's behavior brought to his mind, then the smile departed at the reminder that he no longer had Darvo to depend on.

He had meant it when he'd told Enri Willard that the older man had earned his trust, but Parno would likely never trust anyone to the degree he had trusted Darvo. The old soldier had been his only real father in a time when his family shunned him and the royal retainers followed suit for the most part. It had been a favorite pastime to 'pick' on the royal that no one would defend.

No one but Darvo. The man had never once deserted him, misled him, turned away from him. Always Darvo had been there for him. Always.

But not anymore.

Parno shook those thoughts away. He had no time for this. Self-pity of any kind was as unknown to him as fear for his physical well-being. And right now, he had much bigger things than his -.

"Rider coming, milord," Harrel Sprigs mentioned softly, pointing toward a galloping horse that had just emerged from the woods. Parno hadn't even known Sprigs was nearby.

He squinted at the rider, recognizing him as one of Parson's scouts. The man practically slid to a halt, his horse foaming with sweat.

"Milord, the heathen are no more than five hundred yards out and advancing!" the man reported breathlessly. "Cap'n Parson requests orders, sir!"

"Withdraw to the east and continue to screen the flank against possible infantry attack," Parno ordered at once with no need for thought. "Keep us aware of any danger to our right. We'll worry with the 'heathen' from here on out."

"Sir!" the man nodded and was once more in motion, on his way back to relay these new orders. Parno attracted Beaumont's attention and waved him over.

"We have minutes at best," Parno concluded after repeating the warnings of the scout. "You're ready I presume?"

"That we are, milord," Beaumont nodded grimly. "Ready and waiting."

"Good," Parno nodded. "I want you and your men to be the rear-guard when we withdraw," he told Beaumont and the man literally came to attention in the saddle.

"You'll be there to screen Whipple's men if needed and to prevent a surprise charge from hitting our backs when we're least prepared."

"Thank you, sir!" Beaumont's normally boisterous voice was subdued. "My men appreciate your confidence." Parno nodded and raised a hand in dismissal. Beaumont raised a hand in half salute and returned to scream at his men a bit more, this time encouragingly. Parno chuckled lightly, shaking his head at the man. He really was a force of nature.

"Any last orders, milord?" Whipple's voice made him turn. The Archery Brigadier was sitting his horse beside the Prince, still carrying his bow. Parno decided the man likely didn't realize he was carrying it at all.

"General Beaumont and his men will screen your men as you engage, should it become necessary," Parno told the archer. "Remember, three flights and flee. I want no casualties of any kind that we can possibly avoid."

"It will be so, milord," Whipple nodded.

"Carry on, then, and Godspeed," Parno ordered. Whipple raised his bow to his brow and then hurried back to his own men,

"Quite a pair, aren't they, Harrel?" Parno noted. "More like drill sergeants than Brigadiers, aren't they." It was a statement rather than a question.

"Both came up through the ranks, milord," Sprigs replied. "Whipple had the advantage of nobility in so far as education was concerned, but he entered the army as a private and asked no special privilege. Beaumont actually began his career as a private as well, then left active duty for a while for a posting in the Tinsee militia, after which he was called back to active duty to teach horsemanship. He was commissioned a Captain and placed in charge of the riding school at Donson Academy. From there he managed to gain a field command and since then has worked his way up to his present rank." By the time Sprigs had finished Parno was just staring at him.

"How in the hell do you *know* all that?" Parno demanded. "I got here the *same time you did!*"

"It's my -"

"-job to know. Yes, I've heard that one already," Parno raised a hand to stop his aide. "Do you *ever* sleep?"

"Of course, milord," Sprigs was taken aback by the question. "Whenever I'm tired, in fact."

"Well, you're doing a fine job," Parno told him without a hint of reluctance. "What else do you know about them?"

"What do you mean, milord?"

"I mean are they the kind of men to be led astray by Th. . .my brother's actions, or would they remain loyal to Soulan? Are they trustworthy enough to entrust the safety of the Kingdom with? If it became necessary?"

"With respect, sir, yes I believe they are," Sprigs shocked him yet again.

"Both men have worked very hard to gain their positions, and did so in an environment designed specifically by your brother to keep such men 'in their place'. There will be no lingering loyalty issues with those two." He stopped when he realized that Parno was staring at him again.

"It's my -"

"Job to know," Parno finished for him again. "Yes, I do believe I've got it. Well, assuming we survive the next two or so hours, give or take, it will be your job to extend an invitation to both men to my mess this evening, and ensure that we can properly entertain such men."

"I'll see to it, sir," Sprigs nodded calmly. Parno studied his aide for another few seconds then turned away with a slight shake of his head. It was difficult to rattle Harrel Sprigs.

"Screen returning, milord," Harrel spoke gently. Parno nodded as he caught sight of the screening regiment coming through the trees before them.

"General!" he called to Beaumont. The Brigadier looked to his Prince, then followed the point to see the regiment fleeing from the trees.

"READY FRONT!" Beaumont bellowed at once, turning back to his command. "STEADY!"

"Milord, you should move back some," Berry recommended gently. "We're in the way, here."

"Very well," Parno nodded, pretending not to notice Berry's relief. He resisted the urge to shake his head. Everyone wanted to treat him as if he would break. His escort formed around him as he moved behind Whipple's waiting archers, the Archery Brigadier's attention focused on the front of the battle line. Enri Willard joined Parno's group as they halted well back from the front.

"Are we ready, Brigadier?" Parno asked formally and Willard nodded.

"All in readiness, milord. We've a regiment on the left to watch for any attack from the west, a line of scouts to the right to keep an eye on the infantry that are trying to reform, and all three divisions are in place on line, ready for action."

Parno nodded his understanding, watching the distant tree line through is glass now. He had done all he could in the time he had. Like it or not, he would now have to depend on his commanders.

-

General Brent Stone, commanding the 1st Norland Imperial Cavalry Corps, followed closely behind his advancing men surrounded by aides, runners, and a small escort. His last message from General Wilson was direct and to the point.

Attack and destroy. He meant to do just that.

Stone had grown up riding horses and had always been offended at the notion that the Southrons were just naturally better than his own people in the saddle. The opportunity to prove Norland superiority in mounted action was a gift from above as far as he was concerned.

"Southern forces appear to be in complete flight, General," a rider informed him. "We see no attempt as yet to reform or make a stand."

"That may be a trap," Stone replied. "See to it that all commanders know to maintain the ranks. I want our discipline intact. We will attack as a unified force and not as an undisciplined mob. Make sure everyone knows that." Several runners spurred their horses away to deliver their General's message.

"Send a man to General Taylor and another the General Wilson informing them were are about to engage if the Southrons will offer battle," he told his aide. "Suggest to General Taylor that if he can be prepared to move against their right, with General Wilson's approval of course, that we will attempt to turn the enemy in his direction."

"Yes sir," the aide replied and immediately summoned two more riders. Stone turned his attention back to his own forces. He could see that the tree line was thinning. According to his scouts there should be a clearing ahead. Stone figured this would be the most likely place for the southern cavalry to make it's stand if they intended to make one short of their own lines.

He hoped they would, since his own orders prevented him from pursuing within range of the enemy lines themselves. If the enemy reached their own lines, then his opportunity to engage would be lost.

He saw a slight ripple in his forward ranks and frowned slightly. That shouldn't be happening.

"See what that's about," he ordered the nearest runner, pointing toward the now ragged area of his formation. The man sketched a salute and spurred his horse in that direction. Stone was about to call his aide over when he saw one of the Wildmen, a tribal leader of some sort named Blue Dog, heading in his direction.

Stone despised the heathens from the west with all his might. They were savage to a fault and had no apparent regard for anything other than the blood they shed so willingly. Stone was a soldier and as such he expected to have to shed blood in battle but. . . .

He shook those thoughts away. His Emperor had dictated that he would work with the godless savages, and so he would. That was that.

"General Stone," the man spoke in heavily accented and broken Nor. "You mans losing their line."

"I've sent a man to straighten it out," Stone acknowledged the failure. "We've been in these woods for some time. It was bound to happen."

"Line too long, too much mans," Blue Dog pointed out. "Better to have small line." This was an old argument with him.

"I'm sure it would," Stone tried to be diplomatic. "But we don't have that option in this case. The Southrons are here in force. If we use smaller units or shorter lines, we invite defeat in detail."

"Southmans better at horse war," Blue Dog said flatly. "Fight them their way, lose much mans. Much horses. Better to fight *Tumcah* way. Southmans not so good then." *Tumcah* was their word for themselves, Stone remembered. It meant 'the people' as best he could recall. It had always seemed arrogant to him.

"If we could, we probably would," Stone nodded. "We can't face them in greater numbers like your people. We do not yet have the skill. But we are learning."

And when we have you'll be sorry you ever met us, Stone thought savagely. He knew of the plans to turn on the Western tribes once the southern kingdom was conquered.

Blue Dog turned savage eyes on Stone, regarding him so seriously that for a moment Stone wondered if he'd spoke his thoughts aloud. Then Blue Dog shrugged, turning his horse away.

"We hold Right Horn," he said over his shoulder. "Protect flank. Try save you when time come, but no promise."

"We'll take our chances," Stone managed not to snarl. Arrogant heathen bastard. He ignored the departing savage and turned his attention back to his own forces. His front line seemed to have corrected itself, and was emerging into the clearing it looked like.

"Enemy in sight!" a runner cried. "Southern Cavalry formed ahead, offering battle!"

"Excellent!" Stone almost rubbed his hands together. "All commanders!" he called to his runners. "Dress lines at the tree line, prepare for attack! On the double quick!" The runners took off flaying their horses with their reins, others taking their place in line.

Stone watched as his lines reformed, regaining the cohesion lost in the woods. He was almost close enough now to see the enemy lines.

"Sir," his aide sounded worried as he came to Stone's side. "Sir it appears we are facing at least three divisions of enemy cavalry here. Perhaps the prudent thing would be to await General Taylor and his infantry before we -"

"Nonsense!" Stone cut the man off with a snort. "Our divisions are larger than theirs and better equipped." It was the standard line, repeated so often that it had become truth. The aide was no fool, however, and knew the lie that lay behind the statement. It was well and good to tell the rank and file troops that their training and equipment were superior to the enemy. It gave them the confidence they needed to meet the enemy in the field of battle.

Generals starting to believe their own propaganda was another thing entirely.

"Sir, I must advise caution here," his Chief of Staff, an experienced cavalry commander in his own right, added his concerns to the aide's. "The enemy has done an excellent job screening his movements so far. If we can see them now, it's because they *want* to be seen. And I'm not entirely sure that our divisions are numerically superior, either. With their militia units in the field, their ranks could have swelled considerably by now."

"You're advocating we do not engage?" Stone looked incredulous. "This is the chance we've been waiting for!"

"One the enemy had presented us," his Chief of Staff reminded him. "They wouldn't invite an attack if they weren't ready for it."

"I agree, sir," the aide nodded his agreement. "This doesn't feel right."

"I can't base our plan of attack on superstitions and 'feelings' gentlemen," Stone snapped. "If you have sound facts that should be considered then present them. Otherwise as soon as we hear from General Taylor -" He broke off as a runner galloped up beside him.

"General Taylor's compliments, sir, and he is trying to reform the broken divisions with his own men. He estimates it will take at least an hour to have a suitable force into position. His own men are heavily fatigued from the earlier fighting and have taken considerable casualties in that action. Hartley and Raymond's units are mostly routed he reports, and his men and the Provost are attempting to get them into line again." Another runner approached as the man finished his report.

"General Wilson's orders, sir," the man held out a message for Stone. His aide took it and passed it along to his general. Stone opened the form and read Wilson's terse orders.

"We are to attack as soon as we are into position, not waiting for the infantry to form. They will form as they can on our left and then support the attack if the battle is protracted. He desires that we engage and destroy the enemy cavalry force if at all possible, though our orders to stay clear of their lines remain unchanged." He folded the message and looked at his two subordinates.

"Well, gentlemen?" he raised an eyebrow. "I'm listening." Both men looked away, uncomfortable with such pressure. Orders from so high up the chain of command could not simply be set aside, regardless of their fears. It was well and good to offer advice. Taking responsibility themselves was another thing entirely.

"As I suspected," Stone didn't hide his scorn and the two men flushed but remained silent. Stone searched behind him, locating the three buglers that accompanied him. He waved the young men over. All three looked as if they had yet to need a razor.

"Sound the Ready," Stone ordered without fanfare. "Wait one minute, then sound advance." The men nodded and separated to help their calls carry. Stone looked at his subordinates again, then back to the front. The bugles began to sound, and the matter was out of his hands.

They were committed.

-

"Sounds like they're coming," Enri said softly to Parno. The prince nodded, but stayed silent. His mind was racing far ahead, planning his next steps. If the Nor did this, what would he do then? If they flanked, or tried to, how to respond? Should they break, would he change his orders and pursue?

No, that was definitely out. Pursuit would put them right back into the bee hive they had kicked over this morning. If the Nor offered him the chance to bloody them here and now, he would take it. But there would be no pursuit. He turned to his runners.

"Inform all commanders that my orders not to pursue are not subject to change," he ordered. "We will not, *under any circumstance*, pursue the enemy even if they are fleeing in disorder. We are still vastly outnumbered and a long way from any support. Go!" The runners shot away, galloping for the division commanders. Parno rode to where Beaumont was studying the Nor in the distance.

"Remember that we are not to pursue," he ordered the energetic cavalryman. "We are too far from support and too near their lines."

"Aye, milord," Beaumont nodded. "I'm not so sure we'll see them rout anyway," he added softly. "Appears they are well disciplined sire, and probably better led than we've faced before." Parno nodded his agreement, his assessment of Beaumont rising another peg based on that observation. Before either could say more one of Parsons' men slid in before Parno.

"Milord, we've seen a few Wildmen on the left," the man reported. "We can't as yet determine how many, but there's at least two groups, company strength or better. They aren't probing or attacking but our left is under observation."

Parno nodded. Thanks to the efforts of Edema Willows, he had known that the Nor had made a treaty of some sort with the savage tribes of the west, so he wasn't surprised at their presence here. The question of import was how *many* were here, and would they engage, or merely watch?

"Keep them under observation, but do not attack," Parno ordered. "Notify General O'Hare to detach one regiment to serve as flanking guard if he has not already done so. We cannot allow them to get around behind us." The rider saluted and took off at once.

"That's a bad business," Beaumont murmured. "Murderin' savages on our flank, helpin' these heathen."

"It is indeed," Parno nodded calmly. "Now you see why we're limiting our attack today, General."

"I do, milord," Beaumont nodded respectfully. "And it's a good plan, if I may add."

"Thanks," Parno grinned, then straightened as the first Nor lines emerged from the tree lines. He studied them for a moment, face pensive with thought.

"I think they're going to try and charge us, milord," Beaumont sounded eager as he spoke. "We can meet them mid-way."

"No, I think we'll try something else instead," Parno grinned suddenly.

"Harrel!" Sprigs was next to him in an instant.

"My compliments to General Whipple, and he may engage at will as soon as the Nor charge is in range. He will conserve his fire to be able to lay the covering fire I requested, and will cease fire as soon as the battle is joined. Until then and subject to those conditions, he may use his own judgment."

"Yes sir!" Sprigs nodded and shot away to Whipple's post to relay his commander's instructions. Parno turned to Beaumont.

"You may go out to meet them when they reach the half way point of the clearing, General," he said softly. "Take care that you are not injured, as I desire your presence at dinner this evening. Understood?" Beaumont suddenly gave his commander his undivided attention.

"Understood, milord," he nodded.

"Then I leave it to you," Parno nodded, turning his horse. "Give them hell Buford, and kill all of them you can." With that Parno spurred his horse away, followed by Berry and his runners. Parno motioned for three runners to join him as he rode.

"Inform Generals O'Hare, Bellamy, and Fordyce that they will look to the center. When the center charges, they will join. Remind them once more that we will not under any circumstances pursue beyond the clearing." The three saluted and hurried to convey these last instructions.

Parno noted that Whipple's men were moving into position behind the cavalry in two long lines. Whipple himself was in line, bow at the ready. He nodded to himself in appreciation. Yes, he and Beaumont would do nicely he thought. Very nicely indeed.

"HERE THEY COME!" he heard Beaumont bellow. Parno temporarily set aside his plans for the future as he turned to concentrate on the immediate problem. Unless they won here, his plans for later wouldn't matter much.

-

Stone looked at the assembled Southern cavalry and for just an instant felt apprehension. They didn't look as if they were about to bolt. The warnings of his subordinates came back to him. Perhaps they were correct that caution should be the order of the day. He was on the verge of ordering a halt when the bugles began blowing again, right on time with his previous orders.

His men shot forward. It was too late to turn back now.

-

Parno watched as the Nor cavalry charged across the clearing. He estimated no more than three hundred yards separated the Nor and his own lines, a distance the Nor were eating up as they galloped his way. He looked toward Whipple who had raised his arm holding a tall narrow pole with a yellow pennant flying in the wind.

His men, moving almost as one, drew arrows and nocked them. The cavalry archers followed suit, their own actions smooth enough though not in the same class as the men of the 21st Horse Archers.

Parno watched as Whipple studied the charging Nor intently. Parno noticed that Whipple's lips were moving slightly and realized that the archery Brigadier was counting something. Suddenly Whipple slapped the pennant down to the ground, the signal for his men to open fire.

Over three thousand arrows lofted in near unison over the heads of the waiting Soulan cavalry, flying across the distance. Parno's eyes followed them even as the archers drew new arrows. Those already in flight traveled in a smooth arc across the open ground and began slamming into Nor troopers and horses.

Screams from both man and beast began to reach his ears as the arrows found targets. Many were stuck multiple times resulting in horses and riders tripping and tumbling into the ground. This often caused riders behind them to stumble as well as they collided with those in front who had gone down. The carnage reminded him of the Gap in many ways. A small part of him wished he was more disturbed by it while the rest was grateful that he was beyond that now.

The Nor came on despite the loss of many of their own number. Their training was obviously better than ever before. It was difficult to train men to continue under fire and maintain their discipline. That was something that often came only with experience in battle. Yet these Nor troopers did just that. True, they already had at least some limited experience since the start of the war and it had apparently strengthened their training and their discipline.

The second flight arrived in their midst and then a third, Still the Nor continued the charge. Parno raised a hand and looked toward Beaumont. The Brigadier was sitting his horse, front and center, measuring the distance between his force and the enemy in much the same way Whipple had done. Suddenly his own pennant rose in the air and the men behind him drew swords, lowered lances and tightened reins.

Beaumont allowed two more flights to pass over head and then lowered his own pennant, yelling at the top of his lungs;

"CHARGE!"

His entire brigade seemed to lunge at the order, putting spurs to war mounts that were eager to close with the enemy. On both sides of him similar orders were shouted and bugles rose above the din to pass the orders along the line.

The Soulan ranks looked like a shallow, massive chevron as the center shot out in front, led by Beaumont and his men.

Whipple suddenly raised his pennant again, waving it back and forth to attract attention and his men held their fire, though stood prepared with arrows drawn for any order to continue. Parno noted that Whipple handed the pennant off to an aide taking another, red this time, which he held down toward the ground. He happened to turn Parno's way for a second and nodded calmly to his Prince. Parno returned the nod then brought his attention back to the battle.

The Nor ranks had been thinned some but there were still plenty of enemy cavalry to go around. Beaumont and his men rode straight into their midst, battle cries lifting all along the line. Parno watched as the two lines closed at breakneck speed, each side confident of their ultimate success.

The two lines collided with such force that Parno could literally feel the ground shaking as tens of thousands of horse hooves pounded the soil beneath them, digging deep into the ground to give the huge mounts the traction they needed to propel themselves forward. Parno lost sight of Beaumont as the lines met, the Brigadier concealed by the battle around him.

There was nothing he could do now but watch, and wait.

CHAPTER SIX

-

Stone cursed as he saw the effect of the southern archery against his men. While his cavalrymen had come a long way, there were no mounted archers among his men. It had taken all the training he could squeeze in to make them efficient riders and to ensure they could handle sword and lance. Using a bow from horseback was a unique skill set and few of his men could master it.

The savages of course were adept at horse archery and he had tried in vain to convince both the Wildmen and his own High Command to form at least a brigade of tribal archers for use with his cavalry. Wilson, along with the Army Chief of Staff, had been reluctant to have such a large force of the unruly and barely disciplined savages organized within their own ranks, while Blue Dog and the other leaders of the Wildmen had flatly refused to consider the option. They did not see the need for such organized specialties since most of their warriors could do pretty much anything from horseback.

Now Stone's men and horses paid the price for those refusals as they were assailed by arrows with no way to answer the attack.

But his men never faltered in the face of the enemy archery. Despite grievous losses they kept their lines and continued their charge across that open ground. Once they reached the enemy, things would change. Mixed in among their adversaries, the Imperial troopers would be safe from southern arrows.

He frowned as movement caught his eyes. Raising his glass, he peered through it at the enemy front, and felt himself falter, just a bit.

It seemed that the southerners would not be content just with waiting for his men to reach them after all.

-

Parno watched with heightened anticipation as his men clashed with the advancing Nor cavalry. The Nor general had made an error perhaps, though Parno wasn't yet sure of that. His lines were shorter than Parno's own, which meant that his men might be able to envelop the enemy flanks.

Just as that thought occurred to him, he remembered the report of Wildmen on his left flank. He motioned to Enri Willard, who rode to his side.

"Milord?"

"How secure is our left?" Parno asked at once. "I know there is a regiment there to guard the flank, but is it a good one? Well led? It occurs to me that our men may fall upon the Nor flanks since our lines extend somewhat past theirs. If we do, then our left will be exposed to attack. There may be more of the Tribal horsemen on our flank than we have yet seen."

"I'll look into it, milord," Enri promised and galloped away to do just that. Parno sat watching the developing battle, wishing now that he hadn't sent Karls and the Black Sheep away. If he had them present, then he could send them to the left to -

"Hot day, looks like," Karls Willard said gently. Parno's head snapped around, refusing to believe his ears.

"What are you doing here?" he demanded.

"We got the trains back, safe and sound," Karls shrugged. "When you didn't return, we decided to come back and see what was happening."

"We?" Parno repeated, turning in his saddle. Arrayed behind him at a respectful distance stood the Black Sheep, horses calm even in battle.

"We," Karls nodded. "You look pensive," Karls added, looking at his prince and friend.

"There are reports of Tribal Cavalry on our left," Parno nodded. "At least two company strength groups, but there could be more. I am concerned that they might hit our flank if the left falls in on the Nor. I should have thought of it sooner-"

"So should someone else," Karls broke in. "That's why you have a staff, and why officers are taught to think for themselves." He gathered his reins in hand. "We'll ride over that way and sort of have a look," he told Parno.

"There's a regiment over there already, but I don't know who. Enri has gone to see how good they might be and who is leading. But yes, I was just wishing you were here to send that way."

"Got that one wish and wasted it on us," Karls laughed. "We're on the way, milord." With that Karls moved back to where the Sheep were waiting and bellowed an order. In less than a minute the column was turned and on its way to the left of the Soulan lines. Parno relaxed visibly knowing that his most trusted subordinate, leading his most trusted men, would be there to watch for trouble.

With at least one worry gone, Parno turned his attention back to the battle before him.

-

General Stone felt most of his trepidation slip away as his men finally joined battle with the Southron cavalry. His men *were* well trained and they fought well against their supposedly superior foe. Their experiences coming south, though brief, had given them much needed confidence in themselves and their officers.

The length of his own lines compared to the southerner's concerned him a bit, but he realized that his line, while shorter, was also deeper. Where the Southron's had perhaps three to five men deep on line, his own forces numbered closer to six and seven, depending on the unit. He wasn't sure of the disparity in true numbers, but believed that his men would certainly hold their own and possibly do much more.

As he watched the battle progress, he aide murmured in his ear.

"One of the savages, sir. A runner." Stone looked around to see one of Blue Dog's men approaching. He was shirtless, as were most of the savage Tribesmen, and carried a lance. A short bow was slung over his shoulder. His horse was wiry, with little in the way of equipment the way his troopers had and was decorated along the same lines as the man himself. Stone resisted the urge to shake his head.

"Chief say Southmans work against right," the man reported without fanfare. "No attack, but stronger now. New mans there now, not there when fight start."

Soulanies were strengthening their right? During the battle? Their lines already extended beyond his own, so why move farther out? It didn't make sense, unless. . .Unless they were trying to break another unit into the rear areas of the army. He shook his head at that.

Surely even McLeod could see the folly in something like that. With the Imperial Army by now alerted all along the front it would be suicide. Assuming that McLeod wouldn't order something so sure to end in disaster, that left Stone wondering what they were doing.

Perhaps the southern officers had noticed Blue Dog's men along the right of line and were worried about an attack from that front. While there was no risk of that happening, the Soulanies didn't know that. If so, then anything that tied up their men in fruitless pursuits was a good thing. He turned to the runner.

"I believe that the southerners consider your presence on the flank threatening," he told the waiting savage. "If so, then they would have to move men to oppose any attack you might make. They are certainly more concerned with your fighting skills from horseback than our own." That hurt to say, but was true none-the-less, at least for now.

"Please ask your Chief if he will continue to demonstrate your presence on the right. Allow the enemy to see you, to know that you are still present. That alone will keep some of the enemy troops tied down and out of the battle here."

"I will say," the runner bowed his head in acknowledgment. "Chief may or may not do."

"That's fine," Stone nodded. He couldn't force the damn savage to obey orders. Maybe his suggestion would be enough to convince Blue Dog to do his bidding, at least this once. The runner turned and rode back the way he had come.

"There will come a day," Stone murmured to himself, then shook it away. That day was long in the future and he had plenty to worry about for today.

-

Buford Beaumont was in his element. His position as a Brigadier often meant that he was relegated to official duties that kept him out of battle, or even training. While he appreciated the fact that his skill had seen him rise to his present rank even in an environment that was hostile to him, Beaumont was a fighting soldier at heart and wanted to be with his men in battle.

Right now, his wish was coming true in spades. He was aware that his presence in the line would not go unnoticed by the enemy and that they would try to bring him down if possible, believing that his loss would hurt his brigade's fighting effectiveness. He snorted mentally at the idea.

While he was sure his men would mourn him, his brigade would continue to fight like the soldiers they were whether he led them or not. His absence might eventually play a role in their morale, but it would not hamper them on the battlefield today.

He left that thought behind as a mounted Nor trooper tried to bring his sword to bear on the southern General before him. Beaumont blocked the attack with relative ease, then spurred his large war horse into the smaller Nor mount, knocking the smaller horse to the side. Eyes wide, the Nor trooper struggled to stay mounted, which distracted him from defending himself. He looked up just in time to see Beaumont's sword coming at his chest.

Tearing his blade from the body of the dying trooper, Beaumont looked for another target. He didn't know how long the Marshal would give them before calling the attack off. He didn't want to waste any of it.

-

"I don't think they're gonna do anything," Simmons murmured from his place beside Karls Willard. "If they was gonna attack, they would have done it by now, don't you reckon?" Simmons was one of the former prisoners that had formed the bulk of the Black Sheep. He had risen through the ranks to command a company at the Gap. He was essentially Willard's second for the time being.

"Don't know," Willard shrugged, surveying the wood line with his glass. "But their presence is a threat we have to honor. Especially since we aren't sure how many there are."

"We could move over there and find out," Simmons replied, his voice betraying eagerness.

"No." Willard's voice was firm. "Our orders are to hold right here and protect the flank. If we move off, then if there's another force out there they move right in here where we're supposed to be. They might be letting us see them hoping we do just that," he added, looking at Simmons.

Simmons' training was strictly in the field other than his basic instruction at Cove Canton. The man was very good at small unit actions and had earned his rank in battle, but his experience was limited and he had never been trained to think strategically. His eyes narrowed as what Karls told him hit home.

"Hadn't considered that," he admitted.

"No reason you should," Karls shrugged. "You training hasn't covered things like that, mostly because we haven't had the time. But remember when you're on the flank, you hold the edge of the line. If you move, withdraw, or give in, then the army's line is exposed. A large force sweeping against an exposed flank can roll up unit after unit in detail, never allowing the army to marshal enough forces to meet them."

"When you're the flank, that's what you concentrate on," he concluded the *ad hoc* training session. "Let the rest of the line deal with what's front. All of your attention should be on protecting the flank."

"Yes sir," Simmons nodded, soaking in the information and applying it to what he'd already learned. He knew that Karls Willard was trying to teach him as they went and appreciated it. Most men of his position wouldn't have bothered.

But Willard had been The Colonel's protégé. That was how all the Sheep had thought of, and remembered, Colonel Darvo Nidiad. *The Colonel.* He had won the respect of every man in the unit over time.

So had the prince of course, but that was a different kettle of fish all together. Where the men loved Parno McLeod and would die for him without a thought, they had feared and respected The Colonel. And that respect had transferred at least somewhat to Willard. Colonel Willard might not be *The* Colonel, but he was *their* colonel. And he had been appointed and approved by *The Colonel.*

Simmons pushed those thoughts away and returned his attention to both the wood line and his commander. There might be more to learn here today.

-

Parno watched the battle unfolding before him, gauging the fatigue of his men. It was coming time to break off while they could still fight a withdrawal if needed. They had done well and it as time to take that and go.

"I believe you have accomplished your goal, my prince," Cho Feng said quietly from his side. Parno turned, not having seen Cho ride up. He should not have been surprised to see a blade in Feng's hand. A bloody blade.

"I was just thinking that," Parno nodded. He motioned for a young bugler, who rode to him with a bit of hesitation.

"Prepare to sound Recall and Reform," Parno ordered. "On my command." The young man nodded and licked lips made dry by a number of things, including fear. Parno looked to Whipple, who was looking back at him expectantly. Parno nodded, pointing to the bugler. Whipple returned the nod and raised his red pennant. Behind him the archers raised their bows once more.

It dawned on Parno at that moment that while he had detailed Beaumont's men as rear-guard, he'd also sent them into battle at the center of the line. He had no real force standing ready to cover the withdrawal.

"It will have to be enough," Feng said gently. "Trust your men, my prince."

It never failed to amaze Parno that Cho Feng always seemed to know what he was thinking. But the oriental sword master was correct. It was too late to fix now. He would have to trust his men. He looked at the nervous young bugler.

"Sound Recall," he ordered calmly. The bugler raised his horn and began to play the order that would end the battle.

-

It took a minute for the sounds of the bugle to carry along the line and be picked up by others. Soon however the notes of recall were sounding all along the Soulan front. Soulan troopers broke away from the Nor, helping injured mates to stay mounted or often pulling them up into the saddle behind them when their mounts had fallen.

Disengaging from a battle was as much an art as it was a skill. Only the arrogant commander didn't have his men practice such a drill. Even when victorious an army might have to withdraw while still engaged. The Soulan Army had done well today and they knew it. But their orders were clear and more than that they made good sense. Whatever victory had been gained today, the war was long from over. Preservation of their fighting forces was essential to the survival of their kingdom.

Unlike Parno, Beaumont *had* considered the problem of how to disengage his troopers so that they could cover the withdrawal. Consulting by runner with General Bellamy, commander of the 4th Soulan Cavalry, Beaumont had made arrangements to have Bellamy's reserve brigade support and replace his own so that they might withdraw in good order to support Whipple.

The actual move was less smooth than he might have hoped for, but considering it was essentially an unpracticed maneuver he wasn't all that displeased. The commander of Bellamy's reserve brigade was steady and calm as his men moved up to engage the Nor troopers to Beaumont's front. As soon as they were on line, Beaumont's men began to withdraw, having already been given their orders before the battle was joined.

Beaumont's men reformed to Whipple's immediate front, allowing their winded mounts a moment of respite as they dressed ranks and filled empty positions. The battle might be considered a victory, but that didn't mean they hadn't suffered losses.

Satisfied that his men were as ready as possible, Beaumont sent a runner to his Marshal to inform him of their readiness and then sat patiently awaiting developments.

-

Parno watched Beaumont's actions and realized that the canny brigadier had made plans that he himself had forgotten. Buford Beaumont once more rose in stature in the eyes of the Soulan Army's Lord Marshal. If they survived today, then he was more convinced than ever that Beaumont was the man for the mission he had already half planned in his mind.

"He has done well," Cho Feng noted from his side and Parno nodded absently.

"He has at that. And he thought of something I hadn't, which was how to get his men out of line and ready to cover the withdrawal. I erred badly in that, Master Feng," Parno admitted.

"You cannot think of everything at once, my prince," Feng replied. "You must be able to trust and depend upon those who lead your forces to know how to implement the orders you have given them. You no longer command a mere regiment, or even brigade. You must adjust your thinking to fit your new duties."

Feng was at least the third person today to tell him that, Parno reflected. He had thought himself prepared for the changes that his new rank would necessitate, but today had proven otherwise. He would have to be more aware of both his responsibilities and his limitations. He wasn't accustomed to having limitations, but he'd never been in a position of real responsibility before the war started.

He would have to learn on the job and on the fly, not the best circumstance for an army commander.

"You're right," he nodded to Feng. "I'm working on it, but there's a lot to learn and I'm out of my element."

"You are not out of your element, my prince," Feng stressed. "You are more than capable of performing your duties. It is your mindset that you must change, not your planning or leadership style. You simply must adjust to commanding, rather than leading. And you must begin to think strategically rather than tactically."

"All right," Parno nodded again, his eyes still on the distant battlefield. "I assume you can help me learn?"

"Of course," came the serene reply. "It will be my honor, my prince. We will begin tonight, if you wish."

"Very well," Parno replied. "In the meantime however, it's time for us to end this."

"I agree," Feng nodded this time. "You have accomplished your goal and your men are still in fighting trim. While we could press the attack here for the moment, we know that the enemy is trying to bring their infantry to bear on the right and there are at least some of those Wildmen you speak of on the left. And there is more to victory than possession of the field of battle."

"What I was thinking," Parno agreed. "Here we go," he said suddenly, seeing the forward units begin to withdraw. "We'll see now how good discipline is in these units."

Discipline was very good, it turned out. Soulan cavalrymen were selected from the cream of the army. It took more than horsemanship and fighting ability to gain a position in the most prestigious fighting arm of the Soulan Kingdom. It took intelligence, steadiness, and the discipline to obey orders even if they didn't appear to make sense.

That last item meant that the commanders of those units had to earn the trust of the men under their command. For a soldier to follow orders that he himself might think stupid meant that he had to trust the men above him to issue good orders, regardless of what it might look like from their own perspective.

Bugles began to sound along the line. After a brief hesitation the men engaged directly against the enemy wheeled sharply and spurred their horses, creating an instant separation between themselves and the enemy.

Surprised, the Nor were slow to pursue. By the time their own commanders had realized what was happening the Soulan units were through their own lines and reforming behind the reserve forces who now stood ready to engage if needed.

Flustered by the sudden change in tactics, the inexperienced Nor commanders hesitated. In the interim, as they decided to send runners to request instructions, some of their troopers pursued without orders. They did so in small groups and in fits and starts, with no cohesion, no structure, and very little order.

The results were less than ideal.

-

"Now!" Parno ordered and Whipple dropped his pennant again.

Once more the sky above the battle line was filled with arrows. The broken and uneven lines of Nor cavalry who had pursued without waiting for their comrades paid a heavy price for that impatience. With far fewer targets to choose from, it was inevitable that some would draw more fire than others.

Parno saw at least four horses just within his own view that fell with no less than a dozen arrows protruding from their bodies. Their riders fared no better.

Parno realized suddenly that the Nor lines were unorganized and without leadership. He raised his glasses to look at the enemy's position and saw nothing but indecision and hesitancy. With a start, he understood what was happening.

"They're waiting for orders!" he exclaimed aloud.

"Now is your chance, my prince," Cho Feng's voice, though much calmer than Parno's, might have betrayed the slightest bit of eagerness. "While they are disorganized."

"Sound the Withdrawal!" Parno ordered his bugler. "Right away! And keep sounding it!" The young man raised his horn and began to call.

-

"What in the devil is going on out there!" Stone yelled at no one and everyone at the same time. "Why aren't we pursuing?"

"Runners, sir," his aide called, pointing to where five different horsemen could be seen descending upon their position. Two arrived at roughly the same time.

"Enemy is withdraw-" Both began, then stopped, looking at each other.

"What is it?" Stone screamed again. "Speak!"

"Enemy withdrawing sir, and General Horley requests instructions!" one of them managed to blurt out.

"I already *gave* instructions!" Stone yelled. "We were to pursue the enemy to within sight of their own lines and no further, doing as much damage as we could in the process!"

"We've taken heavy losses ourselves, sir!" the second runner announced even as the other three reined in. They nodded their agreement since that was part of their own report.

"I don't give a damn about our losses!" Stone bellowed. He knew as soon as he said it that he'd made a mistake but he couldn't take it back. "If we don't pursue and destroy the enemy, then our losses were for *nothing*!" he tried to back away slightly, but the look on the runner's faces told him it was too late for that. Before he could speak again another runner appeared.

"General Horley reports that the enemy is withdrawing while fighting, sir!" the man saluted. "They are engaging us with archery fire again and withdrawing by the numbers!" The runner actually had no idea what that meant, but Stone did. He sighed in defeat, realizing that his hesitant division commanders had just cost him any chance he might have had at victory.

"Order all commands to reform on our side of the clearing," he ordered dismally. "This engagement is ended." He looked to his own bugler.

"Sound reform."

-

Whipple and Beaumont sat side-by-side observing the enemy action. A distant bugle call came to them from the far side of the clearing, soon echoed by others. The Nor to their front wheeled almost in unison and started for their own lines. Whipple allowed his men their third volley just to spur the enemy on their way, then raised his pennant again. It was largely unnecessary, as his men were highly disciplined and knew their orders.

"I think we can withdraw," Beaumont observed quietly, and Whipple nodded his agreement.

"I do believe we have spanked them, General," he chuckled. "Our Lord Marshal should be pleased, I think."

"I'll find out tonight, I guess," Beaumont shrugged. "I've been ordered to mess with the Prince tonight." Whipple looked at Beaumont, frowning slightly.

"So have I," he admitted slowly. "I would normally think we were being commended, but. . .my 'invitation' came before this battle was decided."

"Mine came before it was even joined," Beaumont nodded. "So it must be something else, unless Prince Parno is clairvoyant. In which case, we might just win this war," he finished with a grin.

"We'll win, regardless," Whipple stated firmly. "I might not have said that this morning," he admitted. "But now? Now, I'm sure of it. We'll pay a heavy price to be sure, but we will win."

"It does look better than it did just a couple days ago," Beaumont agreed. He was watching the enemy through his glass. "They appear to be reforming, but there's no sign they intend to attack." He made a snap decision and turned to his aide.

"I want our men scouring the battlefield for wounded," he ordered. "Withdraw at the first sign of Nor attack. Don't wait for orders, just withdraw. Hurry now!" The aide turned to send runners away.

"Those aren't our orders," Whipple said softly.

"I won't leave good men to the mercy of those heathen bastards," Beaumont growled. "And we have time."

No sooner had he said that when he heard a high-pitched yelling from his left.

-

"Northmans have failed," Blue Dog said to his own subordinates. "Fight stupid, lose." He watched as the Nor troopers withdrew, noting that there were a few Soulan troopers still on the field.

"We give Southmans battle?" one of his sub-chiefs asked, eyes almost glowing.

Blue Dog considered that. His position as War Chief was held because of his prowess in battle and the fact that he led his people to victory. Attacking now would not be good tactics but it would please his men. And pleasing his men was part of what kept him Chief.

"We attack," he nodded. "Take hairs, take horses. One, maybe two pass, then withdraw. No need make Northmans jealous," he grinned. The others returned it and hurried to their own groups.

Blue Dog had the equivalent of perhaps six companies of Nor cavalry with him, around eight hundred men, total. More than enough to take the flank of this group and allow his men to slake their thirst for blood.

A good day, he decided.

-

Karls Willard had ordered the Black Sheep to withdraw after the flanking regiment assigned by his brother Enri had departed. For some reason Karls was uneasy. They had not seen any sign of the Tribesmen for some time and that worried him. They were uncanny warriors who specialized in striking from ambush. The woods and scrub cover on the army's left provided the perfect setting for their kind of warfare.

Now Karls sat his horse, watching how the rear-guard fared. His men were fairly well concealed at the moment and his own flank was secured by a squad of Parsons' best scouts. Their position was as secure as it could be outside their own lines.

"Sir, I think the rear-guard is going to search for wounded," Simmons told him, pointing to where Soulan troopers could be seen moving back onto the battlefield. Willard resisted the urge to curse.

He of all people knew what it was to be forced to leave wounded on the field of battle. It was a sickening feeling for anyone and more so for a commander. But Parno's orders had been clear. The Army would withdraw at once when the call came. Technically Karls was violating those orders himself, but unlike most others he had a bit of leeway in what he did and when. He was commander of Parno's personal regiment and not assigned to any greater unit in the Soulan Army. Karls Willard answered directly to the Lord Marshal. Who also happened to be his best friend.

"This might be a mistake," Karls began, but was cut off as the wood line erupted with howling savages. Hundreds of Tribal Horseman came boiling out of the woods, intent on attacking the Soulan units as they were divided to look for survivors.

"Double lines, lancers front!" Karls called at once and heard the Sheep behind him moving. "Company Commanders, call ready?"

"Ready!" came the cry from four different voices, in order. Calm. Assured.

"*Charge!*" Karls screamed at the top of his lungs, his own sword now in hand.

He and Parno had often wondered how the Sheep would fare against the Wildmen of the west. Karls figured this was as good a time as any to see.

-

"What the hell!" Beaumont turned to see what was causing the commotion. Whipple ordered his men to reform at once, yelling for his commanders to engage the enemy at will. He recognized the horsemen as Tribal Cavalry, a hated and notorious enemy feared by his people far more than the Nor.

Beaumont realized that his men were caught in the open, separated and cut off. While his men outnumbered the attackers, they were spread across the battlefield searching for injured. They were also fatigued, having been in battle all morning. The Tribesmen shared none of those disadvantages.

Just as Beaumont was sinking into despair at what he had allowed to happen another sound came to his ears. That of still more charging horses, accompanied by a full-bodied yell coming from several hundred throats.

"*PARNO!!*

As he watched, Beaumont saw two solid lines of well-dressed cavalry wearing the colors of the McLeod Dynasty hit the flank of the screaming savages unaware. Lances skewered horse and man alike as the front wave of Prince Parno's Own collided with the oncoming Wildmen. He would swear that a visible shock wave ran through the Tribal horseman as their own tactic was used against them.

A silent prayer of thanks on his lips, Beaumont gathered the men nearest him and rode to engage the enemy.

Blue Dog could not hide his shock. One moment his men had been bearing down on a tired and disorganized enemy that looked ripe for the plucking, the next they themselves were being hit from the flank by a wave of green and black clad horsemen.

The Tribal War Chief looked on as his men were caught in a trap of their own making. A southern cavalry unit using their own tactics against them on an open battlefield. He had no idea where the unit had come from. He had seen the same unit earlier on the southern army's flank, but had watched them withdraw along with the rest. He'd had no idea they were anywhere nearby.

Not only were they nearby, they were very efficiently killing his men. Intent on their own attack against a tired and disorganized enemy, his warriors had never seen the attack coming.

And neither had he.

Karls slapped a lance tip aside with his sword as he and the Black Sheep tore into the Wild's flank area. The warrior to his front looked shocked to see the Sheep and Karls couldn't help but smile as he plunged his sword into the other man's chest. The warrior's smaller mount was pushed aside by Karls' larger horse as the commander of the Black Sheep looked for another target.

His men were faring very well against the Wilds he was pleased to see. The savages had apparently intended to attack all along judging from their paint and decorations, something they rarely did outside battle. While Karls had a sullen admiration for the westerners fighting abilities it was tempered with complete disgust at their lack of honor. They would attack anyone, including women and children, sparing none unless they were taken as prisoners. Karls rarely wondered at the fate of those prisoners. He really didn't think he wanted to know.

Many of the Sheep shared his hatred of the western tribes and their savagery and took this opportunity to dish out severe punishment upon these representatives of that hated people.

For their part, the westerners were not accustomed to fighting troopers like the Black Sheep. Parno's regiment were finely conditioned, as were their horses. Their training in martial arts, swordplay, indeed in all the arts of war was far beyond the average soldier from either side. As a result, the casual contempt that the Tribal horsemen held for both northern and southern soldiers made them careless.

And that carelessness now made many of them *dead*.

Seeing that his men were taking serious losses and that the intended targets were now reformed and preparing to offer battle, Blue Dog knew that he had to withdraw his men. This would mean a serious loss of respect among his warriors, but at least they would still live. Some of them at any rate.

Using the *shaghair* horn around his neck, Blue Dog blew a long single note that carried across the battlefield even above the noise of combat. Though in the heat of battle his men turned immediately and ran for their own lines, leaving the southerners in possession of the field. Karls considered pursuit for only a second before having his bugler sound Reform. He noted the reluctance of his men to return to the line but they *did* return, their discipline holding.

Karls turned at the sound of approaching horses to see the commander of the brigade Parno had selected as the rear-guard approaching with a good many of his men trailing.

"Colonel, I appreciate your timely intervention," Beaumont said evenly. "I made a severe error and only your being here saved my men from paying for it."

"Gather your men and let's move," Karls ordered tersely. "We're exposed here and now that the Army has gone we are alone. We cannot tarry here any longer. Move!"

No one thought to object to Karls Willard giving orders, including Beaumont himself. Chastened, he ordered his regimental commanders to form their units and make ready to depart. Whipple's men were already formed and began slowly moving toward their own lines, staying close enough to support Beaumont should there be another attack.

Karls used his glass once more to examine the Nor lines, now over four hundred yards distant. While detail was hard to get at that distance, he could see no signs that the Nor were preparing for another attack. He shifted his glass to the point where the western savages had disappeared, his glass moving slowly across the area. He stopped short, moving the glass slightly back to his right having seen a splash of. . . .

Sitting alone watching him and his men was a single savage, his body coated in some kind of blue powder. The horn around his neck identified him as a leader of some kind and Karls suspected this was in fact the war leader of the men his own unit had repulsed.

Even as he watched the man in blue raised his short bow overhead. Karls didn't know if that was a salute, a warning, or just a wave, but he raised his own sword above his head, then allowed the blade to lower until it pointed more or less at the bowman in the distance.

The man nodded once, lowered his bow and disappeared into the brush behind him. Lowering his glass, Karls wondered what that had been about. But only for a few brief seconds.

"Let's go," he ordered Simmons, who had been watching the two Soulan brigades of the rear-guard who were now making their way toward their own lines. Tired men on tired horses.

"What are our losses," he asked as he and Simmons rode side-by-side along their column.

"Three men wounded, one serious," Simmons replied. Karls waited for more, then turned to look at his subordinate when there was no more.

"And?" he prompted.

"That's all, sir," Simmons smiled gently. "Got maybe two, three dozen with scrapes and what not, and we lost four horses dead. We're combat able right now," he added.

"Forget it," Karls said at once, recognizing the tone. "We've already exceeded our orders. We're going back."

"Never thought otherwise, sir," Simmons managed to get out without his disappointment showing. "We gave them savages what for, though." Karls smiled at that tone.

"Yes, we did, Major," he agreed. "We certainly did. I think the Prince will be most pleased with us."

"Aye."

CHAPTER SEVEN

-

The Prince was not, in fact, pleased.

"I ordered you to withdraw as soon as the Army was in the clear!" Parno seethed. To his credit Beaumont took the dressing down like a man.

"The fault is entirely mine, milord," he said formally. "I sought to take advantage of the enemy's disorganization to retrieve any wounded we could reach. I should not have done so. Only Colonel Willard's intervention saved my men from paying the price for my error in judgment."

Parno made a visible effort to get control of himself. Beaumont had done nothing that Parno himself might have in that same situation. Leaving wounded behind was anathema to a good leader. And Beaumont was obviously smarting from his lapse. Parno didn't want the man's confidence shaken too badly since he had plans for the fiery brigadier. And nothing Parno could do or say would be more punishing than what Beaumont was putting himself through at the moment.

"In the future, keep what happened today in mind," Parno settled for saying. "We know that the Nor have at least some Tribal Horsemen with them. We know that they have made treaties with the Wild Tribes to provide both horses and instruction. We will likely face them in battle again so always be aware of that fact."

"I will, milord," Beaumont nodded stiffly.

"Very well, General," Parno almost sighed but caught himself. "See to your men, and to yourself. I'll see you this evening."

"Sir," Beaumont snapped a salute and left the tent, leaving Parno alone with Karls Willard.

"And how was it that you came to still be there?" he asked.

"We were watching the withdrawal," Karls replied. "I've been using every opportunity to give Simmons some field training and this looked like a good chance. I'm glad we were there."

"So am I," Parno nodded. "How did you fare?" he asked, almost hesitantly.

"We ripped their guts out," Karls smiled wickedly. "Not a man lost, either, though we have at least two that won't be returning to duty any time soon. Lost four horses and have a lot of scrapes and cuts but otherwise we're in fine fettle."

"Really?" Parno raised a brow. This was very good news indeed.

"Really," Karls nodded firmly. "We caught them by surprise there's no doubt but I estimate they had us by about three hundred men and we still kicked their teeth in. I think the question of whether the Sheep can fight the Tribes has been answered, Parno."

"Good," Parno's voice was firm. "That means the newer units should be able to as well."

"I did see their leader," Karls added. "Odd fellow, coated in some kind of blue coloring. He may have given me a salute of some kind."

"I bet he did," Parno snorted.

"Well, it might have been something else," Karls admitted. "He raised his bow, then pointed it at me. I returned the gesture with my sword. I prefer to think it's respect," the young officer sniffed.

"I'm sure it was," Parno nodded. "But keep an out for him in the future. He'll probably want some kind of payback against you to regain his loss of stature amongst his men."

"That's fine with me," Karls nodded, obviously terrified at the thought. "How about the attack? Do we know our losses yet? Or have any idea at the damage we inflicted?"

"I'm waiting for your brother's report on losses," Parno replied, taking his seat once more. "The reports from the commanders will help us determine how badly we damaged the enemy, but from what I could see we did fairly well. The important thing is that we restored the morale of the Army. At least I think we did." He looked at his friend. "And if not for you, that morale might have been shattered again had Beaumont and his men suffered too greatly against the Tribesmen. Thank you, Karls."

"Ah," Karls waved the thanks away, taking a seat himself. "That's what I'm here for, Parno. To help you any way I can. And I always will," he promised, leaning forward. "Our men did very well, too, milord."

"Your men, Karls," Parno smiled, albeit a bit sadly. "My days of leading the Sheep are over, I'm afraid. If I hadn't realized that before then today taught me that for certain." He leaned back, his face thoughtful.

"Today was good, but I can't tie myself down that way often. I can't even stay here, not permanently. There are other commands I need to visit. I need to see how things are going at Shelby for one thing. And then there's the problem at sea. I can't be everywhere at once. I can't even be a few places all at once."

"That's what staff and commanders are for, brother," Karls said plainly. "You're going to have to depend on them, Parno. You simply don't have a choice. Not anymore."

"I know, but saying that is proving far easier than doing it," Parno nodded. "I need to be able to trust those commanders, but it's not lost on me that I have no idea how many are more loyal to my dearly departed traitor of a brother than they are to Soulan. There are only a handful of people I can really and truly trust, Karls."

"Then find out who you can trust," Karls said simply. "You have good men at your beck and call, milord. Use them to sound out your military. Find the vipers in our midst and get rid of them. We certainly have no time for such things. Not now."

Parno nodded slowly at that, considering. He was not without resources, that was true enough. He rose, walking slowly around the spacious tent he used for his office. Karls watched in silence, knowing that Parno needed the motion to work out his problems.

"I'm going to make some changes," the Prince said absently as he paced, hands locked behind him. "I'm going to organize a new unit. One that can operate behind the Nor lines, raising hell with their communications and supply lines." He looked up. "I'd planned to place Beaumont in command, using his men as the basis for the division, and add Whipple as his second, using his men as well. I had planned to add another brigade of cavalry and perhaps a supporting regiment to their strength and give what support can be had in such a unit."

"He'll do well at such work," Karls nodded. "Today will only make him more alert to the dangers of such a command. It will likely prevent him from making another such mistake."

"You think so?" Parno asked. "I admit that was my first hope."

"I do," Karls nodded firmly. "The man is good at what he does. His mistake today was not so much a mistake as it was a miscalculation. He looked at the Nor regulars and thought he had them sufficiently cowed to gather the wounded. And in his place, I might have done the same," he admitted.

"Not against my orders," Parno shook his head and Karls nodded, conceding the point.

"Still, he meant well and there's no doubt he's learned from that mistake," Parno continued. "I think it will work. I intend for them to take ten, perhaps fourteen days to prepare and then make a move around the enemy's right and into their rear. If nothing else, they should be able to draw the rest of the Nor horsemen away and probably some of those damned Wildmen as well."

"Their presence is a problem," Karls agreed. "Though I daresay that our little set-to today is already passing among the army and making the troops realize that they aren't nearly as formidable as they seem. And that can only add to the mystique of the Sheep, by the way," he added with a grin. "And that will help make your position more secure. Especially when they realize that this is only one battalion of the regiment. Anyone who wants to usurp your authority will know they will have to contend with us in order to do so. That will stop all but the most determined."

"You're developing quite the ego, Karls," Parno chuckled, but his friend merely shook his head.

"Not at all. But don't think that the Sheep aren't looked at with envy among the rest of the Army, Parno. We've already had two dozen junior officers and senior non-coms approach about 'joining'. I don't even know how many troopers. I've lost count, to be honest."

"Have you explained that you can't simply 'join' the Sheep?" Parno asked with a chuckle.

"I haven't personally, but you can bet the troops have," Karls smirked back. "They take their reputation very seriously."

"They earned it," Parno said simply. "They have the right. Paid for it in blood."

"Well, the point is the Army will be getting the idea sooner rather than later. I had thought to mention to you that we might begin to accept recruits for the regiment at some point. Send them to Cove for training. Those that survive would be able to fill the holes left by losses." Anyone else might have thought Karls funny with the mention of survival, but Parno had gone through the training himself. In fact, one of the reasons the Sheep were fanatically loyal to their prince was the simple fact that he *had* endured the hellish training alongside them. He had earned the right to be known as their superior.

"A sound idea," Parno nodded his agreement. "Pursue it at your discretion. It's your regiment now, my friend." He returned to his desk, and Karls stood. Parno had much to do.

"I'll expect you at table tonight as well," Parno told him. "I'll have you and Enri there as well as Master Feng when we meet with Beaumont and Whipple. Be thinking about my plan. If you have ideas I want to hear them."

"Aye, milord," Karls bowed slightly, a small smirk on his face.

"Get out," Parno shook his head. "I have work to do."

-

It was three hours before dinner when Enri Willard arrived at Parno's tent carrying a bundle of papers. The remains of a working lunch littered Parno's table. He kept his face carefully neutral as he looked up at his Chief of Staff. This report would establish how successful his plan had been executed.

"Command reports, my lord," Enri said evenly. "Division and Brigade level."

"Numbers?" Parno asked. Enri didn't even consult the pages in his hands.

"We lost two thousand, three hundred and forty-two men dead or missing and presumed lost," Enri replied. "Another five hundred seventy-two are seriously wounded and will not return to duty soon if at all. One thousand three hundred and ten other wounded of all ranks that can and will return to duty, ranging in time from already reporting to four-to-six weeks. Total casualties four thousand two hundred twenty-two."

"Estimates on enemy casualties?" Parno asked, not sure whether to be grateful his own losses weren't higher or saddened that he hadn't found a way to lessen them somehow.

"Rough estimates are all we have at this point, my lord," Enri said. "We'll have more definite estimates once we receive Regimental reports. However, the rough estimates are that we killed, injured, or otherwise debilitated twenty-one thousand Nor soldiers of all ranks. Both figures include the cavalry clash as well as our attack on their flank." He kept himself carefully neutral but it was obvious he wanted to add something.

"What is it, Enri?" Parno asked.

"Sir, this was an overwhelming victory!" Enri enthused. "Our actual losses are less than three thousand, while the enemy losses are well over *twenty-thousand*! The morale of the army is higher than at any point since the war began, my lord. We inflicted casualties totaling almost ten percent of the enemy's forces!"

"And we won't be able to do it again," Parno said softly, letting the boom down easily. "Today was a great victory, Enri," he nodded. "A very satisfactory outcome. And one borne of complete surprise and ineptitude on the part of our opponent. Something we cannot count on seeing again. And if we do, we can't overlook the possibility that it's a trap."

Willard nodded his understanding but his enthusiasm was not diminished.

"All that may well be true, my Lord Marshall, but nothing undoes the damage inflicted on the enemy, both in terms of outright losses and in morale. Their confidence in themselves and their leaders will be shaken while our own is soaring."

"I suspect that is true," Parno allowed. "Still, let's not deceive ourselves into thinking that this has ended the struggle before us. Or even shortened it. At best it had bought us time to regroup and reinforce our positions. At worst they will hit us in the morning with everything they have in an attempt to end the war right here."

The look on Willard's face said it all. That had not occurred to him.

"All commands will be standing to at one hour before dawn," Parno ordered formally. "Scouts out during the night, bonfires to be set one hundred yards in front and lit at least an hour before dawn. Scouts will return to our lines at dawn or when and if the enemy approaches. The units involved in today's attack are to be assigned to the reserve for two days rest and refit barring their need in repulsing attack." He looked down at his desk and picked up a sheet of paper.

"General Beaumont's brigade and General Whipple's archer brigade are to be separated from service tomorrow and assigned to a new command. The details are here, but I want this order held with you until tomorrow. I plan to inform the two of them at supper this evening. I want you to be there as well. In the meantime, I want your opinion of the basic concept which is outlined there," he indicated the paper he'd just handed over. "Be thinking as well about which other units would be a good fit for the new command. We'll discuss that this evening as well with their input."

"Yes sir," Enri nodded, looking at the brief plan. "With your permission?" Parno waved and Enri retreated, reading as he went. Harrel Sprigs was waiting at the entrance of his tent and Parno waved him inside.

"I've secured a house nearby for tonight's meal, my lord," he said without fanfare. "The owners were glad to offer their home for your quarters as well."

"No," Parno shook his head. "I needed a secure place for tonight's supper because of the plans I'll be discussing, but I won't put someone out of their home just to be more comfortable. Please extend them my thanks and see to it they are compensated for any inconvenience that tonight may cause them."

"Already done, my lord," Harrel nodded. "I have arranged for a room at a local inn, complete with meals and livery as well as a two-man escort to see them there and back in the morning."

"Very well," Parno nodded, returning to his work. "Please have Mister Parsons report to me here."

"Right away, sir," Sprigs nodded again and slipped away. So engrossed was he in his work that it was not until Parsons cleared his throat that Parno realized the man was standing before him.

"Wanted to see me, sir?" he asked.

"Yes," Parno smiled. "I'm going to need you to detach a squad of your men who are familiar with this part of the country to attach to an independent command. They need to be smart, resourceful and able to think on the move. They will be scouting for a unit operating behind enemy lines on a regular and sustained basis."

"How many?" Parsons asked.

"I think ten should be more than sufficient," Parno replied. "They won't be screening the command as your men often do for me. Instead they will be doing work more in line with your actions before the war. They will be General. . .the commander's eyes and ears, so to speak. This is, needless to add, secret information. Select men you trust implicitly. Their actions may mean the difference between victory and defeat. They will certainly be the difference in life and death for several thousand Soulan troopers."

"I'll have it to you this evening, my lord," Parsons promised. "I'll need to ponder on this a bit."

"Morning will be fine," Parno assured him. "We need to be looking for men who can fill your ranks again, Mister Parsons. Hunters and trappers I suppose, but. . .well, you do as you think fit. I can provide incentive to the right men if you think they're worth it. We have to know what's going on."

"I'll see what I can come up with," Parsons promised.

"In the morning," Parno nodded. "One last thing. I need one man, completely trustworthy and able, to carry a dispatch of sorts to Cove for me. I need to send a message and some items to someone there."

"I'll have a man here within the hour," Parsons promised. "By your leave?"

"Carry on."

As the scout leader departed Sprigs returned.

"Time for dinner soon, my lord," the aide reported.

"Very well," Parno stood and buckled on his sword. "I'm actually hungry."

-

The home that Sprigs had arranged for the meeting was very nice, built along the lines of a manor house with a large dining room and well-appointed kitchen. Parno's own staff, such as it was, had taken over the home for the night, with Sergeant Berry and his men standing guard at the doors while other members of the Black Sheep roamed the grounds.

Generals Beaumont and Whipple arrived together trailed by a runner and a single aide each. They would not be included in the meeting but supper would be provided to them along with Parno's own men. Karls and Enri Willard arrived together shortly afterward with Cho Feng having made the trip alongside Parno.

Parno could not begin to imagine where his men had found a ham and didn't ask. Instead he dug into the meal of ham, potatoes and beans with fried bread to the side along with coffee and lemonade.

"Splendid meal, my lord," Whipple commented as he wiped his mouth. "Thank you for inviting me."

"Agreed," Beaumont nodded, his face still showing a bit of embarrassment at his snafu earlier in the day.

"Well, I'm sure the two of you realize that I didn't invite you here to give your opinion of my cook," Parno smiled and the two chuckled. "My aide should have everything set up for us in the study of our host, so if you'll bring your brandy and whatever delicacy you have yet to finish, I'll show you what I have in mind."

The entire party adjourned to the room where Sprigs had set up a map easel and had arranged chairs for all participants. He excused himself as the men filed inside and then closed the doors, isolating the room and its occupants.

"Today was a good start, gentlemen, but there's no denying that's all it was; a start." Both generals nodded their agreement.

"We have other concerns than this army, too," Parno continued. "There is a determined attack underway in Shelby, though the enemy has not yet made its way across the Great River in any substantial numbers. That may or may not last. If they are determined enough, and willing to spend the lives necessary, they may eventually force their way across."

"In addition, there is a large naval force off our coast, somewhere in this area," he pointed to ocean area off the Sunshine Coast. "Our navy is assembling to try and run them down, but until we know they aren't carrying another infantry force capable of landing somewhere on our coast we have to honor that threat. Our fleet will hopefully be able to not only determine that but also engage and destroy or drive off the force altogether. Once their superiority of the sea lanes is established, again assuming they can do so, it will provide us some breathing room in other areas as well."

"Our position is not untenable but it is precarious," Parno told his guests. "Not only can we not afford a mistake, we must take advantage of every mistake our enemy makes, and try to force him to make more. We have to play to every advantage we can and wring every possible advantage we can from each favorable situation we find ourselves in while also mitigating the damages we suffer when conditions do not favor us, preserving our men and resources for when we can get the most use from them."

"The force before us here is by far the strongest thus far committed since the war began. Their numbers are great, their training far above anything we've ever seen from the Nor and their equipment and tactics greatly improved over what we've seen in the past. Unless our fathers have lied to us about how easy it was in the past to deal with the Nor," he grinned and received polite laughter in reply.

"We are undertaking a massive training program," he told the two Brigadiers. "One that will make our army far more formidable than ever before. Unfortunately, that takes time, and we can only train so many troops at one time since they have to be removed from the line to accomplish that. So far we're taking on the best and brightest for inclusion in my own unit, mainly because the training is actually at least as savage as combat." Both men exchanged a glance at that then looked to Karls Willard who returned their gaze steadily.

"We've seen your men in action," Whipple offered finally. "Whatever the training regimen may be, Marshal, it's obviously effective."

"And someday we'll have entire divisions trained up to those standards," Parno nodded. "We'll need them. But for now, we have to buy time. Time to assemble and train our men, time to allow our advances in tactics and training to be applied across the board, and time for our newest inventions to be readied for use across the battlefields wherever they may be. You've likely heard the rumors of our battle at the Gap." Both nodded again, leaning forward.

"They are true, save those references to witchcraft," Parno chuckled darkly. "Though I don't mind the Nor thinking we're using wizardry; the fact is that simple chemistry is responsible for the weapons we employed at the Gap. If it were wizardry, we could utilize it again right away. Since it is not, however, we require time produce those weapons in sufficient numbers to stockpile them for continued and sustained use on the entire war front."

"And that's where you two enter into my plans," Parno brought his point back to the two men he'd chosen to lead this effort. Both leaned in once again, eagerness clearly written on their faces. Parno nodded in satisfaction.

"As of tomorrow morning your units will be detached from your normal command structures and combined to form a new unit. Brigadier Beaumont you will be given a brevet promotion to General, and receive overall command, with Brigadier Whipple as your second. Your respective staffs will be maintained and your commands will remain with you. There will be at least one additional brigade, probably of cavalry, and a support regiment of farriers, engineers, wranglers, supply, medical and so forth."

"You will have two weeks to integrate these units into one command, at which point your mission will be simple; take your command behind the enemy lines between here and the Ohi and raise as much hell as you possibly can."

"Yes sir!" Beaumont positively beamed while Whipple smiled broadly, nodding his approval.

"You will pick your battles carefully gentlemen because you will be a long way from home. My scout master, Mister Parsons, is selecting a squad of his best men, all familiar with this area, to bring you information. You'll have to depend on your own men for screening since there won't be enough of these scouts to do that. You'll use them instead to locate and then destroy isolated units of the Imperial army, outposts along their lines of communications and any supply depots or wagon trains headed south."

"I cannot stress enough how cautious you must be in conserving your forces," Parno continued. "Yet you must also take measured risks in order to be effective. You will at times be tempted to attack when you should not, and to pass when you should attack. You will have to learn to make those decisions on your own, and then live with the consequences of those decisions." The two men sobered as the import of his words sank in.

"You will be completely out of communication with us, dependent upon your own resources and whatever you can steal from the Nor and nothing else. I will try to find a quality unit of Tinsee militia horsemen from this area to accompany you as scouts and flankers to help you in managing your units in the available terrain. I understand that you are at least nominally familiar with the area yourself, General?" he said to Beaumont.

"I am sir," the big man nodded.

"Do not limit yourself to operations only in the Tinsee province, or even the Tinsee valley," Parno added. "Remember that you can range as far north as the Ohi River, but do not attempt to cross over. Not yet," he added. "That will come later on, once we have dealt with the immediate problems."

"Sir?" Enri blurted, caught by surprise.

"We'll discuss that later on," Parno promised, then turned back to the two men he'd just assigned to his pet project. "Questions gentlemen?"

"Black Flag, sir?" Whipple asked.

"Absolutely," Parno replied. "Not just because you'll have no way to care for prisoners, either," his voice was grim. "We've used this same tactic in the past so the Nor will be expecting it. The difference this time will be that we will not be engaging in any of the so called 'rules of civilized warfare'. I intend to teach the Nor a lesson that they are not likely to forget for many generations. Namely that any attack on this kingdom is not only doomed to fail, but be so costly that it's too horrible to contemplate. I have only one rule of war, gentlemen. Win. Understand?"

"We do sir," Beaumont was as serious as he knew how to be, his normal exuberance nowhere in evidence as he received his orders.

"Create havoc among them, Generals," Parno urged. "Make them fear the sound of your horns. Let them sleep fitfully if at all while contemplating being found by their fellows left dead, or simply disappeared without a trace. Remember that your mission is to spread fear and panic as much as it is to wreak that havoc upon their supplies and men. You will use fear, terror even, to demoralize the Imperial soldiers and their commanders."

"They will send men after you. Let them. Draw them in and ambush them. Kill them all. When their numbers are too great, keep moving and disappear into the countryside only to reappear somewhere else, attacking once more. Do you see what I want from you, Generals?"

"Clearly, sir," Whipple replied. "How long do we have?"

"That's up to you," Parno told them. "When supplies start to run low or when you need rest and refit that you cannot accomplish behind the lines, return to our own lines for a time. Stand your men down and rest them and their horses, repair your equipment, replace your losses where possible, and then go again. Give the Nor no rest you can deprive them of. No peace of mind, no mercy of any kind." Parno's eyes grew hard. Flinty.

"This is the dawn of a new kind of war for Soulan, gentlemen. I call it total war. Where we destroy our enemies root and branch so that they can never again trod our soil or kill our people. Now," he finished. "Have I selected the right men for this job? If you do not wish to be part of this project, you may say so and that will be the end of it."

"I'm in," Beaumont said at once.

"Me as well," Whipple nodded thoughtfully. "This may well be the way we rid ourselves of the Nor once and for all."

"That is my plan," Parno nodded. "Expect to encounter Wildmen again," he warned. "If the Nor can convince them to come after you then do your utmost to catch and destroy them. It will merely add to your reputation and further demoralize the Nor soldiers."

Beaumont nodded grimly, his encounter earlier that day still clearly on his mind. He would not underestimate the Wild Tribesmen again, nor be caught off guard by their tactics.

"Then you have your orders," Parno concluded. "May God go with you and before you, Generals." Each man stood and Parno clasped their hands in turn. "I'll have written orders to you sometime tomorrow. Use your time well, and buy me the time I need to make them pay."

"We'll do so, sir," Whipple promised.

"Indeed," Beaumont echoed. "Indeed we will."

-

After Beaumont and Whipple had departed, Enri Willard assisted Parno in drafting their orders and selecting the units who would accompany them on their mission. As they finished, he looked warily at his Commander.

"Milord," he began, not knowing exactly how to give voice to his questions.

"Yes, we will be invading the North, excepting an order from the King not to do so," Parno said flatly. "And I intend to argue for the invasion even if he is against it. If I cannot convince him then I will attempt to convince my brother, Memmnon. One way or another, we will be going north one day. Count upon it."

"Ah, Sir," Enri was hesitant but it was his job to advise. "Milord, we've never before pursued the Nor past our own borders. There is no precedent for it that I know of."

"And that might be why we keep having this problem every generation," Parno nodded grimly. "We drive them away, but we never defeat them. This time will be different," he looked at Enri with eyes that were as flat as death. "They want one kingdom? They'll have it."

"The Kingdom of Soulan will be the one. The only one, once this war is over."

"That's a large marching order, sire," Enri kept his voice respectful. Cautious.

"That's why I need more Black Sheep," Parno nodded. "Many, many more."

CHAPTER EIGHT

"Any questions, General?"

Parno had just completed his orders to General Davies. He, Davies, and the members of each staff were standing in the command tent. It was two days since the cavalry clash Parno had led and it was time for him to be on his way. He had accomplished what he had hoped to here and he needed to see what the situation was in Shelby.

"No, milord," Davies shook his head. "Your orders are clear and will be carried out. Your actions have left us in far better shape, I think."

"Expect reprisal," Parno warned. "If I were the Nor commander there's no way I'd allow that defeat to go unanswered. And be especially concerned with the Wild Tribesmen. If the Nor truly have them under their command, then they may well use them to try and get around you. They could do to us what Beaumont and Whipple are supposed to do to them."

"We already have scouts far and wide to the west, milord," Davies nodded again. "We also have scouts to the east, across the river. Three separate brigades of mounted militia are patrolling heavily in that area to screen Nasil, and I've received a report that the combined Royal regiments and House Guard that His Majesty used at the Gap are now in place to defend Nasil. There's little doubt that if an opening presented itself they would make a run on the Capital."

"Agreed," Parno nodded. "Please see to it that my dispatches are delivered, especially the one to Cove Canton. I should be back in three weeks, assuming all goes as expected, perhaps sooner. I need to see what the situation is in Shelby and confer with General Raines. I will return here after that, though I may have to depart again and head south depending on what is happening off the coast. I hope to hear from Admiral Semmes before then, however." Rafael Semmes was the commander of the Soulan Navy and was leading the combined fleet of the Savannah, Sunshine Coast and Key Horn squadrons in an effort to eliminate the naval threat off Soulan's coast. Seventy percent, give or take, of Soulan's pre-war naval strength were committed to that effort.

"We'll be here, milord, God willing," Davies promised. "And if He's not, then we're doomed anyway."

"Too true," Parno sighed. "May He watch over you all," Parno shook hands with Davies. "Farewell." With that the young Lord Marshal mounted his horse. His staff surrounded him along with Lieutenant Montrose Berry, promoted for gallantry at the Gap and because, in Enri Willard's words, 'Can't have a sergeant over the guard detail of the Lord Marshal'. Berry had gained an additional ten men to supplement his squad as well, which had been a relief. Having been appointed by The Colonel himself, Berry had decided that this was where he would serve until he could no longer do so. He was certain that his young charge was Soulan's best hope for survival, which made this job more important that anything he could be doing elsewhere.

Behind them the Black Sheep waited for the order to ride. While Davies could undoubtedly use their help, they went where Parno went.

"Karls, are we ready?" Parno asked.

"That we are, milord," Karls Willard nodded.

"Let's be about it then," Parno ordered. Parsons and his men were already scouting the trail ahead and had been for the last hour. Karls raised a hand and the column set off for Shelby and the battle raging there. At a walk until they cleared the camp, at which point Karls picked up the pace.

Time was the enemy as much so as the Nor these days.

-

Colonel Bret Chad examined the area below him with his glass, looking for any signs of trouble. He and his men had entered Kenty seven days ago and were now deep inside Soulan territory that was nominally controlled by the Nor. Nominally because they had very few actual troops in the region.

Had he not been on a particular mission, Chad would have set about reducing and destroying those troops and driving them from Soulan soil. At best it would free many people from the terror of Nor raiding parties, at worst it would result in troops diverted from the front opposing General Davies in the west. Not good for Chad but very good for the war effort.

But his orders were firm. Find and retrieve their families and then return to Cove Canton where they would endure the harsh training and acclimation that would see many of them become members of Parno McLeod's personal troops.

"Nothing," he said, lowering his glass.

"Concur, sir," Tom Hildebrand nodded. "Looks clear all around."

"Scouts out, Mister Morely," Chad ordered his aide, a young lieutenant. "I want them checking the surrounding area out five miles in all directions save behind us of course. I expect them back before dusk. We'll bivouac in the valley below."

"Yes sir," Morely nodded and spurred his horse on his way.

"Tomorrow we start gathering our people that we can find," Chad told his second. "Seven days, ten at the outside, and then we're on our way home, Tom. We can't tarry here too long, in case the Nor send another army against the Gap."

"Sir," Hildebrand nodded. "Be nice to take a battalion and raise some hell around here for the Nor that remain."

"And we may do just that," Chad nodded. "But not until we've found as many of our families as we can and ensured their safety."

-

Admiral Rafael Semmes hailed from a long line of sailors and naval commanders. He often joked he had salt water instead of blood in his veins, and being a true sailor he spent every moment he could at sea, enjoying the crisp air and salt spray.

But here, now, there was little enjoyment to be had for Semmes or anyone else. He and his men were moving along the coast in an effort to screen Soulan from an approaching Nor Fleet that had enough ships to contain a sizable landing force. If he could eliminate or even drive off that force, then General Freeman's Corps could be released to the fighting in Tinsee, bolstering the troops there that were, by all reports, being hammered. An entire army corps was being held hostage to this enemy naval force and that was enough to decide the outcome of the war.

"Sails south, Admiral," his aide, Commander Nettles informed him quietly. Semmes shifted his glass, scanning the southern horizon until he found the masts of several vessels.

"That will be the Key Horn Squadron," he nodded in satisfaction. "I estimate we'll have them alongside in two hours or less. We'll have all Captains and Firsts aboard one hour after their arrival, Mister Nettles," Semmes ordered. "Time to get this expedition underway."

"Aye, sir," Nettles nodded and set about ordering the signal for the meeting and time hoisted. The flagship of the Savannah squadron was the cruiser *Wabash*, a heavy ship designed not only to throw but also to ram, using the giant iron reinforced spar that extended from her nose. It was hard on a ship to ram, but *Wabash* was built for it.

She was also built to be a command vessel however, and that was how Semmes used her. He would command the three combined squadrons from her decks as they engaged the Nor fleet. His current plan, dependent on advice from the squadron commanders, was to allow the three squadrons to operate as separate commands of the same action, with his general orders given to the squadron commanders for them to implement as best they saw fit using men and ships they would know best. Time was of the essence and he begrudged every second lost, but without good planning any time advantage would be lost when the battle was joined and their navy defeated.

No, he'd spend the time wisely. And after that he'd give the Nor sailing off his kingdom's coast something to think about.

-

The escort of IG troops ferrying Therron McLeod was some of the best troops under the Inspector General's command. The duty would be rotated among the men so that no one was required to spend more than six to nine months 'babysitting' the former Lord Marshal.

Therron had attempted to bully those troops as soon as they were out of sight of Nasil, but the commander and his two subordinates were well chosen for this mission and the troops hand-picked from among the most loyal in the kingdom. As a result, Therron McLeod found himself isolated in the spartan coach that was ferrying him to the Key Isles. A desolate and isolated area if beautiful, he would spend the rest of his life there, effectively exiled while remaining within the borders of Soulan. His father would not risk Therron being allowed to return at the head of a mercenary army, or that the turncoat son would actually betray them to the Nor.

The men escorting him were well aware of the threat the Nor presented to their kingdom and had been told in no uncertain terms that Therron had almost allowed the Nor to take Nasil by refusing an order of the Sovereign. They knew he was fortunate not to have been executed, and assumed that only the war had prevented it.

All were perfectly willing take Therron's head themselves to prevent his escape. A fact that the Inspector General had taken great pains to explain to the former Marshal. Therron seethed at the treatment but there was naught he could do for now but to take it.

That did not mean that he would always do so. One did not attempt to seize a kingdom without forethought and planning.

Or accomplices.

He was patient, and it was a long way to the Key Horn. Much could happen between Nasil and the Gulf of Storms.

-

Lieutenant General Gerald Wilson listened without emotion as his aide rattled off the damages done by the Soulan Cavalry raid. Two general officers dead along with the majority of their staff. Two infantry divisions crushed, their surviving men and officers useless for anything other than garrison duties. A third infantry division suffering heavy losses but also having held against the enemy and thus their moral was rather high despite everything.

Their commander, Major General Taylor, was preening like a young rooster, conveniently forgetting that his own men would have likewise been crushed had it not been for the intervention of Stone's cavalry.

And the vaunted cavalry that everyone was so proud of! Stone's command had been torn a new one and that was as nice a way to say it as Wilson could find. Just when it had looked as if they were about to catch the Soulan horsemen in a decisive battle, the southerners had changed tactics on them mid-stride and created havoc among what was supposed to be the best trained unit in the Norland army.

The casualty count was horrendous. Infantry losses were somewhere around twenty-two thousand dead and wounded, though there were far less of the latter than Wilson would have believed.

Stone's cavalrymen had lost another eight thousand plus in their brief engagement against their southern counterparts. He could scarcely believe it.

"Enough," he said tiredly, shushing his aide with a raised hand. "I get the gist of it. We got our asses handed to us."

"I wouldn't put it that way, sir," the young Captain didn't stammer.

"Nor should you," Wilson nodded. "Have the reports prepared and then provide me a written summary of losses and damages. The only supply areas they managed to get to were the three infantry units they engaged, correct?"

"Yes sir," the young man nodded. "General Stone's arrival kept them out of the main army's rear areas."

"Well there's that anyway," Wilson sighed. "Send Stone in on your way out."

"Sir," the Captain braced to attention and departed. Stone entered right away, face set in a mask.

"General, I'd like to know why you failed to follow up when the Soulanies began their retreat."

"I screwed up," Stone admitted flatly. "I lost my coordination with my units and that cost us the opportunity. No excuses. It's easy to let communications get messed up in that kind of mess, but I should have anticipated it. Should have prepared for it. And I didn't. The blame is mine."

Stone wasn't going to lay blame on anyone else. His hasty words to the runners that he hadn't cared about their casualties had run through his men like wildfire. It hadn't been the way he'd meant it, but that was how it had sounded. He'd done as much damage control as he could with his senior officers and now it was up to them to explain what he'd actually meant.

He had lost nearly a third of his force in the brief encounter with the Soulan Cavalry. His only happiness in the whole experience had been seeing Blue Dog and his savages get their own asses handed to them by a handful of Soulan troopers. Served him right for trying to attack men who were checking for wounded comrades.

"There's plenty of blame to go around," Wilson assured him. "If it hadn't been for Raymond being completely unprepared for an attack while he sat on our flank, this attack would have been repulsed without such serious losses. Of course he and Hartley both perished in the battle so they could escape the blame for their actions," he added with a snort. "Sit down, I'm tired of looking up," Wilson ordered. Stone took the seat opposite his commander.

"How are your men?" Wilson asked.

"Angry, at me as much as the southerners," he shrugged. At Wilson's questioning look Stone explained his mistake.

"That was bad," Wilson nodded. "Still, I see what you meant. Your subordinates should be able to straighten that out. And you were right," he nodded. "Losses we'd already taken meant nothing without victory. Wasted lives. Are they still able to fight?"

"Of course," Stone nodded. "They were caught by Soulan horse archers which is what caused most of our casualties. We did learn that our horses are not large enough in most cases to compete with their larger war-mounts. Their horses are trained almost as highly as their men. Ramming into our smaller beasts and sometimes literally knocking them to the ground."

"So I've heard," Wilson sighed. "Well, I'm assuming you and your staff are working on a remedy for that?" His tone indicated they had better be.

"We are," Stone nodded. "Nothing but planning at the moment, but now that we've seen a real cavalry battle where we didn't completely outnumber our opponents we know what to expect. We can factor that into our training and tactics, as well as our orders. Next time it will be different, horse archery aside," he added that last with bitterness.

"I know that's a sticking point for you," Wilson said evenly.

"It cost me almost three thousand men by our best estimates, and us with no way to answer it. We just have to take it. We also lost nearly thirty-five hundred horses. Not all are dead, but some are so injured they're not good for much more than the cooking pots." He grimaced at that. No cavalry man liked the idea of losing horses.

"Send any that you think can recover to the rear," Wilson ordered. "We'll not be eating a horse that can one day mount a trooper again, or even pull a wagon."

"Sir," Stone nodded.

"We do have some horse archery training ongoing at home," Wilson continued.

"Lot of good that does us here," Stone shrugged. "If we can get around them, use our mobility on their flanks, we can probably get away from that massed archery fire, which would give us a better chance to close with them. Once we've figured how to work around their over-sized mounts, we'll incorporate that into our training. I'm thinking about maybe adding some crossbows to my units.

Anything to give us a return volley, even if it's just one shot."

"Shoot once and then sling them, or just drop them?" Wilson asked.

"Can't drop them, the follow on horses will trip on them, but a sling would work," Stone mused. "Like I said, anything to give us a way to fight back."

"I understand Blue Dog tried to take advantage of the aftermath," Wilson changed the subject. "How did that work out?"

"Got his teeth kicked in, ignorant savage," Stone smiled grimly. "I hate that bastard with a passion I usually reserve for women and whiskey," he almost growled. "It was good to see him taken down a peg."

"Just remember that we need him. For now," Wilson advised.

"Oh, I do," Stone nodded. "I've bitten my tongue, my lip, my cheek and back to my tongue, but I've been nothing but respectful to the savage or his men. I'm patient. I can wait."

"Good," Wilson nodded. "Well, leave your report with my aide, he's assembling the bad news for me so that I can try to paint a good picture on this for the Emperor. Though I'm sure by now Daly has already sent off a courier with the good news. Gloating bastard."

"You know, men die all the time in battle," Stone shrugged. He left it open and Wilson nodded.

"So they do. We just need to make sure more of their men die and less of ours," he added for anyone who might be listening.

"Like I said, we're working on it," Stone played to the same audience, just in case. He stood.

"By your leave?"

"Dismissed."

-

"Draw!"

Winnie Hubel watched as the newest recruits went through their archery routine. These men had already had their basic training and were in good physical condition when they arrived. That would speed the process of turning them into archers.

So long as they were willing to listen.

Unlike the men she had trained before, these soldiers seemed to completely reject the idea of taking their instruction from a woman. Had she trained a group of men like this the first time she would probably have quit. Having managed to train the Sheep, she found it difficult to be intimidated by these men. Something they had yet to catch on to.

"Hold!" the Captain supervising their training ordered. She watched as the men strained to hold the pull on their bows. A few were shaky, but that would stop in time. This exercise was designed to build the muscle groups they would need to use their bows for extended periods in battle.

Winnie walked through the ranks, occasionally adjusting a trooper's arm or elevation, complimenting on occasion. She sometimes found it difficult to be a young woman surrounded by young men. Many of them made unwarranted assumptions about her which had to be corrected. Usually by one of the Sheep still in camp. Even recovering from wounds the members of Parno's regiment were far tougher than the men they were training.

There were other women around of course, but save for a handful like Doctor Freeman, all were the wives, sisters, or daughters of the Black Sheep. After their action at the Gap no sane man would want to anger one of them by making an offensive remark or action toward one of their women.

Winnie appeared to them to be fair game. She had been amused at first, thinking it a distraction but nothing else. Certainly nothing to worry over. She had been born and raised in the Apple Mountains and was herself as hard as the men she had helped to train. Her skirt hid muscled legs used to climbing rocks and moving up and down mountain trails. Long sleeves in the mountain climate concealed finely muscled arms, developed from a lifetime of hard work and her own archery skills.

All the soldiers could see was a comely young woman. A single young woman who might be safer to pursue. Several had approached her and taken her rebuff calmly, accepting that she was not interested.

Trooper Helm had not taken his rejection as calmly. Tall and handsome with blonde hair and skin browned by the sun, Helm thought highly of himself and felt that Winnie should too. In fact, she should be flattered that he had even approached her at all. She had smirked slightly at his implication as she moved past him, only to stop as he moved to block her yet again.

She had been prepared to let something like that slide but Helm had made the mistake of trying to touch her. That was something Winnie was not at all inclined to tolerate.

As a result, Trooper Helm was now recovering in the hospital after which he would be confined to the stockade for the foreseeable future. His broken jaw, dislocated shoulder and concussion were enough to dissuade even the most determined of other admirers, who now chose to admire her from afar.

"Release!"

She watched as the men carefully released the tension on their bowstrings, noting that a few were still struggling. She made some soft comments to them, giving advise which they nodded their acceptance to. Seeing her shoot had been an eye opening experience for them just as it had been for the Sheep. There was never any question that Winnie Huble knew how to use a bow. Trooper Helm had also learned that she knew some other things as well. The rest chose to learn from his example.

Winnie almost sighed thinking about the fact that her dealing with Helm was a problem in other ways. It would be difficult if not impossible for her to find a husband that would accept that she was not going to spend her life barefoot in his kitchen, popping out babies every year until she was too broken down to do so. She had no objection to having a child, or even two or three, but she was not made for housekeeping duties. She belonged outdoors, free to roam and to do and to see. To feel the sun on her face and the wind in her hair.

She would not give that up for any man. At least none that she had met so far.

"Draw!"

Winnie left those thoughts behind as the exercise continued with her watching. This was her job, at least for now. There might come a time however, when she herself rode to war with her bow.

The very thought was repugnant to most men, though her father had merely nodded his acceptance when she'd told him of her thoughts. He would not want her to, but Whip Hubel had raised a free spirit, much like himself. She would go where she willed. He would worry, he would pray for her safety and he would miss her, but he would not interfere.

So all she had to do was convince Parno McLeod. But she had a plan for that. One that would need a certain ally. One that knew exactly how Winnie felt. One that could speak with much more ease than Winnie herself could.

Fortunately, such an ally was available.

-

"Why?"

Stephanie Corsin-Freeman couldn't hide her look of shock. In hindsight she shouldn't have been surprised, but at that point in time she didn't have the benefit of hindsight and was floored.

"Because I should be able to serve just like they do," Winnie Hubel said evenly. "I thought you would understand that better than anyone," she added.

"I do understand wanting to serve," Stephanie nodded. "But. . .Winnie you're. . .I mean you can't imagine how bad it is," she settled for saying. "It's not clinical like on the firing range. The carnage is horrifying. I. . .I can't adequately describe it," she finally admitted.

"Yet you wanted to go," Winnie pointed out.

"To serve as a medical officer," Stephanie pointed out at once. "Specifically to keep. . .to make sure that. . .I mean. . . ," she trailed off, spluttering.

"Yes?" Winnie pressed, perhaps a little maliciously though not mean spirited. It was well known that the 'Lady Doctor' had set her cap for the Prince.

"Never you mind," Stephanie waved it away. "The point is I wouldn't have been in combat, or even at the front. Just what little I saw from the rear area at The Gap was enough to last a lifetime, and remember that we were ordered away before the final battle. Winnie it's no place for a woman. I had that pointed out to me rather pointedly just a few days ago."

"By who?" Winnie asked.

"By Duchess Cumberland," Stephanie replied. "She told me that my presence would be a distraction to Pa. . .to the men," she caught herself, flushing ever so slightly. "And that would be if I were in the hospital near the front. Imagine how distracted the men would be with you fighting alongside them. What if they were wounded or killed because in their worry for you they didn't pay enough attention to the enemy? How would you feel then?"

Those were the same words, more or less, that Edema Willows had fired at her just days ago. Saying them to Winnie now made Stephanie realize just how accurate that statement was.

"It's not my fault if they can't keep their mind where it belongs," Winnie shrugged.

"I didn't say it would be your fault," Stephanie corrected. "I said you would be a *distraction*. One that men in war don't need, to be honest. It's bad enough as it is. Not to mention there are certain. . .issues that all women encounter that would be difficult at best in the field. Do you think the enemy will stop their operations while you deal with your monthly visit?" Winnie's face flushed pink at the subtle mention of the one thing that she had no answer for.

"I've been working to find a way to get by that," she admitted.

"Well, until you find one I'd suggest you table this idea, Winnie," Stephanie suggested. "Honestly, I think the idea is a grand one, it's just not feasible. Not with things the way they are." She paused suddenly, having a flash of inspiration.

"Have you spoken to anyone else about this?" she asked. "Other women I mean? About the possibility of going to war?"

"A few," Winnie said cautiously. "Here and there."

"What was their response?" Stephanie asked, genuinely interested.

"Mostly favorable," the girl replied. "There are a lot of women here, you know," she said evenly. There were family members, but any Cantonment would attract various 'trades' so to speak, and Cove was no different. The actions of those around the camp were much more restrained of course, since the Black Sheep patrolled their own areas, and they answered only to the Lord Marshal. There wasn't much they couldn't do to someone who was caught cheating at cards or stealing or groping an unwilling woman, or pretty much any other crime.

Of course, a camp like Cove also attracted women who were willing, so long as certain monetary considerations could be satisfied.

"Yes, I know there are," Stephanie nodded. "But how do you think the Sheep would react to having their wives, sisters or daughters in battle? Do they strike you as the type that would want that?"

"Shouldn't what we want matter more?" Winnie asked plainly. "I really thought you'd be more supporting. I mean, you're a woman in what's commonly considered a man's profession. You do the same work as any man, probably better, yet still some look down on you because you're not somewhere sipping mint tea on the veranda. I expected you to understand. To support me." The girl fought to keep the hurt out of her voice.

"Winnie, I do support you," Stephanie sighed. "I'm trying to get you to see the downside of what you're wanting. It's not just about what you want. My being a doctor wrinkles some old man's nose and the only person it really affects is the old man and his nose. What would it do to your father if you were killed, or worse captured, by the Nor? Can you imagine the effect it would have on our men thinking about you or the others dying at the hands of the Nor, or falling captive into their hands? Do you see what I mean?"

Winnie was about to retort when the words sank in. Her father would be beside himself, certainly. She had not thought about being captured. Killed, yes. She had considered that and knew it was possible, but it was just as possible for the men she was training at the moment. She could share that risk.

She wanted to serve. She wanted to do something, anything, to help her believe that she was serving.

"I do see," Winnie nodded. "I still think it's not right," she insisted. "But I can see that you're not going to help me, either," she sighed. "I'm sorry I bothered you Miss Freeman. You have more important things to be doing than worrying with me. If you'll excuse me I need to get back to work." The girl turned and was gone before Stephanie could think of anything else to say.

She hated for Winnie to think that she was denigrating her desire to serve because that was not the way of it. It was simply too great a risk, too much of a distraction for Winnie and other young women to be at the front, fighting.

Surely the girl would see the truth of it if she thought on it a bit longer. Shaking her head Stephanie turned back to the hospital. Winnie was right about one thing. Stephanie had a lot of work to do.

CHAPTER NINE

-

The trip from First Army's headquarters to the river fortifications in Shelby had taken Parno and his men nine days of hard riding. Nine days that Parno spent worrying over what was happening while he was out of communication with everyone else. He was going to have to find a happy medium where he could be centralized if for no other reason that so reports could find him.

He missed the days of being at Cove Canton, where his only problems had been the populace being angry at him for not allowing the soldiers to spend their pay in their establishments and keeping Darvo off his back about...

Thinking of Darvo Nidiad brought a cloud over Parno as it always did. He missed the old man more with each passing day, yet there was no relief for that. He had to press on, more so now than ever before. He had no choice but to do so. In fact, he had very few choices left open to him these days.

"What bothers you, my Prince?" Cho Feng appeared suddenly at his side, having noted the change in demeanor, subtle though it was.

"Just thinking," Parno replied as they moved through the city heading for Third Corps' headquarters at the river. "Too much of that gives me a headache."

"About Colonel Nidiad, no doubt," Feng once more showed his grasp of understanding his young charge. "It is ever painful to lose one's mentor, Parno," he added softly. "You can but carry on as he would have had you do."

"I know," Parno sighed, nodding slightly. "It's not that all of you aren't good enough, Cho," he added suddenly. "I couldn't ask for better people to be surrounded by in all this. It's just that Darvo. . . ." he trailed off, unsure of what he wanted to say.

"Raised you," Cho said it for him. "He was your father in all but blood, Parno. Missing him is natural. It is not something to be unhappy about, ashamed of, or that needs to be put away. He earned your love and it is only proper that you still feel it. Do not let this upset you. Instead, remember the things he has taught you and you will do fine."

Parno was stunned by the words, sounding so much like what Darvo had said from his death bed. Parno decided not to pursue the discussion as Third Corps' Headquarters came into their view.

General Raines and his staff were assembled outside, having been warned of his approach by courier. Parno stopped his horse several feet away and dismounted tiredly. His own staff and escort did the same, though the others remained mounted.

"Welcome, milord," Rained said simply.

"Pleasure to be here, General," Parno nodded, extending his hand. "Parno McLeod," he said, quite unnecessarily.

"Sir," Raines chose not to point that out. "Captain will you see the Prince's escort to their billet please?" he said to the man next to him.

"Sir," the man nodded and looked to Karls.

"Major, the Captain will show you to our quarters," Karls told Seymour.

"Sir," the Major nodded and followed the Captain away, the Sheep following and leading the horses of the others. Berry and his men remained with the prince.

"General, can you bring us up to date on how things set here?" Parno asked. "And maybe rustle us up something to eat?" he added as his stomach growled.

"I'm sure we can feed you," Raines fought a grin and looked to an aide who hurried away to inform the General's personal cook that he'd be cooking for the Prince today. Right now in fact.

"If you'll come in sir, I can show you our dispositions and give you a brief report on how things stand at the moment. Complete reports are available for you at your leisure, or that of your staff."

Parno followed Raines inside. Unlike the field headquarters for First Army, this was Third Corps' permanent home and the furnishings showed it. Not that there was anything fancy or flashy about the building or its interior for it was utilitarian for the most part. But there was a sense of permanency here that a tent in the field couldn't carry off. Parno liked it.

"Our map room, sir," Rained said as he led Parno into a large and well-appointed room. Parno halted at the door, surprised by the sight.

There were maps on every wall, which he'd expected. But there was also a detailed re-creation of the river valley on a larger table in front of him. Parno didn't know the scale, but it ran from BellMonte, Kent all the way to the coast of the Gulf of Storms. Small blocks of different colors littered the board in places.

"Our model of the zone, sir," Raines said when he saw where Parno's attention was focused. "It reminds us of terrain and helps us keep the size of our area of responsibility in mind."

"I'm impressed," Parno nodded. "You did this yourself General?" he asked as he approached the model.

"Well, I had it done," Raines nodded. "A man in my engineering staff designed and constructed the model."

"I'd like to see him while I'm here," Parno ordered and Raines knew he'd probably just lost the services of a very talented engineer.

"I'll see to it, sir," he promised. "These block indicate our troop dispositions," he pointed to one of the colored blocks. "Yellow is cavalry, blue is infantry, gray for mounted infantry. We use the same colors for suspected enemy dispositions, but those blocks are also half black, to indicate they are then enemy."

"Nice," Parno nodded, meaning it. He wished he had such a model for the Tinsee valley. And would soon, if that engineer was able to recreate his work here.

"So what are you facing, General, to the best of your knowledge?" he asked, turning to business.

Raines spent the next half-hour detailing the events along the river up to present, Parno nodding on occasion and only a few times stopping Raines for clarification or to ask a question.

Raines had held his own misgivings about the new Lord Marshal upon hearing of the change in command, but had reserved his opinion until he could form it himself. He was glad now that he had.

With two momentous victories under his belt, Parno McLeod had every reason and right to be cocky and proud, yet he exhibited no signs of either. He was patient, seemed intelligent, asked good questions and had the respect of some fine fighting men if the shape of his personal regiment was any indication. Raines had heard more than one story about the men following McLeod and they had all been good.

Nothing he saw in the young man before him now detracted from that in any way. Parno McLeod just might be all right as the Marshal, he decided.

"Is there any one area that gives you most pause, General?" Parno asked as the briefing came to an end.

"I can't say there is any particular area of itself, milord," Raines shook his head. "Our main concern has been that the enemy would attempt to cross the river by boat and raise havoc behind us. We've not seen any attempt at that so far, but we do have observation posts all along the river to watch for that or any other activity."

"Aside from that threat, the major concern of course is the bridge," Rained indicated the span across the model of the Great River. "I have to say that

I do not believe that the enemy intends to try and force a crossing, milord," he added.

"What makes you say that?" Parno asked, and Raines could almost see Parno's mind working behind his eyes.

"They have made several half-hearted attempts at attacks, but none of them in any kind of force and all of them repulsed. I won't say easily repulsed, because they've been costly to us. Still, we estimate there are at least five divisions of Nor and Tribal horsemen across the river, supported by at least some artillery. They could certainly mount such an attack if they desired. I don't believe they do."

"So what do you believe their goal is, General?"

"To hold Third Corps in place here while the war if fought on the front to the north," Raines replied at once. "They know that as long as they are threatening, we can't afford to send even a single unit to aid First and Second corps. We can't spare them in case of an all-out attack or a river crossing effected by boat. So they threaten, they demonstrate, and we have to honor that threat."

"Excellent," Parno murmured as he nodded. "My thoughts exactly. Unfortunately, we can't afford to act on that because if we pull men away from you and they realize it, then this feint becomes a real attack. Success here would negate any gain we might achieve by utilizing some of your command further north against the field army."

Raines was shocked by the rapid understanding the youngest McLeod demonstrated in his statement. He'd just summed up two hours of intelligence brief in one minute or less. And accurately, too.

"That's the way we see it, milord," he nodded to cover his surprise.

"You've done a fine job here, General," Parno said at last. "I don't believe that better could be asked of you or your men. Well done."

"Thank you, milord," Rained bowed his head slightly. Just then an aide returned and nodded to Raines.

"I think your meal is ready, milord," Raines informed Parno.

"Join me then, General, and let's discuss your options, such as they are."

-

"There's always the option of destroying the bridge, milord."

The meal was good. Roasted pig with potatoes and corn, probably all freshly pulled. Parno hadn't eaten this good in days and it showed in his enthusiasm. But that didn't keep him from shaking his head at Raines' suggestion.

"No, General," he said between bites. "We will need that bridge one day."

Raines raised an eyebrow at the statement but the Marshal offered nothing else on that front, instead turning to other concerns.

"Your patrols along the river seem effective. Have they been? Have you had any reports of raiding or other types of incursions? Any unexplained attacks or incidents?"

"No, milord, we have not," Raines replied, shifting his thoughts back to the matter at hand. "Our patrols are not the only way we're watching, either. We have observation posts along the entire length of the river from here all the way to the coast." Parno did stop eating at that, looking at Raines for amplification.

"Small detachments of five or six men, and in some cases women," Raines explained. "They man spots along the river where crossing might be made easier. These positions are well concealed and can see for quite some distances with the scopes they have. If activity is noted, then two messengers are dispatched to the nearest cavalry post for assistance while the remainder of the detachment continue to watch. We have had many false alarms of course, but we check each one. The enemy only needs one success. We must always be successful."

"True," Parno nodded. "Women, you say?" he asked. "Serving directly or. . . ." He trailed off, unsure how to ask his next question, or even if it were necessary.

"They are considered paid irregulars, sir," Raines admitted with only slight hesitation. "In some cases their husbands are serving at the same posts, or perhaps they are on active duty to the north. Some are younger women, rural in upbringing and just as capable as any man might be, at least for this duty."

"I assure you I know some very capable women myself," Parno nodded, thinking of Winnie Hubel and her ability with a bow. "I dislike the notion of their serving in combat, but in something like this I can't see the harm, especially if they are good at it."

"They are," Raines nodded firmly. "One post just south of here is in fact actually commanded by a woman," he admitted. "The post is on her land and manned by her family and farm hands. Far better than the living conditions at some of the more distant outposts. They simply report for duty on a regular schedule, sharing the work between their normal activities."

"Indeed," Parno grunted. "I assume she does well?" he asked, leaning forward.

"She does," Raines assured him. "Concise and well written reports, always on time and always careful to differentiate between what she actually sees and what she suspects. Honestly, if she were a man I'd have her commanding a scout company. She's very intelligent and obviously well-schooled. She probably wouldn't accept the pay cut, however," he grinned.

"Noble?" Parno asked.

"No, but a large land owner," Rained explained. "Raises cattle and row crops along with a large swine herd. This feast is compliments of her farm, in fact," he indicated the table. "She inherited the farm as a girl when her father was killed by a bull. Has run the entire operation herself since the age of seventeen, in fact. She's a widow, now, but has two sons and a daughter, all of whom are just as smart as she is. One son is away with the militia at present, the other being still a year or so shy of the minimum age. He and the daughter help run the operation nowadays."

"Interesting," Parno mused. "She sounds like quite a woman. If time allows I'd like to meet her," he said suddenly. Raines nodded as if he'd expected that.

"I'll ask her to come 'round tomorrow for lunch," he replied.

"Excellent," Parno nodded, looking to Sprigs who merely nodded and made a note in his ever-present notebook. He then turned back to Raines.

"Now that my stomach and backbone are not so close together, what say we have a look at the enemy, General?"

Parno looked at the distant shore on the far side of the Great River. He had been here once before as a boy, one of the rare trips he had been allowed to accompany his father upon, but that had been long ago. He had decided as he grew older that his impression of the width of the river had been exaggerated by his own diminutive size. He had been wrong. The Tinsee was wide in places, even very wide in a few of those, but nothing like this. He wondered. . . .

"Just over a mile distant, even at the most narrow," Raines commented quietly as if reading Parno's thoughts. "Deceptive to say the least. Several idiots drown each year in an attempt to swim the damn thing. I dare say with so many Tribal horsemen just across the expanse there will be a slowdown of that activity, at least until they are gone."

"Swim," Parno shook his head at the news. "I can't imagine the mental issues that would make someone want to swim against that current," he pointed to a swirl and eddy clearly visible below them.

"And even that is deceptive," Raines nodded. "We've lost more than a few small boats to such as that. Almost always with fatalities. Most fishermen don't even care to know how to swim they say, since it's unlikely to be of any assistance if they're very far from shore. I know I try to avoid being on the water any time I can."

"Why would you need to be on the water at all?" Parno asked, turning to look at him.

"I need to see my defenses from the enemy's viewpoint," Raines shrugged. "I need to see what they see. Look for weaknesses and try to correct them. It's a never ending mission. Plus, watching for erosion to existing fortifications. The current is strong and in flood the river often does great damage. There's always work to do here, milord," he grinned. "No shortage of work details."

"So I see," Parno nodded. "And that boat? There?" he pointed to a medium sized vessel with oars over the side perhaps a quarter of the way across.

"Fishermen," Raines informed him once he'd seen the boat. "They have to make a living," he shrugged again. "And there's no real justification for keeping them from going out. The enemy hasn't fired on the boats that I've been made aware of. Restricting the fishing would simply create ill will for my men. Under the circumstances I felt it better to allow business as usual."

"Sensible," Parno agreed. "Is there much fishing here? Like that?"

"A good bit," Raines replied. "Perhaps not so strong as further down river or on the coast of course, but it is a thriving industry here."

"I'm glad they're still able to work," Parno said flatly. "Retaining any little bit of normalcy is good, especially right now." Abruptly he turned from the view and began following the platform along the fortified area around the bridge. Raines fell in beside him.

"I have heard things are. . .bad, milord," Raines finally broached a subject that had been the source of more than one rumor or speculation. "At least in places."

"It is, indeed," Parno nodded, sighing as he thought of just how 'bad' things were. "We have averted, or at least postponed disaster for the moment General, but make no mistake that our very kingdom rests in the balance. The events of the next few months will almost certainly decide the future of our people." He stopped, turning to look Raines in the eye, then to look at the gaggle of aids following them. All backed away under his gaze and when satisfied they were out of earshot Parno continued.

"My brother's plot has simply made things worse," he said flatly. "At a time when the Army needed him, he has allowed his desire for personal gain to imperil the entire kingdom. His arrogance in believing that we could simply overwhelm the Nor has left us in this mess. We have to clean it up and we must hurry."

"Every day they occupy so much of our crop land is a victory of sorts for them. Their own crop lands are likely being planted even now while millions of acres of our own lies fallow or covered in Nor refuse. It is intolerable and cannot be allowed for a moment longer than necessary to remove them." Parno stopped abruptly as if he had suddenly become aware of how he sounded.

"There is an Imperial naval force off our coast that is threatening the south-eastern shore line with ships that could be carrying more troops. I strongly believe those ships are a ruse to prevent out moving troops from that area into the campaign here in the west. Yet I must honor that threat unless and until it can be proven false. Admiral Semmes is at sea now to try and deal with the problem, but it takes time to assemble his ships and even then he must have favorable winds to be successful."

"And time is our enemy as surely as the Nor Empire right now," Parno sighed, summing up the problem in that one sentence. "We have to commit more men to the fighting on the Tinsee plains or we're going to be pushed further and deeper into the heartland every day."

"I understand you may have stymied that move for a bit before coming here, milord," Raines pointed out.

"For all I know they are attacking this very minute," Parno shrugged. "I won't even know it until it's too late. And one man, more or less, won't make much difference I suppose," he added. "Tell me straight out, General. Can you spare any men from your present command and still be assured of holding should the Nor or the Tribes launch a determined attack on your position?"

Raines stifled his automatic response to such a question. He needed all of his forces to hold his ground here. That was the standard response to any such question.

But this was the Lord Marshal of the Army. Parno McLeod also had two amazing victories behind him already where everyone else was failing miserably. He deserved an honest answer.

"I don't know," Raines admitted finally. "I can only estimate the enemy numbers, milord. And that's essentially what we called an educated guess when I was in Command College. If I'm right about their numbers and they can take the bridge, then I'd need every man I could scrape up and then some to hold the shoreline here."

"If I'm wrong and they have even more men than I think, then it might not matter one way or another in the long run," the General continued. "We'd lose due to attrition if nothing else. That was why I suggested destroying the bridge. With it gone, even boat raids would be of limited use to the enemy. They simply cannot move horses and heavy equipment across this river in barges like they are reported to have done on the Ohi. The current would sweep them downstream and possibly capsize them."

"That bridge is the last of the avenues across this river, General," Parno shook his head. "I need it. Or at least I will. Later on."

"That's twice you've said that, milord," Raines couldn't stand it anymore. "May I ask what you mean by that?"

"I mean that I'll need it," Parno said flatly. "If they destroy it, that's fine, you'll not risk any of your men to prevent it. But we will not fire the bridge ourselves unless it's full of screaming heathens and we're in danger of losing the war. Understand?"

"No, I don't," Raines replied flatly. "But I don't have to understand orders to follow them. It will be as you command, milord."

"One day we'll be crossing that bridge ourselves," Parno decided to share. "We'll be moving across it to put an end to all of this, once and for all. That's why I need it. Now do you understand? General?"

Raines knew that his eyes were growing large but he didn't know that he could help it. Never in history had the Soulan Army marched outside their own borders. Yet the Marshal was hinting. . . .

"This will be the last invasion of Soulan soil, General," Parno said grimly. "One way or another, there will be no more. War perhaps, but not invasion. Our people will not suffer through another occupation. That's why I need that bridge.

Now, can you spare any of your command and still be at least reasonably sure of holding your position here?"

Raines immediate answer was no, but he caught the reply before it left his lips. This Marshal was nothing like his brother. Raines had never had much time for Therron McLeod, having never liked or trusted the man. Raines had been friends with Memmnon McLeod for more years than either would likely want to consider, and he knew for a fact that the Crown Prince had likewise had little time for Prince Therron.

Parno McLeod was another story. Never taken seriously before now, the youngest son had quickly made a name for himself as a fierce fighter and leader. Suddenly he was no longer the Playboy Prince that everyone ridiculed or treated with casual contempt. In a war that had already seen grievous losses and military defeats Parno had produced the only viable victories, both of them as tremendous as the earlier losses.

And that was the man asking him if he could spare any of his command.

"I would need to reevaluate our position to answer that effectively, milord," he admitted finally. "I think we could spare a cavalry division, provided we can use the militia in their place. I've kept a cavalry division in reserve to respond to any sizable incursions along the river. It would be a gamble," he admitted, "but I could release that division to you. It would leave me seriously undermanned in the event of a major crossing by boat, but. . .if we're right and they don't intend to attempt a forcing then we should be alright, at least so long as we can keep up the enemy from discovering that we've weakened our forces here."

"And if they stage a large river crossing to effect a raid in strength?" Parno asked. "Will you be able to ride them down?"

Raines blinked at that. Was this a test? Had he not explained this just now?

"Sir, I don't know," he decided for truth. "It would depend on where they crossed, how much warning we had, and how large a force we had nearby. If I spread my forces far enough and thin enough to cover everywhere, then they run the risk of being defeated in detail if the raiding party is strong enough. And, honestly, the militia won't be nearly as effective in pursuit or in combat as the regular cavalry unit I'm keeping in reserve for that instance."

"True," Parno nodded. He stood looking across the river, apparently lost in thought.

"Your militia, where are they coming from?" he asked suddenly.

"Mostly from Tinsee Province, milord, though a handful are from Misi and Northern Alma. But most of their units have gone south."

"To the gulf," Parno said absently, still looking across the river.

"Yes sir," Raines nodded. "I requested that some help be sent to me before the war ever began to assist with patrolling the river. In fact, I asked that the river south be handled by 4th Corps, to allow me to concentrate here, and to guard the river to the north."

"The response?" Parno asked, looking at Raines finally.

"I received what was supposed to be a brigade of mounted militia from Misi, supplemented by a late forming battalion of Alma cavalry."

"Supposed to be?" Parno raised an eyebrow in question.

"Little more than two regiments worth of men, milord, even throwing in the Alma cavalry. About half mounted and them not well. In a pursuit, they would not last more than two days, if that," Raines replied evenly.

"I see," Parno nodded. "Dismount them and add them to your infantry here," he nodded to the fortifications around the bridge and along the shore. "Use them to man more of your observation posts. Can anything be done with the horses?" Raines was so surprised by the order that it took him a minute to answer.

"I. . .I don't know, milord, to be honest," he admitted. "I haven't had the time to see to them myself."

"Nor should you," Parno agreed. "Have your lead wrangler inspect the animals. If they can be fed up and exercised back into shape, order that he do so and use them as remounts. Any that cannot be used for cavalry or to bear mounted infantry should be used as draft animals for supply trains. Should any be unsuitable for that, you may dispense them to area farmers in recompense for food stores. Even old horses can have uses for stockmen and farmers. If we cannot use them as war mounts or as draft animals, get them off the supply burden. Your fighting here, should it come, will mostly be on foot it appears to me."

"Any attack on us here will certainly be so, milord," Raines nodded.

"Using those men on foot should free up some of your regular mounted infantry?" Parno asked, and almost grinned as he saw the light finally dawning on Raines face.

"It would," he nodded. "But milord, there are political issues with moving militia to-"

"I'll have an order drafted for it as soon as we return," he looked at Sprigs who nodded and make a notation in his notebook. "We have no time for political issues at the moment. Any who try to make them will be dealt with as you see fit, up to and including execution if they refuse reassignment. If you'd rather, I can have my men see to that," he added, his tone kind. "I know it might cause you discomfort."

"It won't be a problem milord," Raines replied evenly. "Distasteful perhaps, but it will be done."

"I don't expect a wholesale revolt," Parno said ruefully. "I simply want you to understand that you are in command, General. I can't be everywhere at once. As I told my Regimental commander a few days ago, I can't even be two places at once. As of now, you are in command of all forces in this area, period. Every man in uniform in this district will answer to you for the duration of the war. No more political 'issues' or interference in your command by minor 'nobles'. Or major ones for that matter." He paused for a moment before making the plunge. Karls was right; Parno had to trust someone.

"Memmnon speaks highly of you, both as a friend and as a commander," he said finally. "Before leaving the front to the north I promoted General Davies to command of the First Field army, combining First and Second Corps. I'm doing the same for you, here. As commander of the Second Field Army, there will be no more political wrangling. If there is a 'noble' among that militia rabble that allowed their horses to be so ill kept, put him to work with the rest. You need work details? Put them to it. We simply cannot afford to have mounted 'dandies' running around while real soldiers do grunt work."

"I agree with that, milord," Raines nodded. "I appreciate your confidence in me as well. I'm glad Memmnon-, the Crown Prince I mean, speaks well of me," he added.

"He should, considering some of the hi-jinks the two of you pulled, if the stories are even partly accurate," Parno grinned, and Raines laughed aloud at that.

"Long ago, milord, when we were much younger and did not have so much hanging over us," he replied. "There is one minor noble among the 'rabble', as you named them. And it's not inaccurate. He is the son of a District Governor in Misi, the Duke of Leeford I believe. He rarely misses an opportunity to remind us of who he is, either."

"Introduce me," Parno ordered. "I might as well get this over with now."

-

Colonel Melton Fisk looked up from his reading to see a young man approaching his camp followed by a group of soldiers. He ignored the soldiers but frowned at this breach of camp etiquette. It was simply rude to walk into another man's command unannounced.

"You there!" he called out as he stood. "What are you doing in my camp?"

"Looking for the commander of this rabble," the young man replied easily. "I've never seen a more disgusting example of soldiery. Who's responsible for this?"

"Who are you to question my command or denigrate my men?" Fisk was white-hot in an instant. "I'm a mind to have you flogged!"

"Be my guest," the young man said easily. "Will you be taking me yourself, or have some of these rejects do it for you?"

"Seize him!" Fisk screeched. "And have someone send for Raines! I'll have someone's head for this!"

Before Fisk's men could react their camp was 'invaded' from all sides by armed men, all wearing the same black and green livery. And all wearing grim looks of combat soldiers, Fisk realized.

"My name," the intruder said easily, "is Parno McLeod." The silence to that statement was deafening.

"I'm told that you led your men here on horses that are barely able to carry your overfed ass," Parno continued. "And that you consistently attempt to use your 'rank' to avoid tasks that you consider beneath you. That ends today, Mister Fisk. You and your men will be moving camp in one half-hour, relocating to the river front where you and your men will assist with maintaining the defenses. Your horses will be reassigned to real cavalry units, assuming they can be rehabilitated from your slovenly treatment."

"You can't do that! Milord," Fisk hastened to add. "We're cavalrymen!"

"No real cavalryman would allow his horses to get into the shape your mounts are in, Captain," Parno shot back.

"It's Colonel!" Fisk almost shouted.

"Not as of this moment it's not," Parno shook his head. "Your men will be assigned to the engineering commander for the duration or until General Raines, Commanding Second Field Army determines you're worthy of a combat assignment. If you refuse or object any more, Captain, I'll have you in the guardhouse until you can be tried for whatever I can come up with under the Military Code. I must warn you that I'm somewhat busy at the moment defending the kingdom *while you sit here on your pompous lazy ass ducking work*! No more!" He had reached Fisk by now and there was a dangerous light in his eyes that his own men recognized quite well.

"We're at war for our very survival and you're treating this like a camping expedition, Mister Fisk. I don't care who you are, or who your father is, you will work or you by God won't eat and you'll rot in prison until every Nor bastard is removed from Soulan soil. After which, if I haven't forgotten you, I'll probably have you executed as an enemy of the Crown, giving aid and comfort to the enemy, cowardice, whatever I can think of. Do you understand me, Mister Fisk?"

Fisk was gaping like a fish out of water at this dressing down. He'd never had anyone speak to him like this. When his father learned of what was happening...

"I'll have your father replaced if I have to," the Marshal said softly, almost as if reading the other man's mind. "Don't think for an instant that I care one whit about a minor governor in the middle of nowhere when good men are dying to protect your fat ass *and* his. Now I asked you a question, Mister Fisk," his voice dropped again. "Do you understand me?"

It finally began to register on Fisk that he was on extremely shaky ground. His father would not look with favor on his son who had attracted Royal ire. Nor would he support that son, either. His gaze dropped to where the Marshal's hand was resting on his sword hilt. Would the Marshal actually attack him? Right here in front of everyone?

"I'm waiting," that same Marshal said, his voice taking on a threatening timbre.

"I... I understand, milord," Fisk managed to stammer. "But my rank, milord. . .I'm a Provincial! My rank was given me by the Provincial Governor himself! We fall under his command-”

"Except in time of war, which in case you've missed it, we are in at the moment," Parno cut him off. "You belong to me now, Captain, and you'll follow the orders of those above you or you'll suffer the consequences and I assure you they will be severe. Now you have twenty-five minutes to strike this pig sty camp of yours and get your men ready to march to the river. Anyone who lags behind will regret it. Follow?”

"Milord," Fisk started, then stopped. He turned to his second in command, a man who now outranked him by Royal Order.

"Major, prepare the men for movement. We have twenty minutes to be ready to march.”

"Our horses, Colo-” that Major was pointing to where the unit's mounts were being cut out by the wranglers of Raines regulars and herded for their own holding area.

"Aren't yours anymore," Parno finished for him. "I said march, and that's exactly what I meant. Your time is running out, Lieutenant.” The 'Major' blanched at having the ire of the Marshal turned on him and immediately went to ushering the men to prepare to move. Quickly.

"If I hear your name mentioned in one dispatch that isn't a glowing review of your contribution to the war effort I'll have you beheaded," Parno spoke to Fisk so softly that only he could hear. "There won't be any more warnings or chances. You'll simply be dead. Try me if you like. I've already killed so many that one more won't matter when I stand before Judgment.”

Fisk had no intention of 'trying' the new Marshal. He's always heard that the Marshal favored nobles of almost any rank and had played on that heavily to avoid any work assignments or danger. He had somehow missed the announcement that there was a new Marshal. One who apparently didn't share his predecessor's appreciation of rank.

"Now get moving," Parno finished. "My men will remain to ensure that you're on the road on time. You may have heard of them," he smiled nastily. "They're called the Black Sheep. Their most recent engagement was against a group of Wildmen that outnumbered them two-to-one. They suffered four injured while killing roughly three hundred Tribal warriors. Feel free to give them a go if you think you and your. . .*men*, are up to it.”

With that Parno turned on his heel, leaving a stunned Fisk staring after him.

"See to it that they get a move on," he ordered Karls, who merely nodded as Parno stalked past on his way back to Raines' headquarters. His own guard followed, as did Enri Willard and Harrel Sprigs. Cho Feng fell in beside Parno, walking silently.

"What is it?" Parno demanded suddenly.

"What do you mean, my Prince?" Feng asked calmly.

"You only walk beside me in silence when you want to make a point," Parno said flatly. "So, make it and be done."

"There is none to make," Feng said evenly. "You did well."

Parno just shook his head as Feng outmaneuvered him once more.

CHAPTER TEN

-

The Tinker led his small caravan into the rear of the camp, his 'pass' issued by the Inspector General of the Army enough to allow him to pass the guard posts. As he rode the last of the way toward the camp, he reviewed his 'orders' once more.

He had not been surprised to receive the missive from Prince McLeod. The new Marshal had promised he would have work for the Tinker at some point and was not shy in financing his waiting. The orders themselves were another thing altogether.

Behind him were five wagons and two ambulances, the result of several days work and expenditure of not a little of the Prince's gold. Two of the wagons held sutler items and tools that the Tinker would use to ply his official trade for the Army of Soulan, the others held furnishings and personal luggage for the people in his caravan as well as certain other 'goods' that would help them establish themselves in camp.

He would sell, buy and trade with the soldiers of the Army while also mending and repairing items of import, much as he usually did. As he did so, he would listen to the chatter of the soldiers, investigating anything that appeared suspect. In the secret pocket of his soft calf-hide boots was another paper from the Inspector General, this one identifying him as an agent of the Crown. Not for the first time he stifled a laugh at the idea of him bearing such identification.

Akin to those orders were the contents of the two ambulances. He had 'collected' several women who made their way in the world with their looks and their bodies. Women who, though of ill-repute, were still educated and cultured enough to attract the attention of even the most fastidious officer in the Army. Women whose dark eyes, black hair and sultry appearances would be able to seduce all but the most reputable of men.

Men who would be likely to talk to such women in times of. . .moral weakness the Prince had called it. The Tinker shook his head at the delicate way the Prince has asked him to basically become a pimp. The women would be well cared for after the war, Parno promised, as would Tinker himself. The Prince needed to know who he could trust and, perhaps more importantly, who he couldn't.

The eleven sultry beauties in those two ambulances would almost certainly be able to gather such information for the Prince. The Tinker knew that such a request had not come easy to the young Prince, whose honor was evident for all to see. He had a respect for women that was unusual, considering his being raised with little female influence. This was another of the things that made the Tinker trust this nobleman when he normally trusted none, noble or otherwise.

What this prince said he would do, he *did*.

So yes, he knew a few women who could fit that description, and most all were willing to risk that the Prince would do as he said. They trusted the Tinker and the Tinker trusted the prince. For people like them, it was enough.

As the camp finally came into view the Tinker turned his thoughts away from that to focus on his new assignment. The first thing would be to find a good location for his. . .business. He shook his head slightly at that. Business indeed.

"What's wrong, sir?" the young man next to him asked. Tinker glanced at the young soldier beside him. Aaron Bell had delivered the message to him from the Prince and then remained to accompany him along the way home. Though Bell was one of the now famed Black Sheep, his regal uniform was stowed away inside one of the wagons, the young man wearing the more common rough dress of a working ranch hand or wagoner.

"Nothing is wrong, Aaron," Tinker assured his young riding partner, pronouncing the name 'ah-rone' as he usually did. "I was just thinking of the work ahead. I must see to some kind of quarters."

"What you need, Mister Tinker?" Bell asked.

"Ideally I need a house," Tinker admitted. "Even better would be a hotel nearby the Army. It needs to be within easy horse ride of the main encampment however. And there must be a clear evacuation route in the event the army is forced to withdraw still further."

"I'll be back in a bit," Bell said after hearing those requirements. "You have to check in with the sutler manager anyway. I'll meet up with you near there in say. . .two hours?"

"Very well, Aaron," Tinker nodded. "Remember," he added with an index finger to his lips.

"Anything for the Prince, sir," Bell nodded and spurred his horse away. Uniform or no, there was no disguising that horse as anything but a war mount. And anything more than a casual glance would assure a studying eye that Bell was no mere ranch hand.

"Mikhail, what are we doing?" a woman's voice called to him and he turned. The lead ambulance was almost to him, the driver a woman dressed in clothing very similar to Bell's, though even rough linen and cotton clothing could do nothing to hide the figure beneath them.

"Rosala, I have asked you not call me that," Tinker said flatly and the woman made a visible effort not to shrink in on herself. "Tinker, Rosala. I am known to them only as Tinker. It will remain so."

"As you wish," Rosa nodded.

"Remain here and try to stay out of trouble," Tinker's smile returned. "I must register with the camp manager. Mister Bell has gone to try and procure our domicile. We will meet him nearby in a few hours."

"Girls are going to want to stretch and look around," Rosa warned. "And there's nature to answer as well," she added.

"Have a care then," he nodded finally. "Circle the wagons out of the way and have Ramone stand guard while Raymond escorts the girls to and from their ablutions."

"They won't like that," she noted.

"I did not ask that they enjoy it," Tinker's voice took an edge though his face was still genial. "I said it would be so, and it will. *Sava?*"

"*Meeta,*" Rosa nodded and turned the ambulance she was driving off the road into a small abandoned clearing. Tinker was a good man to have around, for many things. But he was also a hard man at times and she did not push. She would have to teach the others not to do so as well.

Tinker watched the wagons and ambulances pulling off the roadway and then spurred his own mount toward the center of the civilian camp.

-

Aaron Bell had grown up in the flatlands of the West and was familiar with not only the area but the people. He assumed it was one of the reasons that Mister Parsons had given him this assignment. He admitted that there were worse jobs than escorting two wagons full of gorgeous women around, but he missed his place in the Regiment.

Still, orders were orders.

He rode easily into the small town that was just two miles from the main camp of Soulan Army Field Headquarters. As he had expected, much of the town was empty at the moment as civilians who could flee had done so. He didn't blame them. War was no place for those who couldn't fight. He'd learned that first hand.

He rode through slowly, eyeing the empty buildings. A few had signs left by owners while others showed slight signs of vandalism, also not unexpected.

With things the way they were, people would be scavenging left and right to make ends meet. There would be little game left in the area and no row crops had yet had time to come to bloom. And the army would take priority in stores of food that were available.

He had been to Tate before, but it had been some time ago. Things were pretty much the same if a bit rundown, but again that wasn't a surprise. As he neared the edge of the town proper, he smiled slightly, seeing what he'd wanted.

Perhaps two hundred paces from the town's edge sat a large house that had at one time been a tavern and inn. He had assumed it would still be open for business and had been thinking how he could approach the owner. From the look of things that might not be necessary.

The window shutters were closed up tight and there was no smoke from the chimney. He saw only one horse before the inn, though the barn nearby might have more. He spurred his horse slightly and made his way down the lane to the still place. A tall, wide shouldered man stepped out onto the porch as Bell rode up, shaking his head.

"Nothing for you here, youngster," the man said flatly, though not unkind. "We got nothin' left."

"Kinda figured," Bell nodded sagely. "You the owner?"

"Lock and barrel," the man nodded. "No stock left to speak of though. Ezekiel Watts," he offered his hand. Bell took it.

"Aaron Bell. So what you aim to do, Mister Watts?" he asked, looking around at the building. Yes, this would do nicely.

"Don't know what I can do young fella," Watts shrugged. "Can't get any supply with the Army on top of us. Don't begrudge 'em it mind, fightin' the heathen and all, but still puts a crimp in my wallet. Figure to close 'er up for now and head south, see what I can get into. Maybe I can come back happens this ends well."

"Be interested in leasin' the place out?" Aaron asked. "Got a venture o' my own, but need a place to habitate and operate as my old man used ta say." Bell leaned on his saddle pommel easily. Open, friendly, non-threatening.

"What kind o' operation?" Watts asked.

"Gonna open a bar and maybe a. . .place o' comfort let's call it," Bell grinned broadly. "Maybe serve food and what not. Boss man makes things, does repair work so we'd need a place for him to store his what-nots," he nodded to the barn and the shed behind. "This place would work out pretty well from the look of it."

"Where you aim to get the where-withal to do all this grand schemin' o' yours, youngster?" Watts asked suspiciously.

"Boss has got his ways," Bell shrugged. "Happens you're interested in sellin' he might open to buyin' the place outright, too," Bell added.

"Ain't thought on sellin' the place," Watts shook his head at once.

"Well, we could use someone to run the place maybe," Bell set the hook carefully so as not to spook his fish. "See the boss man he's got all kinds of work to see to. Runnin' a place like this might. . .might interfere, let's say, in his business interests." Bell was laying it on thick, attempting to convince the owner that he was trying to act important to his 'boss', to the point of not quite speaking out of turn. Bell's youth made that a bit easier.

"I might be amenable to such an agreement," Watts said finally, attempting to speak more formally than he normally did. "Don't know that I would cotton to workin' for someone else, but. . .I can't make a go of the place as it is. If he can and is willin' to compensate me properly then. . .I'll listen to what he might have to say."

"That's neighborly of ya," Bell smiled broadly as if he'd just done the man a large favor. "I should be back with him well 'fore sundown. You be here, mind," he added.

"Be waiting right here," Watts nodded and took a seat on the porch.

Bell managed not to smile to himself in satisfaction until he was well away. Mister Tinker ought to be right well pleased.

-

The camp manager gave Tinker little more than a cursory glance as he looked at his authorization to do business around the camp area, issued him the necessary paperwork and passes and then sent him on his way.

As he made his way back to the caravan the Tinker allowed his eyes to flow over the area, taking in things others might ignore. A place like this would attract all kinds of men and women. No one would bother the soldiers and risk the ire of the army, but other civilians would be considered fair game to any predator.

Tinker was not overly impressed with security, but he admitted there was little need of it this far behind the lines, at least not from the Nor as a rule. Any attack strong enough to reach here would not be stopped by a stronger provost. Still, there was a certain lawless air about the area that he found both slightly disturbing yet also full of potential.

Part of his 'cover' would depend upon the impression that he was somehow 'connected' enough to have the goods he'd secured with the Prince's authority, yet that connection to the Prince had to remain hidden to maintain that illusion of lawlessness. It was a fine line to walk, but Tinker had been walking such lines all of his life.

A smiling Bell was waiting for him as Tinker returned to the wagons. A glance to Rosala was rewarded with an 'all is well' nod and Tinker turned his attention to Bell.

"You look very pleased with yourself, Mister Bell," the Tinker noted.

"Found us a place, maybe," Bell nodded, going on to describe the situation. Tinker nodded thoughtfully.

"An established business," he considered. "The man might make an excellent manager for the front operations."

"That was my thinkin', though I admit that I made the offer just to keep him from turnin' me down outright. I figure your persuasion 'll be better'n mine."

"We shall see," Tinker shrugged casually. "We will move," he raised his voice slightly as he called to Rosa. "We may have a place."

"Very fast," she observed as she slapped the side of the ambulance with her fist. An answering knock assured her that all were accounted for.

Without further orders the Tinker set out alongside Bell, the wagons following.

-

"Reckon I ain't a flesh peddler," Watts said quietly as Tinker completed his pitch.

"Nor will you be asked to be," Tinker assured him. "The woman will manage things," he nodded to Rosa. "Her women do not cater to just anyone, Mister Watts. Their clientele will be discriminating as well as discreet. The rear stairs will be useful for that and all such business will come through the back. We will also serve alcohol and food. I need a strong hand for the front, and you are already known to those in the area. I want no trouble in the business. You are no doubt strong and accustomed to dealing with difficulty. I would have you continue to do so. And I believe I can make you a lucrative offer." He named a figure and suppressed a smile as Watts struggled to keep surprise off his own face.

"I can work for that," he nodded. "I live here, though," he added. "Got a room out back. Reckon I'll keep it," he didn't quite challenge.

"That would be desirable," Tinker agreed. "Are there other accommodations on the premise?"

There were. A small servant quarters out back and two rooms over the stable. Nothing fancy, but clean and usable. The main building had a kitchen, large serving hall, three rooms downstairs other than the owner's and eight more upstairs. Two stairways, one front and one back and, most impressive, an indoor bathing room complete with two tubs, a pump for the water and a tank of water heated with wood. Ideal.

The deal was struck and suddenly the women were descending upon the place, Rosa barking orders as the house was set in order. By nightfall they would be well along. By the next night they would be open for business.

Tinker was pleased. The first part of his operation was under way. Rosa would oversee that, having done so before. The brothers, Raymond and Ramone would be their security and assist with the kitchen and stables. A third man, Alphonse, would assist with the kitchen and be 'available' to everyone else if he was needed. Two of the eleven women would operate the kitchen, two others were serving girls and one more would alternate between the two.

The others would be *entertaining* selected officers of the Army. Rosa and the others would occupy the rooms on the upper floor, their clients using the rear stairs to gain entrance to their boudoirs. Gaining such access to Rosa's girls would be difficult and costly. Only the very distinguishing of gentlemen would be able to approach her about it. Just the sort of man who would be in Therron McLeod's nest of vipers.

And Rosa's girls could make a man talk about many things he might otherwise never mention.

With this part of his operation now safely underway, Tinker turned his attention to other matters.

-

Brenack Wysin was unhappy being separated from the Black Sheep and his Prince, but as with Aaron Bell, orders were orders. He arrived in camp followed by three apprentices, each driving a wagon similar to his own that contained tools and materials for their trade, including a small forge. A fourth wagon driven by a man wounded at the Gap carried coal. While he would not use the coal often, he knew getting coal in this part of the country would be difficult. The soldier was a man well enough to be working, but not yet able to stand the rigors of being in the field. Having an assignment after weeks of convalescent leave had been a welcome relief to the man.

"Mister Wysin!" the smith heard and looked around him, finally spotting a waving Aaron Bell who was riding toward him.

"Youngster," Wysin nodded. "Have we a place to work yet?" he asked, straight to business. He was tired, having pushed long into the night more than once in order to arrive as soon as possible. His orders from the Prince were to assist the Tinker while plying his trade for those among the army who could afford to buy custom made equipment.

"That we do, sir," Bell nodded. "Place that was already in operation, in fact. *The Hogshead Inn.* Mister Tinker sent me to lead ya'll into place. Through town and just beyond. Ladies already got it all fixed up."

Wysin snorted at that, wondering how Tinker managed to maintain his sanity around so many women under one roof.

"They ready for us?" he asked, his thick brogue and accent cutting like a knife.

"That they are," Bell promised. "Got a stable for patrons, of which there won't be so many, quarters out back and I managed to lay in a store o' wood two days ago that should make pretty good charcoal. Owner stayed on to run the front, a tavern with a kitchen. Miss Rosa will be runnin' the. . .other," Bell finished.

"Well done, lad," Wysin smiled tiredly. "Lead us on, then. These old bones are in sore need of rest. We have pushed hard to be here so quick."

"Your quarters is already made up and they got hot baths in the inn," Bell promised. "Have to help set up the brewers tomorrow though," he warned.

"We can do that," Wysin promised. "I hear tell the Tinker's harem is a fair pretty picture, lad," Brenack needled slightly and Bell blushed every so lightly.

"Reckon they're pretty, all right," he nodded, trying to affect a maturity beyond his years in such matters. For all of his innate and learned abilities, he was still a very young man in some things and Rosa's niece Briel, one of the serving girls, had caught his eye right away. Slight of build and dark of complexion, the girl was a thing of beauty so far as he was concerned.

She might or might not be returning his admiration. He hadn't quite worked that out yet.

"Well, let's get moving then," Wysin was too tired to kid over much.

"Follow me."

CHAPTER ELEVEN

-

Parno sat across from Evelyn McKenzie at lunch the following day. She gave Raines a full and concise report of what had been happening in her area of responsibility while Parno listened without comment.

She was Raines' age, Parno guessed, but no more. She was strongly built, the kind of woman who would indeed thrive on a ranch and birth healthy children. Her brown hair was cut short, no doubt for utility as she worked her own fields and livestock. Her skin was sun-kissed but not weathered, which Parno credited to the wide brimmed hat she had worn to the meeting and the gloves that sat on the table in front of her.

She'd been accompanied by a gangling teen son who was just now growing into his height and a dark-haired beauty of a daughter who was a carbon copy of her mother, short hair and all. Her dark hair made Parno think of Stephanie and he instantly forced the thought away. He could not afford the distraction and she was deserving of better than him at any rate.

"Mrs. McKenzie, I failed to introduce our guest," Rained said as she finished her report. "He wanted to hear your report first hand without influencing you. This," he motioned to Parno, "is Marshal Parno McLeod. Marshal, Mrs. Evelyn McKenzie of DeSoto."

"Ma'am," Parno nodded politely. The daughter had shown little interest in Parno until the announcement but she sat up straighter now. Parno fought the urge to laugh.

"Milord," Evelyn nodded her head.

"Very impressive what you've done, ma'am," Parno told her. "And I appreciate your efforts."

"It isn't much effort," Evelyn shrugged gracefully. "In truth, we'd be watching the river anyway, milord. For raids, for the water to rise, for trespassers. Idiots come in swarms I'm afraid, and many of them try to steal by river. Most of them drown," she added with a slight smile.

"I've seen the eddies," Parno nodded. "Much different from the Tinsee or Cumberland. Harsher, I should think."

"It can be very harsh," Evelyn replied. "We're seen no real activity other than glimpses of their patrols passing along the far shore. Heathen Wildfolk for the most part, but we've seen the Nor a time or two as well in regimental or battalion strength it appeared."

"Are they taking notice of our shore or just making a patrol you think?" Parno asked. This woman was obviously intelligent. He wanted her opinion.

"For my money, they're going through the motions," she replied steadily. "Even the Wildfolk respect the river, milord. We've seen no sign of attempted crossings, nor even any interest in such. Of course they may just be doing it out of sight, but we do try to keep a steady look out. The men General Raines assigned to the post are constantly on the move."

"Have you any idea how far south their patrols go, ma'am?" Parno asked, leaning forward.

"Usually gone by no more than two days before we seem them return," Evelyn responded. "We can only assume of course, but I'm of the opinion that they go a day's ride south, camp one day, then return. I think they are doing the same thing we are, essentially, just doing it in force rather than using the outposts like we are."

Very intelligent, Parno thought to himself.

"Have they broken their pattern at all?" Parno asked.

"Every so often, maybe one patrol out of three, are gone another day," she nodded. "No idea what they're doing. Perhaps they merely ride further south, but that would be conjecture. We've no way of knowing. Other outposts may pick them up," she added, looking at Raines.

"They do," he supplied. "The post to Mrs. McKenzie's immediate south sees patrol activity about once per week on average."

"That would be about right," she agreed.

"I'm given to understand that we owe you for more than just the look out, Mrs. McKenzie," Parno changed the subject. "I ate a splendid meal yesterday after far too long in the saddle. Fresh food from your farm."

"We supply what we can," Evelyn nodded. "Glad to do it."

"We have some horses that have been ill used by their former owners," Parno told her. "We've checked them and save for general mistreatment and a bit of undernourishment they are healthy enough. If you can use a dozen or so trained mounts, I'd be glad to let them go back with you. We can provide a wrangler to assist you in getting them home."

"If they're able to sit a rider and work then yes, milord, horses are always welcome," McKenzie nodded, her eyes showing a slight surprise. "I wouldn't think you had horses to spare."

"Normally we wouldn't, but as I said, these horses were taken from a group of rabble militia who thought they were just playing soldier. Some are still receiving care and we think most will be able to serve in some capacity once rehabilitated, but the dozen I offer you are well enough. A week, perhaps two, of good feed and grooming to settle them and I think they'll serve you well. Little enough we can do for all you're doing."

"I thank you, milord," Evelyn bowed her head slightly.

"And speaking of food, I think it's about time for lunch," Raines announced. "With your permission, sir?" he asked Parno.

"By all means," Parno nodded, grinning. "I'll never say no to a good meal."

-

Evelyn had heard of Parno McLeod and her daughter's interest in the Prince didn't go unnoticed. She was careful to keep the daughter at arm's length from the Prince and Parno had to stifle a laugh when he realized it. Wouldn't do to offend the woman.

She was remarkably intelligent. He was all but certain she had been to a university somewhere but it would be improper to ask so he didn't. He did enjoy her company for the noon meal then had a man guide her to her new horses.

"Remarkable lady," Parno remarked as McKenzie and her group moved away.

"Every inch of it," Rained agreed. "There's iron in that one, milord."

"I'll be riding out tomorrow," Parno said suddenly and Raines blinked at the abrupt change of subject.

"I had thought you would be here longer, milord," he ventured carefully. Was something wrong?

"No need of it," Parno shook his head. "You're doing just fine without any interference from me. I'll leave a letter for the general of the cavalry division to carry to Davies but he'll know how best to use them I'm sure. Meanwhile, I'll try and make sure you get some help to the south. Also," he paused for a second, "also, you'll soon I hope be receiving a delivery from Nasil for your artillery contingent along with a group of advisers. Listen to them *very* carefully General. The weapons they're bringing helped me destroy the Nor at Cumberland and they'll aid you here as well."

"Ensure that your artillery commander knows to listen to these men. They aren't so high ranking and they're a bit rough around the edges, but they know how to use these new weapons. They also know how badly things can go wrong when proper precautions aren't taken."

"These must be some weapons, milord," Raines mentioned.

"You honestly won't believe it until you see it," Parno shook his head. "Trust me though, if we can get them into constant and reliable production then crushing the Nor just got much easier. General, you're doing a remarkable job here," Parno changed the subject yet again. "You'll have to keep doing it, too. There's no help in the immediate future except what we can do to deceive the enemy. We have men training now, good men who will be even better if they survive the training, but it takes time. Time the enemy won't just give us. We'll have to take it."

"We'll keep them fooled, milord," Raines promised, hoping he wouldn't wind up eating those words someday.

"There's a new unit I formed that might already be in the field by now," Parno continued. "They'll be working their way around the Nor right and trying to cut off their lines of communications as well as disrupt any provisioning they can. Spread terror and confusion where they can't."

"Like the old days," Raines nodded, smiling, but the smile faded as Parno looked at him.

"No, not like the old days," the young prince suddenly looked much older than his age. "It's a black flag operation, General. No mercy, no quarter, no prisoners. You'll extend the same to the enemy here. Raise the flag as a warning if you wish, I'll leave that to you, but we will not be taking prisoners. Interrogate them, get what you can from them, then execute them." Raines had paled a bit at that.

"Milord, we've always-"

"And no more," Parno cut him off. "This attack was planned using all of our history against us. They attack, we defend. They invade, we repulse. Who suffers for this every time? Our people, General. Their own people sit safe at home because the Soulan Army never crosses the River Ohi and always act with honor, returning their captured men even though they kill ours. Well, that's a thing of the past."

"We can't feed them," Parno was brutally honest. "Can't spare the men to guard them, for that matter. And we need to start sending a message to the Nor soldiers. A message they can't possibly misunderstand; you come here, we kill you. Period. Understand?"

"I do," Raines nodded thoughtfully. "It's not without precedent you know," he added suddenly. Parno looked at him questioningly.

"Tyree did much the same once, milord," Raines placed his hands behind him, easing into lecture mode. He had been a teacher at the Army Academy for several years prior to his rise to Corps command. "Early after the Burning, milord, before there was even a kingdom. Was almost his undoing according to what I've read. His superiors at the time were very upset with him. But it worked," Raines added with a slight grin. "We'll do the same here. Do you want any high-value prisoners sent to Nasil?"

"No," Parno's voice was flat. "As I said, get what you can from them, then get rid of them. How, I leave up to you."

"I will see to it, sir," Raines promised. "Where will you be off to next?" he asked, moving away from such a black subject.

"I am unsure at the moment," Parno admitted. "I should ride to Nasil and give a report to the King I suppose. It's too far to ride to 4th and 5th Corps headquarters while the battle hangs in the balance here, but I will be dispatching riders ordering General Herrick to free up a reliable militia division to assist in patrolling the river south of you. Most of that shore line is his area of responsibility after all. Until I hear from Admiral Semmes I can't afford any more than that, just in case that fleet really is loaded to the gills with Nor soldiers. If he can defeat that force, then I'll bring Herrick and 5th Corps north. Freeman will just have to cover the best he can."

"On that note, I'll be sending him your idea here about the observation posts. It should be easy enough to erect such posts along our shores to spy out enemy landings. He can use that to hide his real strength as well."

"Anyway, I appreciate your hospitality General," Parno smiled briefly. "Now I need to meet with my staff and I think I'll retire early. Long ride tomorrow." Without waiting for a reply Parno left the porch, heading for the building where his own staff were working.

Raines had to admit that he was impressed by Memmnon's little brother. For the first time since he'd seen the Wildmen on the bridge, Raines felt as if there might be hope for their survival after all.

Parno walked across the busy street shadowed by Berry and several of his men, now working in shifts to 'keep an eye' on the Prince. Entering the building he'd taken over upon his arrival, Parno noted Enri Willard pouring over dispatches and walked over to his top adviser's side.

"This is two days old, milord," Enri noted the report. "Still quiet to Davies' front. He's seen some movement, but there's been no attempt to attack his positions. This is somewhat older," he picked up another. "Admiral Semmes has rendezvoused with the other squadrons as of seven days ago and was at that point maneuvering for a good position to attack. As of yet they cannot ascertain if the troop ships actually have troops or not."

"Quiet on other fronts as of no more than four days ago," Willard concluded. "A note from Beaumont that he would be heading into the field tomorrow, if his schedule has held. He reported no difficulties and that the units had drilled hard, working well together. He used the time he needed to gather supplies and equipment to allow the units some time to work up as a whole."

"Good plan," Parno nodded. "Send a message to General Herrick," he ordered. "He's to provide one militia division, this one well trained, equipped and behaved, to patrol the southern leg of the Great River. That unit will be under Raines' command until further notice. Make sure that Raines' gets a copy of the order." Willard nodded as his own secretary scribbled furiously.

"Next, send Freeman and Herrick both the general outline of what Raines is doing with his outposts. If they haven't already implemented this plan, they are to do so as soon as possible and then devise a warning system to alert them of any possible incursions by sea. Those veterans too old or injured to be able to serve in a field command can be used to man and command the outposts." Parno paused for a moment, then added; "and they are not to automatically exclude women from that duty, either. Capable women are just as efficient as men at that kind of work, and they free up men who otherwise would be fighting. Their pay and privileges are to be commiserate with any other of its kind. Stress that I will be checking on that and would be displeased to find it was not so."

"Will do," Enri nodded.

"That engineer, Fields I think his name was, I want him going with us to Nasil. Once there I want him working on a model of the Tinsee similar to what he did here for the Great River. I'd like another of the Lovil area if he can manage that using maps and drawings of the area. That model allows a good view of the terrain and the forces in the field. Excellent idea. Ensure that he and Raines are both commended for it." Willard nodded again.

"Issue orders to all posts that Raines is now commanding the Soulan Second Army and is in command of all forces in his theater of operations. The only exceptions to that are the IG, any Crown agents, and the Sheep. If you think of anyone else that should be exempt, add them as well."

"Yes sir."

"And have the unit prepared to march at daybreak," Parno concluded. "Raines is doing a first-rate job here and I am in no way needed. We'll ride to Nasil on the morrow and report to the king, then decide where we go from there. Probably back to the west with Davies, but we'll see."

"Yes milord," Enri showed no surprise at the order to move out. Parno didn't know if he'd expected it or he was just always prepared for it. Either way, Parno was too tired to worry over it.

"And I'm going to bed," he smiled tiredly. "I'm too young to feel this old."

"We all get that way time to time, milord," Enri smiled back. "We'll be ready in the morning."

CHAPTER TWELVE

-

"When are we going to attack, General?"

Wilson bit back a sigh as Daly's voice floated to him across the room he used as an office. He turned to see the arrogant nobleman standing at the door expectantly.

"You'll receive notice of any orders posted, Brigadier," Wilson managed to say calmly, reminding Daly of his own position.

"As the Emperor's representative-"

"I've had no command from the Emperor to treat you as such," Wilson cut him off cleanly. "You were assigned to me as my Chief of Staff, a job you are well qualified for but cannot seem to fulfill due to your constant machinations and intrigues." His voice was cool now. "Should the Emperor inform me to treat you as his representative in the field, I will of course extend that courtesy to you, just as I follow all of my Emperor's instructions or even advice." He picked up a parchment from his desk and held it out to the still smirking Daly.

"It would seem that the Emperor isn't quite as displeased with my actions as you believed he would be," Wilson relished this moment. "He has, in fact, *endorsed* my plan to consolidate our position and strengthen our communications before proceeding. He notes the failures of the past being a result of a lack of foresight in that area and commends our caution as, and I quote, 'necessary and appropriate'." Daly took the parchment as if it would bite him, glancing at the words upon it.

"He does not mention you at all, Brigadier," Wilson fought to keep the smugness from his voice and was mostly successful. "Not as his representative, as my Chief of Staff, nor even as a kinsman. Nor does he mention any of the reports I'm sure you have sent to his offices since this campaign began. Since I cannot fathom any such report viewing me in a favorable light I am forced to assume that the Emperor has simply chosen to. . .ignore you."

Daly's face flushed beet red at that last barb and he fought to keep his hand from trembling as he lowered the parchment, tossing it back onto Wilson's desk.

"So it would seem that your reluctance to attack has infected my cousin," Daly almost sneered, though he was careful not to outright accuse his relative of cowardice. "We are sitting here with a massive, well trained army instead of attacking the Soulanies where they live! What use is an army if we aren't using it!"

"Idiot," Wilson snarled and Daly almost recoiled. Wilson had never spoken to him in such a manner before and it caught him by surprise. "We're destroying Soulan every day we sit here you short sighted moron. Do you not comprehend how many acres, how many *square miles* of their precious farm land we are preventing them from utilizing by our presence here?"

"What difference does that make?" Daly shot back. "Their army is not three miles distant from this spot and yet we do nothing!"

"It's always struck me as odd that you, who has never led men in combat nor seen any yourself, are always so eager to see the blood of our own soldiers spilled to satisfy your misguided notions of what it means to be powerful," Wilson's voice was cutting. "Their army is three miles distant, and *cannot move* for fear of opening still more of their land to us. They are paralyzed by our presence and our other forces in the field and at sea, while we move at our leisure. Movement is everything in warfare, Brigadier, and we have denied the Soulan Army any freedom of movement, anywhere."

"Meanwhile, their planting season is already underway and we are sitting on thousands of square miles of their best lands. Come winter their people will be starving for that food but it will not be coming because it won't have been grown to start with!"

"Despite the ineptitude of Therron McLeod, don't for an instant think that the rest of the Soulan royal family is stupid, nor are their retainers. They know the damage we're doing to them by just sitting here. They will soon be forced to move against us by the circumstances, whether they want to or not. We outnumber them at least three-to-one and we will not be caught in unprepared camps again." Wilson calmed slightly as he walked to the map on his wall.

"They will have no choice but to throw their army against us in an attempt to dislodge our forces and free their lands from occupation. Instead of wasting the blood of our men on headlong attacks against *their* defenses, we'll wait for them to come to us." He turned again to face Daly.

"They will break upon our lances and pikes, Brigadier, and when they have then, *then* Brigadier, we will move south and conquer the so called *Kingdom* of Soulan. Their army will lay in ruins and there will be nothing else to oppose us. Our objective, General, is not to occupy ground, nor to seize cities. No, our objective is to destroy the Army of Soulan once and for all!"

"And with that done, we will hand this place to the Emperor to rule as he does our own lands. There will be no one left to oppose his rightful rule and the only army on this continent worthy of the name will be under his command."

"Now get out," Wilson's timbre changed suddenly. "I've grown weary of your foolishness. Stay out of our way and keep your mouth shut and you may maintain your position and the privileges that go with it. Interfere and we'll see who the Emperor supports more; you, or me."

Stunned, Daly almost stumbled as he turned to leave Wilson's office. Having fancied himself as the 'real' power in the command of the Imperial Army, Daly had just been handed a rude awakening. In a daze of sudden and unpleasant awareness of his insignificance he made his way outside and toward his own camp. As he walked his emotions ran a gauntlet of tides, beginning with embarrassment and shame, then turning to thoughts of how he'd been betrayed by his cousin. Only the luck of birth had given him the throne rather than Daly after all.

By the time he reached his over-sized camp of guards, retainers, hangers on and 'followers', Daly had worked himself into a rage of epic proportions. He decided as he stormed into his own quarters that Wilson would pay for this slight and, if the gods were with him, so would his cousin the Emperor.

Pay very dearly indeed.

-

Admiral Rafael Semmes stood in the *Wabash* ward room looking at the assembled squadron commanders and ship captains sitting around the room. Some faces looked bleak, some looked eager, and more than a few just looked pensive. He could sympathize with that last one, feeling a bit pensive himself.

"Gentlemen, give me your attention," he said simply and what little talk there was died away. Satisfied that he had their attention, he began.

"You know that the enemy fleet is assembled off our shores, apparently escorting a squadron of troop ships. You also know by now that the situation on land is dire to say the least. While three army corps are struggling to contain a Nor army that outnumbers them at least three-to-one if not more, two full corps of the Soulan army, plus their provincial attachments, are standing to in order to honor the possible threat this Nor fleet represents." His face looked grim.

"We are going to eliminate that threat, gentlemen, if it costs us every ship in this assembly." There was a slight stir among his audience but no one objected. He would not have entertained such in any case.

"Make no mistake that the continued existence of the Soulan Kingdom rests on the outcome of this war. And the war could very well be decided by our actions in the coming engagement. If we can destroy the Nor fleet, or at least damage it sufficiently to drive it from our waters, then the majority of the troops in the south can be sent north to fight against the incursion from Kent and the threat against Shelby on the Great River. Those men are desperately needed there and it's our job to make sure they can go without threat to any landings along our coast."

Several heads nodded in understanding. Rumors were that things at home were very bad indeed.

"We will attack by squadron," Semmes turned to the map stand behind him, satisfied that he had made his point. "Squadron commanders will be given general orders, their implementation left to your discretion. We will not have much in the way of real time coordination once the battle is joined so it is absolutely vital that each ship realize not only what is at stake, but what is expected."

"The Savannah Squadron will be the pivot, here," Semmes pointed to the map again. "Our last report was that the Nor fleet was still more or less stationary roughly thirty miles due east of San Augustina. The best information we have on their order of battle comes from a fishing vessel commanded by a former naval officer." He turned again to face his commanders to make sure they understood what he was about to tell them.

"He is convinced that the Nor *allowed* him to get a good view of their fleet before making a half-hearted attempt to chase him away. He is further convinced that had the cutter that gave chase wanted to catch him, it could have done so with ease." He paused to let that sink in.

"They wanted to be seen," one captain remarked softly. "They wanted us to know where they were and how strong they were."

"Indeed," Semmes nodded, pleased that at least one of them was paying attention. "That lends credence to Marshal McLeod's theory that this is a ruse. That those troopships are empty and the Nor fleet is simply sitting there to keep two full corps of Soulan soldier out of the decisive battles to the north."

"Begging your pardon, Admiral," Commodore Anthony David, commanding officer of the Key Horn Squadron raised a hand. "That could also indicate that this is a trap designed to lure our fleet in and destroy it."

"That is correct," Semmes again his pleasure at the observations of his commanders. "The enemy had been very clever indeed this time, gentlemen. They have presented us with an issue we cannot ignore, regardless of their intentions. They have managed to place us in a position where we have no choice but to attack them. With that decision taken from us, as well as the place of the engagement, we have only two items left that we can influence."

"When we attack, and how," Thomas George, Commodore of the Savannah Squadron nodded firmly. "We must choose the time of the engagement and set the terms for it."

"Precisely," Semmes nodded. "The 'when' is as soon as possible. With that in mind, we strike anchor tomorrow at sun-up. We should have moderately favorable winds for most of the day, but we will also make use of the oars where necessary because time is our enemy and a Norland ally. Every day we allow this engagement to be drawn out and left undecided is another day that the southern corps cannot ride to the aid of the northern army groups. We cannot allow this situation to continue. It will be a race as it is for our men to arrive before news of the Nor fleet's defeat reaches their army in the west."

"This will be our plan of attack." For the next twenty minutes Semmes outlined his plans. When he finished he had the expected results. Some were anxious to go, others showed concern.

"This is a complex attack plan, Admiral," Hampton Rhode, Commodore of the Sunshine Squadron noted with a frown. "If our timing is off, we run the risk of being defeated in detail."

"I know," Semmes nodded. "Understand gentlemen, our defeat, even our destruction as a fighting force, is acceptable so long as those troopships are sunk. If they have soldiers aboard, then most will perish in the sea. If they are empty, then we'll know that too. So long as our messenger cutter survives to carry that news to the Prince, we will have done our duty."

Somber faces looked back at him from around the room at this declaration.

"I know that your training dictates the conservation of your ships and men when and where possible," Semmes said gently. "Further, the loss of even a single man should be anathema to a good Captain, as should the loss of a ship under his command. In any other situation that would be true but *here*," he slapped the map with his right hand, "that situation is different. We cannot win this war ourselves, out here on the sea. We *can* decide who wins on the land, however, with this engagement. Therefore, we will prevail, even if it means the loss of every ship and every man in this fleet. If you do not believe that you can follow those instructions, now is the time to say so."

"I will not punish a man who thinks he cannot do his duty to crown and kingdom in this one instance," he said flatly. "You will be returned to shore and reassigned to some other duty. There will be no mark against a man who chooses that path."

There would of course. It wouldn't be official and the Admiral himself, should he survive, would not hold it against a man professionally, but any Captain who walked away from a threat to his land would not be forgiven by his peers. Those present at the battle would forever look upon him as having deserted his ship and mates, while those not present would be angry at his having passed over the opportunity they themselves would have given all to have. That was the way of fighting men the world over. Many things might differ from nation to nation, but the honor and dignity of the men who did the actual fighting would remain in some form no matter what banner they fought under. There were a few unwritten rules that applied almost everywhere.

No one asked to be replaced. Instead a grim aura of acceptance settled over the room as the assembled commanders looked at friends, classmates, former ship mates and in some cases kinsmen, wondering silently if they would have the opportunity to sit together at the same table in this lifetime.

"Squadron commanders, you have your specific orders for the general outline of out attack. How you implement them I leave to you, but make sure your best signal men are on deck when the action starts. Also, should our timing be good and all squadrons arrive in time to attack in concert, watch *Wabash* for general orders to be issued in the event that opportunity or threat presents itself. Are there any questions?"

"If they strike colors?" one man asked.

"Sink them," Semmes replied flatly. "All operations of the Soulan military as of this moment, actually as of near two weeks ago, are now Black Flag operations. There will be no quarter offered or accepted. We will fight to the last man, to the last drop of Soulan blood, to throw these heathen out of our lands for good."

"Marshal McLeod issued such an order?" Commodore David looked surprised.

"Marshal *Parno* McLeod issued such an order, yes," Semmes dropped his final bombshell on them. "Marshal Therron has been relieved of his duties for health reasons. Prince Parno McLeod has taken his place. And before any of you rush to judgment," Semmes raised a hand, "you should know that Prince Parno has produced the only victory over the Nor forces to date in this conflict." News of the cavalry battle had not yet reached Semmes as he was at sea.

"In a battle for the Cumberland Gap, Prince Parno and his personal regiment, along with a short brigade comprised mostly of militia and two battalions of regulars, destroyed a Nor army some ten times their size. Details of that battle are not yet available to me, but the general description I received was that less than twenty percent of the Nor force in that battle survived. They are even now being run to ground and eliminated."

Looks of shock and a few whistles of surprise echoed around the room.

"The Black Sheep prince has claws, gentlemen," Semmes smiled grimly. "And we will as well. You have your orders, so report back to your vessels and brief your men. Ensure that we are prepared to get under way with the coming of the sun. I expect it to be a long, warm day."

-

Fleet Admiral Jason Selvey had always been an early riser, and today was no exception. As the sun came up in the east he was on the command deck of the Imperial naval cruiser *Indina*, his command vessel for this operation. Though there was nothing to see he still swept the horizon all around with the powerful glass on the swivel near his 'sea' desk. Selvey preferred to remain on deck as much as possible, to the point of conducting business there when weather conditions permitted.

He noted the wind was westerly today. That was both good and bad. Good in that it might prompt the apparently reluctant Soulan Navy to seek engagement, and bad in that his ships would be at a disadvantage if battle were joined while the wind was at the enemy's back.

"Morning sir," Captain Caleb Merrill said as he climbed the stairs to the deck where Selvey stood.

"It is indeed, Captain," Selvey nodded. Merrill was the *Indina*'s commander and Selvey's Flag Captain. While not officially of any higher rank than any other ship Captain, his position as Flag Captain placed him in a position that transcended time in grade. And he had earned his position with merit and skill rather than political influence, a sign of the changes brought about by the current Emperor.

"I notice the wind might favor the Soulanies this day, sir," Merrill said casually. "If they decide to come out and face us, that is."

"Oh, they will, Captain," Selvey said firmly. "Never doubt that. Whatever they may be otherwise, the Soulan Navy are not cowards. But neither are they stupid." Selvey turned to face Merrill. "Our force is a large one, Captain, larger than any we've ever put to sea in fact. Their forces are strung out in penny packets along their coastal waters to prevent smuggling and raider attacks. Assembling a force sufficient in size to tackle us will take time. That being said," Selvey returned his gaze to the horizon, "I think they've had time to do so by now. And this wind will certainly encourage them to seek engagement. We'll conduct readiness exercises this morning in order to be prepared for such an eventuality. See that those orders are posted, if you please. Signal the fleet to be ready at oh-eight-thirty hours to commence a full fleet drill by squadron if you please."

"Right away, sir," Merrill nodded and left to order the signal be sent. He wasn't sure he approved of such a drill at this point, believing it better to be prepared for the appearance of the Soulan fleet at all times. He was not the Admiral, however, and would never oppose Selvey's orders.

Merrill shared his generation's contempt of all things Soulanie, something Selvey discouraged among his commanders any time he had the opportunity. Merrill believed in being respectful of an enemy's capabilities, but he also had the arrogance that came with indoctrination that had yet to be tempered with actual combat. While Merrill had great respect for Selvey, he did not share his commander's wariness of the Soulan fleet.

The Norland Imperial Navy had never known defeat. The fact that this wasn't strictly true was not taught at the Imperial Fleet Academy where Merrill had been educated. True, no fleet engagement of this size had ever been lost by the Imperial Navy, but then no fleet engagement of this size had ever been *fought* by the Imperial Navy, either. That little tidbit was often overlooked by many.

In wars past, the Imperial Navy had won a number of smaller engagements against Soulan naval forces, always with the element of surprise. Attacking in strength against a divided and unprepared enemy was not the same thing as inviting attack by a prepared and organized enemy fleet led by competent officers and fought by well-trained men.

Merrill objected to their orders in general, though he was careful not to voice those objections. Dangling the fleet out here just a few miles off shore of the Soulan coast seemed a waste of resources to the young Flag Captain. Had he been in command, the Imperial Fleet would be attacking shore installations this very morning, using their Marine contingent to sack Soulan ports and do as much damage to Soulanie infrastructure as they could before putting back to sea.

The largely empty troopships that were part of the deception simply added to the complication of this operation in his mind. Lost on him was the fact that those troopships were the only reason for their presence off the Soulan shore. It didn't occur to him that the Soulan Army would have to honor the threat those troopships might represent. He likewise didn't consider that the presence of those very troopships would be what spurred the Soulan Navy to attack the Imperial Fleet.

While Merrill was a satisfactory ship captain, and even Flag Captain, he was not a strategic thinker. Few officers in the Imperial Fleet were. While the Emperor had gone to great lengths to select only the best possible men for leadership positions in his revamped military arms, those like Merrill were still a product of the Imperial thought that Size Mattered. The Imperial Navy was larger, ergo better, than the Soulan Navy. Simple as that.

Even as he passed the Admiral's orders along, Merrill's thoughts were that the whole thing was a waste of time.

-

"We are making good time, sir," Nettles mentioned quietly as Semmes paced the command deck of the *Wabash*.

"I'm aware of that, Commander," Semmes nodded, his voice not as curt as his words might indicate.

"Beg pardon, Admiral," Nettles said easily.

"No pardon needed, Commander," Semmes assured him. "I am anxious to see this done, that's all."

"You don't expect us to prevail, do you sir?" Nettles asked carefully. He was on thin ground here, but part of his job as Semmes' aide and Flag Secretary was to give the Admiral a private sounding board. He was good at his job, even at the risk of the Admiral's ire on occasion.

"I expect victory, Pyrrhic though it may be," Semmes surprised him. "Our mission is to sink those troopships, or prove they are empty. Either is a victory for us, Commander. But their forces outnumber ours by a smart ratio, perhaps two-to-one in total vessels. Hopefully some of those ships really are troopships, but still; those are long odds. We will have one good pass with the wind at our backs, but after than we will be at the mercy of the fortunes of war and weather. Should the wind abandon us, or worse shift to the Nor's favor, then we will be in dire straits, make no mistake."

"We can always wait for better conditions, sir," Nettles suggested, knowing that it wasn't true.

"No we can't, Commander, and you well know that," Semmes chided gently. "I've known since this started that our forces would be fortunate indeed to escape this engagement with more than a corporal's guard. That being said, we still have no choice. If we are to survive as a kingdom, sacrifices have to be made. The Army has been making those sacrifices since the war began. You've seen the same dispatches I have." Nettles nodded his agreement, reluctant though it was.

"Today is our turn," Semmes continued. "The Nor have acted very shrewdly indeed, Mister Nettles," Semmes was almost in lecture mode. "They have followed the Art of Conflict very carefully, placing themselves in a position that we cannot allow them to retain, therefore we must attack. Even if we know that we are doomed to fail, we must make the effort because the survival of our kingdom, our way of life, is at risk. Very shrew indeed," he repeated.

"Why is it they attack us, Admiral?" Nettles asked suddenly, changing the subject. "I've never been able to grasp why it is that the northerners insist on attacking our people so often. We've given them no provocation, have we?"

"They need none," Semmes almost spat. "For as long as there has been a Southern Kingdom and a Northern Empire, there has been aggression by the Nor. They insist that we belong to them, to the Empire, that we should be subject to their Emperor. They desire our land, our people, our resources for themselves, Mister Nettles, and they have spent many lives and much treasure over the centuries to acquire them. This time, however, they have added a new element. One lacking in all previous attempts to subjugate us."

"What element, sir?" Nettles asked, interested in Semmes discourse.

"Intelligence," Semmes said flatly. "The North has always been led by fools, Mister Nettles. Attacking when they should withdraw, committing blunders of strategic importance even while making tactical advances. This time their leadership has been very careful with planning and implementation of that plan. In the past it has been the Imperial way to attempt to simply bowl us over with sheer strength. They have come close a number of times in doing just that, mind you," he admitted. "But always they have over committed, trusting in numbers rather than in training and skill. As I said, this time things are different." He stopped pacing suddenly, looking at Nettles.

"I've no direct knowledge of how we came to have advance warning of this attack, but consider this, Mister Nettles; had we not had these several months to prepare, what would our situation be like? Even with that warning we are desperately pushed just to hold what we can. What if such an overwhelming attack had been launched while we were still on a completely peace time footing?"

"The war would likely already be over," Nettles admitted. "There might still be isolated fighting with the southern corps and supporting militia, but most of the kingdom would lie in Imperial hands by now."

"Indeed it would," Semmes nodded firmly as he resumed his pacing. "As I said, this time is different. And that means we must fight differently. Hence the Black Flag order. We cannot afford leniency or mercy this time, Commander. We stand on the verge, on the very precipice of disaster. Defeat. Only savagery and abandon can win this war, Mister Nettles. Prince Parno had proven that already."

"You admire him, don't you sir?" Nettles asked. Like most, he had only peripheral knowledge of the youngest member of the McLeod family. That knowledge was less than ideal.

"Never met him," Semmes replied flatly. "Heard a great deal about him of course, as I'm sure you have," he added. "But his victory at the Gap was decisive, Mister Nettles. Bloody to be sure, and also Pyrrhic in that he lost something like eighty percent of his command if early reports were correct. But he utterly destroyed a force ten times his own and sent the survivors into full flight, protecting the heartland and the Royal City from almost certain destruction. That alone might have ended the war before it had really begun."

"I hadn't considered that, sir," Nettles admitted.

"No reason you should," Semmes nodded absently. "You're trained to fight at sea, Mister Nettles. Trained as well as we can manage it, in fact. But fighting here, on the ocean," Semmes' arm swept the water around them, "if a far cry from battle on land. Whatever Parno McLeod's failings might be elsewhere, he is a fighter, have no doubt. No man who was not a fighter could have managed that. Especially with a regiment of men taken from prisons and wanted posters," he added.

"Sir?"

"Parno McLeod's 'personal' regiment is comprised almost entirely of prisoners and wanted criminals, supplemented by army rejects and near wash-outs," Semmes told his aide. "Yet the Prince took those men and transformed them into a force that was capable of destroying a foe many times their own number. True, he had terrain on his side," Semmes allowed, "but that does not negate the fact that only a superbly trained force that was extremely well led could have defended that position against such an overwhelming adversary." He stopped his pacing again, once more giving Nettles his undivided attention.

"And now that man is leading our military against the Norland invasion," he said flatly. "That was the first piece of good news I have received other than word of his victory at the Gap." Semmes looked toward the front of *Wabash*, the heavy cruiser cutting the sea with her iron reinforced bow.

"Now, we have to do at sea what he did on land. And we cannot expect our costs to be any less than his own."

"The good commander must consider all costs in war, young prince." Cho Feng's voice was gentle, meant only for Parno's ears as the column walked their horses for a few minutes.

"But if we try to fight the war on a budget, we'll lose," Parno objected.

"That is true," Cho acknowledged. "The admonition to be aware of the cost in treasure is meant for the commander who takes his army into the field as an aggressor. For the present, you must survive, regardless of the cost in coin. If your kingdom falls then the cost will not matter anyway."

"You're talking about later," Parno said gently and Feng nodded.

"Indeed. You must be completely prepared before you step foot across either river to confront your foes in their own territory. All preparations must be made beforehand. Nothing can be left to chance or else you invite disaster. And remember this," the older man warned grimly. "You are not alone in fervor for your home land. The soldier who fights only average well in a foreign land might well become a rabid animal in defense of his own. Do not assume that the mediocrity of your enemy will continue once you have invaded his home."

"Point," Parno nodded. "I've wondered more than once if the Nor haven't made a mistake in invading in the spring. Had they waited and come right before harvest, they could feed their army without worrying about such long lines of supply and communication."

"One wagon of the enemy's supplies is worth many more of your own," Feng nodded. "A wise stratagem. Tell me, why do you think he did not wait?"

"Time, I suppose," Parno shrugged. "By attacking early in the spring, he has most of the year to press his attack. His army is less acclimated to the heat that we often face in summer, especially further south, so perhaps that was part of their thinking as well. But for me I think it's time. They want this to be over soon. Meant for it to be," he added, thinking of the attack he had helped thwart at the Gap.

"Excellent," Feng almost smiled. "You are now thinking as your enemy. In order to be assured of victory, you must know your enemy, young prince. You must know yourself as well. One who does so will almost always be assured of victory, providing he takes all things into consideration."

"My 'invasion' will need careful planning," Parno nodded. "I'd already known that, at least in theory, but you've given me something else to think on."

"Good," Cho Feng nodded again as the column halted to remount. "Remember that all things must be considered. You must have the moral law on your side as well. Your people must be prepared to follow you regardless of the cost. They must believe in their sovereign, and in the rightness of his actions. Believe to the point that they are willing to perish, if needed, to bring about his wishes."

"I'm not the 'sovereign', Master Feng," Parno grunted out as he mounted his horse. "My father is now, and one day my brother will be. I'm just. . ." he paused suddenly, his face a study of concentration.

"Yes?" Feng asked as the column prepared to continue their ride toward Nasil.

"I don't know," Parno finally shrugged. "I started to say I'm just a soldier, but that's not really accurate, I suppose. I am the war leader, the Marshal of the Army," he admitted. "I suppose the men have to have confidence in me as their commander just as they need that confidence in the King. I hadn't really thought about that, to be honest. I've been fortunate that the men I've led have followed me the way they have."

"Not so fortunate," Feng disagreed as he spurred his horse forward. "You have shared the same hardships as your men, including combat. You have led by example as well as by intelligence. That inspires confidence, young prince. You have also led them to victory. This too inspires the common soldier as well as the educated officer. But that success is also a trap that you must avoid falling into," he warned.

"What do you mean?"

"Your men will grow to expect victory under your leadership," Feng pointed out. "They will expect victory because they are confident in your ability to provide leadership that will place them in a position to be victorious over their foe so long as they do what is asked of them. Thus you must take great care, my prince, to ensure that your decisions provide them that opportunity. Setbacks and defeats will shake their confidence in you. Too many and it could break. That is to be avoided. Morale of the army is of great importance on the battlefield."

"So I have to keep winning to keep winning," Parno snorted.

"That is over simplified, but not incorrect," Feng agreed.

"Right now I'll settle for surviving."

-

"The exercise looks good, sir," Merrill noted. His own First Officer was in command of the *Indina*, an opportunity for him to gain some experience in command that freed Merrill to be with the Admiral.

"So it does," Selvey agreed, his scope traversing as he examined his ships. "They are responding well to signals and keeping their formations. This is good. Discipline will often win the day with all else being equal."

"We don't really expect things to be equal do we sir?" Merrill asked. "We do outnumber the Soulanie fleet by a goodly margin."

"So we do," Selvey nodded. "And that means little if those number are not employed effectively. We've learned in wars past that there is no substitute in battle for good planning and leadership, Mister Merrill. Hard lessons, learned at great cost in men, material, and treasure."

Merrill nodded at that, aware of the lessons of wars past. That was something that current training was careful to emphasize so that those mistakes would not be repeated.

"Once we've defeated the Soulan fleet, what then, Admiral?" Merrill asked. "What are our orders after that?"

"We should not assume that we will be in any shape to pursue any course of further action once the coming engagement is decided," Selvey replied flatly. "I expect we will have many wounded men and damaged vessels if the Soulanies have gathered sufficient forces to attack us. While we may be victorious, do not assume that the costs won't be harsh, Mister Merrill. But," he lowered his glass to regard the younger man, "should we still be combat capable, then we will begin reducing whatever ships and fortifications remain from here north along their coasts while maintaining watch for the remainder of their fleet to approach and offer battle."

"How likely do you believe that to be?" Merrill was mostly successful in keeping the disdain from his voice.

"How likely would we be to marshal any available forces to oppose an enemy at our door, Captain?" Selvey asked in return, and noted with satisfaction the red creeping up Merrill's neck and face. Good.

"Point taken, sir," Merrill acknowledged the hit. "I didn't mean that they would not-"

"Sails!" a cry from above them cut off the rest of Merrill's reply. "Sails west! Many ships west!"

Selvey immediately turned his glass toward the west, scanning the horizon. Nothing.

"They are still too far to be seen from the deck," he said at once. "Get a qualified officer aloft at once to surveil them and get an accurate count as soon as possible. I want a breakdown of the ship classes and numbers as soon as they are in view. And signal the fleet to begin closing up! We cannot meet them strung out in squadrons like this. Move man!" he stressed as Merrill seemed to freeze for an instant.

"Right away, sir!" Merrill stammered and ran to carry out his orders.

-

"Enemy in view, Admiral," Nettles reported, much more calmly than his counterpart among the Imperial Navy.

"So I hear, Mister Nettles," Semmes nodded, taking up his own glass as he ascended to the command and observation deck of the *Wabash*. "Can our lookouts spot our northern and southern forces?"

"Not as yet, sir," Nettles admitted. "Doesn't mean they aren't there, however," he added hopefully.

"Have the steward release green smoke, Mister Nettles," Semmes ordered far more calmly then he actually felt. "They should be able to see it clearly in these conditions I should think, and close in when they do."

"Right away, Admiral," Nettles nodded and began issuing orders to runners waiting along the edge of the deck. Below decks, the stewards would be maintaining the stove, the only source of fire still burning aboard other than the torches used by the artillerymen to light their pitch rounds once battle was joined. Dumping sponges and cloths soaked with green dye onto those glowing coals would send a stack of green laced smoke into the air, alerting the other ships that *Wabash* and her sister ships were in contact with the enemy.

If they were close enough to see it, that is.

Forward, the chase ballistas were loaded with large bolts also soaked in pitch or designed to carry lengths of chain intended to tear sails and rip lines from masts on enemy ships. Battle at sea was one of finesse until the actual exchange of fire started. At that point things devolved into a dirty backstreet brawl that would see a terrible toll in both men and material. Below the decks of each ship physicians and surgeons were standing by to treat the wounded that would certainly result from the coming battle.

Along the rails Soulan Marines gathered, arbalests in hand, prepared to engage enemy sailors and marines as their ships passed each other in combat. Other marines waited along the decks to either repel boarders or to board enemy ships themselves, swords still sheathed for the moment. Few of them had seen real action and most were scared though their discipline held. The few experienced men among them were grim faced with determination. They knew that no amount of skill would spare them from the misfortunes of naval warfare that could see an errant ballista bolt or arbalest bolt glance off an iron stay or railing and puncture leather armor that could never hope to withstand such force.

Long-bowmen gathered around small torches with arrows drawn, waiting for the time when they would be within bow-shot of the enemy when they would light their arrows and loft them toward the wood and canvas of enemy vessels, hoping to do more damage to the enemy than the enemy would do to them.

Through all of this Semmes maintained his composure, watching the enemy forces as they moved on the horizon and occasionally checking north and south for signs of the rest of his ships. He hoped he had not erred in his battle plan. The one squadron around the *Wabash* would not last long against the combined Imperial Fleet.

CHAPTER THIRTEEN

-

Tinker was working on a piece of chain mail, repairing a link that had begun to rust and was threatening the integrity of the mesh metal 'net' that its owner hoped would protect him from an arrow or a sword tip. Chain mail wasn't used by everyone, despite its protective value, simply because it was heavy and difficult to maintain. The soldier who owned this particular vest had obviously tried to keep it in good shape, but weeks in the field had left it weakened in one spot despite those attempts.

As he finished replacing the damaged link the soldier, a career sergeant in the 1st Heavy Infantry, continued to cast dispersion on the Army High Command.

"And for that matter, we should be attacking right now instead of wallowing in this mire," the heavy muscled swordsman was saying. "This kind of camp is just begging for dysentery or cholera. You can't keep this many men in a camp this long and not get hit with disease o' some kind I'm tellin' ya."

"So it is said," Tinker nodded neutrally as he crimped the new wire together and placed it on the small anvil he used for such things. He carefully wrapped a piece of softer wire around the joint, then took a piece of burning coal from a small bowl and laid it over the metal vest. Soon, smoke was rising from the anvil as the wire melted, effectively welding the link closed. While not as good, nor ultimately as strong as if it had been welded in a forge, the repair work would make the vest considerably stronger than it had been with the damaged link still in place.

"And it's true, too," the sergeant nodded firmly. "I've seen it more than once and yet we never seem to learn," he shook his head. "You'd think that the Army would put that into the officer's training manuals as many times as we've had to learn it the hard way."

"Perhaps it is there," Tinker shrugged gently, removing the vest from the anvil and allowing it to cool. "It may simply be that there is no effective choice for the moment but to maintain the defensive posture the Army has assumed and that means keeping camp."

"That's true," the sergeant agreed reluctantly. "There's no doubt they outnumber us by a right smart. And damn me if they don't fight better'n they ever have, heathen bastards," he added bitterly.

"Your own men are fighting well, too," Tinker reminded him.

"That they are," the sergeant perked up a bit. "The new Marshal made sure o' that, now, didn't he? Takin' the whoreson cavalry right into the lion's den so to speak. Was good to see that bunch do some fightin' for a change."

"You don't care for the cavalrymen?" Tinker asked, one eyebrow raised.

"Ah, they got their place, sure," the sergeant waved a dismissing hand. "But how hard can it be to ride a horse all day?" he asked in near derision. "Ain't a one of 'em could last out a day in the infantry," he added proudly.

"I suppose that would be accurate," Tinker said with a straight face, thinking of how tough the Prince's soldiers were, cavalry or not. "Still, fighting from horseback can't be easy."

"Not against other horsemen prob'ly," the infantryman admitted. "But against a man on foot he's a right terror." Tinker could hear the truth behind the sergeant's declaration. He had the foot-soldier's fear of a cavalry charge, and rightly so.

"I would think that is accurate," Tinker nodded and held the vest up, examining the work. "I think this should do nicely," he said to the sergeant, handing the equipment over for inspection. The man took the vest and made his own examination, nodding sagely at the work.

"Can't hardly tell where it was done," he said approvingly as he handed over the two coins the Tinker had charged him. His prices were, in fact, far cheaper than many of the others and his work superior to most of them. It made him very popular with officers and enlisted alike.

"A grand compliment indeed," Tinker smiled. "And I thank you for your patronage," he bowed slightly.

"Ain't a better man in camp for this kind o' thing to my knowledge," the sergeant said earnestly. "I'd rather trust you with it than some o' the idiots we got in our unit, and that's the truth."

"You aren't well cared for by the Army?" Tinker asked carefully. "I would think they should be taking great good care of their fighting men, especially now."

"Oh, we do fine," the sergeant nodded absently. "Better now thanks to that new Marshal, to be sure. But the quality o' work you put out is high and above the average fella in the service battalion, don't doubt it. I could likely have got this fixed there for free, but I reckon a man gets what he pays for, and my life might depend on this thing," he shook the mail vest. "Worth it to me to pay for better."

"I can imagine that," Tinker smiled. "I am relieved to hear that you are in good care, however," he cast his line carefully so as not to alert the fish.

"Can't really complain, especially in a camp such as this," the sergeant waved a hand around them. "Ain't as good as bein' in barracks, but the Army rarely slides in makin' do for us. And like I said, the new Marshal has shook things up a good bit. A lot o' officers that was being right harridans to the men have calmed down a bit since Lord Parno took over. He don't cotton to such foolishness, ya see? They knows it, too, so they've taken to bein' a bit more gentlemanly of late. Glad for it, myself," he added almost as an afterthought.

"Surely they weren't mistreating the men they lead into battle," Tinker commented casually. "That would be foolishness to my way of thinking."

"You'd think the idiots could see that, would ya not?" the sergeant replied. "But there's a good many of 'em that's from 'high' families, and to them we're on the same level as their family servants. Man like the last Marshal, he might have encouraged that kind o' thinkin', but not this new one. Men like him, too, I'm here to say. And it said a lot about him that he led that cavalry battle, too. Old Marshal wasn't never in hearing of the front lines and there Lord Parno was, out in the enemy's front door. Well, side door, as it were," he grinned.

"I've heard good things about him," Tinker nodded. "It is good to know that the men respect him so well. I arrived here expecting to find things in much worse shape," he admitted, since that was true.

"Likely would have been, not for the new Marshal," the sergeant admitted. "Well, I better get back, I reckon," the man straightened again. "Thanks again, Tinker. Know you're busy."

"Never too busy for you, my friend, or for any of your mates. Ensure they know that. Some of us are highly appreciative of your service, and especially at times such as these."

"I'll do that," the man promised and then was off, back to his unit. Tinker cleaned away the slight mess he'd made working, considering what he had learned. The attitude change in the officers would be good news for the Prince, but the fact that it had been necessary would not be.

Still, his brother's actions now made it possible for Parno McLeod to make inroads with the Army's rank and file by merely treating them correctly in the first place, something that would not have been possible without Therron McLeod's slip-shod management of the Army of Soulan during his tenure as Marshal. His musings were interrupted by the approach of another potential customer.

"Good day, my friend," he smiled. "How can I serve you today?"

As he looked at the helm offered him by a young officer, Tinker pondered how he could 'fish' this one.

-

"All squadrons signal that they are closing in, sir," Merrill reported as he joined Selvey on the command deck. "And Commander Rickett is aloft to spy out the enemy numbers and composition."

"Excellent," Selvey nodded, his own glass still fixed on the western horizon. "We should have plenty of time to reform. We'll meet them as a single unit, and that-"

"Sails!" the cry came again, cutting off Selvey's comments. "Sails to the north, off the starboard bow! Many sails!"

Selvey turned his glass that way but again the enemy was still too distant to be seen from the deck.

"Two forces?" he mused. "I need a report from Rickett right away concerning size and make-up of the enemy. It's possible that our intelligence about the number and whereabouts of the Soulan Fleet was in error, Mister Merrill."

"Sir!" Merrill hurried away to the messenger line running to the look-out posts where Rickett was already posted. A steady man with a good eye, Rickett was an excellent choice for the role. Merrill found a message descending as he made his way to the main mast of the *Indina*. He took the note and read through it, ordering a message to be sent in reply that Rickett should get a glass on the new force.

The enemy to their due west was comprised of at least three cruiser weight ships and six frigates, though Rickett's terse message warned there was at least one more line of sail behind that which he could not yet make out. Merrill felt his stomach ease at the news as he made his way back to the Admiral. Nine ships? Maybe a few more? Even if the new force had the same amount, the Imperial Fleet had a near two-to-one supremacy. They would get hurt, as Selvey had noted, but victory would be all but certain.

-

"Northern force in view, Admiral," Nettles reported calmly. "Red smoke from the force, sir. They've seen our smoke and are making turns."

"Good," Semmes nodded. Lookouts were still cataloging the enemy, but so far it looked like his men would face three-to-one odds. If the Keyhorn Squadron closed up those odds would drop some, but he couldn't be sure that all of the Norland ships were accounted for yet.

"Orders, sir?" Nettles prompted carefully.

"None needed for the moment, Mister Nettles," Semmes shrugged. "We will continue to close and seek engagement as quickly as possible. If we can distract them, then the Imperials may not notice the Keyhorn ships until they're in full view. Assuming they arrive in time for it to matter," he added grimly.

"About the target selection, sir," Nettles began, but stopped at a raised hand from Semmes.

"We will target the troopships, Mister Nettles. Destroying them, assuming they do carry troops, takes precedent over self-defense. If they prove to be empty, then we'll engage the warships and do as much damage as we can. Those orders will not change," he added with a stern look at his Secretary. "Our entire objective today is to sink those ships or prove they are not a threat to the Kingdom. Anything else must come after that."

"Aye, sir," Nettles nodded. He was reluctant to sacrifice their own ships and men and felt the Admiral should be as well. Semmes made no other reply. In his mind, none was needed.

-

"Green smoke from the north, Commodore!"

Commodore Anthony David used his glass to spy out the smoke.

"Right where they ought to be," he nodded to himself. "How about that?"

"Sir?"

David turned to Commander Jonathon Riddell, his flag secretary.

"I said they're right where they should be," he smiled slightly. "Signal all ships to come north, and have our heading set to. . .zero five zero, I should think," he said after a brief pause. "That should do nicely."

"Shall I order red smoke in acknowledgment, sir?" Riddell asked.

"No," David said firmly. "If the Admiral could see, then so could the Imperials. Let us keep our presence here a mystery as long as possible. It might save the day if we can catch them unprepared. I almost wish the wind would shift slightly to our south, but that might make the Admiral's job harder. Make sure that our rowers are ready, but do not unship them until we must." He turned back to the horizon.

"Assuming the Imperial commander places his warships between the Admiral and the troopships, we just might be able to slip behind him and engage the troopships early on. If we can do enough damage, then our mission will be achieved regardless of the final outcome."

"Sir," Riddell nodded and hurried to give the orders. David took an extra minute to think over his own orders. Should he have signaled the Admiral? How would Semmes react not knowing if the Keyhorn ships were on their way. Would he fight the engagement differently?

David shook his head. It really didn't matter. Their orders were to destroy as many troopships as possible unless they could prove they were empty. Any opportunity to do that, regardless of risk or costs, had to be taken. No, Admiral Semmes would agree with his decision if he were here. It hadn't been something they had discussed, but it was still a good idea.

"Red smoke further north, sir," Riddell returned, slightly winded but grinning. "Sun squadron is replying to the Admiral."

"Excellent," David smiled now himself. With both the northern groups to contend with, the Imperials might actually not see him until it was too late. And that was worth the risk, he judged.

-

"Enemy to the north has at least four cruisers and six frigates, Admiral," Merrill reported. "Western force now in view with five cruisers, eight frigates and two sloops. The sloops are hanging back, however. They're only barely in view."

"Ships of that class aren't much good in an engagement like this," Selvey nodded slowly. "No sense in having them on the line. Why bring them at all, I wonder?" he mused.

"Might be their command vessel, sir," Merrill offered.

"No," Selvey shook his head. "He couldn't see from that far back. And signaling would be too difficult," he added. "No, there's another reason. Perhaps they have medical personnel on board." This more to himself than to Merrill. "Not a bad idea if so," he nodded absently. A sailor ran up with a message for Merrill.

"Northern force now approaching abreast, sir," Merrill read the message. "Six cruisers, seven frigates. No sloops or other ships in view with this force," he added.

"Eleven cruiser weight ships and fifteen frigates," Selvey said aloud. "That would account for most of their eastern navy." The assembled Imperial Fleet had a total of eighteen cruisers and twenty-four frigates protecting eleven troopships and three cargo ships. Just about right for an invading army. Of course, those ships had only a handful of Marines aboard other than their crews.

"Numbers are more even than I expected," Merrill admitted. He had counted on outnumbering the Soulan fleet elements heavily in this engagement. That wasn't looking to be the case, now.

"Always a safe bet to assume that your enemy outnumbers you, Captain," Selvey replied. "You avoid surprises that way. Signal the fleet, Mister Merrill. Line abreast, primary targets are the cruisers. Soulan cruisers are built to ram so we need to keep them off balance as much as possible. I don't need to remind you that the wind favors them in this first pass?"

"No sir!" Merrill replied. He was already moving to where sailors awaited with flags to hoist for signals to the other ships. The Imperial Fleet was divided into three squadrons, but all ships would take their orders from the *Indina* rather than from their squadron commanders. It was something Merrill had argued against, but Selvey would not be moved in that. He did not trust his squadron commanders to act in the best interest of the navy overall rather than themselves, so he would issue all orders to all ships.

Of course, if something happened to Selvey, or the *Indina*, then there would be a time of confusion among the Imperial Fleet until command structures were back in the squadron commanders' hands.

A lot could go wrong in those moments.

-

"We should slow slightly," Semmes almost murmured. "Allow the Sunshine Coast contingent to catch up. But sacrificing that speed would cost us."

"Sir?" Nettles asked.

"Talking to myself, Mister Nettles," Semmes shook his head. "Ideally, we should slow our advance to allow Commodore Rhode's ships to catch us. But doing so would make us slower when we hit engagement range and I don't want that. I'd rather have gone in together."

"Is the loss of speed worth the gain from waiting, sir?" Nettles asked.

"Excellent question," Semmes nodded. "The truth is I don't know. We have no real idea what the Imperial ships are capable of, to be honest. Oh, we know roughly what they can do," he added as Nettles started to object, "but what is the accuracy of their weaponry? How drilled are their men? How well trained are they? See what I mean? All those are unknowns to us for the moment." He paused, considering.

"Signal the squadron to drop the three-quarter sail," he ordered finally. "That should allow us to maintain enough momentum while allowing Commodore Rhode the time to come up in support." He raised his glass to the south, searching for the Keyhorn ships of Commodore David's command.

"Perhaps they'll see us soon, sir," Nettles offered as he departed to relay the signal orders.

"Perhaps," Semmes said aloud to no one. He swept the southern horizon once more before turning his attention back to the Imperial Fleet.

They would soon be in theoretical range of ballista and catapult. Things would certainly liven up then. Perhaps he should slow to half-sail, allowing his gunners more time to engage before resuming ramming speed.

-

"Total Soulan count remains at eleven cruisers and fifteen frigates, sir," Merrill reported.

"I can see that Mister Merrill," Selvey replied calmly. "I expected more ships," he added after a moment. If he noticed Merrill's red face he ignored it.

"Perhaps their king rushed them to attack with whatever they had," Merrill offered, almost hesitantly after the last retort from his Admiral.

"That is a possibility," Selvey nodded. "No doubt we're putting pressure on them with our presence here. But why would he order them to attack us with numbers so small that our victory is all but assured?"

"Sir, is it possible that this is all there is?" Merrill asked cautiously. "We were at peace for a long time, and we were talking peace right up until the war began. Maybe they had drawn down their forces and this is all they have."

"Again, that is possible," Selvey mused. "But judging from the readiness of their army, we dare not make such an assumption I fear. I think your first suggestion would be closer to the mark, Captain. We have put such pressure on the southerners that their King has ordered them to do the impossible."

Selvey continued to watch the approaching enemy, unable to completely overcome the unease he was feeling. He told himself it was only natural to feel that unease. He was about to lead his ships into battle against a worthy opponent. If he failed, he might well perish. If he failed and lived, he would be a prisoner at best. Should he live and escape, he would then be at the mercy of his Emperor, as would his family.

Yes, there was plenty of reason for his unease. And not all of it was due to the number of ships his opponent was mustering.

-

"Sir, top lookout is seeing sails to our northwest," Commander Riddell reported. David nodded sagely, still considering his options.

"Any idea of the count?" he asked, not expecting one.

"Not as yet, but the enemy is facing west it appears, and there are two lines of vessels," Riddell replied. "It's possible their troopships are the second line, sir," he added.

"So it is," David nodded. "That would be a great good fortune, would it not?" he almost grinned. "If we could take the troopships unaware, before their warships can intervene?"

"It would indeed, sir," Riddell nodded. "But. . .our frigates aren't really rigged for ramming, sir," he continued hesitantly.

"I'm quite aware of that Mister Riddell," David replied.

"Their throw weight isn't great enough to sink a very large troopship, either, sir," Riddell continued despite his reluctance to do so.

"Make your point, Mister Riddell," David's voice was slightly brittle now.

"Sir, if our frigates attempt to ram such large vessels, they're almost sure to sink along with them," Riddell took the plunge.

"That they are," David nodded. "And we will do our duty if it costs us every ship in this squadron, Mister Riddell. The navy exists for the sole purpose of protecting the shores of Soulan." He turned to look at the younger man. "You may have been taught that at Savannah. No?" Riddell's face reddened at the slight barb, but he nodded.

"Then there should be no doubt that our frigates will do what's required of them, should there?" David turned his gaze back to the northwest. "We will do what we came here to do, Mister Riddell. Make no mistake about that."

"Sir," Riddell nodded his acquiescence, thoroughly cowed by his Commodore's quiet scathing.

"Carry on, Mister Riddell," David ordered. He looked at the sails above him, noting they were billowing more than before. The *Ocoee*, sister ship to the *Wabash*, was cutting through the water at a fine clip now.

"Signal line abreast, Mister Riddell," he ordered suddenly. "The wind appears to be in our favor for the moment. Let's take full advantage of that."

"Will do, sir."

"Wind appears to be shifting," Merrill noted the same thing aboard the *Indina*. "This may favor them more, Admiral," there was no need to add.

"So it may," Selvey nodded. "Nothing we can do about the wind, Mister Merrill except pray that it changes to favor us in time of greater need."

"Sir," Merrill acknowledged.

"We'll open fire at maximum range," Selvey ordered. "Ships may maneuver at will to unmask batteries, but line positions are to remain constant. Present broadsides as though needful but do not break formation." He turned to look at Merrill.

"At times such as these, it is discipline that will win the day, Mister Merrill. We must maintain."

"Yes sir," Merrill nodded. "I'll have the signals sent."

"Carry on."

"Imperial ships are maneuvering, sir," Nettles reported. As with so many of his 'reports', it wasn't really needed or necessary, yet it was his function to make sure that his Admiral knew everything there was to know.

"So they are, Mister Nettles," Semmes nodded absently, observing the Imperial ships himself. "They intend to open fire at long range," he added after a few seconds. "Signal all ships, make full sail," he ordered. "By the time they decide they have us, we'll be gaining speed again. That will throw them off a bit at least for the first round or two."

"Full sail, aye sir," Nettles replied and nodded to a runner standing close by. The man nodded and took off toward the signal officers who were already hauling down the current signal flags.

"Order chase weapons to ready as well," Semmes added after no more than a few seconds. "Ship captains are to allow chase weaponry to fire as soon as they believe they can achieve accuracy. They know their men better than we do."

"Yes Admiral," Nettles nodded. This message he carried himself, because of its importance. His other runner for the moment was a teenager who was so scared his face was white.

Nettles hurried to the signals officer, a commander who had been at sea longer than the young runner had been in the world, and quickly explained the order. The man nodded, making a quick note in his log even as he snapped out orders. His signalmen hurried to attach these new orders to the second of three lines used to replay signals. By the time Nettles had returned to his Admiral's side the signal flags were on their way up the line.

"Signals made, sir."

"Excellent," Semmes nodded. "We'll soon be in the fire, Mister Nettles," he added. "I assume you've made ready?" he asked suddenly.

"I have, sir," Nettles said gravely. "Today is as good as any other."

"And perhaps better than some," Semmes nodded again, in approval this time. "Soon it will be in the hands of the men, Mister Nettles. Our job is to give them a chance. To put them in position to win. Once we've done that, it's all up to them from that point on."

"We have good men, sir," Nettles agreed.

"That we do."

CHAPTER FOURTEEN

-

There was little elegance to it, in the end. The Royal Navy of Soulan made full sail directly into the Imperial Fleet's line and the Imperial Fleet stood by to receive them. One side fighting for their home, the other for an ideal, or in some cases for their continued well-being.

Men of both sides prayed that their officers, their ships or their luck would see them through the coming battle. Their officers prayed they would give a good account of themselves, save their ship and be victorious. A rare few looked at the battle with a gleaming eye, hopeful for glory, reward and fame.

The ships themselves creaked and groaned under the strain of moving through water that was much heavier than themselves, bows splitting the ocean to allow the ships to pass as they prepared for battle. They were proud vessels, made by proud men and sailed by those who took great pride in the ship they served. Ships made for the art of war at sea, designed to outlast the enemy before they succumbed to damage themselves. A few of the ships, and a select few men on both sides had seen naval combat, but never before had the combined navies of each power faced each other in such a duel. The commanders on both sides were in uncharted waters here and had nothing but training, theory and discipline to fall back upon.

Each hoped it would be sufficient.

-

"They intend to ram, Admiral!" Merrill almost shouted as the fact dawned on him.

"I believe you were taught that Soulan cruisers were built to ram other vessels, Mister Merrill," Selvey replied calmly. "This tactic should not be unexpected."

"Our ships won't be able to stand those blows, sir," Merrill stressed.

"In all likelihood they will not," Selvey admitted as the first catapults fired from his most forward ships. "That is why we have artillery, Mister Merrill. We must trust to our men that they will damage the enemy, at least some of them, sufficiently to prevent them from completing their runs. And they only get one," he added, raising his glass again. "Once they've shot their bolt, it will be sword and arbalest and pike. Ballistas and boarding actions. You've trained for this Mister Merrill." Selvey lowered his glass suddenly and looked at the younger man.

"Surely you didn't think we would escape unscathed from this battle, did you?" The older man's tone was slightly condescending, but also the tone of a teacher. An instructor.

"I. . .no sir, I knew we would take losses," Merrill replied, swallowing hard. "I just. . .I didn't expect them to come right at us this way."

"And why not?" Selvey returned his eyes to his glass, looking at the approaching enemy vessels as the first shots began to land among them. "We threaten their homeland, Mister Merrill. I warned you many times, did I not? Say what you will of them, the Southerners are not cowardly nor are they ignorant."

"Taking fire, Admiral," Nettles reported.

"So I see," Semmes nodded. "We'll soon see-" He was cut off as the forward mounts on the *Wabash* fired, hurling half-barrels of flaming pitch and red hot iron at the Imperial ships.

"- how effective our own fire is," Semmes finished as crews forward raced to reload their weaponry. "Would you be so good as to find Mister Hoag for me, Mister Nettles?" Semmes asked calmly. Wayland Hoag was the sailing master of the *Wabash*, making him the senior sailing master, or maritime expert, in the fleet.

"At once, Admiral," Nettles nodded and sent two runners scurrying to find the requested man, adding himself to the search on the after decks so he was still within hearing of his Admiral.

Two minutes later Wayland Hoag appeared, his shirt sweat stained and face grimy.

"Admiral?" he almost demanded. Unlike the others, Hoag was not an officer, but the senior enlisted man in the entire fleet that was now at sea. He had more practical sailing and shipping knowledge that all of Semmes' officers could muster combined. Experience in command they had. Experience in actual ship handling they left to seasoned hands like Hoag.

"Mister Hoag, I've had a thought," Semmes said evenly. "I need your input before I signal the order, but I'm afraid I must have your answer forthrightly as time is of the essence."

"About?" Hoag was wary now.

"I'm curious about our speed..."

-

South of the battle, the Keyhorn Squadron continued to close at full sail, benefiting from a favorable wind for the moment.

"Lookouts report seeing fire to the north, sir," Riddell reported to Commodore David. "Enemy is engaging with fire."

"Very well," David nodded, his eyes never leaving the horizon. Only his lookouts could see the enemy as yet, but his own ships were closing quickly.

"Signal all ships to maintain position," he ordered suddenly. "Front rank will take whatever fire the enemy can muster in our direction once our presence is known to them while the rear rank will concentrate on the troopships as they come into view." He gave Riddell his full attention for a few seconds.

"All frigates are to ram the nearest troopship to them that is still unengaged."

"Sir," Riddell began but David's look stopped him.

"You have your orders, Mister Riddell. Carry them out."

"Aye, sir," the younger man nodded and headed for the signals officer.

Anthony David turned back to the horizon, looking toward an enemy he himself could not yet see, but he knew was there, nonetheless.

-

"Admiral, it's not that this won't work, but understand that you'll lose enough speed that it will affect your follow through," Hoag said flatly. "You won't have the speed to continue on once the cruisers ram, sir."

"As I suspected," Semmes nodded. "Still, we can at least succeed in the first attack, still. Yes?"

"Yes sir," Hoag nodded carefully. "Barely," he forced himself to add.

"That is acceptable Mister Hoag," Semmes nodded. "I thank you and you may return to your post."

"Sir," Hoag stiffened slightly and hurried on his way.

"Admiral," Nettles began, then stopped himself. He had overstepped enough for one day, he decided.

"There is only one condition of victory here, Mister Nettles," Semmes said softly. "We are here to determine the status of this enemy force. If they have troops, we must sink them. If they do not, we must know it, and so signal the cutters behind us. Fail and we lose this battle, regardless of whether we survive or not."

"I for one would rather die succeeding than simply die fighting," he finished.

"Yes sir," Nettles nodded, admitting that he felt much the same though he would highly prefer surviving as well.

"Prepare the signals," Semmes returned to business. "Prepare for moving broadside."

-

Hampton Rhode looked at the signals message with a frown. Had Semmes lost his reason?

"Sir?"

He turned to see his runner waiting.

"Send the signal, son," Rhode handed the message back. "Quickly now. You!" he pointed to a runner standing by waiting for orders. "Advise Commander Layton to prepare ballistas for moving broadsides."

The runner nodded and took off at a run.

Rhode could only shake his head and hope his Admiral knew what he was doing. Rhode certainly didn't.

-

"We're overshooting," Merrill observed. Selvey almost snorted at the unnecessary comment, but managed to stop himself. It wasn't dignified, after all.

"Their commander increased speed as we prepared to open fire. Excellent tactics."

"We'll get the range, sir," Merrill said and once more Selvey had to stifle his reaction to the unneeded comment. Sometimes Merrill really wore on him.

"I'm sure we will, Mister Merrill," he settled for saying. "Unless and until their commander does something else unexpected."

-

"Their shots are scoring, Admiral," Nettles said, using his glass to scan their own ships. "*Belle* and *Seawitch* have taken hits. *Belle*'s foresail is aflame."

"Very well," Semmes replied, not looking for himself. "They'll carry on as best they can I'm sure."

Nettles said nothing else, continuing to look across at their own ships. He would keep Semmes apprised of their damages so that Semmes could concentrate on issuing orders to the fleet.

Forward, the *Wabash*'s chase weapons fired again, the thrump felt and heard throughout the ship. Their own artillery was getting the range as well.

-

"One of their ships is aflame, sir!" Merrill sounded more enthusiastic.

"Yes, I can see that," Selvey fought to maintain his calm. "What of our own vessels, Mister Merrill? The enemy is turning fire."

"Sorry sir," Merrill's face reddened at the dressing down as he turned his glass to their own ships.

"Well?" Selvey asked when Merrill didn't immediately reply.

"Sir, *Sorcerer* is ablaze," Merrill said quietly, his earlier enthusiasm gone. "*Stitch* and *Velvet Glove* are also burning," he added. "Their men are good shots."

A cruiser and two frigates burning, possibly out of action. In return, the enemy had one frigate burning and another that had minor damage. Not the best exchange.

"Signal all ships to stand by rowers," Selvey ordered a runner. "We'll have to move soon," he added to himself more than anyone else.

He turned his attention back to his enemy. His very capable and resourceful enemy as *Indina's* weaponry hurled another volley across to every narrowing expanse of water.

-

"Two enemy ships ablaze, sir!" Riddell read the message from the lookouts. "Two of our own appear damaged as well," his face fell somewhat as he continued. "Second line of ships match silhouettes for known Nor merchant and troopships, sir."

"That's our target," David said at once. "Signal the squadron to make full sail at once and stand by rowers and chase weaponry. We will fire the moment the enemy seems to take notice of us."

"Sir," Riddell nodded and ran to issue the orders.

"Hold on Admiral," David said to the horizon. "We're coming."

-

"Now," Semmes ordered calmly to the signals officer standing by to raise the orders he posted. The man ran the banners up the main signal mast quickly, tying the line fast.

The Soulan fleet trained its ship commanders and sailing masters hard. Command went to those officers who could think on their feet and showed a talent for handling their vessels under pressure. Sailing masters were the most seasoned sailors the Royal Navy could muster from all walks of the kingdom, selected for their knowledge of ships and seas.

But there was no way to communicate from ship to ship that didn't involve visual cues. Flags were a time proven way to get orders out, but they took time to disseminate through the fleet. That meant that only the most general of orders were usually given, the individual ship commanders being left to implement those general orders as best they could given their conditions.

Despite all the training and preparation however, a fleet of ships under full sail simply could not turn on a line. Orders would be a few seconds ahead or behind another ship and turns would be faster or slower depending on ship size, weight, and the skill of her handlers.

Problems were bound to occur. Semmes was hoping for the least possible amount of those problems with this set of orders, made on the fly.

He was to be disappointed at least somewhat.

"Sir, *Seacat* is hit!" Nettles reported. "The *Warrior* has rammed them in the turn, Admiral! *Seacat* is listing and *Warrior* has lost her momentum."

"Understood," Semmes said gravely. He had hoped to avoid that, but had known it was possible. Another frigate lost, and a cruiser, the *Warrior*, without enough momentum left to stay with the line. It was a loss, but hopefully it would not be decisive. As that thought hit him, the starboard broadside of the *Wabash* fired in unison, shaking the cruiser from bow to stern.

Shaking off the losses, Semmes raised his glass to see the result of his change in orders even as his ships began to heel to starboard to expose their port broadsides.

-

"What-"

"Mister Merrill, if you cannot cease your babbling then kindly call for your relief and remove yourself from this bridge!" Selvey had finally had enough.

"Sir-" Merrill began, then cut himself off, trying to regain his lost calm. He was not acquitting himself very well in the Admiral's eyes so far, and that could have negative consequences for his career.

"Damage report?" Selvey demanded, again reminding Merrill of his responsibilities.

"Sir," Merrill said again, quickly moving to survey their ships.

-

"Good hits on first volley, sir!" Nettles reported. "Two enemy cruisers and three frigates are hurt badly!"

"Well done, lads," Semmes said softly. "Prepare the signal for ramming speed as soon as the port broadsides are expended. Fire from chase weapons to resume as soon as they bear."

"Aye sir!" Nettles raced to the signal platform where the fleet signals officer was already prepared to hoist new orders. The *Wabash* fired again before he made it.

-

"*Illini* and *Razor* are listing heavily, Admiral," Merrill managed to maintain his calm this time. "*Rouge*, *Gypsy* and *Wind Jammer* likewise heavily damaged. *Rogue* is likely lost," he added. "At least three other ships hit but still capable."

"Very well," Selvey kept his own calm voice as well. Again, his enemy had caught him unaware. Even as he watched, the Southern Fleet continued to turn, unmasking their port batteries.

"Signal fleet to execute scatter!" Selvey ordered at once, but still far too late.

-

"Port broadsides away, Admiral," Nettles returned. "Orders posted to resume course and speed."

"Excellent," Semmes nodded. "Damage report?" The Imperials were still firing.

"Their targeting is off because of the turns, sir," Nettles reported. "*Wasee* has taken a hit but is still in formation. *Webb* and *Donovan* are hit, *Webb* falling away and on fire, *Donovan* still in formation for the moment but also with sails alight. *Agamennon* also has after sails ablaze but the fire appears contained."

Better than he'd hoped. Another cruiser hit, still another with a sail on fire but both still in line. A frigate surely lost, another burning but still fighting at least for the moment.

It was in the hands of his captains, now. He had done all he could for the moment. He raised his glass to see what the latest volley had accomplished.

-

"*Sorcerer* and *Razor* are gone, sir," Merrill reported quietly. "Both are hulled and sinking. *Illini* is listing, but the fires will get her first. *Vagabond* and *Wanderer* are now hit as well, with *Vagabond* burning."

"They've had their turn," Selvey's voice was grim, almost savage. "They can't risk another turn like that to unmask without losing more speed than they can afford. Our weapons should bracket them now."

"Sir," Merrill nodded, keeping his eyes on their own ships this time. Selvey's none too subtle reminder of his place was still ringing in his ears. He felt the *Indina* shudder as her weaponry fired a volley at the approaching enemy.

-

"*Tinsee* is lost, sir," Nettles reported flatly. "*Holton* is fully ablaze but her sails are still full, I think Captain Ring will still try to ram before the fire can destroy his ship. *Vaughan*, *Forsythe* and *Willis* are now falling out of line as well. I think *Forsythe* is lost sir, and *Willis* may be as well. Two others have fires aboard but are still in line."

The report finally ended and Semmes tried to keep his face impassive. He'd known it would be rough, he reminded himself. He'd lost half the ships he'd entered the fight with and was still not quite into ramming range. Atop of that, the troopships that were his target were still safely behind the remaining Imperial warships.

He had to face the fact that he might have failed his Sovereign.

"Sails! Sails south!"

-

"What?" Selvey snapped as the warning came.

"Many sails South-Southwest! Ships in view! At least ten ships abreast!"

"How the hell did they get so close!" Selvey bellowed.

Above him, his lookouts had been watching the battle and not watching the horizon. The fires had obscured their vision as well, forcing many to cover their faces in order to breathe. Whichever cause was responsible for their inattention, that negligence had allowed Anthony David's Keyhorn ships to approach to striking range unnoticed.

"Signal the fleet to close in!" Selvey shouted. He had just issued the order to scatter in order to avoid the expected broadsides from the Royal battle line and some of his ships were still maneuvering. Now they would have to reverse course and do it quickly in order to meet this new attack.

Selvey's insistence on issuing all orders himself was about to cost him and his men heavily.

-

"I think they see us, sir," Riddell grinned in spite of the possibility of his approaching demise.

"I'd have to agree, Mister Riddell," David grinned back. "Orders stand. Signal all ships to fire at will."

-

"It's David!" Nettles cried out. "The Keyhorn ships are behind the enemy front!"

"Well done, Anthony," Semmes breathed. His losses had not been in vain if David could get at the enemy troopships.

"David only has four cruisers, sir," Nettles reminded him.

"I am aware of that, Mister Nettles," the Admiral replied calmly. "He knows his duty, as do his men. Signal all ships to close and ram, then stand by for close action. And raise the black flag, I suppose," he added. "Give them something else to think about."

-

Selvey watched the black flags appear one at a time above the Soulan ships, his mouth set in a grim line.

I should have expected that, he told himself savagely. *We're threatening their homeland. Of course they'll fight to the death.*

"Sir, the troopships are taking fire," Merrill reported. "The new ships are concentrating on them for some reason."

"You can't possibly be that stupid, Mister Merrill," Selvey sounded tired. "Those troopships are the sole reason for our being here, you little moron! If they can get word back to. . ." He stopped, turning back to see. . . .

Yes, the two cutters were still there. Through his glass he could just make them out. Sails down, oars out, waiting.

Waiting to tell their leaders if there really is an army aboard these ships.

The thought hit him solidly even as Merrill babbled yet another useless report. The damned Soulanies never intended to fight him in a real naval duel they knew they couldn't win. They were sacrificing themselves in an attempt to sink the troopships. Even if there were soldiers aboard, if the ships were sunk then the troops would largely be lost in the ocean.

And if the southerners discovered there were no troops, then Selvey's mission would be a failure. Complete and abject failure.

"Signal the fleet to protect those ships at all costs!" Selvey yelled directly to the *Idina*'s signal officer. "Disregard all other concerns and protect those ships!"

-

"We're hurting them, sir." Riddell reported. "Three ships on fire and another listing sharply. Hulled, I think."

"Any sign of enemy troops?" David asked, looking for himself.

"Not as yet, sir, though there should be, considering. They should have men ready to repel boarders or deal with damage to the ship if. . ." the younger man trailed off suddenly, recognition dawning.

He directed his glass to the troopships' water lines, ignoring their minimal weapons and deck actions. He went swiftly from ship to ship, surveying all of them in his view.

"Sir, none of those ships are riding heavy," he said finally. "I. . .I don't think they're carrying anything other than their own crews and stores."

"I do believe you are correct, Mister Riddell," David nodded as he lowered his own glass. "We can't make that assumption just yet, however," he added sadly. "We're going to have to see for sure."

"Yes sir," Riddell nodded.

"Have Captain Ball direct us to the nearest vessel and prepare to ram," David ordered. "Inform Major Bromley that we'll probably have work for his Marines shortly. And then prepare the proper signals for the Admiral. If these ships are empty, he has to know that in time to send the message out. Move!"

Riddell scurried away, already shouting orders in every direction. It took only two minutes for David to feel the deck of the *Ocoee* shift beneath him as her Captain, Luther Ball, turned his ship toward the nearest troopship, which just happened to be the largest as well.

"Always the show off, aren't you Luther?" David grinned slightly. Well, considering the likely outcome of the next few minutes, David didn't see the harm.

Just this once.

"Dammit, I want ships interdicting those ships now!" Selvey swore at the hapless signals officer.

"Signals have been sent, Admiral," the Commander risked saying. "All ships, defend transports and merchant hulls. Disregard losses."

"The Soulanies have raised the black flag, Admiral!" Merrill reported, running up to Selvey nearly breathless.

"Mister Merrill, please remove yourself from my presence," Selvey said far more evenly than he felt. "I cannot abide your incompetence any longer. Open your mouth again at your own peril!" he added when Merrill seemed about to speak further.

The young Captain stood there another few seconds then stiffened to attention, whirled on his heel, and departed. Having left unsaid that the westward Soulanie battle line was about to make contact.

He'll know soon enough, won't he? Merrill thought savagely as he made his way to the wheel deck to take command of his own ship once more.

Behind him, Selvey continued to bellow orders to the signal section, demanding actions and information that they simply could not provide.

-

"Brace, brace, BRACE!" the call went throughout the *Ocoee* as her target loomed large to her front. David pocketed his own glass and sat upon the deck, taking firm hold of the railing and bracing his feet against the deck rail to his front.

Ramming was never enjoyable.

The *Ocoee* slammed her iron-reinforced bow into the port side of the Imperial Transport Ship *Pontoc*, her nose slicing neatly through the standard wood side of her target. The *Pontoc* was a merchant vessel more or less, and had never been intended to be anywhere near actual naval combat.

And she never would be again after today.

The *Ocoee* scarcely slowed as she cut the *Pontoc* neatly in two, leaving a destroyed and sinking vessel in her wake.

"As you will, Mister Ball!" David called down to the command deck beneath him, releasing Ball to select his own targets from that point on. Ball waved in reply and barked out orders to the two sailors manning the wheel of the *Ocoee*. Once more the cruiser shifted her direction, metal still screeching and wood continuing to splinter as she pulled away from the rapidly sinking *Pontoc*.

David surveyed his squadron from his position on the observation deck, a grim smile decorating his face. Two of his frigates, the *Greggs* and the *Piper*, had successfully rammed transports equally as large as the *Ocoee*'s first victim, their Captains sacrificing themselves and their ships to protect the Kingdom. Both ships were badly damaged though somehow still afloat. David ordered signals to both ships to withdraw and make for shore if possible. They had done their part for King and Country today.

His other three cruisers had likewise made good on their targets. Two were continuing into the flock of merchant vessels, though the last, the *Pinola*, appeared to be hung up on her target. Marines and sailors flooded her decks attempting to clear away the damage as archers and arbalests fired bolt after arrow at the enemy, preventing them from attacking the work crews.

There was a decided absence of soldiers among the ships they had rammed. No soldiers on the decks helping defend the ships, none in the water after their vessels had been rammed. David took the time to scan the entire area again before making his decision.

There weren't any soldiers here, after all, he sighed. So much lost for nothing.

"Mister Riddell!" David shouted. "Order the signal sent at once to the Admiral! Transports are empty! Raise the signal, and instruct all ships to raise it in repeat as well!"

"Sir!" Riddell replied and made for the signal officer.

We probably won't win the battle, David thought to himself with macabre satisfaction, *but we just might win the war, now.*

The Royal Navy had done her bit. It would be up to the Black Sheep Prince now.

-

"David is really taking it to them, sir!" Nettles said. "Three, no five transports sunk and another damaged! Two of David's frigates appear to have rammed and are now turning away, listing."

"So I see, Mister Nettles," Semmes nodded. "Is there any-"

"Signal from *Ocoee*, sir!" Nettles interrupted. "Transports are empty Admiral! There are no troops! Signal being repeated by all Keyhorn ships in view! We've done it sir!"

"Signal the cutters at once with orders to return at best speed with their orders," Semmes said at once, a sense of urgency creeping into his voice. "Nothing is to stop them. Nothing."

"Yes, Admiral!" Nettles snapped and ran to obey. He would need to hurry, Semmes decided, looking forward. *Wabash* was about to throw her own weight around, and her target was not a transport.

An Imperial cruiser loomed large to their fore, broadside exposed.

"This should be interesting," Semmes decided as the command to brace passed along the ship.

-

"Hard to starboard! Engage port rowers, push!" Merrill shouted, trying to maneuver *Indina* out of the path of the coming Soulan cruiser. Selvey's orders had left Merrill's ship exposed in the most amateurish of ways and now Merrill and his men were about to suffer for it.

"We're not goin' ta make it, sor!" the helmsman offered in his thick brogue. "Rudders right heavy!"

"So I see," Merrill nodded, suddenly calm. "Brace!" he called. "Brace for impact and prepare to repel boarders!" The call was picked up by others and ran the length of the ship.

"Best hold on to something Spivey," Merrill told the helmsman. "This will probably hurt."

-

Selvey wasn't looking when *Wabash* crashed into *Indina*'s starboard side. He was concentrating on the battle to save the transports and had forgotten to watch the battle line. Merrill would have been doing that for him had he not been sent away, but he had, and Selvey had appointed no replacement for him.

As a result, the blow took him completely unaware. He had ignored the Bracing call, so occupied he had been with bellowing at the signals officer with constantly changing and often conflicting orders.

And so it was that Admiral Jason Selvey suffered a severe whiplash as *Indina* was rocked violently by the ramming action of the Soulan cruiser *Wabash*.

His neck severely injured, Selvey was unable to right himself, or prevent his being catapulted into the waiting ocean beneath him. His lungs, already robbed of air by the blow he'd taken in the initial ramming, were empty when he hit the water, robbing him of any buoyancy.

He never resurfaced and there was no one to help him as he sank into the depths of the ocean.

-

The battle raged for over an hour, weapons still firing whenever they could be loaded and find a target. Archers fired and fired and fired until the barrels of bolts and arrows went dry, sweeping decks of enemy ships clear time and again, only to see sailors and marines from below take the place of those just slaughtered.

Wooden decks were slippery with blood as ships lost their momentum and were forced to engage oars or 'tack' into the wind in order to move. The butcher's bill for this unnamed sea battle would never truly be fully known as men fell into the sea never to be seen again or fell with horrible injuries received either at the hands of the enemy or from the kind of crushing that accompanied a close fought naval engagement such as this one.

Semmes, blood streaming from a cut on his forehead and cradling his broken and useless left arm inside his tunic, surveyed the scene, sick at heart for the loss of so many of his men and ships.

"Mister Nettles!" he called, only to have an unknown lieutenant appear in front of him.

"Beg pardon, Admiral, but Mister Nettles is gone, sir," the young man stammered.

"I see," Semmes fought off the wave of sadness that enveloped him at that news. "Are we capable of signaling, Lieutenant. . ."

"Taylor, sir," the young man supplied. "And yes sir, I believe so, sir."

"Then signal for all ships to disengage and make for shore bases as best they can," Semmes ordered. "Order every ship that can to repeat and relay those orders."

"Right away, sir!" Taylor snapped and hurried off to get the word out.

Semmes could only guess at his losses, but he knew that the Soulan Royal navy was essentially destroyed. True, the Gulf Squadron was not involved in this action, but her two cruisers and nine frigates were no match for a true combat squadron, the Gulf ships more concerned with smuggling and pirates than with invading Imperials.

Semmes had taken fifteen cruisers and twenty-one frigates into this battle. Not a single ship was undamaged. Many were already gone, sinking beneath the depths of the ocean. The *Wabash* was still afloat but was listing slightly and had suffered twice from fires. Other ships were either equally damaged or worse off than his flagship.

Semmes counted a few hulls, but stopped as he realized his fleet had lost at least twenty vessels. Twenty ships completely gone, many taking a large part of their crews with them.

Crews. That made him think of the men in the water, the men still on board ships that would not be able to make enough way to escape. Their fate was as sealed as if they were already beneath the waves.

But he could not save those men. They were beyond his help at the moment, and probably for all time. All he could do was save what he could of his command. His men and ships had accomplished their mission. The cutters carrying the message to Lord Parno were long out of sight, making their best speed for shore with the news of what he had paid so dearly to learn. What his men had paid so dear a price to know.

He continued to watch as *Wabash* heeled around, making toward Savannah. She might make it or she might not, Semmes didn't know. He did know that many berths at Savannah, Jackson and Minimi would be empty for a long time to come.

But at least now the troops held motionless by the threat of this Imperial fleet could move north. Semmes hoped it was worth it.

He really, really did.

He would not realize it when he lost consciousness and fell to the deck.

CHAPTER FIFTEEN

-

Parno and his men made their way into Nasil without fanfare, just ahead of dusk and nearing exhaustion. Moving at once to the barracks near the palace, Parno's men were met by members of the Palace Guard and the King's own, men moving to take over the care of tired horses for the tired men who had ridden them.

Parno made his way to the palace without pause, trailed by Enri Willard, Cho Feng and Harrel Sprigs. Memmnon was already in the council chamber when Parno arrived, having been made aware of his brother's arrival minutes before.

"Hello, Parno," Memmnon smiled slightly, embracing his younger brother slightly. "You look worn out."

"Nearly so," Parno admitted with a nod as he sat down heavily. He looked to where the others waited.

"Well, sit down," he ordered and the three took seats of their own, Parno shaking his head at their hesitation.

"How are things in the west?" Memmnon asked, settling into his own chair.

"Raines has done an excellent job," Parno said at once. "One reason I'm here so quickly. He has no need of me there. Well, he did have one issue that I solved for him," Parno amended, "but he needs no assistance in keeping the Nor at bay. He's fine."

"I'm glad to hear that," Memmnon nodded. "We also received word of your victory at Dreeden," the elder McLeod frowned. "Parno, you simply cannot continue to take such risks. Not at a time like this. We absolutely cannot spare you-"

"I've already had this lecture," Parno cut him off with a raised hand. "Multiple times, in fact," he shot a glare at his trio of followers. "That was a necessary risk I took. And no, I like as not won't be doing it again. I've too much to do elsewhere. But we needed a victory to raise the army's morale and set the Nor back on their heels. We got it."

"Yes, a very great victory by any standard you care to apply," Memmnon nodded. "Well done, brother. Well done. I was not criticizing your actions as much as your risk."

"I was never in any danger," Parno rolled his eyes.

"The after-action reports indicated that your regiment was involved in combat with Tribal cavalry!" Memmnon objected.

"Not with me leading them," Parno replied. "That was Karls. Outnumbered probably three-to-two or so at that. Caught them flanking the rearguard and tore them limb from limb."

"Really?" Memmnon leaned forward, his eagerness apparent as he seemed to forget his 'lecture' to his younger brother.

"Really," Parno nodded firmly. "Our men are their equal or perhaps their superior, with the training regimen that Cho Feng and... .and Darvo developed for the Black Sheep."

"I understand you have a new group undergoing that same training now?" Memmnon asked.

"Yes, a full brigade of cavalry," Parno replied. "They should be well under way by now, but it's not a quick process. It should go faster for them since they have basic instruction already behind them. That will speed things along. Also, many of the Sheep had to learn horsemanship which is something else that won't be a problem."

"As we train new instructors, we'll be extending the ground training to infantry units as well," he finished. "Again, not a rapid process, but one well worth the efforts."

"You proved that at the Gap," Memmnon nodded. "Your man Finn has been working almost non-stop since his arrival, by the way," the Crown Prince changed the subject. "We've provided him with everything he's asked for and given him the old foundry south of the city proper. He requested something out of 'blast range' of the city and its occupants. I am not familiar with that term, to be honest," he admitted.

"Many of Roda's toys can be. . .explosive, I think, is the word we use to describe them," he looked to Sprigs for confirmation and received a nod. "The damage his inventions can cause is somewhat mind boggling, to be honest," he returned his attention to his brother.

"These are the 'sorcery' you used at the Gap, I take it," Memmnon grinned at the term.

"I've heard that the Nor describe it so," Parno grinned back tiredly. "Truth is it's nothing but pure science. Practices of the ancients that Roda and others like him have dug up from the ruins."

"Yes, such as the. . .semaphore, I think the term was, towers and signals. We're still consulting with the Royal engineers about their construction, but I admit it looks promising. Learning the signals may require some degree of schooling, but the theory is very intriguing. If successful it could literally transform the way important information is passed."

"We'll need to guard the codes closely," Parno warned. "Only the most loyal and trustworthy of men should be given that training."

"A sound suggestion," Memmnon agreed. "I will see to it. What are your plans now?" he asked.

"I will sleep tonight," Parno laughed dryly. "Tomorrow I will see Roda Finn. I have an engineer I stole from Raines that I will want to confer with the Royal Engineer Corps for information. He constructed a model of the Great River for Raines that is an excellent tool with many uses, not all of the military. I want him given whatever he needs to construct such a model of the Tinsee Valley, and eventually the Ohi as well. Once we've cleared the Nor from our lands, we will develop a new military command for that area and such a model will be beneficial for the commander there."

"I received your orders combining 1st and 2nd Corps under Davies' command," Memmnon mentioned. "How did Graham respond to that? He was one of Therron's favorites, you may know."

"He made that apparent," Parno nodded. "General Graham and I reached an understanding. He will respect my authority and show his loyalty to the King, and as a reward for doing so I won't kill him."

The words were spoken flatly, a simple declaration. From his tone, Parno might just as easily have told him brother that he'd acquired a new horse.

"I see," Memmnon settled for saying. "I'm sure that will work for now," he added for lack of anything else to say.

"If it doesn't, I'll destroy him and place someone else in command of 1st Corps," Parno shrugged as if it were of no consequence. "I have organized a new unit that should already be behind enemy lines, harassing their lines of communication. Since it's nowhere near harvest, the Nor must depend on supplies from their lands to sustain them. Beaumont and Whipple will interdict those lines when and where possible, while also destroying isolated units they encounter."

"A sound strategy," Memmnon nodded.

"It is my hope that their actions, along with the successful attack we launched before I departed, will stall their offensive long enough to prepare offensive movements of our own. At the least it should, hopefully, give Roda more time to resupply our artillery and train them to use their new weapons."

"You believe you will be able to launch an offensive?" Memmnon asked, surprised.

"If Admiral Semmes has been successful, or will be at any rate, then yes, I will," Parno replied. "I will be bringing both 4th and 5th Corps north, save for some militia units that will patrol the shores and the southern leg of the Great River. With their strength added to 1st Army, yes, we will launch an attack. I'd prefer, in all honesty, to absorb a Nor offensive using Roda's weaponry before we attack, but I've no idea if that will come to pass. We will have to see what happens."

"A bold gamble, brother," Memmnon kept his voice neutral. He did not want Parno thinking he was interfering with the youngest McLeod's running of the military.

"We have to gamble, Memmnon," Parno shrugged. "We face two large forces to our North and West. If we do not consolidate our forces and try to dislodge them, then protecting the coast will be of no use to us. We need to push them back, and then punish them."

"Punish them?" Memmnon's eyebrow rose at that.

"That is for later, and assumes we will be victorious," Parno waved the idea away for now.

"What do you need from me?" Memmnon asked.

"Continue to support Roda and the others in his group," Parno said at once. "The things they uncover will be priceless to us, both in war and in peace. They need and deserve our support."

"They have the full backing of the Crown, and each has two Royal Marshals in attendance to ensure they get whatever they need," Memmnon promised. "Finn has objected to the number of women working in the Foundry, but he understands that we lack the men to fill all the positions he has, or that others have. Our women are strong and independent, and many have demanded to be allowed to assist in the war effort. It seemed beneficial not to deny them."

"Not to mention keeping certain of the noble women happy," Parno grinned.

"That too," Memmnon grinned sheepishly. "And honestly, Parno, they are doing excellent work. There's no good reason to prevent them from serving in these roles."

"I agree, and have given orders to include women in the observation and warning posts along the river and the coastlines," Parno replied. "I would also expect to see women medics soon, if Stephanie has her way."

"'Stephanie', is it?" Memmnon grinned broadly at his brother, who flushed.

"Memmnon," he said warningly.

"Just making an observation, brother," Memmnon raised a hand in placation. "Well, your apartments are ready for you," he rose. "You and your men should rest. If there is a need, let me know and I will see to it."

"Thank you."

Sherron McLeod watched from the shadows as Parno departed the conference room, leading his foreigner and other lackeys along. Including the traitorous Enri Willard who had once been so close to her cherished brother, Therron. As Memmnon emerged behind them, Sherron set upon him.

"So it is true," her voice cut across the hallway. Memmnon turned to see her standing there.

"What is true?" he asked. "What brings you out so late, sister?"

"Father has replaced Therron with Parno?" Sherron asked, eyebrows climbing high on her head. "Where is Therron, by the way?"

"Therron has been sent away Sherron," Memmnon told her flatly. "He defied the King one time too many and is paying for it now."

"Defied him? How?" she demanded. "We're at war and he replaced his Marshal with Parno of all people? Has father lost his senses as well as his courage?"

"Mind your tongue!" Memmnon snapped, somewhat more harshly than he'd intended. "And where do you get the idea that our father has lost his courage, sister? That is perhaps the most ridiculous thing you've ever said. Given your track record, that is making a statement all its own."

"Father feared Therron and so did you!" Sherron accused. "Both afraid that his popularity among the nobles and the army would make him more powerful than you! So you contrive to have him removed and 'sent away'!"

"Sherron, I must assume that your delusions of conspiracy are the result of listening to Therron speak about himself too often," Memmnon replied acidly. "Too much of that will rot your brain, as you seem determined to prove. Therron defied a direct order from the King himself. Doing so very nearly cost us the war before it was well underway. If not for Parno, you would likely be dead or in captivity at this very moment, along with the rest of us and this city lying in Nor hands. That is why he was 'sent away', dear sister. I assure you that our father lacks nothing in the arena of courage, either. It was him that faced Therron down and pronounced judgment on him." He took a step closer to her.

"And you would do well to keep your voice down when speaking so, since father has allowed the story that Therron is ill to be repeated rather than let the truth be known. That is far more than he deserved, considering all of his actions."

"You still fear him, even now," Sherron mocked her older brother. "You reek of it, Memmnon. Fear that your younger brother would surpass you and rule in your stead. Shameful."

"For the record," Memmnon fought to control his temper, "he could have the crown so far as I'm concerned. But he would need no heir in all likelihood, since he would almost certainly be the last sovereign of Soulan. His 'rule' would be ruinous and result in our being bowled over by the Nor heathen in short order while Therron preached to all and sundry that our forces were superior and we could not be beaten. That is all he did for most of the winter as we tried to prepare."

"We will never fall to the Northern Heathens!" Sherron snapped. "Soulan has stood since the time of Tyree and will continue to stand long after the last Nor bastard is rotting in the earth!"

"Yes, that's exactly the sort of thing Therron was saying," Memmnon nodded. "Of course, the reality is somewhat different, sister. The 'heathen' are far better prepared than at any time in our shared history. They have trained and equipped a massive army that you may have heard is now camping out on *several thousand square miles of Soulan soil*!" Memmnon's voice rose steadily as he spoke. "Prime growing areas for that matter. Every day they sit there is another day lost to growing season on some of the best producing lands in our kingdom. And that leaves aside the loss we've already suffered in livestock that was left behind to feed the damn Norlanders!"

Memmnon worked to calm himself, suddenly aware of how loud his voice had become. He looked around him carefully, ensuring that no one had heard him speak.

"Look at you," Sherron hissed when she saw his actions. "Lurking and spying to see if anyone can hear us talk about the fact that Therron is the one who should be making these decisions and not you!"

"I'm not making any decisions, you ignorant twit!" Memmnon snapped back, no longer concerned with preventing a scene. "The *King* is giving the orders you ignorant child, not me. If not for his leadership we'd already be Nor slaves! If we lived at all, of course," he added. "You'd make a *fine* prize for some Norlander's harem, would you not? 'Daughter of the last King of Soulan!'" Memmnon's voice rose as if introducing a dignitary entering a ball room. "Yes, that would be quite the fashion accessory in Norland, Sherron! Assuming he didn't just keep you locked away for his own use, or to share with others on special occasions!" Memmnon stopped again, working to calm himself.

"You are as deluded as Therron was," he added quietly. "At least you aren't in a position to ruin the kingdom with your rabid ignorance. I tire of this fencing match, sister." With that he wheeled on his heels and started for his own apartments, tired from more than just arguing with his ridiculous sister, or a day of labor.

"You'll *rue* the day you betrayed Therron!" he heard his sister almost screech behind him. Appropriate considering, he decided. She was as hateful as a banshee for certain.

"You'll see, Memmnon!" Sherron's voice was louder now as Memmnon drew away from her. "Therron is the heir we need for Soulan's future! He will be seated upon that throne and *not you!*"

He can have it, Memmnon didn't bother saying aloud. At the moment, having his own small ranch of horses and a few fat cows looked very appealing to the Crown Prince of Soulan.

Very appealing.

-

"I must say, I do find them women very appealing," Ezekiel Watts murmured, almost as if afraid of being overheard speaking well of Rosa's 'girls'.

Aaron Bell gave a short chuckle, shaking his head at Watts' reluctance. In the two weeks since the Tinker and his entourage had taken over the Hogshead Inn, business had been brisk to say the least, and Rosa's girls weren't the only reason, or even the main reason. Only a very few got to spend time with any of the women.

The majority of the customers were soldiers and townsfolk who came to drink and eat, both pursuits were hard to come by in a town beset by one army and threatened by another. Where the Tinker came from was still a mystery to all but his most trusted associates. Of which, Watts was not a member.

"What?" Watts looked at Bell.

"You're the only man in this town who'd look at them beauties and say they were 'very appealing' as if he were ashamed to be heard saying it," Bell laughed softly. "Go ahead and admit it, Zeke, you like havin' 'em around."

"Never said I didn't," Watts sniffed loftily, adjusting his belt as he stood straighter. "Said I wasn't no flesh peddler, that's all. Don't mean I can't appreciate a fine lookin' woman as much as the next man."

"It's not like we're a brothel, Zeke," Bell rolled his eyes. If Watts knew what was really happening he'd likely be more approving, but that was something no one could be trusted with who wasn't a part of it. One slip was all it would take to ruin the entire operation.

"We're closin' fair to it," Watts replied, though without heat. "It just don't set well, with me, that's all," he continued after a moment. "Women ain't things, boy. They deserve better, that's all." The older man was clearly bothered by the situation.

"They're treated better than most women anywhere," Bell pointed out. "Safer than in their mother's arms, they are, and you know it for a fact, seein' as you're part o' that. And, if it makes you feel better, I agree with you. Thing is," Bell leaned in, lowering his voice, "this is what they know, that's all. You see how some of the town folk look down on the women who just work here in the Inn. They're looked down on because of some kinda hate ag'in their blood. Those girls are as fine a bunch o' women as I've known, but they won't never get any real respect cause of who they are."

"So, they choose to profit off that hate," he shrugged, straightening out.

"They make hypocritical bastards that wouldn't be seen with 'em in public for no 'mount o' money pay handsome like just to be in their company in private. Use that hate and hypocrisy against 'em. That's all."

Watts eyes shown with new understanding as Bell finished speaking, nodding slightly more to himself than Bell.

"Hadn't thought along them lines," he admitted. "I ain't never been one to hate on folks cause o' who they are. Guess since I don't do it, didn't think on others doin' it neither."

"It's hard to stomach," Bell nodded. "Makes me want to punch some of these sons flat, it does, but . . . ain't mine to do or to make decisions for them, either. They live their life by their rules, that's all."

"Can't blame no one for that," Watts agreed. "I appreciate the education, youngster," he said with a slight grin. "Reckon I can learn a bit now and again, provided you use a big enough hammer on me head."

"You're not so bad," Bell replied. "And it speaks right well of you that you don't think along them lines yourself, you know? It ain't no bad thing not to be familiar with that kind of thinking, so far as I'm concerned."

"I appreciate that too," Watts chuckled. "Well, reckon I better get out there and check on the brew. We'll be getting busy soon."

"Imagine we will," Bell noted the sun sinking. "Guess I better get busy myself. Tinker ain't prone to look kindly on slackers."

"That's a hard man right there, too," Watts nodded. "Good one, I'd wager, though I ain't known him long. But there's a hardness to him a man would be smart not to go testin'."

"You said a mouthful there, brother," Bell agreed completely.

-

"Your license is in order it appears," the Provost officer said, returning the Tinker's paper with a seeming reluctance. "Mind you stay on your manners. Never have cared for your kind," he added darkly.

"My kind?" Tinker raised an elegant eyebrow in reply. "By that I assume you mean a man who is willing to work for a living? Do manual labor or trade his services to others as a means of supporting himself and his family? That kind?"

"You watch your mouth, vagabond," the officer almost snarled. "I won't have none of your back talk, you hear?"

"Oh, I hear you, officer," Tinker replied in kind. "And by the end of the day every soldier I've helped with any problems will know it as well," he smiled thinly. "As will the officers who use my services or visit my Inn. One of whom I believe is your immediate superior? No, I think he is actually your superior's superior." He paused, allowing the threat to hang between them. The officer tried to maintain his stance, but the threat of his commander, let alone the General, was a bit too much to ignore.

"Now you're threatening a member of the Provost?" he blustered.

"I've made no threat of any kind," Tinker was instantly back to the affable vendor he normally portrayed. "Merely pointed out that I heard you, and well enough to repeat it. You asked a question and I answered."

"Is there a problem here?" a new voice entered the conversation. The provost officer turned rather quickly to see a man behind him in officer livery.

"Just doing my inspections, Brigadier," the provost informed the cavalry officer. The man was dirty faced, carrying a saddle that was trailing a broken cinch strap.

"Are they finished?" the man said testily, shifting the obviously heavy saddle in his grip. "Some of us have need of this man's services. Rather urgently," he added pointedly.

"All finished, sir," the inspector nodded hastily. "I'll just be on my way." With a last glance at the Tinker, the inspector scuttled away.

"Revolting creature," the young officer said darkly.

"I'm sorry for the inconvenience, sir," Tinker smiled, taking the saddle himself and placing in a wooden horse. "I was trying to assure him that his threats were understood."

"Threats?" an elegant though dirty eyebrow rose. "What bloody threats?"

"I'm afraid that my ancestry is an offense to the inspector, sir," Tinker replied calmly.

"What kind of rubbish is that?" The man demanded. "This isn't Norland! See here, Tinker. Can you repair that strap for me?"

"Of course, sir," Tinker nodded at once. "Perhaps an hour? Maybe a little more."

"Perfect," the young commander nodded. "Meanwhile we'll just see about this ancestry business," he growled darkly. "And if that creature bothers you again, I want to know it at once, you hear?"

"I do sir," Tinker bowed slightly. "I will do as you say."

"I'm not giving orders to you, Tinker," the man's tone softened. "But by the Crown, I'll not see that kind of talk in this camp so long as it comes from below my rank. There's no place in Soulan for that kind of silliness in peace time, let alone with an enemy at the bloody door!"

"I did not take it that way, General, I assure you," Tinker soothed the ruffled young man. "I appreciate your kindness."

"Well, you work on that saddle while I work on this other matter," the man ordered. "I'll be back."

"Of course, General," Tinker smiled brightly. "I'll get right on it."

Tinker whistled slightly to himself as the brigade commander stomped off to 'deal' with something that had offended him almost personally.

-

Buford Beaumont sat his horse just inside the tree line atop a ridge far to the north of where the Soulan Army now sat blocking the Imperial invaders. His glass in hand, he surveyed the area below with a patient eye, taking in details that would be important later on.

"What's doing, Buford?" Horace Whipple asked as he rode up, reining his horse in beside the other man.

"Just havin' a look," Beaumont replied, lowering his glass. "There's a station of some kind down there," he pointed, passing his glass to Whipple. "Have a look. There's at least four dozen horses there, probably more I can't see, and a good company of men. I see smoke that's likely from a forge, too. I think this is a way station of sorts for the Nor supply line. Replace lame horses, repairs to wagons and shoe draft animals and what have you."

"Agreed," Whipple nodded after a moment, returning the glass. "Many of them are in uniform and appear to be standing post, too."

"Where?" Beaumont asked, having overlooked that. He followed Whipple's point and raised the glass once more. Sure enough he spotted a picket post. Then another. Having an idea of where to look now, Beaumont soon had nearly two dozen pickets spotted and a squad of videttes patrolling around the site between the picket posts.

"Not enough to stop us if we attack," Beaumont declared. "Things is, do we strike now, or try to wait a day or so and see if we can catch a supply train here first?"

"We've no idea of their movements," Whipple mused, considering the question. "We could leave a squad here to monitor the post, keep a record of trains through here which would give us an idea of how often they send them, how large they are and how well guarded."

"And we do what in the meantime?" Beaumont asked, frowning.

"Well, we can loop well around to the north and watch the trail," Whipple offered. "We might catch a supply train on the trail and take it."

"Wouldn't that make leaving an observation post here nil?" Beaumont asked, considering the suggestion. "Once we strike, they're like as not going to change the route or add more security."

"I've considered that and have an idea. It's a bit risky I suppose, but everything we do is a risk at the moment, wouldn't you agree?" Beaumont nodded.

"We would do well not to advertise our strength at first," Whipple continued. "I suggest we use company and regimental attacks, always just large enough to get the job done and then leave survivors to tell the tale. That might make their leaders suspect that we're nothing more than a guerrilla band roaming the backwoods."

"Survivors are apt to just increase the numbers to make themselves look better," Beaumont shrugged.

"We leave civilian survivors," Whipple countered. "Drivers, drovers, things of that nature. Kill any soldiers we find, but tell the civilian 'survivors' that we don't make war on civilians. Let them get a good look at the company or battalion that attacked so they know how many there are. Some of them will be able to tell it factual. And be more inclined to do so if we show them mercy."

"We're committed to the Black Flag," Beaumont reminded him.

"I didn't say we make it a policy," Whipple's grin was cold. "Just for a while. Just to spread the word. They won't stop driving if they think all they have to do is surrender and we'll spare them. We can probably take a lot of the wagons intact. Make use of whatever we can, then hide or destroy the rest. If we can find a safe place to stash them, we can take them with us when we head back for refit and to leave our injured."

Beaumont considered that for a minute. It was a good plan and he liked the idea of taking plunder back to their own lines. Anything they could manage to get to their own lines would likely be a help somewhere along the line.

"Poll the division," he ordered finally. "Find those with experience handling cattle and horse herds and any teamster experience. We'll ask Mister Parsons' men if they can locate a suitable place to hide any plunder until we're ready to make use of it or head back. While you do that, I'll take one battalion and raid this place," he pointed to the station below. "We'll use your plan there as well. Anyone not fighting and not in uniform will be spared to spread the word."

"Might want to ditch the coats at least for this first one," Whipple nodded to Beaumont's uniform. "Let them think we're brigands to start. That will explain why we're taking the wagons and whatever else we can. We're thieves taking advantage of the situation," he smiled coldly. "As the word of our numbers increase, the number of troops they have to commit to protecting their supply trains will increase as well. As they do, we simply use more of the men and continue inflicting casualties on the enemy. They'll bring themselves right to us instead of our having to constantly be on the move looking for them."

"You are one devious son-of-a-bitch, Horace, you know that?" Beaumont grinned in return. "Makes me proud to know you!"

"Likewise."

****

Abel Chambers was not by nature a patient or forgiving man. Raised in the northwestern reaches of the Empire, he was as hard as the woods and the winters of Lakeland could make a man. He was quick to anger, and to strike, always boasting of his prowess and his ability to 'take any son among ya!' to those who worked under him.

Running Farrier Station Eleven was a demanding job, but Chambers figured he was just the man for the job. He got the maximum amount of work out of the dregs he'd been given to work with, and managed to keep trains moving along by having horses always ready to replace lame or exhausted animals and then returning the animals left in his care to health as soon as possible.

When there was nothing else to do, he kept the company at work making stores of supplies and parts that they used most so that repairs would be quicker and easier when damaged wagons rolled in. Transoms, axles, trace chains, anything that could break and hinder a wagon on a train, you would find a replacement quick and clean here at Station Eleven. No problem.

He had been fortunate in having a good team of smiths assigned to his farrier company, men who knew their business and had no need of supervision from him. He was careful not to antagonize them as he did his common laborers, either. While he was himself a hard and strong man of the north lands, a man who swung a hammer all day soon built muscles that were as hard as the iron he molded in his forge and on his anvil. Chambers had no interest in seeing if he could best one of them the same way he rolled the hostlers and wranglers that worked for him. The smiths didn't need any encouragement from him to do their jobs, anyway.

He was expecting a new train through anytime, tomorrow most likely, the next day for sure, and he wanted to be ready for it. He already had several draft horses rounded up out of their pasture area, ready to replace any horses that were going lame or showing signs of exhaustion. There were some harsh standing orders about maltreatment of horses in the Imperial Army, and the punishment was carried out on the spot in many cases. One General had made the flat statement that he had plenty of soldiers but not nearly enough horses. The implication being that the life of a soldier being forfeit for damaging an animal beyond use was perfectly acceptable to him.

Chambers didn't necessarily agree with that, but he liked his head right where it was, a resting place for his hat. Thus, he ensured that all horses under his care were well seen after, and any that came to him suffering from neglect were recorded in his ledger as such, along with their treatments and recovery record. Chambers had no intention of suffering for some other man's inability to follow orders.

In keeping with his intention to run the best station in the Army, Chambers was currently plodding his way out to the corral where the best horses on hand were already contained, awaiting any need that might present itself with the next train.

"Morning, sir," the young wrangler at the gate nodded.

"Yeah," Chambers growled back. "What's the count?" he demanded without fanfare.

"Forty-two, sir," came the reply. "All fit for service, soon as-."

"You just let me decide that," Chambers shot back, cutting the younger man off short. "You lot wouldn't know a decent horse from a livery plug, anyhow."

The young man nodded but made no verbal reply, accustomed by now to Chambers' attitude toward his subordinates. The wrangler was one of the rare northerners to grow up around horses, thus having the all too seldom found knowledge of equine matters that the Imperial Army so valued in its new incarnation. Still, he knew that Chambers would not be happy unless he looked the herd over himself, likely finding some flaw or other, more imagined than not, for which to castigate his men for.

"Look at this," Chambers confirmed less than a minute later, holding a draft horse's hind right foot up, exposing a hoof and shoe that needed a nail. "You call this ready for service?" he demanded.

"We're taking all of them out at a time and checking them, sir," the wrangler promised. "He's already been inspected. See that chalk on his flank?" he pointed. "That tells the smith's apprentice that he needs shoeing. They're taking them in turn, now. We're already set their hooves to right and made 'em ready to help speed the process."

Chambers eyed the chalk mark with a surly and jaundiced eye, trying to find something wrong with the man's report but failing. Dropping the leg with a huff he continued his inspection. He was about half way through when he heard a shout from somewhere front of the station proper.

"What's that idiot saying?" he demanded over his shoulder, not bothering to look around.

"We're under attack!" the wrangler shouted back, running for cover. "Picket posts are being attacked!"

"What? Ridiculous!" Chambers replied, releasing a horse he'd been checking and storming his way out of the herd back toward the gate. He could hear shouting and sounds of a fight and assumed that some of the soldiers left here for security were into a brawl. Well, that Lieutenant that was in charge would have to sort that out. His men, his mess; that was the rule that Chambers lived by when dealing with the Army.

As he cleared the gate however, he realized that the 'idiot' soldiers were, indeed, under attack. Under attack and falling like flies for that matter.

"Alarm!" he shouted, despite his surprise. "Sound the bell!" he yelled toward the smith at the forge. The large man instantly began hitting the iron bell with his hammer, the ringing reverberating across the small valley.

Off duty soldiers came running from their own barracks, hastily throwing on coats and equipment to answer what they assumed was a drill. The Lieutenant was a stickler for that kind of thing, damn his ambitious little heart.

Most of them died still thinking it was a drill, Soulanie arrows buried in their chests as they struggled to get their equipment on and shake off the sleep they had been enjoying only a minute before.

Chambers watched as the last of the soldiers set to guard his outpost fell, mouth agape as he watched a gaggle of ill-dressed horseman converge on his station.

"You aim to give us any trouble?" a large man in the front of the crowd asked Chambers, studying the civilians carefully. "We don't aim to kill no civilians we don't got to, but won't hesitate to do it you get in the way," he warned.

"Who the hell are you!?" Chambers found his voice. "This is an Imperial

Army way station! You're messing with the Imperial Army here, boy!"

"Boy, is it?" the large man's eyebrows rose at that. "And we know who you are. Why the hell you think we're here? Figure you got food, horses, maybe even money here. We aim to help ourselves to it since you being here has put a crimp in our normal activities. Boys, search the buildings, round up everyone still standing and bring 'em out here. Clem, you and your boys start movin' 'em horses, hear?"

"Yes, boss," several voices replied in unison.

"These horses belong to the Imperial Army!" Chambers stood his ground.

"Not no more they don't," the big man laughed. "Get out that way while you can old man."

"Old man, is it?" Chambers roared. "I'll beat the tarnation from you, you southern scum!"

All pretense at friendliness left the large man at that. The smile and laughing disappeared, replaced with an icy stare. He dismounted suddenly, tossing his reins to a man next to him and moving to stand face to face with Chambers.

"Southern scum?" the man's eyes were almost glowing. "Did I hear that right, you northern pig peeler?" Pig peeler was a polite way, sort of, of saying that Chambers had intimate relations with pigs. His face went red with rage.

"I'll-"

Whatever he intended to threaten never got said as the large man drew his sword in a swift move that saw the blade rip upwards, slicing Chambers open from his belt to his chin. Eyes wide with surprise, the surly station manager slowly fell backward into the dust, his blood creating a red stained mud beside him.

Cleaning his blade on the dead manager's pants leg, the large man turned to see the now fully assembled staff of the way station looking at him in horror.

"Now. Any o' *you* want to call me southern scum?"

Nope. No sir. No one wanted to offer anything like that.

"Good," he nodded firmly. "Now you bunch behave for a few minutes and we'll leave you unharmed and hale. Bother me, just one o' ya, and I'll kill tha bunch. Got it?"

Every head nodded in silent unison. The big man had to turn back to his horse quickly to hide his grin at the comical look the men presented. His temper had gotten the better of him for a minute causing the scene with the loudmouth, but he was back in control, now. He mounted his horse again, taking his reins back.

"Which one o' ya 's in charge?" he demanded.

"Uh, he was, sir," a tall, thin young man declared, pointing to the man the bandit had just gutted.

"Figures," the big man sighed. "He have a second?"

"The Lieutenant," the young man replied, pointing to a now very dead Imperial officer some yards away.

"Well, anyways," the leader sighed again. "We'll be takin' them horses, that wee herd o' cattle and any useables we might find and then burn them buildin's," he declared. "Reckon you want to get your possibles, you better hurry. Mind you, any one o' ya shows with a weapon drawn, we'll kill the lot o' ya, so bear that in mind."

The civilians counted themselves lucky to be granted such favor and hurried to get their things. In two minutes they were back, assembled in a rough formation.

"Box o' hardtack," the large man said, pointing to a wooden box his men had thrown out as they passed. "Better make it last, I reckon. Long walk north. Don't know how far to the next station."

"Fifteen miles," one hapless apprentice offered, then swore under his breath.

"Thanks for that," the man grinned. "Well, we thank you, gents, for increasing our worth this fine day. Have a good walk. Don't come back to our neck o' the woods, hear?" With that he put spurs to his horse and headed back toward the heavily forested hills, his men following as they drove the liberated horses and cattle on the hoof.

Once the raiders were gone, the wrangler let out a long breath, glad to be alive.

"Reckon I'll head north, boys," he said at last and started that way, stopping only to fill the two canteens he carried around his neck and then drink his fill. Slowly the others fell in behind him, repeating his actions and then following him up the road.

North toward home.

-

"I enjoyed that entirely too much," Beaumont said as he galloped away, speaking to no one in particular.

"We noticed, sir," a captain behind him laughed. "Really got into the roll, too."

"Always wanted to be an actor!" Beaumont howled. "Let's get this plunder put away and head out. I think I'm gonna enjoy this job, boys! Yessir, I believe I am indeed gonna have a fine old time of it back here."

Behind him several of his men exchanged glances but said nothing, knowing that when Beaumont was having one of his 'fine old times' there was nothing to be done but hold on and endure.

And survive, if possible.

CHAPTER SIXTEEN

-

"Are you planning to visit home while we're here, Parno?" Karls asked over breakfast.

"I'd like to, but we'll have to wait and see what happens," Parno nodded. "Right now, I'm hoping to hear from Admiral Semmes sooner rather than later. I can't really do anything until I know that we aren't facing an invasion somewhere along our seaboard."

"How likely do you think that is?" Karls asked. "They're arrayed a lot of men against us already."

"True, but they have a much larger population than we do as well," Parno sighed. "If Semmes can determine those ships are empty, or better yet defeat the Nor fleet in battle, then our options are much better."

"Good morning, brother," Memmnon said as he entered the small dining area. "I trust all of you slept well?"

"Good morning, Memmnon," Parno nodded. "Can't speak for everyone else, but I slept like a rock." The others nodded agreement as they continued to eat.

"When you are finished, please come to my office," Memmnon said evenly. "There is something I need to discus with you. Something of a. . .private, nature," he added.

-

"I already know she hates me, Memmnon," Parno shrugged when his brother finished telling him of the confrontation with their sister the evening before.

"It's beyond hate, Parno. For you, for me, or for father." The Crown Prince sat back, releasing a long breath. "She's unstable."

"I've no doubt," Parno replied dryly. "I still can't see where this is an issue. For me, anyway."

"She's determined to seek revenge I believe," Memmnon told him flatly. "She was obviously privy to Therron's plans, as she practically accused me of fearing him. And said we all know that he deserves to sit upon the throne rather than myself."

"Why would anyone want to?" Parno asked. "No offense, brother," he added.

"None taken, I assure you," Memmnon snorted lightly. "Believe me, I've had the same thought myself. At least once a day, and that's on the good days. But Therron intended to take the throne, by force if necessary. By the way, your findings in Bingham last year?" Parno nodded, remembering. "Well, it was my constables that unearthed a part of that plot, as then Governor Keen was in it up to his eyeballs. It's my belief that allowing that strife to build was one of the tools Therron intended to use to turn any supporters against the King, if it was needed. He spent a lot of time working on this plot of his, Parno. Even now we've no idea how deep into the kingdom his rot has spread."

"I've had that thought where the Army is concerned," Parno nodded. "I've taken steps already to find out and cut that rot out wherever I find it. I can't really help you with respect to the rest of the kingdom," he added apologetically.

"Nor should you be forced to," Memmnon nodded. "That is for me to see to. You have enough to worry about as it is. I tell you this merely to let you know that even in his absence, Therron's plot may be alive and well in the form of idiots like our sister."

"Surely there isn't much she can do, is there?" Parno asked.

-

Sherron McLeod was unaware that her brothers were discussing her at the moment and would likely not have cared if she were. At that very moment she was making her own plans to right the wrong that had been done to her beloved Therron.

Sherron's mental illness was something that was closely guarded. She knew that her way of thinking would be frowned upon at best by the Royal physicians, and likely result in her being 'put away', as the polite way of phrasing it went. She had no desire to be locked in a cage, gilded or otherwise, and had been careful all of her life to guard against anyone knowing her true self or her innermost thoughts.

She had fully supported Therron in his bid for rule, having planted the bug in his ear herself some years ago. She and Therron were very close as twins, though much closer, perhaps, than anyone knew. As the 'girl' of the line, she was mostly ignored. With three sons, even if one of them were Parno, the odds of her ever ascending to the throne were nil. There had been female rulers in Soulan, of course, but they were rare in the extreme. Most kings through the ages had produced at least one male heir, even if by adultery. In the world she found herself living in, even a bastard son was deemed more worthy to occupy the throne than Sherron would be. This in spite of what she herself considered to be a superior intellect compared to most of the men around her.

She was about to prove that one way or the other she knew.

"Do you understand my instructions?" she demanded. The man before her had been a loyal retainer of her brother Therron, and herself, since birth.

"I do, milady," he bowed slightly. "I shall place it in his hands myself."

"Good," Sherron nodded firmly. "The seal should eliminate any interference as well as prevent others from hindering your way. Have you any questions?"

"No, milady."

"Then go and let nothing stop you!"

The man mounted the horse behind him, one of the best in the Royal Stables, and was soon galloping away at a good clip. Not so fast as to arouse suspicion but fast enough to carry him out of the city quickly.

Sherron watched until the man was gone, then departed. She had other preparations to see to.

She had worked too hard for too long to see her dream cast aside so casually. She would find her brother and return him to his rightful place. Therron would be King of Soulan, she promised herself.

And she would be his Queen.

-

Even as Sherron's rider was departing, another was entering the Royal City, his horse exhausted as he himself nearly was. Around his shoulder was the strap of a courier bag. His horse carried nothing else. The courier dropped to his feet, nearly stumbling before the Sergeant of the Guard caught him.

"Thanks," the man mumbled. "I've an urgent dispatch meant for Marshal Parno," he told the sergeant. "I need to have it relayed on to him at once."

"No need," the sergeant told him. "Lord Parno is here in Nasil, has been since last evening. Come on, I'll get you to him."

The courier straightened, following the sergeant on legs that didn't really want to carry him. His mission was almost completed, however. Soon he could rest.

"Please take care o' my horse," he asked the guards behind.

"We'll see to him," one promised, already leading the weary animal away. "No worries."

-

"My Lords, there is a courier here with an urgent dispatch for Lord

Marshal Parno."

The two brothers had barely finished their discussion of Sherron's mental illness and consideration of what she might be able to accomplish. Both looked up at the steward's interruption.

"Show him in," Memmnon ordered at once. Parno stood, taking the bag from the exhausted man at once.

"What can you tell me?" he asked.

"Dispatch from the Fleet, milord," the man said tiredly. "Sent by courier from the fleet while they was still engaged. Like as not be a full report behind me somewhere, but this, whatever it is, was deemed urgent enough to send alone."

"Very well," Parno nodded, opening the bag. "Get him something to eat, a chance to clean up and a comfortable place to sleep. He's excused duty for the next thirty-six hours."

"Thank you milords," the man bowed as the Steward all but drug him from the office. Parno ignored it, opening the single note inside and reading quickly.

"Message relayed by flag from Semmes, repeated by all ships in view," he read aloud. "Enemy troopships empty. Repeat, enemy troopships are empty. Fleet still heavily engaged. Message ends." Parno lowered the letter, passing it along to Memmnon with a sigh of relief.

"There is no invasion force," he said at last. "Please excuse me, brother. I have messages of my own to send."

-

"Three messages to each man, understand?" Parno ordered. Sprigs nodded as he finished writing the orders for the two southern corps of the Army.

"Aye, milord. They'll be on their way shortly," the secretary promised. "Best horses available."

"Good. Nothing is to stop them."

Sprigs nodded again as he ran to secure horses and couriers for his Lord Marshal's message. Parno turned to find Cho Feng standing behind him.

"Master Feng."

"My Lord," Feng nodded in reply.

"What is it?" Parno sighed, resisting the urge to shake his head.

"What do you mean?"

"You only call me 'My Lord' these days when you think I'm making a mistake."

"Not so, Parno," Feng shook his head. "You are the Lord Marshal. It is appropriate to address you as such."

Parno eyed the small oriental with suspicion for a moment, as if waiting for the punch line. When Feng's facial expression did not change, he accepted it and went on.

"We may ride for Cove in the morning," he said. "We'll see to Master

Finn first of all. Perhaps he will have good news for us. Perhaps very good, even."

"That is possible," Feng nodded. "If he has been successful then his work may well be that which we need to turn the tide."

"That and two new corps from the south," Parno nodded, walking back toward the palace. "With them, I can return Raines' men to him and still have sufficient forces to handle what's before Davies. Especially with anything that Roda has managed to put together."

"Then what is it that bothers you, young Prince?" Feng asked.

"There are many things that bother me," Parno answered evasively.

"Yet there is perhaps one thing that bothers you most?"

"No, they pretty much bother me in equal measure," Parno admitted with a heavy sigh. "I'm taking a great risk in bringing the others north. Especially not having heard yet from Semmes about the aftermath of the battle. Then there is still the risk that the enemy across the bridge at Shelby will actually mount an attack while I have the bulk of our army gathered north. There is also the possibility that our attack against the northern force will not succeed, leaving us at best in a bloody stalemate, and at worst completely defeated."

"Assuming we are victorious there, and can drive the Imperial Army out of our lands, then there remains the prospect of their western army invading to take the pressure off their retreating northern force. Add to that my plan to strike north at some point in the future. And, finally," he paused, drawing a deep breath and looking around him. Feng waited.

"Finally," Parno continued after a moment, "there is my brother, Therron, and his twin, our sister Sherron." He looked at Feng.

"My sister is quite probably mad. Therron may be as well. He is certainly convinced of his superiority to the rest of us. Certain of his right, not to mention his fitness, to rule. My father's decision to banish him may backfire, Master Feng. I only hope it does not cost us dearly."

"This isn't your responsibility, Parno," Feng reminded him softly.

"No, but someone will have to pick up the pieces and you can bet I'll wind up being that someone."

-

"I cannot possibly allow both of you in here at the same time."

Roda Finn was standing in front of his Foundry, thin arms folded across his chest. Memmnon and Parno, flanked by their retainers, stood in front of him, their way inside blocked.

"We merely wish to see your works Master Finn," Memmnon said reasonably. "No one expects you to be ready for some kind of inspection, I assure you."

"I am not concerned with inspections," Finn rolled his eyes. "Lord Parno, you know how volatile my creations are. Allowing the both of you inside where a catastrophe could occur at literally any minute is tantamount to treason!"

The brothers exchanged a glance, Parno looking chagrined at the reminder.

"He's right, Memmnon," Parno nodded. "I should have thought of it myself. It would be very irresponsible for the two of us to be here at the same time."

"It is that dangerous?" Memmnon asked, clearly skeptical.

"Very much so," Parno nodded. "You should return home, brother. I'm sure that Master Finn will be glad to entertain you at another time. Perhaps arrange your visit for a time when the Foundry is inactive?" he added with a glance at Finn.

"That would be for the best," Finn acknowledged. "And I would be happy to do so at the first opportunity."

"Very well," Memmnon sighed. "I still do not see why all this is necessary," he added.

"I will prepare a demonstration for you when you visit, milord," Finn promised. "When you see it, you will know that our caution was deserved."

Memmnon departed, his guard surrounding him as he traveled back to the palace. Parno turned again to face his 'wizard'.

"Please tell me you have some good news, Roda?"

-

"We already have several thousand of the Hubel Arrows either finished or laid out for completion," Finn pointed to a small assembly line as he escorted Parno and his retinue through his small kingdom. "As soon as we have a sufficiency for battle we can begin sending them north."

"Keep stockpiling them for now," Parno ordered. "I'll send someone to secure a holding facility between here and the army where they can be stockpiled. What about other. . .ordnance, wasn't it?"

"Yes, milord," Finn was noticeably pleased at Parno's recollection of the term. "We have begun casting the rounds for our catapults and trebuchets, and our laboratory is producing the solution that makes them explode. Small amounts for now, similar to what we were able to accomplish at Cove, but we are increasing production every day. We will begin seeing substantial quantities in another fortnight or so. We will repeat our transportation method from Cove and ship the rounds and the solution separately. For safety."

"I assume you're training crews to safely assemble the components once they reach the front?" Parno asked with a raised eyebrow.

"You may safely make that assumption," Finn nodded. "Also were are working with a team of veterans from the battle at the Gap who are not yet well enough to return to full duty. They in turn are training men to safely handle the ordnance and employ it in battle. We do not have as much time as we did at Cove, but we know more than we did then so it balances out."

"We hope," Parno snorted.

"Fervently," Finn replied. "I believe we should have enough ready ordnance for a protracted battle within a month, though it will take another ten days or so to get everything safely in place. Your acquiring a safe staging area might cut down on that time considerably, however. We would be replacing spent ordnance as you used it, keeping the supply up as high as possible."

"I will not be ready to act for at least a month," Parno admitted. "It would be well to have some of your gadgets on hand in the event of a full-fledged attack on our northern positions, or the western emplacements at Shelby for that matter, but I'm doing all I can to buy time for that to happen."

"We will not let you down, milord," Finn promised. He almost said something else, but withheld it at the last second, not wanting to promise something he might not be able to deliver.

"You've done well, Roda," Parno said quietly as the tour ended. "I'm in your debt."

"Hardly, milord," the fussy little man waved the comment away. "I am in yours. And Soulan is my home as well."

-

"It appears that things are going well," Feng remarked as they returned to Nasil proper.

"Looks that way," Parno agreed with an absent nod.

"If we can make another month, or better another six weeks, we'll have a marked advantage," Karls said.

"We'll have the start of an advantage," Parno corrected.

"Agreed," Enri nodded. "It's fine to think of our advances as helpful, but we cannot expect the enemy to do things as we want. No plan survives contact with the enemy." He sounded like a lecturer at the War College.

"So it doesn't," Parno nodded. "Until Soulan soil is free of Imperial presence, we'll assume only that we're losing. If we're preparing for the worst, expecting the worst, then we won't be surprised when it happens."

"Well said."

-

"I've sent two men north to secure a forward staging area for Roda's gadgetry," Parno informed his brother that evening. "He's beginning to build up an inventory so I want it out and gone as he does. It will also make resupply easier to have a forward supply area. Not to mention making Nasil safer by not having so many of his. . .creations, in the city," he added.

"I still find it difficult to credit all these precautions," Memmnon looked skeptical.

"Once you see the demonstrations, you won't," Parno promised. "His work can literally change the course of the war. Change how we fight in the future for that matter. You should send for him sometime when he is not busy and allow him to speak to you of what he has discovered. He cannot reproduce even a tithing of it, but even that tithing is. . .substantial."

"Very well," Memmnon nodded. "You are off tomorrow?" he changed the subject.

"I am," Parno nodded. "We're heading to Cove for a few days, then back to 1st Army headquarters. I'm expecting it to take at least a month, perhaps as much as six weeks for 4th and 5th Corps to make it there. I've ordered each man to detach his absolute best militia units to remain in the area, patrolling and garrisoning vital outposts. I won't leave the area completely uncovered."

"Good," Memmnon nodded. "Father would like to see you before you go," he changed the subject again and Parno stiffened. Despite a reasonably good relationship with his eldest brother, Parno was not of a forgiving nature. He held both of them at least partly responsible for what had happened to Darvo Nidiad. And he still blamed Memmnon for not supporting him when Therron had lied to the King about him and his troopers.

"What does he want?" Parno tried to keep his voice neutral.

"He wants to visit with his son," Memmnon said evenly, careful to maintain eye contact with his younger brother. "He is not well," Memmnon added with a slight shrug.

"I know this," Parno nodded curtly. "Does he think to make up for a lifetime of maltreatment now that he might be dying? Do you, for that matter?" he challenged suddenly. Memmnon's face reddened slightly but he accepted the barb as a fair shot.

"I can never make up what I've done and said to you," he told Parno flatly. "I will not insult you with the effort. All I can do is treat you better now, and try to build a better relationship with you as adults than I bothered with as children. I can do no more. Nor can I ever undo the damage I have done prior. One must accept his limitations and work with what he has."

"You're telling me that he actually desires my company?" Parno's expression couldn't have been more bewildered if Memmnon had suddenly told him that he would have to assume the crown himself.

"Yes, he does," Memmnon said, nodding. "If you can spare it."

"Well, since he always had time for me," Parno's sarcasm was thick, "I suppose the least I can do is return that favor, isn't it?"

-

Parno entered his father's apartments after the evening meal, actually surprised that his father had not dined with them. When he thought about it, he realized that Tammon McLeod had been absent completely from all meetings, most unlike him.

"Prince McLeod," Physician Smithe's voice preceded him out of the dim light of the King's apartments. His tone was not one of welcome.

"Doctor," Parno nodded. He was long passed being intimidated by anyone. Even Stephanie's old and cantankerous uncle.

"The King simply cannot entertain you this evening I'm afraid," Smithe's voice was adamant. "He must rest."

"Well, that's a problem then because he sent for me," Parno replied evenly.

"I'm sure he did," Smithe didn't bother to hide his disdain.

"I believe we may have gotten off on the wrong foot, Doctor," Parno said gently. "I no longer bow and scrape to you and the others of this household. Nor will I ever do so again. So long as he lived, Darvo Nidiad did his utmost to keep me in check and prevent me from retaliating against those whose maltreatment demanded that I seek satisfaction for it." Parno paused for a moment to make sure he had Smithe's attention.

"You may recall that Darvo is no longer with us."

"Are you threatening me, Prince?" Smithe demanded.

"Yes, I am," Parno replied simply. "I couldn't care less about your opinion of me, Doctor, as I will like as not die before this war is over, so please spare me your whining as I simply do not have the time for it. Now, kindly step aside. I have no real desire to be here, but my father has asked for me and I leave with the rising of the sun tomorrow."

Smithe's mouth opened but despite motion from his lips no sound emerged. He clearly had expected the somewhat browbeaten Prince he had come to know as the King's Physician, not the man who stood before him now as Lord Marshal of the Royal Army.

"I won't ask again, Doctor," Parno kept his voice even but his eyes clearly dared Smithe to continue to challenge his right to be here. Wisely, Smithe decided not to push the issue and stepped aside. Parno walked by him without another word and entered his father's bedchamber. The sight that awaited him there shocked him.

Tammon McLeod was pale and drawn as he lay upon his bed. Despite that his eyes were clear as he saw Parno immediately and motioned for him to approach.

"Hello, my son," Tammon managed a weak smile. "It is good to see you."

"Hello, father," Parno managed to sound warm, having no wish to upset his obviously sick father. "Doctor Smithe tells me you are feeling poorly this evening," he settled for saying as he sat carefully on the side of his father's large bed.

"Yes, well, he needs me to feel poorly so he can keep a job I suppose," Tammon shot back and Parno grinned in spite of himself. "How goes it, my son?" he asked, more serious.

"We are holding our own for the moment," Parno promised him. "We've had a bit of good news today, two bits actually, with hopefully more to follow." He briefly explained the news from Semmes and from Finn, as well as his orders to bring the two southern corps northward.

"Semmes is from a good family," Tammon nodded at the report from the Admiral. "Been sailors all the way back to Tyree as I recall. I knew his father, years ago. Good man, good family."

"He seems to have done well," Parno nodded. "I have promoted General Davies and given him command of the newly formed 1st Army. His own command and 1st Corps. I did the same with Raines in Shelby, though he will have to settle for his own Corps and attachments as 2nd Army. I may form 3rd Army with the two southern corps when they arrive. I haven't decided yet."

"Herrick is a solid man, but a womanizer," Tammon warned. "He's not a bad man, but he'd tell a whore his entire battle plan if he thought it would impress her. Bear that in mind. Freeman is a solid book soldier but not inclined to think outside his manuals. He's also prone to ride the coat tails of others. That doesn't make him a bad general I guess, but it might keep him from being a great one."

"Why have such men in such important posts?" Parno asked.

"I let Therron handle those things, Parno," Tammon admitted. "I should not have, but in my defense I had no idea at that time that I had sired a snake. Two of them if my house spies do not deceive me." He gave Parno a knowing look.

"They do not," Parno confirmed. "She is an agitator and instigator. I suspect that she will continue to advocate for Therron behind the scenes so to speak. Attempt to create a crisis or even an uprising, somewhere."

"How will you deal with that, my son?" Tammon asked, not even bothering to pretend that Memmnon would be the one to confront them.

"I'll kill them," Parno shrugged. "We cannot do otherwise now, father. We stand on the cusp of ruin. To allow that kind of deceit and treachery in our ranks would be courting disaster."

"How will you know who to trust?" Tammon asked, curious.

"I already have people working to determine that," Parno said grimly. "And, if I can't decide one way or the other, I shall err on the side of caution."

"I'm truly sorry, Parno," Tammon said suddenly, his face drawn. "For so many things, but especially for placing you in such a position. You deserve better."

"Yes, I did," Parno didn't pull his punches. "That is behind us now, however. I will do as I must to contain this problem. There will be a throne in Soulan, and Memmnon will sit upon it," he all but swore. "Whatever it takes. We will not be the family that loses the crown. That day may come, but it is not now. Not us."

"I do not deserve a son such as you," Tammon smiled faintly. "I cannot tell you how proud I am of you. I know that I had no part in making you the man you are, but I am proud of you nonetheless. And I have something for you," he added, pulling the cord beside his bed. A chamberlain appeared before the cord stopped moving.

"My King?"

"Bring my valise, please, Ben," Tammon said. "I have need of it." The man disappeared back into the shadows, only to reappear within the minute, handing a leather satchel to the King before withdrawing. Tammon rummaged inside for a moment before withdrawing two pieces of parchment.

"I have done something that should have been done long ago," he admitted, looking at his youngest son. "Darvo Nidiad has been added to the peerage, posthumously," he handed the first paper to Parno. "There is a small land grant along with livestock and a stipend. He would have laughed in my face had I offered it to him," Tammon chuckled, "but I wanted Dhalia to have it. Whatever her future is will be for her to decide. She will not be forced to do anything she does not wish to."

"Thank you," Parno nodded. "I will place this in her hand myself."

"And this," Tammon lifted a second, heavier scroll, "is yours." He passed it over to his son. "You have been deeded the lands around Cove Canton. All of them. You may select any title you wish though I doubt you will be interested in one. Still, your offspring should be able to claim peerage rights, my son, since if there is still a kingdom it will be due to their father more than any other."

Parno looked at the scroll but did not open it.

"I have no desire to hold a peerage, and have no plans to raise a family," he told his father, seemingly in the verge of handing the scroll back. "Not that I do not appreciate the thought," he added, seeing the look on his father's face. "It is simply that I do not expect to live through the war. And I have no prospects with which to raise said family. No father worthy of the name would want his daughter married to me," he grinned wryly.

"I have heard that said myself," Tammon chuckled. "I think you will find that changing now days."

Parno thought of Evelyn McKenzie's efforts to keep her daughter from him at Shelby and wondered how true that was. Not that he had designs on the younger McKenzie female.

"Perhaps," he allowed with the same wry grin. It cost him nothing to appease his father in this, and it might make him feel better.

"Take it," Tammon ordered gently. "Do not assume that you will not survive, or that you will have no life outside of war. No man knows what tomorrow brings before the sun sets upon him, Parno. You are young and may have a very long life." He paused, studying his youngest son. "There was a saying that came down to us from the old world," he continued at last. "That saying was that some people walked between raindrops."

"What does that even mean?" Parno asked, grinning.

"I don't know what it originally meant," Tammon admitted. "But I always thought of it as someone who could move through the storm without suffering from it. There is no doubt that a storm is upon Soulan right now, Parno. The worst perhaps since the Burning. But do not surrender your hopes and dreams to that storm, my son. The storm may take them, that is true. But *make* it take them. Make it work for them. Don't just give them up." He looked intently at his son.

"Walk between the raindrops, Parno."

Parno considered that for a moment before nodding slowly.

"I will remember, father," he promised. "Now," he said, pulling a blanket up closer to his father's head. "You should rest. And I should get some rest as well, since I'll be riding again in the morning. When next we meet I hope to tell you that the Imperial Army is in retreat, heading to its own lands. Or better still that it lies in ashes upon our own. I'll settle for either."

"Luck in battle, my son, and fortune smile on you," Tammon said, his eyes fighting to stay awake.

"Thank you, father."

Parno waited until his father closed his eyes before leaving the bed chamber. Smithe was sitting outside, waiting.

"I intend to speak to the Prince about your threats," he said at once.

"Go right ahead," Parno shrugged. "Keep in mind that I'm the one who is safe guarding his kingdom for him right now. He may just side with me, considering that." Parno continued on his way without a backward glance for the surly old doctor.

He was sure he would get an earful from Stephanie over this, but that was fine. It might make her come to her senses.

-

The morning was clear. It was still early enough in the year that a chill permeated the air. Steam from the nostrils of hundreds of horses created a false fog around the assembled men of Parno's Company as they awaited their leader.

Parno walked out of the palace accompanied by his brother, stopping to look at his sibling in the light of the lamps at the door.

"Take care of yourself, Parno," Memmnon said quietly. "Remember that we cannot afford to lose you now."

"My loss will not make or break the kingdom, Memmnon. That much I know if nothing more." Parno's grin was almost infectious.

"Do not sell yourself short, brother," Memmnon refused to be humored. "You have produced our only victories to date. Whatever else you may or may not be, you are a leader. One we desperately need right now."

"I'll keep that in mind," Parno nodded. "We'll stay in Cove a few days, see that things are going well, then return to Davies' Headquarters. Herrick and Freeman should be arriving soon after I hope. Watch yourself with Sherron. She would put a knife in your ribs if the chance presented itself."

"You know, I think she might," Memmnon said seriously. "But she would bury it in your head," he grinned.

"Without hesitation," Parno agreed. "Farewell for now, brother," Parno shook hands with his brother. Memmnon almost tried to embrace him, but thought better of it. Instead he merely placed a hand on his brother's shoulder and squeezed gently.

Parno swung easily into the saddle, taking the reins from his enlisted runner.

"Karls, are we ready?" he asked.

"That we are, milord," Karls replied as always.

"Then let's ride."

CHAPTER SEVENTEEN

-

The ride to Cove took two hard days. Normally it would take three, but the column was eager to reach home and pushed as much as their horses would bear. As a result, it was a weary column of men who straggled into Cove Canton late into the night. Their arrival created something of a stir among the camp, initially among the guard and then among the soldiers there for training, and finally among the families awakened by the noise.

Family members streamed out of their houses in hastily donned clothing to welcome home husbands, sons, brothers and friends. Lt. Colonel Dory Leman, formerly the commander of the 8th Tinsee Mounted Infantry, was now the commander of Cove Canton, what remained of his unit having been absorbed into Chad's command. His lesser wounded men were now part of the staff at Cove Canton and would, when recovered, go through the same training Chad's men would endure before officially becoming Black Sheep.

Leman had men out working in minutes to care for the column's horses so that the tired troopers could go home to their families. He was watching the activity when Parno limped up to him.

"You look lame, milord," Leman said straight faced.

"If I was a horse you might have to have me put down," Parno nodded. "How are things going?"

"Well, sir," Leman assured him. "Training is on schedule and the men look good. Brigadier Taylor is also participating in the training alongside his men," Leman fought off a grin. "He is less than enthusiastic about that, sir. Or about someone of lower rank commanding the post."

"Well, life is tough all over these days," Parno grinned. "He'll live. Probably," he added. "I'll be in my house. My men are officially on leave as of this moment. Three days, starting tomorrow. After that we'll work up a day or so, refit, and probably be gone again in six to ten days."

"Sir," Leman nodded.

"If any messengers arrive for me, send them to Captain Sprigs. He can decide if they need to see me. I may sleep for two days, myself."

"Understood, sir," Leman grinned.

"You'll carry on as usual, Colonel," Parno said as he walked away. "This is your post. We're just visiting."

"Very well, milord."

-

Parno was reclining in a bed of grass near one of the many streams in the area around Cove Canton, reading various reports that only half-registered, his mind wandering all over the kingdom reviewing military deployments.

Who would have imagined even a year ago that he would be in command of the entire Royal military apparatus? He knew that he lacked the real training for this post, and certainly lacked the experience. Experience he wasn't likely to get, at least not the easy way. This job was strain enough without the incredible burden of assuming command during war time. More so when the war was not going your way.

Those troubles were far away for the moment, however. The sun was beaming today, bringing the warmth of late spring to Parno's shoulders as he leaned against the large rock he'd thrown his saddle blanket over. At times like these he could place the war and it's concerns aside, at least temporarily, and take time to recharge.

A rumble of thunder came out of nowhere, surprising him. He looked to the sky but could not see a cloud anywhere. Odd. Still, thunder usually meant rain, and he was a twenty-minute ride from Cove. He'd managed to give Berry the slip this morning, though he was sure to get a lecture from Enri Willard when he got back, not to mention a tongue lashing from Karls and a frown of disapproval from Cho.

Thunder rumbled again and he looked once more for the source as he stood and prepared to head back. Still nothing, but perhaps the storm was out of sight, blocked by the trees along the creek.

"Parno! Parno McLeod!"

He heard the voice, calling as if far away. Apparently, someone had finally noticed him missing and was now searching for him. He sighed, not really angry, but a bit disappointed. He would have rather rode back alone, having just a bit more time to himself. It was odd that he had to literally steal time for solitude.

"Parno McLeod!" More thunder as the voice continued to call. "Open this door!"

Door? What the hell was that about? And was that a woman's voice? There shouldn't be any women looking for him, should there? Those days were long gone, left behind him when he'd taken command of Cove Canton. He'd been a good boy for most of a year now-

"Parno!"

Parno shot straight up from his bed, blinking away sleep, trying to get his bearings. Slowly he realized he was in his own house, in his own bed for that matter. The thunder hit again, only this time he recognized it as someone literally beating on his front door.

"Parno, open this door right now!"

He groaned as he realized that Stephanie was at his door, no doubt beating her fist raw. Where the hell was Sprigs? He was supposed to keep people away from here, at least until Parno could get some sleep. He stumbled from his bed and pulled a robe on as he made his way down the stairs, accompanied by the continued beating of his door.

"All right!" he yelled as he got to the bottom of the stairs. "I'm coming, for Crown's Sake!" He stomped over to the door and unlocked it, yanking it open just in time to get a small fist in his eye.

"Ow!" he stepped back, covering his left eye. "What was that for?"

"Parno, I'm so sorry!" Stephanie Freeman's hand shot to her mouth in shock. "I was trying to knock on the door!"

"Knock it down, you mean?" Parno shot back crossly. "What is so important that I can't wait for me to get some sleep?"

Stephanie's shock at hitting Parno was instantly gone, her anger returning in a flash.

"So important?" she repeated. "What's so important?" her voice rose slightly. "How *dare* you not tell me you were back!"

"What?" Parno was trying to blink away the tears from having his eye almost poked out. "What are you talking about? I just got here!"

"You got here last night!" Stephanie shot back, entering the house and slamming the door so hard that the glass rattled.

"You know, that glass is hard to come by up here," Parno noted. "I'd appreciate it if you could not break it while you are abusing my house and myself ooophh-" His mini-tirade was cut off as Stephanie's mouth cover his in a deep kiss, her arms circling his neck. Somewhat shocked by that, Parno responded almost automatically, wrapping his own arms around her and kissing back.

Just as suddenly as she had kissed him, Stephanie broke the kiss, pulled back slightly, and slapped him across the face.

"What the hell was *that* for?" Parno yelled, ears ringing.

"That's for not coming to see me the minute you got here!" she told him hotly. "How dare you not at least send someone to get me when you arrived!"

"Two days ago, I was in Nasil," Parno told her, still rubbing his jaw. "I rode here in two very hard days and was exhausted when I got here. We all were. The only thing on my mind last night was sleep. I'm very sorry that my being on the verge of falling from the saddle is such an inconvenience to you, Doctor." His voice was brittle as he finally began to shake off the sleep stupor he was in. Now he was leaning toward angry.

"You could have at least had someone come and tell me," she shot back, sounding more hurt than angry now. "I would have welcomed that news, just knowing you were all right."

Parno opened his mouth to retort, but held it as he noted the dampness in Stephanie's eyes. She was on the verge of crying, something he didn't know she was capable of.

"Hey, now," he soothed, placing his hands on her shoulders. "There's no call for that. I'm fine. Surrounded by hundreds of baby-sitters who never let me out of their sight. There's no need to worry about me."

"There's every reason to worry!" she replied sharply. "You are entirely too prone to involving yourself in the combat around you, Parno," her voice softened. "I. . .I would die if something happened to you," she added softly. "I couldn't bear it."

Parno studied her for a long moment of silence, not knowing exactly what to say.

"Come and sit down," he settled for saying at last, guiding her into the small sitting room and leading her to the couch. She sat, grasping his hand as if it were a rope and she a drowning victim.

"I'm sorry," Parno told her with genuine contriteness. "I was so tired, we were all so tired, that all I was thinking about was rest. Being able to sleep in my own bed again, in my own house. I'm sorry if that seemed selfish. I didn't mean it to be."

He really didn't know what to do or say in a situation like this. He'd never had anyone show this kind of concern for him. Not like this. It was a new experience for him, and he wasn't sure what to do at this point.

"I'm sorry I over-reacted," she said finally, wiping at her eyes carefully with a small handkerchief. "When I awoke this morning and saw all the commotion, I didn't think much of it. There are thousands of men here, after all, and hundreds of women. I'm used to seeing large numbers of people. But when I went to the hospital, I overheard others talking about your being on the post, and I... I'm sorry," she settled for saying.

"It's okay," Parno shrugged. "I always enjoy waking up to be punched by a beautiful woman," he grinned, and in spite of herself, Stephanie laughed.

He pulled her into an embrace and she fell against him. Suddenly he felt her shaking and realized with a start that she was crying. He held her tighter, one hand rubbing her hair along the back of her head.

"It's all right, Stephanie," he whispered to her gently. "I really am fine. And like I said, I'm surrounded by people who rarely allow me the dignity of the latrine without benefit of an escort." Her giggle at that comment warmed him.

She pulled back, looking at him now with a smile.

"I am so glad to see you," she told him softly, her hand tracing his face in a much gentler fashion. "I have missed you so very terribly."

"I would have thought that you would be too busy to miss me," he grinned at her.

"Things are very busy," she admitted. "We are of course training new surgeons, plus still caring for the worst of the wounded from the Gap. And there are training accidents all the time of course. And we've had three mothers deliver new babies, too-"

"How 'bout that?" Parno smiled.

"It was a great event, each time," she nodded, smiling brightly. "How long will you be here?" she asked, changing the subject.

"A week, perhaps a bit more," he told her, seeing the light fade at the news. "We're taking a short leave while awaiting the troops from the south to arrive. After that, we'll begin trying to push the Nor out of our land."

"So, you'll be back where the fighting is," Stephanie's face fell.

"No, I won't," Parno shook his head. "It's been pointed out to me from many places that I cannot take the lead or 'risk myself' in any way. Even Memmnon says I'm too important to the kingdom," he snorted. "Can you believe that?"

"Yes," she said simply. "I can."

"What time is it?" he asked suddenly, looking to the clock on his mantle. "Eight fifteen?" he sounded dismayed. "So much for sleeping two days," he said wryly. "I need to visit Cumberland House," he told her suddenly. "I'm sure Karls will want to go as well, but I need to see Dhalia. I have news for her about something from my father. Are things in the hospital set enough that you can accompany me? We would be there at least overnight," he warned.

"Absolutely," she nodded, thrilled with the idea.

"Well, allow me to clean up a bit and send a runner to Karls, then," he stood, pulling her up as well. "Meanwhile you can get ready and we'll try and ride in an hour or so. Sound good to you?"

"Very," she nodded, smiling brightly once more. "I'll be ready by then."

"Excellent," Parno nodded, then called for his runner.

-

"Colonel, we're about finished here."

Bret Chad turned to see Major Hildebrand standing close behind him.

"Good," Chad nodded. "We've been here too long as it is. We're lucky not to have been spotted or engaged."

"I don't think it's luck, sir, to be honest," Hildebrand shook his head. "The Nor were pretty soundly beaten here. I'm sure there are a few bands of unorganized Imperials still running around but we're not an isolated town or unprotected farmstead, either. We're a full battalion of armed men."

"Escorting a vulnerable wagon train of women and children," Chad nodded as if Hildebrand had just made his point for him. "We need to get out of here."

"We'll be ready to ride in ten minutes, sir," Hildebrand promised. "I've already got scouts out riding our road home."

"Home," Chad mused. "This used to be home," he said absently, waving a hand about him.

"And it will be again," Hildebrand said firmly. "Prince Parno will see to that, Bret. We just have to do our part."

"Yes," Chad nodded. "I believe he will. And our part right now is to get our people home, and then retrain and refit so we'll be able to do our part, as you call it."

He followed Hildebrand to where Morely stood waiting with the reins to his horse. Taking them he mounted up, instinctively looking back down the line to where his wife and two daughters sat on a wagon with their most cherished possessions. The rest, if it survived, would be waiting when they returned. If not, they would be rebuilding and replace what was lost.

The most important things in his life were sitting on the bench seat of that wagon, anyway.

"All in readiness, Colonel," a sergeant reported.

"Very well, Hardy," Chad nodded. "Take the point if you will. Let's get out of here."

"Aye, Colonel, let's do just that," Hardy nodded back and led his squad of troopers forward to ride point for the train.

"Tom, let's get moving. Sitting still we're a target, battalion or no."

"Ready to move!" Hildebrand called, though not nearly so loud as he might have. They had worked out a system where commands would be relayed down the line without the usual yelling and bellowing that might normally accompany a column like this if it were purely military in nature. Hildebrand watched as heads turned to pass the order, then raised an arm, motioning the front wagons forward.

"Move out," he called calmly to the nearest group. In fits and starts the long, winding group began its slow trek back to the Gap, and from there to Cove Canton.

Chad considered what Hildebrand has said about Kent being home again, after the war. He wondered if it would be for him and his men. Technically they were now part of Parno McLeod's personal regiment. They had earned that position in combat, but not yet through the brutal training regimen that Parno's own men had survived to become the elite fighting force they were now.

If he and his men were able to complete it, they would be considered a permanent part of the Prince's Own regiment. Would that make Cove Canton their new home?

Of course, for any of that to matter, he had to survive the war. And for that to be more likely, he needed the training that awaited at Cove Canton. Which meant he needed to reach Cove Canton, where his family would also be as safe as possible.

"First things first," he said to himself as he spurred his horse forward. He would concentrate on getting this train of wagons to the Gap, and then on to Cove. Safely. Then he would worry about the rest.

Well, after a good night's sleep anyway.

First things first, after all.

-

"Sir, you should not be venturing about without your escort," Berry insisted as forcefully as he dared.

"We'll be accompanied by Lady Freeman-Corsin's escort, Lieutenant," Parno smiled. "Perfectly safe. And you and the others can remain here and rest and enjoy visiting with your families."

"Sir, I will not be able to relax knowing you are going about the countryside without a proper escort," Berry replied.

"Berry, relax," Parno ordered, a bit more sternly. "We'll have forty troopers accompanying us. More than enough to fend off even the most desperate band of brigands. And Colonel Willard will be with us as well," he reminded his chief protector.

"Sir-"

"Enough," Parno's voice took on an edge that Berry knew quite well. "You'll all be in danger soon enough, trying to keep me safe. This is a social call with only a bit of official business on the side. Nothing more. We'll be a scant ten miles away, and surrounded by well-trained men." Most of the escort were members of the Black Sheep who were now well enough to rejoin the Regiment in the field, and would be with them when the Lord Marshal returned to the battlefield in the west. For now, they were more than ready for any kind of distraction from camp life. A gentle ride through the countryside wasn't exciting, but it wouldn't be Cove Canton, either.

"Now go, and enjoy your leave," Parno ordered. Berry stiffened to attention and saluted, then whirled and stalked away.

"Shouldn't be so hard on him, Parno," Karls said gently from nearby.

"You and Enri shouldn't encourage him to be so stubborn, either," Parno shot back. "I've surrendered more than enough of my private life to my new 'position'," he made the word sound like a curse. "There are four squads of highly capable soldiers assembled to ride guard. There's no reason to think they can't deal with whatever we might encounter between here and Cumberland House."

"True enough," Karls sighed. "He's just trying to do his duty," he added.

"No, he *does* his duty," Parno corrected. "And quite well, at that. There's no reason for him to doubt that. Make sure you tell him that when we return."

"Why me?" Karls showed his surprise. "It would mean more coming from you, I'm sure."

"Don't underestimate your influence on all of them," Parno replied. "Including Berry."

-

Edema Willows had finished lunch and was sitting on her front porch when one of her hands ran up the walk.

"My Lady, there is a small column approaching," he said breathlessly.

"Who are they?" she asked, looking at the giant bell that hung from the porch. In an emergency she would ring that bell for a full minute or more to alert the estate and surrounding area of trouble.

"Don't know exactly as yet, but they're carrying the McLeod banner, My Lady," he reported.

"Probably Doctor Corsin then," Edema allowed herself to relax. "Take a glass and make sure however," she ordered. There was no sense in taking chances.

"Already got a man on it, My Lady," the man promised. No sooner had he spoken than another servant came racing into the yard on horseback. He left the saddle before the horse had stopped completely.

"My Lady!" he called excitedly. "Lord Parno is with them!"

Edema's face brightened like a cloudy day when the sun had finally broken through to shine it's light.

"Parno!" she almost laughed. "That's wonderful! Hank, alert the stable that we'll have guests, their horses will require care. Joseph, make sure that the empty bunkhouse is clean. Their escort will need lodging. I need to alert the kitchen we'll have extra hands for supper. Go on now!" she shooed them away. Both ran off to obey.

"Dhalia, dear!" Edema called as she entered the house. "Dhalia we're about to have company!"

-

Dhalia Nidiad stood alongside Edema on the porch as the column approached the house. She always enjoyed visiting with Stephanie, and of course it would be good to see Parno again. But what Dhalia most desired to see was Karls Willard riding up to that gate to see her. Maybe with-

Her thoughts cut off as she watched one of the leading figures take shape, and her mouth dropped open in surprise.

"Karls?" she almost whispered. "Karls!" she shouted louder as she ran off the porch and down the walk.

"That girl had got to learn some patience," Edema sighed in mock exasperation. "At least make him think she hasn't missed him that bad."

"Karls!" Dhalia shouted again as she tore through the gate and began running to meet the approaching horsemen. One figure broke away, galloping to meet her.

"Karls!"

-

"You didn't really think I'd ride all the way over here and not bring him with me, did you?" Parno asked, grinning.

"Thank you, Parno," Dhalia said with heartfelt sincerity. She was nestled in Karls' arms across the front of his saddle, happier than she had been in weeks. "Thank you so much."

"Anything for you my sweet," Parno assured her as they arrived at the gate. Parno dismounted, then assisted Stephanie in doing so since she had insisted on riding horseback with him rather than following in her ambulance. The ambulance followed along further back in case of inclement weather, though Hiram Wiggins, the Cove Canton 'meteorologist', as he preferred to be called, had assured them of decent weather for at least three to five more days.

Karls lowered Dhalia to the ground and then dismounted himself, handing his own reins over then taking Dhalia by the hand.

"Hello Parno, dear boy!" Edema gushed as she embraced him, kissing his jaw. "Oh, it is so good to see you. Hello Stephanie dear, how are you?"

"I'm very well, Lady Cumberland," she bowed slightly, only to feel the wrath of Edema's fan.

"Oh, stop that!" she ordered. "You're practically a member of this household. And you, young man," she turned to Karls, "I expect to spend all of your time with this young woman," she indicated Dhalia. "She has pined for you since the day you departed."

"Edema!" Dhalia protested, her face going beet red. Karls' face was nearly a match though he remained silent. He was not on first name basis with the Duchess of the Cumberland.

"You know it's true, dear," Edema said, her voice ringing with authority. "I'm sorry Edward is away, Parno," she turned back to the prince. "He'll be sorry he's missed you, but he is actually in Nasil. There was a need for transport services by the Crown and he has taken the bulk of our people to try and help."

"Interesting," Parno mused, knowing of only one transport need at moment. He made a note to have Sprigs send a message that Edward Willows was not to be on any wagon carrying Roda's 'solution'.

"Well, come in, come in!" Edema waved them all into the house. "I'll have something to drink brought. Are you hungry? I'm afraid we've already had lunch ourselves, but there is always food here somewhere."

"I could eat," Stephanie nodded, blushing slightly. "I've had a rather busy morning."

"I'm sure you have, dear," Edema grinned knowingly.

"It's not like that."

-

"Dolly, before you run off into the trees, I've got something serious to discuss with you," Parno said as he and the others finished their light meal.

"Parno McLeod," she all but growled, but he continued on anyway.

"I spoke to the King before I left Nasil," he told her gently. "He has awarded Darvo entrance to the peerage, posthumously, and bestowed upon you a title, through that grant." He passed over the parchment he had received from his father for her.

"I... what?" the girl was cleared floored.

"You are now the Countess, or maybe Viscountess?" he looked at Edema, who smiled and nodded. "Anyway," he looked back at Dhalia, "you are now Viscountess of Wolf, a small steading south of here, a few hours ride. It comes with some livestock and an annual stipend. I'm sure that Lady Edema can assist you in handling such affairs," he looked again at Edema who nodded once more.

"Parno, what. . .how. . .what do I know about anything like this?" Dhalia was floored. "I don't even know where to start!"

"Well, as for that," Parno nodded in Edema's direction, "you're sitting beside the best possible teacher, right now. I'm sure she'll be glad to put up with you a while longer so that she can teach you to act like a lady instead of a barracks solider," he teased.

"I'll show you lady, you miserable-" she began, face red, then she stopped, glancing at Karls. She had been about to act exactly like a soldier would before she thought.

"It's all right," Karls said softly. "I want to strangle him at least once daily myself," he added in a mock whisper where everyone could hear.

"Such thanks I get," Parno let loose a long suffering sight, shaking his head. He then turned more serious.

"The King felt that your father would have laughed in his face at the offer, but he was adamant that this be given to you. He insisted that your future be your own to choose, Dolly, and that you have the means to do so." He took her hand gently.

"This is little enough to do for the daughter of the man who helped me save this kingdom, dear Dhalia. Do not think for even a moment that it isn't deserved. I know you would trade it all to have him back, and I would gladly take his place if I could, that he might be here with you instead of me. I am so truly sorry," he finished, his own eyes growing damp in spite of his best efforts.

"Damn you, Parno," Dhalia said softly, hugging him to her tightly. "You're making me cry. I hate to cry."

"I know dear heart," Parno hugged her tight, his love for the woman he considered his 'real' sister stronger than any embarrassment. "I'm sorry for that too."

"Stop it," she slapped his arm as she pulled away. "Stop apologizing for everything," she ordered. "Do you think he'd have been anywhere else? He was a soldier, Parno McLeod. He died doing what he loved, beside a man he loved like a son. Fighting for his kingdom, his sovereign, and for me. I would never deprive him of that, even if it were possible." She looked at him closely.

"See that you do not follow him," she ordered. "At least not for a very long time."

"I will do my best," he promised, meaning it. "Now, you and Karls are no doubt itching to explore the barns around here or something so I won't keep you. Let Edema put that scroll in a safe place for you. I'm sure that Karls would enjoy taking you down there to see your new lands before we head back." He gave Karls a look that said he had better enjoy it, though it was unneeded.

"I would indeed," he told her, smiling. "We can head down day after tomorrow if you like. How would that be?"

"I... I'd like that," she admitted. She stood, hand out to him.

"Come, soldier. Escort your Viscountess around the estate!"

"By your command, madam," Karls stood and bowed, then took her arm.

"We'll go explore the barns," he winked at Parno, only to get a slap on the arm from Dhalia.

"We'll do no such thing!" she squealed, her face beet red.

"Go on, enjoy yourselves," Parno ordered. "Take what time we have," he added softly. The two departed, leaving Parno with Stephanie and Edema.

"Did you have anything to do with that?" Edema asked once they were out of earshot.

"No," Parno shook his head as he sat back. "I had made my own arrangements with Memmnon to see that she was taken care of, but Tammon the Terrible did this of his own volition."

"Parno!" Stephanie gasped. "Have some respect."

"That was my respect," Parno told her evenly. "I should tell you both as well that I am now officially the owner of Cove Canton and the surrounding area," he added quietly. "Allowed to choose my own title, even."

"Parno, that's wonderful!" Edema exclaimed. "You'll be nearby even after the war."

"That is possible," he nodded absently. "Anyway," he forced himself to brighten. "I'm glad he allowed me to be the one to inform Dhalia. That has brightened my day considerably."

"Did your day need brightening that badly?" Edema asked. Before Parno could answer, Stephanie interrupted.

"Edema, will I be in my usual room tonight?"

"Of course, dear," Edema nodded. "It's always there for you."

"If you don't mind I'd like to go and freshen up," she said evenly. "Will you excuse me," she looked to Parno.

"Of course," he smiled gently. "Hurry back," he added as she departed. She smiled slightly over her shoulder and disappeared into the house.

"Parno, you are going to have to start being more careful of your words," Edema said at once.

"What? Why?" Parno looked bewildered. "What did I do?" The *now* part of the question was unspoken but still there.

"It should be Stephanie that 'brightens' your day, Parno," Edema fought the urge to sigh in exasperation.

"She does," Parno agreed. "Why should that mean that giving Dahlia some good news can't also make me happy? She's as close to me as any sister could be. Certainly more so than my own."

"I know but that's not my point," Edema replied. "That young woman is very taken with you, Parno, and you know it. And I believe you are with her in equal measure. Now," she leaned forward. "Am I wrong?"

"About me?" Parno shrugged. "No. But. . . ." he stopped for a moment, his gaze wandering across the landscape around Edema's home.

"I'm not a good prospect for her, Edema," he said finally, turning his gaze back to her. "She's a wonderful woman. Someone I could easily lose myself in, to be honest. Smart, brave, strong and strong willed, and obviously beautiful."

"Then why is there a 'but' in this conversation?" Edema demanded. "Why are you not courting her as is proper?"

"Edema we're at war," Parno reminded her. "A war that we're still losing. I may be able to turn that around soon, but then again I may not. And I have other enemies much closer to home, as well. I may not live out the war. Hell, I may not live out the year," he said grimly.

"Now you tell me," he looked at the woman who was as much a mother to him as if she had raised him. "Is that any kind of future to offer her? Link her to a man with my reputation only to see her left a widow, or worse left the 'woman' of Parno McLeod? Her reputation and standing in the circles she travels in would be destroyed. That's not right, or fair."

Edema smiled gently at Parno's words. She knew she had been right.

"Parno, don't you think she's considered all of that already?" she asked softly. "Don't you imagine that she's played over everything that can happen in her mind, waiting every day to hear word if you're alive or not? She visits me on a regular basis and her loneliness for you is no less than Dhalia's for Karls Willard. She is almost desperate for any kind of sign from you that you reciprocate her feelings, and you are completely avoiding giving her that sign. Deliberately."

"I had at first thought that you simply weren't aware, but now I think you are aware, which means you either don't care or that you are afraid," Edema told him. "I know that you care, dear child. You may can hide it from her, but not from me. So that means you are afraid."

"If you fear death on a battle field, which I doubt, then that is not reason enough to withhold your affection from her, Parno. There are hundreds of thousands of men on those same battlefields, and many of them have women at home hoping and praying for their safe return. She will not be alone in that."

"I know that," Parno almost whispered. "I'm the reason most of them don't return, remember?" he looked up at her sharply. "Every time I issue an order, men die, Edema. No matter what I do, no matter how carefully I plan, men die. Every time. I can't stop it, I can't even diminish it, and soon I'll actually make it much worse." He leaned his head back against the chair, looking at the roof of the porch.

"Before this is over, I will be responsible for no telling how much death and destruction. I may even be forced to kill my own brother and sister for plotting against the crown." He looked back to her abruptly.

"Now is that the kind of man she deserves?" he demanded, though not unkindly. "Is that the kind of man that deserves her heart? I think not, Edema."

"That is not for you to decide, Parno," Edema shot back at once. "Her heart is her own, to give to whom she wishes. You can accept it or not, but if you turn her away because you don't believe she's made a smart decision, then you call everything she does into question. You insult her intelligence if you think she isn't fully aware of what's fallen on your shoulders. She may not like it, nor do I if I'm honest, but she's aware. She can't not be, surrounded by wounded men and soldiers training to join you in battle."

"I'm not saying she isn't intelligent," Parno defended himself. "She obviously is or she wouldn't be a doctor, would she? I'm just saying that I'm a miserable, poor choice for a suitor for any woman, let alone one of her quality."

"You sell yourself short, child," Edema shook her head, almost scolding him. "You are more than a stupid reputation, no matter how well earned it was. And there are very few, now, who speak of you with other than deep respect. Your actions at the Gap alone have seen to that."

Parno considered that, mind working furiously. Was he being unfair to Stephanie even while trying to be as fair and thoughtful of her as possible? Edema was right in that Stephanie was intelligent enough to know what she was getting into with someone like Parno. She was quite possibly the smartest woman of her age Parno had ever known.

And perhaps his reputation was beginning to wear away. He had worked diligently to put it behind him, knowing that only good service at this point in his life would undo the damage of his childish behavior before.

He sighed, rubbing his face in a scrubbing motion with both hands. He finally looked at Edema and nodded.

"All right," he told her. "I'll try," he said simply. "I'm not good at that kind of thing, but I'll try my best."

"Just be yourself, dear," Edema beamed. "Just be yourself. That's who she loves, after all," she almost whispered as Stephanie reappeared. Parno felt like a heel when he noted the carefully disguised redness around her eyes. Was he really that bad?

"I need to step away for a bit," Edema told them, standing. "I have to make sure that we have enough food cooking for so many. We are roasting a beef this afternoon, which will be excellent. We've killed the fattened calf since the prodigal has come home," she smiled.

"Ha ha," Parno laughed half-heartedly. Edema departed, leaving the two younger people alone.

"Stephanie," Parno said. She looked at him immediately, and he had to fight a wince at the look in her eyes.

"Yes?"

He didn't know what he'd intended to say, but the look in her eyes made him forget all about it.

"Would you like to take a walk with me?" he said instead, standing and offering her his hand.

"I'd like that very much," she smiled despite her surprise, taking the offered hand. Parno led her off the porch, then walked side-by-side in silence for a few minutes, gathering his thoughts and thinking about what Edema had said to him. Maybe she was right?

"Stephanie, I-"

"You don't have to say anything, Parno," Stephanie said softly, cutting him off gently. "I already know."

"Know what?" he asked, confused.

"That you don't return my feelings for you," she said flatly. "Edema and Dhalia had convinced me that you did, and I've made a fool of myself today over your return, and I'm sorry for that. Please forgive me."

"They did, did they?" Parno mused. "Well, it just so happens, Doctor, that they were right," he said it before he thought. "At least, I have feelings for you. I don't know your exact feelings for me, of course, so I can't say that I return them. I never thought of this as something you could measure," he smiled at the ground before looking up at her, tightening his grip on her hand slightly.

"I've been unfair to you I think," he decided to follow Edema's advice, especially since she had worked so hard to put him and Stephanie together. "I've been trying to be more than fair, in my defense. To protect you from my-"

"Parno McLeod if this is some kind of 'weaker vessel' speech then you better stop, right there," Stephanie warned darkly, storm clouds brewing suddenly in eyes that seconds ago were laced with sadness.

"Could I finish?" he asked, and her eyebrows rose as she nodded.

"Protect you from my somewhat tarnished reputation," he continued. "Not to mention the fact that the odds are somewhat favorable that I won't survive the war. I have enemies on every side, Stephanie, and not all of them are from the north, either. And I can't always be watching all of them. I surround myself with capable people, but it only takes one mistake," he shrugged.

"The last thing I would ever want in the entire kingdom would be for you to be hurt, in any way, because of me. Whether it's being left alone after I'm. . .gone, or by someone trying to get to me through you. That's what I've sought to protect you from. That is not a 'weaker vessel' argument, but a simple statement of fact. Another statement of fact is that I am almost certain that I'm in love with you," he admitted in a near rush.

"Almost certain?" she asked, more to cover her shock than anything else.

"I've never had much experience in love, Stephanie," he shrugged. "I've only ever loved three people, really, and all of them were like family, not. . .not romantically, if that's the proper term. Edema is like a mother to me, has treated me so much better than my own family that I would kill anyone who offended her and die defending her."

"Dhalia is more a sister to me than Sherron could ever think of being, and someone else that I would die for without thought. And her father might as well have been my own. He raised me from the time I was out of diapers for the most part, turning down promotions and good postings to stay with me because he knew I needed him. When I said I would gladly take his place, I meant it."

"I know you did," she nodded slowly, her voice soft. "So does Dhalia."

"The point is, all of that is familial in nature," Parno told her. "I've never had. . .I have never felt for anyone the things I do for you," he admitted with difficulty. "I'm sometimes confused by those feelings, distracted by them even." He smiled suddenly.

"When I was in Shelby not long ago, I met a very capable woman named Evelyn McKenzie. She lives south of Shelby in a place called DeSoto, and operates an observation and listening post on her land that lies along the Great River. She came to lunch one day at Raines' invitation so I could speak to her. Because of my talk with her I've ordered that women be considered for all such posts if they are interested."

"She must have made quite an impression," Stephanie fought to keep her voice even.

"She did," Parno ignored the tension in her voice. "She had a daughter, maybe two years younger than me. Pretty girl, much like her mother. Smart, hard working. She had no interest in me until she discovered who I was. After that it was almost comical to watch her maneuver, and watch her mother work to keep her away from me."

"I'm sure," Stephanie's voice had an acidic quality to it now.

"Thing is, when I looked at her daughter, I started comparing her to you without much thought," he told her, smiling at her discomfiture. "In fact almost any woman I meet ends up being compared to you, and always falling short. No matter how smart, how attractive, whatever the case may be, they always fail to measure up to you."

"What I'm trying to say is that you dominate my thinking, Stephanie. No matter where I look or what I'm doing I always seem to find something or someone who reminds me of you or makes me think of you. I've heard it said that absence makes the heart grow fonder, and I'm convinced that is very true, because I have missed you a great deal."

"You have a funny way of showing it," she replied, not quite testily. She wanted to believe. So much.

"No, I have a way of avoiding it," Parno did not allow her comment to detract him. "When I'm afraid of something, I avoid it," he admitted. "I don't know what else to do, in all honesty. And the way I feel about you scares me."

"What?" her testiness was gone suddenly. "Why?"

"I've never had anything to lose," he told her plainly. "My whole life I've never had anything that I cared about enough to worry over whether I lost it or not. I never had to learn how to deal with that kind of fear. Until now," he stopped and looked her directly in the eyes.

"Now, I think I love you. No," he corrected, "I know I love you and think I'm *in* love with you. Only, I don't know what to do, and I don't know what to say, and I'm ashamed of how people think of me for the first time in my life because of how it might affect you, and the last thing I want is for the poor general opinion people have for me to be transferred to you in any way," he rambled in one long sentence.

"I tried to keep you at a distance because I don't deserve you, and you certainly deserve someone better than me." He stopped there, not sure if he's said too little, too much, or somewhere around enough.

Stephanie looked at him in silence, looked deep into his eyes, and Parno let her, maintaining eye contact with her.

"Parno McLeod," she said finally. "I'm a highly intelligent woman. Ask anyone who knows me and they'll verify that. I'm not bragging, just stating fact. I'm smart enough to know all of that. I know your reputation, but I also know you. My mother said that you were nothing more than high-spirited and that wasn't a bad quality in a man. My mother is also fairly smart," a smile tugged at the corner of her mouth.

"I'm well aware that people will talk, of what they'll probably say in fact, and I don't care. I know the real you, Parno. I know the Parno that hurts for his men who fall in battle. The Parno that was willing to die alongside those same men to protect a land full of people who think poorly of you and a family that is completely undeserving of your service and devotion."

"I know the Parno that has made a home for men and their families who might not have anything otherwise. I know the Parno who fought a duel against Soulan's most feared swordsman to defend the honor of someone he loved. I know the Parno that has won the love and devotion of a group of men who cannot be bought or bribed but must be convinced though effort that you deserve the right to command them." Her hand came to his jaw then, caressing it gently.

"I know the Parno who has worked to make life better for his people. Even the people who would speak ill of him for no other reason than it's fashionable in certain circles. Most of all, I know the Parno that is loyal to the bone to those loyal to him and that Parno is the Parno I have come to love. The Parno that has won my devotion and loyalty as surely as you have my heart."

Parno was somewhat overcome by her speech and without much thought he leaned in and kissed her. She responded at once as he drew her into an embrace, pouring every unspoken emotion running through him into his actions, just as she did in return.

As he kissed her, Parno realized that yes, he now had something to lose. Something too precious, too priceless to name. But in that same instant he realized something else.

He now had something to fight for. Something to live for.

CHAPTER EIGHTEEN

-

Colonel Frank Callens had commanded Prince Therron's personal regiment for just over four years. In that time, he had become close with the Marshal, and as such was completely privy to the Prince's plans. He also heartily approved of them and had of course added his own sword to the gathering group of supporters behind Therron McLeod.

The Prince's arrest less than a month past had come as a shock to say the least. He and his men had been neatly mousetrapped by a brigade of regular cavalry on the day Prince Therron had been taken from them and held at bay until well after the Inspector General had departed with their royal charge. Callens had chafed at the attitude of men like General Davies toward the Prince's Own in the intervening weeks, and chafed more at the knowledge that Parno McLeod, Prince Therron's hapless younger brother had been appointed in his place.

He knew of Parno's victory the second day of his presence on the field, but wrote that off to good planning by Enri Willard, the traitorous jack, and good execution by Davies. He flatly refused to consider or entertain any notion that held Parno in any way in a good light.

As a result, he and his men, now no longer a Royal Regiment but merely a well-dressed and equipped cavalry regiment, had been shuttled from one crap job to another all over the camp. Picket duty, guard posts, even herd detail for Crown's sake! The humiliation of being demoted hadn't been enough. No, now his elite men were replacing wranglers guarding the horses.

The message in his hands offered him the opportunity to change that. He read the message once more, slowly, more to ensure himself it was genuine than because he hadn't understood it the first time. He looked warily at the courier.

"Do you know what this is?" he demanded.

"Yes, Colonel," the man nodded. "Milady also entrusted me with another delivery," he handed over a saddle bag of fine leather and silver. "I do not know the contents of this. I was to hand it to you after you had read the message and then await elsewhere for any reply."

"Very well," Callens accepted the bag. "See my aide outside and he'll get you a tent and something to eat."

"Thank you, sir," the man bowed and left the tent. Callens waited until he was gone to open the valise.

The scent from the bag hit him at once as he recognized Sherron McLeod's perfume. Inside the bag he found another, more detailed note that was to be burned after reading, and an item of clothing that still smelled of the Princess even after two days of riding.

"Damn her," he growled softly as he fingered the garment before reading the second message again, committing it to memory. The woman was a witch, he was sure. She taunted and teased him with promises that she never quite delivered on, yet he could not refuse her anything she asked. Had one of his own men been so besotted with a woman, even Her Ladyship, he'd have had him removed or killed as a security risk.

He knew that he should ignore both messages. Toss them both into the fire outside his tent and then arrange for the courier to vanish somewhere in the wild areas between Nasil and the battle front, never to be seen or heard from again.

And even as he acknowledged that was what he should do, he knew that he would not. He sighed, placing the delicate garment in an interior pocket of his jacket, almost as if it were a talisman to ward off the reprisal sure to come if he were caught. He walked outside his tent and tossed the private message from the Princess into the flames, watching to ensure its destruction before turning to his aide.

"Company commanders to my tent in fifteen minutes," he ordered briskly. "And find Major Garren at once." The aide nodded and hurried away. Callens remained where he was, staring at the flames.

Thinking of the flames sure to come.

-

"I'm sure you're all tired of how we're being treated," Callens said without fanfare. His company commanders nodded silently, their anger almost tangible.

"I'm about to do something extremely risky," he told them flatly. "I want you and your men to come with me, but I'm not going to order you to. I'm going to find Prince Therron. I'm going to find him, and see him atop the throne of Soulan or die trying. If you have no wish to accompany, all that I ask is that you remain silent as to what I'm doing. I hope I've earned that much from you."

Every head nodded, acknowledging that Callens had earned their loyalty.

"We are Prince Therron's own regiment," he told them forcefully. "His protection is our duty. Our burden. It is for us to find him, free him if he's being kept prisoner, and return him to his rightful place in this kingdom. I want everyone ready to ride in half-an-hour. Arrangements have already been made for our provisions further south. Our men need rations and feed bags for three days, so see to it that each man has it. Ten pack horses per company, no more. We travel light, and fast." He paused, eyeing each man in turn.

"Make no mistake that we'll be hunted and hounded by our own as we do this. We'll try and keep casualties to a minimum, but Prince Therron is our objective and nothing can be allowed to stop us. Make your preparations, and do so quietly. We must get out of this encampment without arousing suspicion. Go."

The men saluted stiffly and departed in silence, minds already running through what they needed to accomplish in the next thirty minutes.

Callens watched them go, then nodded to his aide to begin their own preparations. Callens packed his own saddlebags, mind racing as he did so.

So much could go wrong in this. So many things work against them despite good planning, and short notice like this did not promote good planning. Or much of any kind of plan, for that matter. He remembered a lesson from his days at the Royal Academy of War; a good plan, violently executed, was preferable to a great plan that never left the drawing table.

So it would be violent, Callens thought grimly as he secured his bag. The rewards were great enough by far to warrant the risk. His reward in particular might be very fine indeed, though he suspected that, as always, there would be a catch.

With a deep sigh he hefted his bags and took the first step of what would certainly be consider a traitorous act by most.

He was going to find his sovereign.

-

"Syn is a good name for you," Major Beau Garren smiled at the woman lying on the bed beside him. "A fitting name for a woman who could make a priest forget his vows," he chuckled. The dark haired beauty beside him smiled, her bright teeth a stark contrast to her deep tan skin and jet black hair.

"You do know how to flatter a girl," she said, raising up to prop her head on one hand as she allowed her left hand to play over Garren's belly. "And I have to admit, you cut a very appealing figure in uniform, Major," she lowered her head and kissed his chest, trailing her lips down his stomach and around his navel.

"I doubt that I-" He was interrupted by a furious pounding at the door. Frowning, he looked at his companion.

"Only someone needing you urgently would be allowed up here," Syn shrugged, pulling a sheet around her. Garren did the same and stomped over to the door, opening it just enough to see his regimental Color Sergeant standing outside.

"Begging your pardon, sir, but we're assembling right now," the man saluted, ignoring the fact that the Major was decidedly out of uniform. "Colonel's orders, we ride in twenty minutes, sir."

"What the devil?" Garren almost exploded but caught himself at the last second.

"Can't say, sir," the man shrugged. "Word is we're headed south, though. All I know. We got word from a courier a short time ago, that is the Colonel did. Soon as he read the message, he issued the order. We have to hurry, sir," the man stressed. "Your horse is being saddled now. I'll be waiting for you out back."

"Very well," Garren nodded, still surprised. He shut the door and turned back to his companion.

"I'm afraid I must cut my visit short, dear," he apologized, grabbing his uniform. Syn allowed her sheet to fall and walked to him completely naked, wordlessly assisting him in dressing. The last item was his sword, which she held out to him with both hands. He had to pause for a moment at the erotic vision she presented, her naked body glistening with sweat, holding his sword. He shook his head to clear it and took the blade.

"Please be safe," she said softly, her hand caressing his jaw slightly. "I would miss seeing you."

"I'll be fine," he assured her, forgetting for a moment who she was. What she was. He was soon out the door and heading down the stairs. Syn counted the minutes, giving him time to get down the stairs and be gone while she washed. Donning a simple shift, she was out the door at the five-minute mark, heading straight to Rosa's room to report her highly unusual evening that had ended far earlier than it was supposed to.

Minutes later Aaron Bell was on his way to find the Tinker. A few minutes after that, one of the men who had accompanied Brenack Wysin was on his way to Cove Canton as fast as his horse could carry him. Tinker was casually mentioning the departure a few minutes later to an officer in the Headquarters unit who was surprised to hear that the former Royal Regiment was on the move and decided to nose around to try and find out why.

All of this was accomplished before Colonel Callens and his men had made ten miles from their camp. While his exact mission was unknown, Colonel Callens' movement had not gone unnoticed. The hoped for day or two lead would not be forthcoming.

-

Beaumont looked over his command with a critical eye, Whipple beside him doing the same thing. The two of them were rarely together, and never in battle. The theory behind that stratagem was simple enough; no single attack would be as likely to see both of them dead or incapacitated leaving the unit without a commander.

"Status?" Beaumont asked his second.

"We've lost thirty-five dead, we have seventy-four wounded, a few severely," Whipple informed him quietly. "We've also acquired somewhere around eight hundred head of cattle and just under three hundred horses from our endeavors," he added. "We have twenty-nine wagons full of equipment and supplies we've taken, as well."

"Our own supplies, particularly arrows and medical supplies, are low," he admitted. "We've still got plenty of foodstuffs, but most of it requires cooking and we're reluctant to do that at present. We need somewhere that we can rest and refit, take a few days to jerk some of the beef and maybe parch some corn or cook other foods that we can store and carry."

"Overall fitness of the command?" Beaumont asked.

"Other than fatigue, we're okay at the moment," Whipple replied. "We've had a few horses come up lame, but other than that we're good."

Beaumont nodded as he considered all that. He could ask Whipple for his suggestions, but Beaumont wasn't one to pass the buck, as the saying went. He wondered for a second where that saying had come down from then cast it aside as irrelevant. And Whipple had already given his input in a way.

They had been in the field for seventeen days and thus far been in nineteen engagements of varying size, never allowing the entire command to be seen. The Imperial Army was already taking precautions to protect their trains and outposts because of the raids. Beaumont smiled at that. His plan to keep the size of their command hidden was going to pay off with that. No matter how many troops the Nor added to their details, he and Whipple would still be able to overpower them. Until the Imperial Army committed real troop strength to the effort, they would continue to prevail.

But his men had to eat, and they needed to rest. Better than two weeks in the saddle or on the ground, one eye constantly open to attack or discovery, the constant strain caused by the fear of that discovery, all of these things would take a toll. Better to take their gains and solidify them than risk defeat or disaster.

"Let's make for home," Beaumont said suddenly, decision made. "We'll stand down for a few days while we refit, then we'll come back."

"Yes sir," Whipple grinned, sketching a salute before turning to their runners. Soon activity flared all around them as the group prepared to move. The going would be slower than normal with so much livestock to move, but some of the wounded couldn't stand a fast trip anyway so that wasn't a problem.

A half-hour later the well-disciplined group was underway, outriders and scouts protecting the column from prying eyes as they started for their own lines and a few days of relative peace and quiet.

After which they would start again.

Raphael Semmes swam up out of the black of unconsciousness slowly, his eyes blinking back tears at the harshness of sunlight. He raised a hand to block the light and realized that it was bandaged along his forearm. As his vision cleared he could see that he was in a small room, on land somewhere, probably a hospital. Even as he wondered where, the door to his room opened and a harried looking woman with wisps of blonde hair falling about her face entered carrying a bowl and towel. Her eyes widened at the sight of the Admiral moving about.

"How do you feel, sir?" she asked at once, setting her bowl aside to come to his bed side.

"I feel like I was hit by an angry bull," he admitted ruefully. "Sore all over. Where am I?" he asked, looking up at his care giver. She was quite pretty, he decided absently.

"Base hospital in Savannah, sir," the nurse informed him. "You've been here for six days, out cold until now." She held a hand to his head, then took his wrist, then lifted his arm and checked the bandage, first looking and then sniffing.

"What are you doing?" he asked, though not unkindly.

"Checking you for signs of infection or fever," she smiled slightly. "You're in good shape for the moment, Admiral."

Semmes took a moment then to assess himself. A process of testing and elimination determined that he still had all limbs and digits. His side hurt terribly, however, and made his breathing painful.

"What happened to me, do you know?"

"Not precisely what happened, no," the nurse shook her head as she retrieved her bowl and towel. "But you suffered at least three broken ribs, a severely bruised spine, a hard knock to the head that probably caused a concussion and had a nine-inch splinter buried in your left forearm," she nodded to the bandage. "You're going to be sore for a while I'm afraid." As she spoke she pulled back his bed sheets, exposing him completely.

"What are you doing?" he demanded, trying and failing to grab the sheet and re-cover himself.

"I'm bathing you," the woman said simply as she took a rag and wet it.

"No, you're not," Semmes shook his head. "This is most improper."

"Admiral, at this point you don't have a thing I haven't already seen," the woman smirked slightly but in good humor. "It's my job, Admiral, so lay back and let me do it. I promise I don't bite. Not even handsome war heroes," she added with a twinkle in her eyes.

"It's not your bite I'm concerned with," he told her, refusing to budge. "I'm fully capable of tending myself, thank you. And if not then a male orderly would be far more appropriate, especially for a bachelor."

"Admiral, you can't do this with that bandage," she nodded to his arm. "And you can't bend because of your ribs," another nod went toward his tightly wrapped midsection. "As for male orderlies, they're all gone, sir. There's a war on and men of all walks of life are gone to fight it."

"I'm afraid it's just us chickens here now," she smiled.

Semmes tried stare the woman down, but failed miserably. Whoever she was, she had a spine of steel.

"Very well," he acquiesced, reclining once more on the bed to give his ribs some relief.

He endured the indignity of having an attractive woman whose name was still unknown to him bathe him as if he were a small child. He also endured the inevitable reaction that was a result of that process with a quiet dignity born of discipline and training, but his face was still very red by the time she was finished.

"All done, Admiral," she announced gaily as she spread the sheet back over his body. She tucked it carefully in around his chest, looking at him the entire time. Suddenly she knelt a bit lower and kissed him on the forehead briefly.

"Bless you," she said softly and gathered her things.

"Please inform my staff that I'm awake," he told her before she could run out of the door. "I need to make sure things are going well and that messages are sent."

"I will," she promised.

Semmes settled back to wait. There was nothing else he could do for the moment.

-

"Do you have to leave?"

Parno sighed slightly as he heard the pleading in Stephanie's tone.

"You know that I do," he told her. They had spent as much time as possible together over the past six days, but now he had to get back. His men were already saddling horses. As soon as the sun was up enough to see, they would be on the road, headed back to 1st Army headquarters.

"I thought you were going to stay longer," she said quietly.

"I told you a week, no more," he reminded her. "Six days and we're leaving on the seventh. It's the best we can do for now. I have to get back. I have a complete field army on the move right now and I'm still waiting to see what the result of the naval battle was in terms of losses. I'm needed in three or four places right now, but I can only be in one. I've got to go."

"I know," she admitted, still crestfallen. "I'm sorry," she added.

"Nothing to be sorry about," he said honestly. "I wish I could stay. I wish I could stay and never leave here. Maybe when the war is over I can. I don't know."

"How old are you Parno?" Stephanie asked suddenly. Surprised, Parno turned to look at her again.

"What?"

"How old are you?" she repeated, her face a mask of concern.

"I'll be twenty-one on my next birthday," he told her slowly. "Why?"

"So young for so much responsibility," she said softly, her hand easing out to caress his face gently. "It's too much," she added. "Too much."

"It may be," he shrugged. "But it's mine to do. Why is my age a factor, anyway?" he asked, eyebrows raised. "I've always had a thing for older women," he grinned. Suddenly Stephanie got her first good look at the rogue prince. Handsome, devil-may-care, unconcerned with propriety or protocol. She laughed out loud at his sudden change.

"I should be angry at that," she told him, lowering her forehead to his shoulder.

"Probably," he agreed, embracing her. "So does this mean you're not interested in me anymore?" he teased. "I mean in a romantical way," he added. She pulled her head back and looked up at him, eyes twinkling.

"I've always had a thing for younger men," she gave as good as she got. "And you're not that much younger."

"How much then?" he pressed, still teasing.

"Not enough to matter," she evaded, still laughing. She stopped suddenly, giving him an evil eye.

"I see what you're doing," she told him sternly. "Trying to make me laugh. To distract me."

"Is it working?" he asked hopefully.

"Partly," she admitted, returning her forehead to his shoulder. "Please, Parno. Be careful and don't take risks. I don't know what I would do-"

"You'll go right on doing, that's what," he told her firmly. "No more of that talk. I can't think about it, and neither can you. And I will be careful. That is a promise, too," he added when she looked at him in near derision. "I told you, I've been ordered, no less, to avoid risk. And I've got far too many people around me ensuring that doesn't happen for me to get in trouble."

"Somehow I doubt that will matter to you if you see the need," Stephanie's voice was tinged with a slight bit of disbelief.

"There won't be a need," he assured her. "There are men far more able than I to swing a sword or ride a horse. I'll just be giving the orders." He kissed her suddenly and she responded at once, wrapping her arms around his neck as he took her back into his arms. Reluctantly he pulled back, looking at her again.

"Time for you to go," he told her gently. "It's bad luck to watch us out of sight," he added with a grin.

"It is not!" she shot back, then asked; "Is it?"

"It's what they say," Parno shrugged. "But I have work to finish and I won't do it so long as you are here, so go on now. I'll see you again as soon as I can. I promise."

"I will hold you to that, Parno McLeod."

"I wouldn't have it any other way."

With the coming of the sun the Black Sheep rode out, their numbers swelled by the return of several men who had been allowed to rejoin the ranks after healing from wounds sustained at the Gap. Enough men to allow a restructuring into five companies instead of four.

"I'm glad to get so many men back," Karls remarked as they left the gate and approached the column.

"Me too," Parno agreed softly.

Cove Canton watched them go, families of the men leaving and those who were training with hopes of one day joining them. Those men looked at the Black Sheep with varying thoughts. Some trying to compare themselves and see if they measured up, others looking and deciding that they were already their equal or even better. Their instructors hadn't hesitated to hold the visiting unit up as an example to the trainees, and as always there were one or two who simply couldn't accept that the Sheep were all that was described.

Several of them discovered that challenging one of Prince Parno's men, on their home ground no less, was simply not a good way to behave. Most of them were even now recovering in hospital.

With the battalion gone out of sight, the place returned to business as usual and remained that way until late afternoon the following day when the guard announced a rider approaching at a dead run. The rider was passed through and LTC Leman was waiting for him when he dismounted.

"Message for Lord Parno, sir!" the man tried to brace to attention but failed. He'd been in the saddle a long time.

"You missed him, son," Leman shook his head. "He's been gone since sun-up yesterday." The man sighed in despair, almost collapsing. Then he straightened.

"Can I trouble you for a fresh horse, sir?" he asked. "Mine is about done in."

"So are you, son," Leman replied. "I'll have a man carry the message after him. You need to get cleaned up, get some food, and then rest. You can return to your post tomorrow or day next."

"I'm beholden sir," the man admitted. "I honestly don't know that I can go another round right now."

Less than an hour later a man was on his way after Parno's Company with a message that two men had already carried almost non-stop. Despite the quality of the horse and rider it would take nearly two days to catch him, since the courier dispatched by Leman had to stop at the trail off the mountain due to darkness.

Thus it was that Parno was about to make camp when the rider came up on their rear, his horse foaming and flecking. After narrowly avoiding a lance from the post behind the column, the rider was escorted forward to Parno.

Parno read the message twice, cursing to himself as he did so. He almost tore the message to shreds in a fit of rage, but managed to simply hand it to Enri Willard instead.

"Incredible," the elder Willard shook his head as he passed the message to his brother. "I would never have imagined it."

"I thought Callens had been dealt with by the IG," Parno admitted. "I should have checked."

"Begging your pardon, milord, but you shouldn't have to," Enri sighed, rubbing the bridge of his nose trying to avert the headache he felt coming. "That's what you have staff and subordinates for, sir. We failed you."

"No more than anyone else, or myself, Enri," Parno shook his head, his mouth twisting into a mockery of a smile. "We'll have to deal with this as soon as possible."

"We'll start at first light and make best speed to the camp," Karls said. "Let's get our men and horses fed and rested as tomorrow will be a hard day in the saddle."

"Agreed," Parno nodded, turning his horse over to an enlisted man who led the animal away to be cared for. Soon fires were going and men were digging rations from saddlebags and 'ride behinds' to make themselves a meal. Parno opened the small box that Stephanie had prepared for him and removed the last sandwich she had fixed him. The ham and bread was going dry now, but it was still good and he was hungry. He chewed wolfishly in silence, brooding over the latest news.

He should have expected this kind of thing, especially knowing his brother. Or his sister, for that matter. He shook his head slightly in silent recrimination, then exhaled in anger, his nostrils flaring. Where the hell was Memmnon in all this? Did Parno have to take care of everything?

"There are others who can do some things, my Prince," Cho Feng said softly, so that only Parno could hear.

"Supposed to be," Parno nodded without looking around. "Yet here I am, having to catch it all."

"Let them go," Feng advised. "Let the Crown Prince worry over this. It is his crown to protect, after all. And while your brother may be a threat, his one regiment and his scheming ways pale in comparison to the army that now encamps on your sovereign soil. Unless you can deal with that, your brother's machinations do not matter. Will not matter."

"Everyone thinks that Therron was removed and replaced because of ill health," Parno snorted in anger. "He can use that, once free, to spread his lies and deceit to those who might well support him in his efforts."

"That may be, but I maintain that it is for your brother to deal with," Cho insisted. He decided to try another track.

"Perhaps a judicious message to your brother, offering him the use of one of your better cavalry units to chase this man, Callens, to heel? If he lacks forces capable of doing so?"

Parno considered that, his gaze going at once to Karls Willard, sitting across the camp from him, talking quietly with his own brother.

"The only group I could trust with something like that are the Sheep," Parno said finally. "And I need them with me, just in case. If we have a catastrophe, they're the only troops that I can depend on to stand fast. Not to mention help me maintain order in the Army if Therron and Sherron manage to get their little rebellion off the ground."

"I would suggest there are at least two other groups you could count on to pursue and detain or destroy Callens," Feng said gently. "Men who would be absolutely loyal to you, regardless of what they encountered." Parno turned at last to look at his oriental mentor, sitting so calmly beside him despite the furor that the message had created.

"Beaumont?" he asked, eyebrows raised. "Behind enemy lines and out of reach at the moment," he shook his head. "Same for Chad, if that's who you're thinking about. And they don't have the numbers, either," he added.

"They can swell their numbers with the men still in camp," Feng reminded. "For that matter, those in training could go as well, if it were necessary."

"No," Parno's voice was firm. "That's out. I need them training. I can't afford to put that off just to chase down this fire. For that matter Chad's men are supposed to go through that training when they return. I'd rather have them doing that than chasing Therron."

"Then let us proceed to camp and see what can be spared, or if your brother even needs assistance. Send him the message in the morning to save time," he temporized, attempting to force his prince to focus on the more pressing threat.

"Yeah," Parno nodded finally. "That's a good idea. Harrel!" he called out and Sprigs appeared as if by magic. Parno quickly dictated the message for his brother with orders to get the courier on his way as soon as it was light enough to ride.

Thoroughly disgusted, Parno went to bed, wrapping himself in blankets as if they were a talisman against his traitorous brother and sister.

-

"Good morning, Admiral," Hampton Rhode said quietly as he entered Semmes room. As senior Commodore, Rhode had assumed command in Semmes' absence. Rhode had one arm in a sling and an angry bruise on the left side of his face.

"Perhaps you should be here instead of me, Hampton," Semmes offered, managing a slight grin.

"Just a trivial matter, sir," Rhode assured him. "Nothing to worry over. How are you feeling?"

"I've been better," Semmes admitted, sitting up straighter. "What is our status?"

"We're shore-side for the time being, sir," Rhode admitted. "We'll have three frigates ready for service by tomorrow afternoon, and we have five cutters standing ready."

"That's it?" Semmes tried to keep the grimace from his face.

"For now, sir," Rhode nodded. "Our losses were heavy, sir," the other man admitted as he took a seat and removed a small notebook from the inside pocket of his jacket. For the next five minutes he droned mercilessly over the list of losses. Eleven cruisers either lost or so damaged that repair would be more costly and time consuming than new construction. Thirteen frigates lost, another five probably beyond salvage. Only the three that were nearly ready for deployment had escaped damage serious enough to keep them in harbor more than a week.

Three thousand seven hundred and twelve sailors and marines either confirmed dead or missing and presumed dead. One thousand nine hundred and eighty-four in hospital. At least in tents around the hospital. There wasn't nearly enough room for them all in the Savannah clinic. Rhode had brought all surviving ships to Savannah, the nearest port to the site of the battle.

Semmes felt a dark shadow fall over him as Rhode read the losses. His fleet had been essentially destroyed in the battle.

"Imperial losses?" he asked, looking out his window.

"Fifteen cruisers sunk or sinking when contact was broken," Rhode smiled slightly. "Same for sixteen frigates and eleven troop transports or merchant vessels in their supply train. Three hundred and seventy-nine prisoners. Impossible to estimate their losses in men, sir. It had to be high," he added.

"Their fleet might still be strong enough to attack the shore line," Semmes noted.

"Admiral, they didn't have much in the way of undamaged ships when we broke contact, or else they would have given chase I believe," Rhode argued. "However, I had planned to send David out with our surviving ships tomorrow or the next day just in case. His cruiser's damage is slight enough that she's sea-worthy at least. Not perfect, but able."

"No," Semmes shook his head. "Keep them in until they have enough to make a good fight. If we use them here, the shore batteries can help stand off the ships the Imperials throw at us."

"Might try to land a raiding party somewhere sir," Rhode pointed out respectfully.

"We probably can't stop them from doing it, so we won't try. Savannah is one of our largest shipyards, Commodore. We must keep it safe. We need ships more than ever, now."

"Yes sir," Rhode nodded, agreeing with the tactic and the need. "I'll see to it."

"Has a report been sent to Marshal McLeod?" Semmes asked.

"I sent a report of results and losses sir, but didn't attempt to file a report of the battle on your behalf," Rhode reported. "The doctor assured me that you would recover, with God's grace, so it wasn't my place I felt to do so."

"Very well," Semmes nodded. "Send Mister Nettles. . ." he broke off, remembering that Nettles had perished in the battle. "Send me a secretary to dictate my report for His Highness," he forged on. "And help me consider someone to assume the duties of Commander Nettles. Proper candidates to choose from and so forth."

"I'll solicit two names from each squadron commander, sir," Rhode offered. Semmes nodded, still gazing out the window.

"Have the secretary report as soon as possible."

Rhode departed, leaving Semmes to soak in his despair at the destruction of his navy. Again, he prayed that their sacrifice was not in vain. For the Royal Navy, the war was essentially over, at least for the foreseeable future.

It would be a land war, now.

CHAPTER NINETEEN

-

Memmnon read the report with an increasing furor. By the time he got to the end of Davies' report he was furious.

"Damn it all!" he managed to turn his exclamation into a quiet curse, though his desire was to scream it at the top of his lungs. Callens and his entire regiment had slipped out of camp and deserted. No doubt answering a summons from either Therron or Sherron. His eyes narrowed at the thought of his near deranged sister. Where was she? He turned to his aide who was never far from him.

"Where is my sister?" he asked, his voice dangerously soft.

"I do not know, milord, but I will send someone to find her at once," the man replied, a questioning eyebrow raised.

"No," Memmnon shook his head. "Send me Chief Constable Grey," he ordered. "Now," he added. The aide bowed and hurried to dispatch his own staff in search of the chief of the Royal Constabulary. Memmnon sat down at his desk and hurriedly wrote out orders, his anger resulting in having to start over twice as a broken pen tip punched through the paper he was using. As he was writing another aide entered his office, passed through by his secretary.

"Yes?" he demanded without looking up.

"Message from Lord Parno, milord," the man offered, holding out the sealed leather bag. Memmnon took it as carefully as if he knew there to be a serpent inside, assuming it was more bad news. He relaxed slightly as he read of Parno's offer to send a unit after Callens if Memmnon needed it.

"Very well," Memmnon nodded. "I'll prepare an answer when I've made a decision. Won't be long," he assured the man.

"Milord," the messenger nodded and left the office. Memmnon exhaled sharply as he sat back, rubbing his hands down his face. This was a complete mess. Thanks to his father's desire to 'keep down scandal', Therron was still alive, and in exile rather than prison. Where he could conveniently be freed and allowed to create rebellion among his supporters, since everyone by now 'knew' that Therron had been replaced due to 'ill health'.

"What a mess," he gave words to his thoughts just as a knock sounded on his door.

"Enter!"

Sebastian Grey entered the office, tall and imposing in his black and green uniform. Grey was the commander of the entire Royal Constable forces of the Kingdom of Soulan.

"You sent for me, sir?" Grey's deep voice nearly shook the desk Memmnon sat behind. He nodded, pointing to a seat. He spent the next ten minutes explaining to an increasingly agitated Grey the situation. By the time he had finished Grey was alternating between shock and outrage.

"What do you need me to do?" he finally asked, unable to really say anything else at the moment. When in doubt, ask for orders.

"First, I want my sister confined along with her entire staff," Memmnon ordered. "Nor is she to have access to that staff under any circumstances. I want that staff questioned thoroughly to see what knowledge or involvement they have in any of these matters, no matter how small or slight. They are to remain confined until I vet each one, after which they will be released both from confinement and from service. We can't afford to have them here any longer."

"Yes sir," Grey nodded. He had known Memmnon a long time, had answered to him directly for several years now. He had never seen the Crown Prince any angrier than he was at this moment.

"You will search my sister's apartments for any damning evidence before confining her to her rooms. You still have female Constables, do you not?"

"Of course, sir," Grey nodded.

"One will be assigned to. . .no, two will be assigned to her rooms directly at all time, with two male counterparts outside her doors at all times. She is under no circumstances allowed to leave those rooms without my express permission. Each Constable selected for that duty must be carefully vetted as well to ensure that none of them will show allegiance to my sister or brother and assist them in any way." Grey started to bluster at the implication that his subordinates would do such a thing but a raised hand stopped him.

"I can't afford any more mistakes," he said simply. "The very existence of the Kingdom is at stake, Sebastian. If they are allowed to make this happen, there is no way the Imperial Army won't conquer us. I have to get this under control as quickly as possible. Understand?"

Grey did understand and nodded his reply. He had not thought about the problem beyond his own duties. He could now see the immense pressure that Memmnon was under. With Tammon's health failing more each day, Memmnon was forced to assume more and more responsibility, and he could not depend on his remaining family for assistance that was rightfully his to demand. Well, other than young Parno, he allowed. That one had matured nicely in the last year it seemed.

"Then get it done as rapidly as possible," Memmnon ordered. "It may already be too late."

"At once Milord," Grey rose and left at once, headed to follow his orders. Memmnon rang the bell that summoned his personal secretary and the man appeared in seconds at his door.

"Milord?"

"Have Inspector General Brock summoned to me at once," he ordered briskly. "No matter what he is engaged in, he is to report to me immediately."

"Sir," the man nodded and was gone. Memmnon sat back again, once more rubbing his face with his open hands.

Today had started out such a nice day.

-

Sherron checked her bag once more, satisfied that she had all she needed for now. She would be back, after all, she smiled to herself. She indicated the final bag to her footman and he took the luggage and departed. With a final look around her rooms, Sherron was out the door, where she ran straight into Sebastian Grey and a half-dozen Royal Constables, three of them women.

"What is the meaning of this?" she demanded, despite the cold feeling in the pit of her stomach.

"I'll have to ask that you return to your rooms, your Highness," Grey said, his voice soft but unyielding. "There's a matter that we need to discuss with you."

"It will have to wait," Sherron said smoothly. "I have a previous engagement."

"It's been canceled, your Highness," Grey's voice grew cold. Behind him Sherron could see her footman protesting as two more Constables seized her bag and detained him.

"Release him at once!" she ordered loudly, trying to move around Grey only to have him side-step her and block her way once more.

"That isn't going to happen, Princess," he told her flatly. "Your staff has been detained for questioning until further notice. Now please return to your room. At once," he added.

"Step, aside, Constable." Sherron bit her words off. "Now."

"Ladies, please escort the Princess back inside and establish your watch," Grey gave up the pretense of respectful address. The three uniformed women moved as one, seizing the Princess' arms and propelling her back into her suite.

"My father will hear of this!" Sherron shouted as she struggled against them, but these women had been selected for their size and strength, then retained for their intelligence. The struggle was lost before it began.

"He certainly will," Grey agreed, following behind.

"I'll have all of your heads for this!" Sherron hissed in fury.

"I seriously doubt it."

-

Just entering the palace grounds, Sherron McLeod's footman heard the commotion as his fellow retainers were gathered together, protesting loudly at their treatment. Slipping into the shadows, he watched as Royal Constables gathered Her Highness' staff and as many of Prince Therron's as remained, escorting them away. Further into the palace grounds.

That could only mean arrest. The footman swore softly to himself. His mistress' plans had been found out!

Was there a traitor? Or had she merely been careless? Was there anyone left he could trust? Would they be looking for him? Since delivering her message he had been keeping a low profile, but he had served the twins all their lives. He would be known.

She would want him to notify Callens, but what to tell him? That her Ladyship was being detained? He didn't know that for a fact, but it was easy enough to infer. What he couldn't do was confirm it. If he showed his face he would join his fellow servants in captivity.

Nor could he inform the Colonel where Lord Therron was at present. Despite her Ladyship's best attempts, they had no idea where the Prince had been taken. If he went to Callens empty handed, the Colonel might kill him to help hide his own part in the plot.

But Callens and his men represented the last chance that the Prince might have. He might be risking his life, but someone had to know what was happening.

Decision made, the servant made his way carefully through the night toward the Royal stables. He needed a horse.

-

General Wilson, commander of the 1st Imperial Field Army, glared at his cavalry commander. General Stone stood before him unflinching.

"Can you explain to me why the ever to be damned southern cavalry are wreaking havoc on my supply lines, General? More importantly, can you explain to me why you and your cavalry haven't stopped them?" Wilson's voice was rising steadily.

"I don't think it's cavalry, sir," Stone reported evenly.

"What the hell do you mean it's not cavalry?" Wilson demanded. "Of course it is!"

"Every survivor so far reports that the men are not in uniform and show little organization, other than the one they call 'boss'. There appears to be no chain of command, no discipline as we would expect in a military unit, nothing to identify them as anything other than garden variety bandits."

"Garde-" Wilson cut himself off, trying to get control of his temper. The Emperor was, so far, still on his side, but his messages to Wilson indicated a growing impatience for action, despite the risk. Wilson needed his supply lines to be safe and secure.

"Your garden bandits are stripping our rear areas of supplies, equipment and manpower!" Wilson grated finally. "Seems a bit much for mere bandits, Stone."

"They are sizable and well led," Stone allowed, "but I still maintain that they are not a part of the Soulan military. The evidence so far argues against it, sir."

"I don't give a good flying damn what they are or who they answer to, I want them gone!" Wilson had finally heard enough. "I'll give you two weeks, at the most, to report back to me that they've been dealt with, or I by the Emperor will deal with you!" he threatened. Wilson stiffened to attention and saluted.

"Yes, sir!"

"Get out," Wilson ordered stiffly and Stone whirled and departed. Wilson sat heavily in his chair, angry still at this and so many other events that were conspiring against him. He looked at his map and frowned. He had to get his offensive moving again, and soon. Waiting for the southerners to attack was a good plan unless they didn't attack. Then it became a first class way to get beheaded. He couldn't wait any longer. Every day the army sat here was costing his Emperor a huge sum. It couldn't last forever.

Decision made suddenly, Wilson called for his aide to summon his staff. It was time to make some adjustments.

-

As a rule, Edward Willows did not often accompany his wagons unless he was making a trading trip of some size. A routine mission to ferry equipment and supplies, even in time of war, would not usually qualify as important enough to rate his presence. This mission had turned out to be anything but routine, however, from the very moment it had begun.

Having answered a call for transportation services to the Crown, Edward had arrived in Nasil with thirty wagons, plus three more with camp gear and supplies for his drivers and scouts. A total of almost one hundred men and women. Edward had never employed women as teamsters before but manpower was in short supply with the reserves and militia all having reported for duty, and he needed drivers. There were actually several women from Cove Canton among his crew in fact as wives, daughters and sisters of Prince Parno's men had applied for work with the Duke of Cumberland.

No sooner had his train arrived than the IG himself had ordered his train sent to the south of Nasil under heavy escort. Edward had wondered at that as two full companies of cavalry seemed like a large escort for so small a wagon train, but the IG has been notably quiet as to the reason.

The next day Edward had been introduced to a very fussy little man named Roda Finn and told that he would be in charge of the operation. Finn was blunt and not a little rude at times, but Edward soon recognized that this was due to the immense strain the man was under. Edward's own wagons were added to another twenty-two wagons that would be operated by Crown teamsters and other men, a fair few of which were wearing the livery of Parno's personal command. That puzzled Edward, knowing that Parno was now the Lord Marshal and as such was probably a long way from Nasil, but again information was closely held.

The next surprise was when Finn reported that he expected the trip to take almost three weeks. Edward, used to deadlines and turnarounds, had scoffed at that notion once he looked at the map.

"We can make this in ten days or less!" he had exclaimed, only to have Finn shake his head.

"You will make less than ten miles per day, weather permitting," the little man had assured him. "Faster invites disaster."

Edward thought this completely ludicrous, but he had already been informed that the speed of the column would be established by the screen commander, not himself. There would be no deviation from the marching order, either. Wagons would be spaced at one hundred yards apart at all times, including in camp. That order went against every possible security measure, but also explained why the screen was so large. The train would stretch for more than a mile with so much room between wagons.

He had watched as each wagon was loaded, the people from the Foundry taking great pains to do so slowly and carefully. So much so that it took two full days to load the train, ensuring that they would not be able to depart until the third morning after.

The last surprise had come when Major Willis, commander of the escort, had informed Edward that by order of the Lord Marshal he, Willows, would not be allowed to ride with the wagons. At first he had been taken aback by this, assuming that this was some lingering animosity for the unpleasantness between himself and the prince that had occurred over the winter. His emotions ran a gamut until he arrived at angry, but Willis had cut his tirade off curtly by assuring Willows that Lord Parno's orders were to ensure Willows safety and nothing more. Though still somewhat rankled at the order, Edward recognized that he did not have much choice but to follow the Major's orders. Parno's orders.

So it was that a train of nearly sixty wagons and well over one hundred horsemen set off from Nasil on a three-week trip to the front, with Edward Willows no closer to getting any answers than he had been when he had arrived. He watched as scouts poured over the roadway before the train, with pioneers ranging ahead in specialty wagons to repair damage to the road and ensure a smooth road bed for the wagons that followed. All of this simply increased Willows' curiosity, but no answers were coming from Willis.

As he chafed under the tight restrictions of the trip north, Edward wondered if he'd get any answers when he arrived.

-

General Raines watched the other side of the bridge and the surrounding land across the Great River from the observation tower through his glass, noting that activity was slight with the rain. The rain impeded his own actions, but it was a small price to pay for a few days of relative quiet for his men. Continually on edge by the presence of a large enemy force so close at hand when they had no help available was starting to wear on his men and their commanders.

He knew how they felt.

Confident he could hold for at least a time against even a determined attack, Raines was under no illusions that he could maintain his position indefinitely against a full scale assault by his opposite number in the Imperial Army. He simply did not have the numbers on his side. If the Imperial commander on the western side of the bridge decided he was willing to accept the casualties that such an assault would bring him, all Raines could do was inflict those casualties for as long as possible. He could not withdraw, so he would hold until his men were overwhelmed. His only hope was to inflict so many casualties on the enemy that their force was unable to capitalize on their victory once 2nd Army had fallen.

He lowered the glass, fighting to keep a sigh from escaping his lips. Wouldn't do for the young Captain in charge of this mission to see his General so frustrated and forlorn, after all.

"Sir?" He turned to see that very Captain standing behind him.

"Yes?"

"Wagons approaching from the east, sir, down the old trade route."

"From Nasil?" Raines asked. This might be the help promised him by Marshal McLeod.

"That direction, yes sir," the young man nodded. "Several men in the Lord Marshal's livery with them, as well," he added.

"Excellent," Raines felt some of his despondency leave him. Parno had promised that this help might make holding his position much easier. And much more costly for the Nor as well.

"They're making camp well outside, sir," the Captain noted. "Almost three miles back and more. And they aren't bunching their wagons despite orders to do so. In fact, they've requested a regiment of horsemen for security, stressing that it needs to be solid men with a smart commander."

"Send Brigadier James, then," Raines ordered. His nephew was about as smart as any commander he had. "Tell him to listen to the wagon master and follow his instructions. I'll be along presently."

"Yes sir," the Captain nodded and disappeared down the ladder to deliver the orders. Raines watched him go before turning back to the view once more. Taking a last look at the far side of the river through his glass, he put it away and started down the ladder himself.

He wanted to see what it was that gave Prince Parno such confidence in their ability to repel an attack.

-

General Davies watched Marshal McLeod dismount with the slightest bit of trepidation. He had been informed of Callens and his regiment having departed south, but had not taken any action of his own, believing that it was more prudent to keep his forces arrayed against the Imperial Nor army. He knew he was about to find out if that were accurate.

"General," Parno was friendly enough despite his obvious fatigue and ire. "I understand my brother's former regiment is in the wind?"

"I'm afraid so, milord," Davies nodded, bowing slightly as he waved Parno into the command post. The small house was heavily guarded. Parno stepped inside, followed by Davies, then by Enri Willard, Cho Feng and Harrel Sprigs, who remained at the door.

"Our scouts report a good deal of activity along the Nor front, milord," Davies motioned to the map set on a central table in the main room. "Based on their activity, I believe that they are preparing to attack our lines, perhaps within days."

Parno studied the situation for a moment, nodding absently at the notations on the map. Finally, he looked up at Sprigs.

"Right away, sir," the young man nodded before Parno could even speak and ducked outside. Parno frowned slightly, then returned to the map.

"When did this flurry of activity begin?" he asked.

"At least three days ago, milord," Davies replied. "To be honest, I don't know why they've waited this long. They clearly have us at a disadvantage."

"They won't much longer, I hope," Parno informed him. He quickly outlined the results of the sea battle and the movements he had ordered based on that outcome. Davies pursed his lips at that, thinking.

"Herrick will likely get here sooner," he said at last, moving to a map along the wall that showed the entire kingdom. He touched the southern Alma/Misi border and traced an old trade route still in use by the kingdom. "He has a shorter distance to travel. I would think he can be here within three weeks of receiving his orders, assuming no difficulties in getting under way," he continued, more to himself than anyone in the room. Finally, he turned to face Parno.

"I suspect we will have to face this attack without their assistance, milord," he said finally. "I'd love to have them here, even in reserve, but I don't see any possible way for Herrick to be here in less than two weeks from today and three is more likely. There is almost no way we'll have three more weeks of inaction on this front. Not with this level of action," he motioned again to the table map.

"Agreed," Parno sighed heavily. "That means we'll have to face them with what we have and what we can get in the next few days. We'll need to-" he broke off as Sprigs returned with Parsons in tow.

"You wanted to see me, milord?" the scout asked.

"Indeed, Mister Parsons," Parno nodded and indicated the map. "Please take a look." The scout moved forward and studied the map for a moment, frowning slightly.

"Lot of movement, milord," he said finally.

"So it is. I'd like you and your men to take a look, based on what you see here, and tell me how long you think we have before the Nor are prepared to strike. I can give you one day, tomorrow, and afterward I want you back here reporting in. Understood?"

"I do, milord," Parsons took his own map from his shoulder bag and made a few notations in short, quick strokes of a pencil. In less than a minute he returned the map to his bag.

"I'll get right on it, sir."

"Carry on then," Parno nodded. "And do be careful, Mister Parsons."

"Will do, milord," Parsons smiled gently and then was gone.

"Let's look at our own lines and see what changes we can make," Parno said, returning his gaze to the table. "Harrel, inform Major Lars I'd like to see him as soon as this meeting is done."

"Sir," Sprigs nodded and hurried out.

"Enri, have Karls send someone from the Sheep to see if we have a train on the way from Roda, please," Parno ordered after a minute's silence. "That would simplify things a great deal."

"Right away, milord," the swordfighter nodded and went to find his brother.

"Train, milord?" Davies asked.

"I have a surprise for the Nor, General," Parno smiled wanly. "Assuming it arrives in time, anyway. If it does, then perhaps we'll make a start on throwing the heathen out of our lands very soon."

"I'd like that milord," Davies almost growled.

"Let us see what we can see, then."

-

Edward Willows watched as the first wagons began easing into the area south of the main camp. There were three buildings there, a small house, a shed and a larger barn. Already two fresh companies of cavalry were patrolling the area, ensuring privacy. As he watched, the first wagon rolled into the barn. Perhaps thirty minutes later, it rolled out again, noticeably lighter and moving faster.

"At this rate it will take all night to offload," he groused to Major Briggs, the escort commander. The two had become something of fast friends on the long slow trip here.

"That is the schedule," Briggs admitted. "We're to-" Whatever he was going to add was cut off when three of his men rode up accompanied by a man wearing the Lord Marshal's colors. His personal colors.

"Sir," one of Briggs' men saluted. "This man claims he's a courier from the Marshal."

"I don't claim a damn thing," the man in question snarled. "Lord Parno wanted to know if your train had arrived. If so, he wanted word of it right away."

"You are?" Briggs asked/demanded.

"My name is James," the man said amiably enough. "Lord Parno's personal command," he added with a tinge of pride. The others looked a bit more wary, now. James looked at Edward Willows.

"Lord Cumberland," he nodded. "The Marshal will be pleased to see you safe."

"You know this man?" Briggs demanded, looking at Edward. Willows nodded.

"Yes. He's visited my home more than once as part of Lord Parno's escort. I've seen him there more than once. And at Cove Canton, for that matter," he added. He hadn't known the man's name, but he had recognized him as one of Parno's escort.

"Very well then," Briggs nodded. "You three will accompany Mister James back, escorting Lord Cumberland to the Marshal's headquarters. Once there you may return so long as Lord Edward has no need for an escort back."

"Sir," the sergeant saluted. Briggs turned to Willows.

"It was a pleasure having your company along this trek, sir," he said easily. "Fortune favor your road." He extended his hand.

"And yours, Major," Edward grasped the hand, smiling slightly. "And yours."

-

It was the work of many hours and not a little sweat to get roughly one third of the train's stores brought to the waiting artillery areas of the Royal Army's defensive positions. It was difficult to see as open flame was far too risky around Finn's 'goodies', thus the workers had to make do with reflected light and dimly illuminating safety lamps.

The work continued with the sunrise and went through most of the next day as roughly another third of the stores were placed in a purpose built bunker that had been lined with logs and then covered with dirt. While the loss of one of the storage areas would be horrible, it would not be a catastrophe. All would not be lost.

The guard on each place, whether at the artillery site, the bunker, or the small headquarters for the newly formed 'Ordnance' department of the Army of Soulan, security was tight, a full company of men on duty at all times. In all, an entire battalion of men separated from the army to defend these areas of vital supplies.

Soldiers complained bitterly about being uprooted from their camps, wondering why they had drawn the short straw on some stupid guard duty of some general officer's personal harem or race horses or whiskey stash, or whatever rumor made the rounds over the next two days.

None of them had a hint of the truth. In all the camp, less than two hundred men knew that Roda Finn had just helped even the odds against a struggling Soulan Army.

-

"Are we ready?" Wilson demanded, looking at his corps commanders. "We had better be," he added testily.

"All but our cavalry," his senior commander, General Milton Fairmount nodded.

"We won't have Stone's cavalry for this attack," Wilson told them flatly. "Soulanies have been raiding the rear and he's gone to put a stop to it." *I hope*, Wilson didn't have to add.

"Taking a risk, sir, not to have Stone guarding our flank, "General Darrell Thomas, commander of the 3rd Corps remarked. "Soulanie's horsemen could get around our flank without them."

"Soulanie horsemen are in our rear areas," Wilson bit out. "Long way from us here. Stone will keep them occupied. We haven't seen a southern horseman since the last battle to amount to anything. A few pickets and couriers, but no real cavalry force. No probes, no reconnaissance-in-strength, nothing to indicate they have more than a corporal's guard of cavalry left in their camp."

The four assembled commanders looked uneasy at that report but said nothing. Their fifth counterpart was absent from this meeting because it had been his generals that had allowed the flanking attack some weeks ago that had all but decimated his own command. Wilson had been extremely angry since then and none of them wanted to attract his ire.

"Tomorrow, sixteen divisions will attack the Soulan lines," Wilson indicated the map behind him. "Well over one hundred and twenty thousand well trained, well led men with the best equipment we can give them. I expect them, and all of you, to give a good account of yourselves in battle. The southerners are behind fixed fortifications, from here," he indicated a slough of the river, "to well past this small town, here," he indicated a place called Gleacin. "Our estimates are that the Soulan units arrayed against us total no more than fifty thousand men, and that's being generous. Their losses at Loville and the retreat from there were heavy, and we've seen nothing as yet to indicate that they've received substantial reinforcements."

"We're going to hit them before they can get help and roll right over them," he said grimly, looking back to his commanders.

"We've taken over a month since our last action to put new plans into place, to train some of our greener recruits, and to stockpile supplies. In that time we've been forced to send more and more men north to protect out supply lines. At this rate, if we don't attack soon, the Soulanies will outnumber us!" he grinned to show that part was a jest, but he was serious about no more delays.

"I want complete quiet come morning," he ordered. "Lines will form an hour before light, in silence and the dark. Have regimental and company officers out today inspecting where their men will be, familiarizing themselves with the ground. I want no mistakes, and I don't want the southerners to know we're coming until they see us coming out of the fog. Noise discipline will be strictly enforced for this. If it's broken, kill the offender."

"Three Corps will be in reserve along with our actual reserve Corps," he went back to the map. "Thomas, I want you poised to capitalize on any breakthroughs or any weakness in the Soulanie lines that we can exploit." General Thomas nodded.

"The Reserve Corps has the rough equivalent of two divisions," Wilson informed them. "If any of you get into a bind, I can probably send you assistance, but it won't be more than a brigade, and will likely be short. Figure two regiments at most. Don't plan on that help, gentlemen. Plan to do this yourselves. But know that some limited assistance is there for the asking in dark times." All of them nodded, grateful for any help.

"Any questions?" he asked. There were none. Each man here knew his job well.

"Very well then, gentlemen," he nodded. "Be about your work. See to your commands and be ready an hour before sunrise coming morning. Dismissed." The men filed out of the small house until it was just Wilson and Fairmount remaining.

"What is it, Milt?" Wilson asked.

"Big gamble, sir," Fairmount said at once, looking at the map.

"I don't think so," Wilson shook his head.

"Soulanie cavalry is out there, we're screwed," Fairmount tried again.

"They're not," Wilson shook his head stubbornly. "They're tearing up our rear areas right now, probably."

"At least see if the savages will cover our flank, then, Gerry," Fairmount took advantage of a decades old friendship to urge caution once more. "Better than nothing," he added with a shrug.

"We've not been successful in getting the Tribe's assistance in endeavors like this," Wilson shrugged. "But I will try," he added when he saw a frown starting to form on Fairmount's features. The frown lessened at the statement.

"It's a good plan," Fairmount offered, almost in way of apology.

"We'll see come morning."

-

"We can expect an attack at any time," Parno told his assembled generals that evening. "It could come as soon as dawn for that matter," he added and saw several nods.

"With that in mind, we will be standing to an hour before dawn every morning, beginning tomorrow," he continued. "Scouts will deploy in a screen ranging out to two hundred yards, with bonfires lit starting at one hundred yards. One of the tricks the Nor liked to use at the Gap was to approach in darkness, trying to keep sound to a minimum. Only good scouts prevented it from surprising us."

"Our engineers have been deploying some of the new weapons that we first used at the Gap," Parno indicated his own men, Seymour among them. "Major Seymour commanded my crossbow company at the Gap and has briefed your own men this afternoon on what they're looking for and when to fire." He waved for Seymour to speak.

"Your crossbowmen will need to be near the front ranks, but cannot engage the enemy directly until their mission is complete. Those of you who watched us deploy this afternoon saw their targets," Seymour pointed to a table where an inert clay mine sat.

"I know that it looks harmless," he grinned. "I assure you it is anything but. We have a great many more of them than we did at the Gap, but there is a great deal more territory to cover as well, so the screen is thin to say the least. While the mines will be important, and will play a major role in blunting the attack, they won't win the battle by themselves. Still, don't allow the crossbowmen to be diverted to other missions until the mines are exhausted." With that Seymour stepped back to his place along the wall.

"I know it seems ridiculous," Parno resumed his briefing. "When you see them in action you'll understand. Not all of them will work, and some bolts won't hit the target, but at least the first round will be worth something for shock value alone. We've seen it before, and I assure you it will work, at least once. Even if the survivors of the Gap have told the Imperial commanders what to expect, they will have to see it for themselves to believe it. They won't want to believe it, otherwise, and will look for any other reason as the excuse for their defeat in the east."

"Hopefully our cavalry battle a few weeks ago have given them that excuse," he grinned again, to several chuckles from the men in the room. "Archers have been issued a new kind of arrow as well," he continued. "Your archery commanders were allowed to see a few of those arrows in use this afternoon, so they know what to expect. Each division has a full battalion of archers armed with these new arrows and orders on how and when to use them. As Major Seymour noted, they aren't to be interfered with. They might make a great deal of difference in the coming battle, so long as they last. Again, we've used them before to good effect. They aren't going to be as damaging as the mines by themselves, but launched in flights by four or five hundred expert bowmen you can expect them to get results."

"We're outnumbered," Parno said flatly. "Heavily so. We expect the odds to be at least three-to-one if not higher. Not insurmountable, but a concern nonetheless. We have help coming, but not soon enough. In a perfect world, we would use our cavalry to skirt their flank and counter-attack them, but we simply don't have the manpower. As a result, the 4th Cavalry will be posted on the left as a guard against the same kind of attack from the Nor, as well as a screening element against any possible incursion by Tribal warriors in the Nor's employ."

"The 2nd and 6th Cavalry will be deployed here, and here," he indicated the positions on the map behind him, "as both reserves to counter any breakthrough, and a ready force to press any advantage we happen to find. The 9th Cavalry, on loan from Third Corps, will be stationed further back as a guard against a deep flanking incursion.

The line will be as it is now, centered on the infantry and mounted infantry units, with artillery deployed all along the rear in support. Major Lars," Parno looked to another of his own men. The bulky Major Lars stepped forward.

"We have a good deal of special ordnance for our artillery to use against the Nor," he said without preamble. "Similar to the mines, these weapons will make a major impact on the Nor. We've seen it ourselves, and the damage the weapons inflict, along with the shock value, will be tremendous. As with the mines, however, it will not win the battle for us."

"The new ordnance has been distributed to the best artillery battalions from each Corps. We've taken them to the rear and made sure they are aware of the care that must be taken in handling these weapons. I cannot stress enough how careful they must be. Some of my own men who are experienced in their use will be assigned to each unit as advisers. For all our sake, please listen when they speak. They know all too well what can happen if things go awry with these weapons." Like Seymour had, Lars stepped back without taking questions.

"These new 'gadgets', as they've often been called," Parno resumed, "will be helpful, but make no mistake that we're in for a brawl. I don't have to tell you that the Nor have a much better trained army than at any time in our recent history. They're tough, and fairly well led." Heads nodded around the room.

"They're also somewhat predictable and a bit too locked into that training," Parno continued. "They don't seem to think well when presented with a scenario they aren't trained or prepared for. Since we haven't used these weapons here yet, they may well assume we either don't have them, or we've used them all.

Either way works for us."

"But as I said, we're still in for a brawl. We may manage to break their first attack, or even the second, but they will keep coming, and will probably reach our lines eventually no matter what we do. There's no point in thinking for even a minute that this won't come down to sword, pike and shield. It will."

"For many of you, this will be the first pitched battle of the war. It's hell. I learned that the hard way. Expect losses, and expect them to hurt. They will. There's no way around it that I can find, and I've looked hard. We are going to get hurt." He paused, letting that sink in.

"But we're going to win," he said flatly, finishing his miniature pep talk.

"Are there any questions?" he asked after another pause. One man raised a hesitant hand.

"Yes?"

"If we have to withdraw-"

"We won't be withdrawing," Parno cut the man off. "We don't have anywhere to go. The Nor have gone as far into our territory as they're going to. This is where we stop them. Anyone else?" his tone left no room for discussion.

"Very well then," Parno straightened when no one else had questions for him. "Each command will be responsible for their own runners. Any orders from me will likely be carried by one of my own men. Unless something happens, your runners can find me here," he indicated a central point behind the main line. "If I move, someone will be there to let your runner know where. Do not look to me for orders, however. Your immediate superiors have my full confidence and know all of my plans."

"We will kick their ass, gentlemen," he almost growled, his eyes glowering. "We've had quite enough of this foolishness, and it stops here. See to your commands, gentlemen," he dismissed. The men stood, came to attention as a group, then broke apart, heading for their own commands surrounded by their subordinates as plans were finalized even as they walked.

Parno watched them go as Davies approached him. He nodded to the older man.

"General."

"Milord," Davies returned the nod. "Do you wish to make plans for a counter-attack should the opportunity arise?"

"No," Parno shook his head. "Not until Freeman and Herrick get here at any rate. With their strength, then yes. We'll definitely be launching our own attack. Not until then."

"Very well," Davies nodded, almost relieved. "These weapons are quite something, milord," he changed the subject. He had seen one of the mines hit, as well as the Hubel arrows.

"They are that," Parno grinned wryly. "With any luck, they'll be the difference tomorrow. Or whenever the attack comes."

"But you think tomorrow," Davies said.

"I do, and have no idea why," Parno admitted. "We'll see soon enough, I suppose. Parsons should be back soon."

Almost as if he'd conjured him, Parsons arrived less than five minutes later. He was sweat stained and dirty, but looked triumphant.

"Good news then?" Parno asked with a hint of sarcasm.

"Depends on your definition, milord," Parsons admitted. "But I can show you where most of the Nor army is at the moment," he spread his map out on the table. "And I can tell you that they were issuing field rations to their men."

The staff still in the room exchanged glances. Issuing field rations was only done when commanders expected an army to be on the move. Soon.

"Show me, then," Parno ordered.

It would be a long night.

CHAPTER TWENTY

-

Callens paced back and forth near the fire, his back to his tent. He and his men had been on site for a week with no word from either Prince Therron or Princess Sherron. He shook his head slightly at his own foolishness in obeying her orders to start with. Now here he was, having led his men in what even the most generous soul would see as treason, with no one to answer to for his actions other than himself.

Not for the first time he cursed his affliction for Sherron McLeod. Damn the woman. If not for her he wouldn't be in this mess. He shook his head again, angry now at himself.

He was in this mess because of his own weakness and nothing else. Again he had the thought that if any of his men were so besot with a woman he'd have long ago gotten rid of them, and this was why. A man addled by a woman was a risk to himself and his fellows, and he'd just proven that be-

"Colonel, the pickets have apprehended a rider," one of his company commanders interrupted his train of thought. "He claims to be a servant of Her Ladyship."

"Bring him," Callens ordered briskly. Perhaps he was about to get some answers after all. Minutes later he was looking at the same rider he'd seen two weeks earlier, though this time looking dirty and disheveled.

"Well?" Callens demanded when the man looked at him.

"Her Ladyship appears to have been detained, Colonel, along with most of her staff," the man reported. "I observed this from just outside their reach. I cannot confirm that the Princess herself is actual being held, but my fellows have all been detained by Royal Constables inside the Palace." Callens felt a cold finger trace down his spine at this report.

"So, we're discovered then?" he demanded, taking a step forward.

"I do not know," the man admitted reluctantly. "I know only what I've reported. I cannot ascertain where Prince Therron is, either. It is being circulated throughout the Palace and the city that he is ill, and has been sent South for his health, but. . .that covers a lot of territory. I've found no one that can tell me where he might be. If he truly is ill, then that should narrow-"

"He isn't," Callens cut the man off. "He's been removed from his place because of his popularity, and that of Her Ladyship." He watched the man carefully, but all he got in return was a nod.

"I assumed as much," the servant replied.

"Did you see Her Ladyship at all?" Callens demanded. "In custody I mean?" he clarified.

"No, Colonel. I did not."

"Probably in her suite, then," Callens said thoughtfully. "We need to get her out. Do you think you could get myself and some of my men inside the Palace?" he asked.

"I can," the man said at once. "Fairly easily."

The faintest glimmer of a plan began to form in Callens' mind. He motioned toward his tent.

"Join me," he ordered. "We have a great deal to talk about."

-

"What are you doing?"

Stephanie turned to see Winnie Hubel standing behind her, watching as one of the soldiers assigned to her escort loaded her bags into the ambulance she used as a transport.

"I'm. . .I'm taking a trip," Stephanie told her haltingly, resisting the urge to fan away her blush. "What are you doing?"

"Watching you squirm," Winnie teased. "Where are you going?" she asked more seriously.

"Just. . .off and away for a few days, that's all," Stephanie waved the question away as if it were a bird or a bug.

"You're going west to see Parno," Winnie accused. "That's why your doctor's bag is going," she pointed to the large cowhide bag with Stephanie's initials on it waiting to be loaded.

"I always carry that," Stephanie reminded her. "And I haven't been to see my family since I got here. I'm caught up in my duties and classes are out until the next batch of students show up. . .and why am I explaining myself to you?" she caught herself finally.

"Probably because of the guilt," Winnie replied in a conspirator's whisper.

"Guilt!" Stephanie sputtered. "What guilt?"

"About going against Lord Parno's wishes and visiting him at the front, of course," Winnie replied at once. "I don't blame you for feeling guilty. After all," she batted her eyes, "you're bound to be a distraction. Right?"

Stephanie felt her face go redder, though she hadn't thought that possible. This had seemed like such a wonderful idea yesterday. Head for Nasil with visiting family as the pretense, then, well since she was so close to the front, no reason not to pop over and inspect the hospital there, make sure everything was up to caliber for Parno- the Kingdom's soldiers. And if she happened to see Parno while doing her inspection, well it surely wouldn't hurt to spend an evening in his company before resuming her trip.

"Fine, you caught me," she admitted, losing her pretense. "Yes. If I can get there, I'm going to visit. First to inspect the hospital, though. Once that's finished, then if I can see him, I intend to, even if it's just for dinner. Satisfied?"

"I wouldn't think Colonel Leman would let you go," Winnie remarked, to which Stephanie snorted.

"I do not answer to Colonel Leman, missy," she replied in a near huff. "For that matter, I don't answer to anyone here."

"Must be nice," Winnie sighed, leaning against the carriage. "How long do you think you'll be gone?" she asked suddenly, eyes growing bright. Stephanie looked at her for a moment before grinning suddenly.

"Ten days, perhaps, counting travel time," she answered. "Be a nice vacation, I suppose," she added.

"Sure would," Winnie nodded, looking off into the distance. Stephanie knew that look, having had it herself more than once.

"How long have you been here, Winnie?" she asked suddenly. The girl looked back to her.

"A year, I guess," she shrugged. "I stopped keeping up with it a while back. One day is like any other around here, most of the time."

"You haven't left the post that whole time?" Stephanie asked. "Gone to visit your family?"

"Papa is the only family I have," Winnie said, her voice even. "There's nowhere to go, really."

Stephanie made a decision suddenly.

"Pack your things," she ordered the younger woman. "Gather your things and get back here in an hour. I'll see Colonel Leman and make sure he knows where you're going and that it's all right."

"Really?" Winnie looked like a small girl for a moment. "How will you do that?" she asked.

"I'll pull rank," Stephanie grinned. "Hurry now," she shooed the girl away. "I want to be on the road soon enough we can get off the mountain before dark."

Winnie ran away without another word, heading to the small house she shared with her father when he was present on post. Stephanie watched her go, then steeled herself for a trip to see Colonel Leman.

She did hope he'd listen to reason. She hated to pull rank.

-

Parno watched the setting sun sink slowly behind a distant tree line, his mind racing ahead to consider his options. He didn't really have many.

Truthfully, he didn't have any at the moment. While recent events had been good, the timing wasn't the best. He had several thousand trained men coming north to bolster the army and give him the strength he needed to try and launch a counter-attack, but they weren't here now. Wouldn't arrive for ten days or more. And while he had no real proof of it, his instincts were screaming at him that he didn't have ten days. He was almost certain that he could expect the Imperial Army to come calling with the return of the sun.

He had three infantry divisions, two of which had suffered heavy losses in the fighting to date, along with two mounted infantry divisions in support. One of those had also suffered losses in the retreat to this point, leaving him only two intact divisions on line while the others were hovering at just over half strength for the most part. Those losses had been made good, to a point, with the addition of militia units, but those units were not near the caliber of the men they were trying to replace. Still, it was better than nothing.

He also had four cavalry divisions, the three that had been involved in his own attack a few weeks prior plus the one on loan from Raines command. All three of Davies' divisions had suffered losses in the earlier action, and Parno had taken Beaumont's brigade from one of them. For that matter he had attached a mounted infantry brigade to Beaumont's command as well, which took their strength from his main lines. For a second he wondered if he'd done the right thing with that effort, but shook off the thought almost as soon as it had formed. Right or wrong, it was done now so there was no point in rehashing it.

He had known the Nor would attack again sooner or later. He'd given them two sharp surprises that had bought him time, but that couldn't last forever. In all honesty he was a bit surprised that it had taken them this long to get back on line. He had to assume that the length of the delay had been used to strengthen the Imperial Army and close up the weak areas that Parno had already exploited.

There were two full battalions of artillery armed with Roda Finn's 'gadgets', ready to pummel the attacking Nor with fire and iron. The others would use traditional shot and pitch to supplement that fire. There were also nearly one thousand mines ready, with half of them already deployed for use. And two full battalions of longbowmen armed with the Hubel arrows would also help disrupt the Nor attack plan.

But this wasn't the Gap. He did not have terrain on his side here as he had there. He could be flanked if he wasn't careful. The odds were far better here than he had faced at the Gap, but he had a lot more ground he had to cover. And his command had to survive this time. He could not afford to sacrifice the army the same way he'd been forced to plan sacrificing himself and his men at the Gap. There were no reinforcements close enough to catch the surviving Nor as they pressed southward should he fail or fall.

The army had to hold here. Period. They had to stand strong and prevail until Herrick and Freeman arrived with their Corps. Once they were here, Parno planned to take them and the cavalry he hoped to preserve during the coming battle and strike north, attempting to drive the Imperial Army back as far as possible. With luck he could push them all the way back to the Ohi. If he could trap them against the river, so much the better. There might be an opportunity to destroy them with their backs to the water.

And that would leave the north wide open to invasion. He would marshal his armies and strike into northern territory, destroying anything he could and leaving ruin in his wake. If he showed the Nor the horrors that the southern kingdom had been forced to endure, then perhaps the people there would resist future efforts to strike south for fear of reprisal. And Parno planned to create a buffer zone of Imperial territory controlled by the Soulan Army that would protect their home against future invasion efforts. They would have to fight through their own nation and people just to get to his.

If he couldn't manage to destroy the Imperial government completely. He had been very careful not to reveal all of his intention in the brief glimpses he'd given others of his plans, but Parno had every intention, should he find it possible, to conquer the north completely and bring it under Soulanie rule. There would be no more Imperial invasions because there would be no more Imperial anything if he managed to get his way.

But all of that was for the future. For the present, he had to make sure that the Soulan Army survived the coming battle and threw back the Imperial attack. After that was done, then he could start thinking about how he would conquer the north once and for all.

-

General Wilson slipped away from his headquarters before sunset to ride the length of his lines, accompanied by his aide and three men as an escort. He didn't let anyone know he was going and kept a low profile to avoid any fuss over his presence. He wanted to see his men and get an idea of how they were faring on the eve of battle.

Until the cavalry attack a few weeks prior the Imperial Army had had things pretty much their own way for the most part. Yes, they had suffered losses, but time after time they had forced the vaunted Soulan Army to give ground. Something no other Imperial force in recent or recorded memory could honestly lay claim to.

Since that cavalry attack however, things had stalled. They had suffered heavy losses in that battle and the men's confidence had been shaken. Add to that the increasing strain on the supply efforts and the drain of manpower that had caused, and you had a recipe for poor morale and slipping attitudes.

Wilson needed to get things back on track and do it quickly. In order to make that happen, he needed a victory. A major victory. A decisive victory. He needed his army to deliver for him.

He quietly made sure that his men were being well cared for, receiving hot food and rest. They would be awakened around one in the morning to begin preparations and forming ranks. By four in the morning they would be on line, preparing to move forward.

By sunrise they would be in battle.

Guard posts were being manned by men from the reserve Corps, unassigned regiments replacing the normal standing guard so that everyone would be well rested. He hoped not to need his reserve units in the coming battle, but if he did they would have to make do. His combat units had to be rested and ready.

He knew by now that everyone was aware that they would be in combat in the morning. Even if announcements hadn't trickled down, the fact that they weren't standing their regular picket posts would be enough to alert most of his men that something was in the wind. It wouldn't take much thinking to make the leap forward to imminent combat in the offing.

By dusk Wilson had quietly ridden the length of his lines and turned for his own headquarters. The men looked good, looked ready for battle. There was nothing else to be done except to execute his plan well and give his men the opportunity to give him the victory he needed.

He was fairly confident he could do that. A few hours would prove him right or wrong, he knew.

-

On one side, the men knew they were going into battle with the coming of the sun. On the other, they knew that their officers were antsy with anticipation, which meant they knew something was in the offing.

For their part, the officers on the Imperial side of the field knew they would be heading into battle in a few hours, while the Soulan officers knew only that their new Marshal suspected they would soon face an attack. For several that was enough, though for others they scoffed, determined to wait and see.

But one group was already gone from the lines, creeping out into the dark in twos and threes, making their way across the distance between the two armies. Royal scouts formed a basket weaver pattern between the two armies making it impossible for any Nor soldiers to make it across without alerting someone.

The most adventuresome scouts crept to within actual seeing distance of the enemy, crawling on their bellies to the point where they could see the winking of camp fires and often hear raised voices. Beyond that point the scouts risked colliding with Imperial picket posts, so they stopped there for the evening, making themselves as comfortable as possible in the dark while maintaining their watch.

Some slept in place, the way a hunter would sleep while waiting for a deer to enter his area, listening even as he slumbered for something out of place. Others thought of home, or family. Of women, left behind in one fashion or another. Of where they would be right that moment if not for the Imperial attack on their homeland. Of what they might do if they survived the war unharmed.

The Imperial pickets cursed the luck that had them guarding posts all night, though at the same time thankful that the duty would see them in the reserve tomorrow. While not a guarantee of safety, it was a lot better than being in the front lines.

Two groups of men, separated in some cases by only a hundred yards. Uniforms, lifestyles, people so much different one from another, yet with surprisingly similar thoughts on their minds as they waited for the sunrise that would be the last many men on that field would see.

Neither side imagining for a moment that his opponent was anything like himself.

-

"Oh goodness!" Stephanie exclaimed as she got down from her carriage. Winnie was behind her but wasn't nearly as tired.

"That wasn't so bad," she shrugged.

"Not for you perhaps," Stephanie nodded. "I felt every bump those last few miles. I'm glad we're here."

'Here' was a small inn just off the mountain, one that also doubled as a courier station for Parno. Two of Stephanie's escort had ridden ahead to secure lodging for the two women and ensure that the stable was prepared to care for four dozen horses. As the two entered, stable hands were already leading the ambulance team to the barns while the escort saw to their own mounts.

The station had obviously been forewarned that Lady Stephanie was a person of importance to the Lord Marshal since a good meal was waiting for the two women, along with a hot bath and private room. They would share a room for the night, Stephanie seeing no reason that the two of them needed more than one. Part of her escort would sleep inside as a guard while the rest bunked in the barn.

After a meal and good bath, both women were feeling the fatigue of the trip, even though Winnie was too excited to feel very sleepy.

"We'll get an early start tomorrow," Stephanie said as she prepared for bed. "It will still take two more days to make it into Nasil. I wish we were going straight to the field, but that will look a bit suspicious," she sighed. Winnie chuckled softly as she polished her bow.

"What's so funny?" Stephanie demanded, though not with any heat. "Do you carry that thing everywhere?" she added, pointing at the bow.

"Yes," she said simply.

"Why?"

"Why do you carry your doctor bag?" Winnie shrugged in reply.

"Point," Stephanie nodded. Winnie was a woman, but she was mountain raised by a father who was all but a living legend when it came to a bow. Winnie was good enough to train even the best archers in the army. She might not be a physician, but Stephanie could recognize a professional when she saw one.

"You enjoy what you're doing?" she asked thoughtfully.

"Yes, though I wish I was making a more adequate contribution," Winnie nodded.

"How is it you think you can do that?" Stephanie asked. She had thought about how to approach this for a while now and this might be just the opportunity.

"By fighting of course," Winnie replied at once.

"And do you think one bow, no matter how good, will make that difference?" Stephanie questioned.

"I can't know until I see."

"Consider how many soldiers you've trained to be better archers so far, Winnie," Stephanie pressed on. "Five hundred? A thousand? More?"

"I don't know, to be honest," Winnie said after a moment to think. "A lot," she admitted.

"And could anyone you've met so far, aside from your father, have trained them as good as you? Let alone any better than you have?"

Winnie was longer considering that question, as it was something she hadn't thought about before. Finally, she shook her head.

"I suppose not," she finally answered.

"So how do you think you can top that contribution to the war effort, then?" Stephanie challenged. "Yes, your bow might come in handy at the front, but how many men will fight better because they've had you to train them? How much of an impact can a thousand or more bows that have been taught by a real expert make on the outcome of a battle?"

"I. . .I hadn't considered it like that," the girl admitted thoughtfully.

"I thought not," Stephanie carefully kept any hint of victory from her voice. "That was the point made to me when I wanted to be at the front, too," she added. "That the surgeons I trained would ultimately save more lives that I could on my own if I were to leave them and go myself. While I don't like it," she admitted, "I have come to see the truth in it. I've already trained many medics and army surgeons to a much higher standard than the army has enjoyed to this point. They will do much better work because of the work I've done with them in the school we've established at Cove. So, while it's not what I wanted, I'm still doing a great deal for the army even though I'm not actually with them in the field."

"That's true," Winnie mused. "Maybe you're right," she said after another minute. "I just wanted to go so badly I never thought about that. All I could see was that I was a far better archer than any of the men I'd sent to the army so far.

That was all I was looking at."

"You are better," Stephanie nodded firmly. "And that's what makes you so valuable to Parno, and your father, right where you are. Do you think your father could be away assisting Roda if he didn't have you to carry on the training at Cove? If you weren't there, who could he leave in charge while working off site?"

"True," Winnie agreed. "All true, Lady Freeman," she smiled brightly. "I know you planned that a while. I appreciate you showing me my worth without belittling my desire to serve."

"I respect your desire, Winnie," Stephanie told her plainly. "And your bravery. It's simply that we're in a terrible spot at the moment. Literally against the wall with nowhere to go. Parno needs archers that only you can train. He needs you where you are for now. He needs men trained to the level that you can train them so that he can use them to defeat the Nor and drive them from our homeland. There are thousands who can serve in the army. There are very few who can train them as well as you can. Only a handful."

"I see why he likes you so much," Winnie teased slightly, causing Stephanie to blush, but she grinned.

"Well, let's put that away and get some rest," she ordered. "We've a long day ahead tomorrow."

"Yes, milady," Winnie grinned when Stephanie sputtered.

-

"We'll leave with the light," Callens ordered his assembled officers. "We have to assume that the word has gone out by now, so we'll be hunted if we're seen. I'll take a small force and head into the palace to try and free her ladyship. Warren, you'll take the regiment south and wait for us here," he indicated a spot just out of the city. "We'll join you as soon as possible. Stay out of sight and send a man here," he indicated a meeting place, "to lead us to you. We'll wait for night to make our move so it will be late when we arrive. Be ready to move out as soon as we get there in case we're pursued. Any questions?"

There were none.

"All right then, make sure we're ready to go as soon as the sun is up. I need to meet with my team and let our inside man brief us. Carry on." Warren waited until the others were gone before speaking.

"Big gamble, sir," he said softly. "What if this goes wrong?"

"Then it falls to you to find Prince Therron and free him," Callens said flatly. "He is depending on us."

"Yes sir," Warren nodded. "Any idea where he may be?"

"No, but I suspect Her Ladyship will know, or be able to find out," Callens replied. "If we can get her out and meet up with you then we'll leave straight away and go to him. If you can find a carriage and horses along the way, bring it with you. Her Ladyship will need one if this is a long trip."

"Slow us down," Warren pointed out.

"There's no help for it," Callens sighed. "She'll never make it on horseback. And we can use the carriage or wagon for a few supplies as well, so it's not a wasted effort. We won't be able to depend on much help."

"I'll see to it, sir," Warren promised. "I'll make sure everything is in order," he added and departed to check on the rest of the command, leaving Callens to plan his 'rescue' of Princess Sherron, and eventually Prince Therron.

-

Memmnon McLeod paced up and down the hallway outside his offices late into the night. Hands locked behind him, head down, he made the trip so many times that if he'd been counting he would have given up at some point. Two guards stood at each end of the hallway, allowing the Crown Prince space to be alone, yet not unprotected.

So far Grey had turned up nothing in his investigation into Sherron. Her servants were fanatically loyal to her, just as Therron's had been. How had the two of them been able to keep all this a secret for so long? Probably because everyone was always so focused on Parno, he admitted. That wasn't much of an excuse though. The truth was that no one would dare investigate a member of the Royal family except someone else in the Royal Family. His father hadn't thought Therron a threat until it was almost too late, and Memmnon hadn't thought his sister a threat at all until news of Callens' departure from the front had reached him.

Now, just when the kingdom needed order the most, things threatened to descend into chaos. Tammon's health was continuing to deteriorate, leaving Memmnon with increasingly more burdensome duties without the actual power to rule as yet. He knew that his father was considering an abdication due to his health issues, but this was not a good time for the kingdom to see weakness in the king.

Still, something would have to give soon. Things simply could not continue like this for much longer. And atop all of this intrigue and betrayal was the fact that a huge Imperial Army was encamped on Soulan soil with another threatening invasion from the west. Memmnon once more cursed the weakness in his father that had allowed Therron to live without denouncing him as a traitor. At least then everyone would know that his brother was a lout and not to be trusted.

As it was, however, he was simply ill. Now he could return at a time of 'great need', sacrificing in service to his people, a great hero for all to dote upon. Memmnon shook his head as anger threatened to undo him.

General Brock, the Inspector General of the Army, had already dispatched an additional company of IG soldiers to Therron's home of exile in the Key Horn, but there were precious few troops of any kind to send away at the moment. Tammon and Memmnon's own personal regiments were also serving as security for the city as well as helping the Palace Guard secure the palace and its grounds.

Manpower was in short supply and would continue to be for the foreseeable future.

Hopefully the moves Parno was making would give them some breathing room soon, even if it wasn't much. Any relief at all would be welcome at the moment. But with so many pieces in motion, Memmnon had to worry and wonder if that relief would come in time to matter. He continued to pace long into the night, his mind swirling over all of this and so much more.

No answers would come, however.

CHAPTER TWENTY-ONE

-

"Milord."

Parno was instantly awake, a very pleasant dream of Stephanie Corsin fading from view as he saw Harrel Sprigs' intense face looking down at him.

"Scouts are returning milord," Sprigs said without fanfare. "Movement front. All along the line."

"What time is it?" he asked, rising to a sitting position and rubbing his face to try and come completely awake.

"Half of four, milord," Sprigs replied. Parno nodded, getting to his feet.

"Give me a minute and I'll be out and about." Sprigs nodded and withdrew, leaving Parno to attend matters and dress. Less than five minutes later Parno was before the fire in his small camp, a bowl of oatmeal thrust into his hands. He took it gratefully and began to eat as Enri Willard filled him in.

"Scouts began returning about a half-hour ago, milord, reporting mass movement within the enemy camp. Bonfires were lit on their way in and some scouts are still out between the fires and our own lines to give us whatever warning they can."

"Your opinion?" Parno asked around a mouthful of oatmeal.

"Sir, this much activity at this time of the morning almost has to indicate an attack forming," Enri replied reluctantly. "It's possible it's merely a drill, but. . .I can't see it, sir."

"Nor I," Parno nodded. Before he could speak further Generals Davies and Graham arrived.

"Gentlemen," Parno nodded to them. "How goes it?"

"We're ready for battle, milord," Davies reported for both of them as Army commander. "Men are eating, but on post and ready. Scouts are still out and sending reports in relays every five minutes or when anything happens. No changes as yet since initial reports of movement in the enemy camp. We're ready to receive them all along the line."

"Very well," Parno sighed as he scraped the last of his oatmeal from the bowl. "We'll await their pleasure, then. Enri, please ask Mister Parsons to have a few of his men investigate and patrol our far left. If the Imperial Cavalry are out there, I don't want them being able to get into our rear."

"I'll see to it at once, sir," Enri nodded and set off to find the scout master. Parno turned to his two generals.

"I suspect they will try to move closer before sunup. That was the tactic they used at the Gap and I suspect you've seen it so yourself, General," he said to Davies, who nodded. "We'll try to let them think they've caught us unawares for as long as possible. Maybe they'll get careless. With our special weapons, we'll use the mines first, then the arrows, and finally the artillery. You may engage with standard artillery at your discretion, but allow me to initiate the special weapons fire. I want to make the maximum impact possible with it. Once we start using it, we'll hammer them pretty steadily. Our supply is far greater here than at the Gap. We should have at least three day's worth of supply, barring any misfortune."

"Very well, sir," Davies nodded.

"Back to your commands then, and Godspeed," Parno said gently. The two saluted and were gone into the dark. Parno stood in silence for a minute before turning to look at Cho Feng.

"Well, I guess we'll see what happens now," he remarked.

"You have a good plan and your men are in a good position," Feng replied. "All you can do is all you can do," he added philosophically.

"That's true enough," Parno nodded. "Let's head over to the tower, I guess," he blew out with a breath. "It's likely to be a long day."

"That it is," Feng agreed as he fell into step with Parno. Berry and the rest of Parno's guard formed a shell around him as they moved to the tower Parno had ordered constructed upon his return. He had learned firsthand how important it was that he be able to see. Davies had one of his own further down from which to command the Army. Parno would not have to be responsible for everything today.

Just the outcome.

Lars joined him along the way, still stuffing his shirt into his trousers.

"Late start Major?" Parno grinned. Lars snorted in the dark as he, too, fell into step with his commander.

"Late night is more like it, milord," he admitted. "Any last minute instructions?" he asked.

"Not that I can think of," Parno admitted. "We'll let the mines go first, then the arrows. Watch for the pennant to fall and then you can unload on them. I'll leave it to you to fix ranges, but remember what happens when the rounds fall short," he cautioned.

"Won't likely ever forget that, milord," Lars admitted ruefully. "Will you be wanting to try the trick with the pitch again?"

"I don't think we can reach anything that will burn that well from here," Parno admitted, remembering the lay of the land. "I'll leave those decisions to the commanders of the regular batteries I imagine. And to their generals. I'll depend on you to watch the two special units and how they fire."

"I'll see to it, milord," Lars promised, sketching a salute before he moved away into the dark.

"Harrel, get our runners into place," Parno ordered Sprigs. "We'll need mounted runners today."

"Already on the way milord," Sprigs assured him as they arrived at the tower.

"Wait here for General Willard, then, and bring him up when he arrives." With that Parno started up to the platform, Cho Feng following. It was cooler on the tower where the slight breeze was more noticeable. From here he could see the faintest bit of light back to the east.

It wouldn't be long.

-

"All commands report on line and ready to advance, sir," Wilson's aide reported softly into the dark. "Awaiting your orders."

"We start off on the hour," Wilson nodded. "As ordered. No changes. Advance in silence to contact. Have the artillery standing by to fire as soon as contact is made."

"Yes sir."

Wilson couldn't see anything yet, but soon the light would be rising and his men would be visible. He wanted them to close with the Soulan Army before that, to get as near them as possible before being discovered. Surprise, coupled with their superior numbers, should give them the advantage.

Wilson needed a win, and he needed it today. Even if the Soulanie forces were just forced to surrender more ground, that was a report he could send to the Emperor without fear of reprisal. And it would be a boost to his men's morale as well. Something he hadn't needed up until now, but found himself in need of after a serious round of setbacks.

"Good morning General," Daly's voice came out of the dark and Wilson bit back a curse. The annoying bastard hadn't been around much since he'd been cut down to size, but it was foolish to think that a member of the Imperial family wouldn't turn up at a time like this. And Daly was still, technically, his chief of staff even if he'd been effectively cut out of any significant role the last few weeks.

"Morning, General," he managed to reply amiably. "We're about to set off. Glad you could join us."

"Oh, I wouldn't miss it, General," Daly's oily voice wore on Wilson, but he took it in stride. "I assume we know what we're facing?" he continued.

"We do," Wilson replied abruptly. "The southerners have stripped their cavalry from their army to try and raid our rear areas, so they have little or no support behind their line. One good break and we'll pour through into their rear and at the least force them to withdraw. With any luck, we'll be on them so quickly that it will become a rout."

"I see," Daly's smug voice made Wilson want to slap him. "You're certain the southern cavalry is out of play? I understand it's been quiet in the rear areas for several days now."

"We believe they are laying low for the moment, adjusting to the changes we've made in our routes and security. It would not surprise me if they tried to attack us somewhere today, in fact. But General Stone will be ready and waiting for them if they do, and that will be the end of that."

"Assuming Stone does better there than he did here," Daly's reply was still smug.

"He will," Wilson bit out. "He knows the penalty for failure."

"We shall see, I suppose." With that Daly rode on forward, followed by his retinue of ass-kissers, all of whom Wilson would be pleased to see dead at the end of the day should it happen. But then, he didn't have that kind of luck. And he wouldn't waste any he might have on Daly and his followers.

That he would save for his men.

-

"Time to-" Stephanie stopped in mid-speech as she realized that not only was Winnie already awake, she was up and dressed, ready to go.

"Well," she temporized as Winnie grinned at her.

"Have to get up early on post," Winnie shrugged. "Not that I ever slept in before then. When you have to work to get your meals, you don't spend a lot of time laying around," she laughed.

"I suppose not," Stephanie agreed. For all that she worked hard and felt like she did not allow herself to be coddled, Stephanie had never once had to worry if there would be food on the table when she awoke. She was seeing now that wasn't always the case for others.

"I'll be ready shortly," she settled for saying and quickly set about preparing to resume their journey. Winnie departed with her bags, saying she would see her below for breakfast.

Fifteen minutes later Stephanie was downstairs, her bags being loaded by a member of her escort. She took a seat at the table and fixed herself a much smaller plate than her friend, eating quickly so that they could set off. The sun was not yet up but would be soon and she didn't want to waste a minute of it.

Winnie ate with the hearty appetite of someone accustomed to working for a living. Stephanie couldn't help but envy the younger woman a metabolism that allowed her to eat so well and still maintain a nice figure. Maybe she should start doing some manual labor herself. Or at least some type of physical training . . .

Soon that was forgotten as they prepared to set out. It was still a two-day trip to Nasil.

-

"Sir, those fires are not in the Soulanie camp," Wilson heard from out of the dark.

"What?" he turned to see the figure of a runner in the growing light. "What did you say?"

"The fires, sir," the man's arm raised to point to the points of light in the distance. "Those are bonfires, set to the front of the Soulanie lines, sir. At least one to two hundred yards. Our men will be spotted moving against them."

"Why didn't we know that?" Wilson demanded harshly.

"Orders were not to approach the enemy lines, sir," the runner shrugged helplessly. "So as not to give away our intent."

Wilson stifled a curse as he recognized his own orders, given for that exact reason.

"There's no help for it now," he said at last. "Orders are unchanged. Continue the advance."

"Sir," the runner sketched a salute and returned with the orders. Wilson watched him go, unease spreading though him. This was a bad start to the day.

-

"And there they are," Parno said softly as his glass swept the bonfires to his front. He lowered his glass.

"This is going to be close," he declared. "Runners to all crow-bow companies targeting the mines; Fire as soon as you can target the mines with the enemy even with them. They have to get their licks in before the Nor envelop the mines and they can't see them clearly enough to shoot."

"Sir," Sprigs nodded and relayed the order to the waiting runners below. Soon riders were hurrying across the field to issue new orders.

"It's going to be close," he said again, this time to himself more than anyone on the tower.

"It will have to be enough," Enri shrugged. "Their aim will be true."

"Won't help if they can't see," Parno reminded him. "I should have thought of this. At the Gap we were out of mines by the time they tried this," he admitted. "I should have considered that today. I did consider the likelihood of this being their strategy, just not how it would affect our using the mines."

"All you can do is all you can do," Enri shrugged again, echoing Cho Feng's earlier statement.

Parno resisted the urge to snap, knowing it wasn't helpful. He returned his glass to the field, trying to get an idea of what he faced in the dim light of the fires. In the distance he could see at least three lines of enemy troops that ran the length of his vision right to left, moving slowly but steadily forward. He couldn't begin to estimate their number.

"How many do you think?" he asked those assembled around him.

"No way to say in this light, milord," Enri admitted. "I'd estimate at least thirty thousand that we can already see, but that's a guess."

"A conservative one," Feng agreed softly. "This general has many more troops than the one at the Gap, and he will not commit them piecemeal. Expect him to maintain a small reserve to exploit any breach in our lines, but to commit the rest to the battle without hesitation."

"What I'd thought," Parno nodded thoughtfully. He raised his glass again.

"Their front rank is approaching about where the mines should be," he said aloud.

-

Major Seymour watched through his own glass as the Nor army crawled through the growing light. He could only just make out the mines along the front and didn't know if the crossbowmen could do so yet or not. He lowered his glass and picked up his own bow. His orders were to fire as soon as the first mine went off.

Now he had to hit that mine. If he missed, then his men would miss the signal to fire, and by the time it got around the Nor would have enveloped the mines and hidden them from view, robbing Marshal McLeod of their effectiveness.

No pressure at all, there, he grimaced.

"You two," he ordered the man to either side of him. "You fire when I do, just in case. Sight carefully since a lot is riding on this." Both nodded and readied their own weapons.

Seymour took a deep breath and slowly released about half of it, then, sighting carefully, squeezed the trigger.

The chunk of the bolt leaving the rails was followed by a similar sound to either side of him as his men fired right on his heels.

For better or worse, the battle was underway.

-

"What in the hell was that!" Wilson demanded as a cloud of fire and smoke rose from the front of his lines. Before anyone could try to answer, the scene was repeated all along his lines as fireball after fireball erupted as far as he could follow it down the line to either side of him. As the din of the explosions fell, he could hear the screams of his soldiers that had been injured in those blasts as well as the shouts and cries of the rest of the army as they milled in confusion in the face of this unexpected threat.

"What the hell is going on?!" Wilson screamed to those around him.

"Sir, it's the weapons we were told about from the Gap!" one man offered in near panic. "It's witchcraft!"

Wilson turned and struck the man so hard that he fell from his horse, stunned. Wilson glared down at him for a second before looking around him.

"Any of the rest of you think it's witchcraft?" he demanded icily. "There's no such thing as witchcraft you idiots! Now find out what the hell caused that before it happens aga-"

His tirade was cut short as it happened again, just as he'd feared. All along the lines fireballs erupted yet again, more sporadic this time but no less effective.

"Stop whatever that is!" Wilson demanded again, waving his arm forward. "GO!" His staff started forward, showing great reluctance in doing so but more afraid of Wilson's fury than whatever form of wizardry awaited them at the front lines.

Wilson watched them go, furious that the same thing he'd berated Brasher's scouts for reporting was now happening to him.

-

"Mines are having a good effect," Parno noted. Beside him Enri Willard stood silent, mouth agape at the destruction he'd just seen laid out before him. Parno turned to look at him, grinning slightly.

"Something else, isn't it?"

"Milord, I. . .," the elder Willard tried and failed to find the words to describe his reaction.

"Yeah, hits everyone like that the first time," Parno nodded. No one outside the Gap veterans and the few allowed to see yesterday's demonstrations had ever witnessed the power of Roda Finn's creations. It did tend to have a silencing effect on everyone at first.

"One more round," Parno noted, turning back to the advancing Nor lines. Ragged gaps had appeared in their lines as they struggled to continue on their way. Hundreds of men in view were either dead or wounded after the two strings of explosions had rippled across their formations.

"About now-" Parno mouthed right as the next and last line of mines were set off by crossbow bolts. Once more the Nor line rippled as still hundreds more of their number visible from the tower fell to the iron ball laced mines.

"Arrows will be next," Parno nodded to himself even as the first flights of regular arrows launched from behind a solid wall of pikes, shields and barricades. Before the first flight had struck the second was already on the way.

"We'll give it about two minutes before using the Hubel arrows," Parno mused, repeating the instructions he'd given his commanders.

-

"I think whatever that was, it's over with now," an unidentified voice told Wilson. "They're using archers now, sir. We're getting hurt of course, but . . . our men can deal with arrows."

"I still want to know what that was," Wilson ordered. "We'll like as not face it again and I want to know what it is and how we counter it!"

"We're looking for any kind of source, sir," the staffer nodded. "I'll see if there's been any luck."

"I don't want luck!" Wilson screeched in rage at the departing back of the speaker. "We trained for years to avoid the need for luck!" Those still nearby looked at each other uneasily at Wilson's growing ire. This wasn't their fault. No one had known about anything like this.

Of course, that wasn't really true. The survivors of Brasher's humiliated command had reported the 'wizardry' that had decimated their ranks to any and every one who would listen. They had been jeered and laughed at for their reports and sentenced to go home in shame as cowards of the Empire.

Several people were rethinking that policy very strongly right about now.

"Our men are pressing on, sir. Whatever the source of those fireballs, they seem to have run out of tricks, now."

Even as the words left his mouth, thousands of much smaller explosions erupted everywhere along their lines, with men screaming in agony once more.

-

"Not as impressive perhaps, but still effective," Parno nodded to himself as the first of the Hubel arrows impacted the Nor. Even as he watched another flight of the damaging arrows hit the Nor lines along with a flight of regular barbed arrows.

"My God," Enri almost whispered.

"Not like reading it, is it?" Parno asked gently. He had seen this kind of raw combat, though not on this scale. For all his experience and expertise, Willard had not. Even his own combat at the Gap had been in the mopping up action. He'd not experienced anything like this before.

"No, milord," Enri agreed.

Parno watched as the Nor managed to grow closer despite the continuous deadly fire from his archers and decided it was time to allow the artillery to engage. He nodded to the staff officer standing at the rear of the platform and the man instantly lowered the red pennant, the signal for Lars to open fire.

"Things will pick up now," Parno predicted. "If they're rattled enough from what we've done already, this might break them. It won't last, but I'll take whatever help we can get."

Even as he spoke the catapults and trebuchets loaded with Roda Finn's exploding wonders sent their shot sailing over the Soulan lines and into the approaching Nor army. The results were nothing short of what Parno expected.

-

"Mother of God!" Wilson exclaimed before he could stop himself as fireball followed fireball, walking down his lines wreaking death and destruction on his men as it went.

"What in blazes?" a dozen voices asked the same question though perhaps in different ways as those near Wilson reacted just as he himself had to this new devilment.

"Have they got a dragon or something?" one man asked aloud, his voice betraying his wonderment. Wilson looked around for the offender but could not find him.

"Get our damn artillery up here and start laying some damage on those lines!" he demanded. The trouble with their lines being so far away was that his army had to advance in order to make room for his artillery to be able to move up and range on the Soulan positions. Now that his men had done that, it was now possible.

He heard the order being relayed and wondered why he, the commander of the entire army, had been forced to issue that order when he'd given precise instructions on how things were to be handled once the battle was joined. What the hell were his people doing that they couldn't handle their jobs, simple as so many of them were?

Another line of massive explosions walked down his forward lines, answering Wilson's unasked question for him. His people were all but struck dumb by the hell being unleashed on them this morning. A morning that should have seen the Soulan Army broken yet again and forced back if not destroyed entirely.

Now that plan was in serious jeopardy if he couldn't get his people out of their shock and back on track.

-

Enri Willard watched as yet another salvo of the exploding artillery rounds shook the ground even from two and three hundred yards away as Lars' men laid their fire not into the first or second ranks of the Nor that had already been decimated, but into the follow on ranks still closing up.

"Their lead ranks will reach our fortifications," Enri noted to his Marshal. Parno nodded in reply.

"There was never any real hope of preventing that unless the shock broke them. I didn't expect that it would," he admitted. "But we've damaged them a great deal and their first wave won't be nearly so strong as it might have been. Plus, Lars and the archers are still laying into them. It will be up to our pikes and swords now, though."

Below and to their front, Parno watched as the now ragged line of Nor infantry finally made it within reach of the Soulan fortifications. Imperial archers were firing now, though their own ranks had been just as hard hit as the infantry had. Still, their arrows found targets and Soulanie soldiers began to fall.

Pike armed soldiers on both sides fought at the front, Imperial ranks trying to gain a purchase on the Soulanie breastwork, Royal pikemen trying to deny them that purchase. Blood began to flow in earnest on both sides of the line as the battle was well and truly joined, just as the sun finally cleared the tree line to the east.

Blood and tears would greet this new day from both sides of the battle.

-

Tinker heard the explosions from his room at the Inn. He calmly made his way to the front as the others screeched around him, trying to get outside and see what was happening. Unlike them, he, Bell and Wysin knew exactly what was happening.

"Looks like the war's back on, Tinker," Bell said calmly from a chair that he had tipped back against the front wall of the inn as he sat on the porch.

"I believe you are correct," Tinker nodded slowly. "Perhaps it would be prudent to be prepared to depart here in the event the army is unable to stop the advance," he suggested more than ordered.

"Already done," Bell nodded. "Wagons are hitched and everyone was ordered to have a bag packed and be ready to go at a moment's notice. Can't save everything, mind, but we can make sure we get our folk out of here, happens there's a need."

"Very good, mister Bell," Tinker nodded. "I believe I will see what is happening elsewhere, then. Should you be forced to abandon the inn before I return, we will meet at the first alternate in two day's time."

"Yes sir," Bell nodded. The first alternate was a hard ride from here and should be safe enough for a meeting place if needed.

As Tinker departed, Bell sat on the porch, listening to the distant sounds of battle, both glad he wasn't there, and wishing that he was.

-

General Fairmount cursed under his breath as reports of mounting casualties came to him in a nearly never ending stream. His men were only just now making contact with the southern lines and already some of his best regiments had been decimated by the hellish devilry unleashed by the southern army.

"We're about to make contact, sir," his aide reported. "Our men are within yards of their lines."

"Good," Fairmount nodded. "Once we're in contact their devilry won't help them! It will be our strength against theirs and we know we're stronger! Order all divisions to press the attack to the hilt!"

"Sir," the man nodded and turned to waiting runners. It was too dangerous at this point to use mounted runners, as Soulan archers picked them off horseback with ease. So, young men with strong legs would run through the battle with orders for divisional commanders, who in turn would send more young men to brigade commanders, and so on down the line until finally the soldiers actually doing the fighting would be given orders that they were, in all likelihood, already trying to obey.

Fairmount watched them go even as he continued to get frantic reports from his subordinates about fearful losses and horrific injuries among his men. Whatever the source of those earlier weapons, they had wreaked as yet untold havoc on his men. Fairmount could only estimate, but his most optimistic assessment was that he had lost at least a quarter of his strength to the combination of attacks that had struck his men before they had even reached the enemy lines. His own archers were returning fire, but. . .no one in their right mind believed that the damage inflicted by mere arrows had equaled what they had endured just getting to this point.

Even as that though completed itself, another string of explosions rattled Fairmount's teeth as Soulan artillery delivered another walking barrage behind his current position, inflicting losses among the follow on units and creating havoc in the rear areas where medics worked to assist the wounded and provosts worked to marshal men back into line that had broken under the noise and fire.

"What the hell is that?" someone asked off to his left, and Fairmount looked to see a young staff officer pointing at what looked like a bee hive made of mud. Grass and sage that had been used to hide it had fallen away as Imperial soldiers passed it by.

"Sir, that might not be a good idea," his aide cautioned as Fairmount moved to take a closer look.

"Don't be absurd," Fairmount waved him away. "There's no danger with them pushed back like they are. If this is what they're using, then this is an opportunity to figure out what they're doing to us, and perhaps how to stop it."

He bent down, peering closer at the strange object.

-

Micheal Sanders had turned seventeen years old the day before the battle. An uncommonly good shot with a crossbow, young Sanders had earned a place with Major Seymour's sharpshooters in a competition designed to find the absolute best shots in the army. He was very proud of that, and rightly so his mates had told him. Separated from his original militia unit and forwarded to Major Seymour's battalion, Sanders had found it difficult to adjust to new surroundings as he left behind friends and neighbors he had known most all his life. Most of the men around him were hardened veterans and gave young Sanders little more than a glance, paying him no mind at all otherwise.

As the battle had started, Micheal had managed to hit his first and third targets but had found his second to be obstructed. Reloading after the third round, he had hunkered down behind a log structure, hoping for a shot at his last mine. Technically he should be helping repulse the attack, but he knew the importance of setting off the mine if possible, if for no other reason than to keep it out of the hands of the Nor.

So far he had narrowly escaped death or injury a half-dozen times by sword, pike, or arrow, but he refused to give up, stubbornly holding until the last second in case his target became visible. Already he'd had one opportunity ruined when a Nor soldier had stepped in front of a perfectly aimed bolt just in time to take that bolt in the leg and prevent it from striking the target.

Stringing his last flint tipped bolt, Sanders had settled in to wait for his one last chance.

Suddenly the Imperial lines opened for just a brief time, almost like clouds parting to allow the sun to shine through for a few minutes. Micheal could see a group of Imperial officers around his target, examining the mine with great curiosity. Grimly he took careful aim.

This would be his last chance not to fail...

-

Fairmount was aware of the force of the explosion as it hit him in the chest. He felt the impact of the iron balls on his body but strangely no pain to amount to anything as he was hurled backwards, away from the strange clay structure his staff member had found.

He didn't realize it at all when passed from this world into the next, his mind still working to explain what was happening when it ceased to work at all.

The Imperial 1st Corps had just lost its commander and three-quarters of his command staff.

-

"We're in contact all along the line," Enri read several messages that had been sent up the tower. "The line is holding, for now. We're taking losses, both to archery and to melee combat, but our men are holding."

"Good," Parno nodded. "They'll have to withstand a great deal today. The Nor commander is obviously putting his entire command into this effort and he started with sun-up. Unless we can find a way to break their spirit and make them run, we'll have to hold most of the day or-"

Cries from along the line cut Parno's statement off as Imperial Artillery began falling among his lines. Parno reacted at once, turning to a runner.

"Compliments to Major Lars, and he is to interdict that artillery at once!" he ordered. "His choice of rounds and unit, but I want it done immediately!"

"Sir!" the officer in charge of Parno's runners nodded and turned to find the artillery runner.

"Can we afford to take Lars' fire away from the battle?" Enri asked.

"We can't afford to allow that enemy artillery to range on our lines unimpeded," Parno replied flatly. "They can undo us in a matter of minutes if left unchecked. We learned that the hard way at the Gap. All that's letting us withstand their attack is Roda's gadgets and our fortifications. If they manage to force a breach, they can literally force their way through no matter what we do. They can afford more losses than we can and still retain enough strength to win the field. We can't let that happen."

Enri nodded grimly, agreeing with his Marshal's opinion. Like it or not, they had no choice but to turn their artillery fire toward the enemy's own and try to contain it.

"Artillery units are taking enemy fire, sir!" Wilson's aide reported. "Losses are mounting!"

"They must maintain their fire!" Wilson ordered, shaking his head at the unspoken request to withdraw. "Tell them to continue."

"Sir, we were unable to locate General Fairmount," a runner stumbled up, looking dazed. "That is to say. . .I think we found him, sir, but. . ."

"What is it, man!" Wilson demanded in frustration.

"Sir, I found what was left of a man wearing a general's uniform and markings, along with several other officers of various ranks, but. . .they're gone, sir. If I had to guess, I'd say one of those fireballs got 'em, sir. I tried to locate his senior divisional commander but could not. The line is a mess, sir. I did ask several of their men to locate a general officer and inform them of General Fairmount's demise and ask him to send a runner here informing us of his whereabouts."

Wilson nodded absently at that, still processing the fact that Milton Fairmount, one of his oldest and most trusted friends and subordinates, was gone. Just like that.

Death was part of being a soldier, of course. War meant casualties and Wilson knew of no way to prevent that. No one did. But officers of Fairmount's rank rarely died in combat save in a total route. It just didn't happen. Command of that stature meant by necessity that you were far behind the lines so that subordinates could find you for orders and to pass along information when needed. That distance from the fighting usually meant that it was all but impossible for you to die at the enemy's hand.

But the Soulanie army had managed to create some kind of. . .of bottled *hell*, and that hell had now claimed the life of his most able Corps commander. He remembered Fairmount's reluctance the night before, his misgivings about their plan of attack. His old friend had felt uneasy. Had he had some kind of premonition concerning his impending death? Had he felt Death's icy hand upon him last night as the two of them had studied the map one last time?

"Sir?" the runner interrupted Wilson's train of though. "Orders, sir?" he asked hesitantly. Wilson realized that he had to lay that aside for now. His friend would still be dead tonight, when he could spare the time to mourn him. Right now, his army was still engaged with a desperate enemy on their own ground.

"Very good," he nodded absently. "Wait here for their runner to find us and then send them back informing whoever is senior to take command of 1st Corp and continue to press the attack."

"Sir," the man nodded and moved away to wait. Wilson continued to stare off toward the front, still reeling inwardly from this sudden turn of events.

What else would go wrong today?

CHAPTER TWENTY-TWO

-

Stephanie sighed as her ambulance hit another rough spot along the roadway, wondering if her driver was trying to hit every hole along the route. Winnie heard her and grinned.

"Rough ride, yes?"

"Very," Stephanie nodded. "I don't like to complain, but I asked for this thing to be well sprung to avoid this kind of discomfort. Ambulances are supposed to be a better ride than this so as not to make the pain worse for the wounded they carry."

"Good thing we aren't wounded then," Winnie snorted to contain her laughter. The ride was rough for someone of Doctor Freeman's upbringing, but for Winnie it was just fine. Much more comfortable than her normal travel arrangements, which was usually either horseback or buckboard wagon.

"Isn't it though," Stephanie nodded. "Still, I can't really be that upset. I did ask for as quick a trip as was possible."

"You expect to make Nasil tomorrow then?" Winnie asked.

"Hopefully by dinner if everything goes well," Stephanie nodded. "That was why it was so important to get down off the mountain before dark so we would be able to avoid that part of the trip today. From the inn where we spent the night we can just about make Nasil by suppertime if there are no problems. And as rough as this is, it's much better than when I first made the trip to Cove. Parno has had crews working on the route all that time, trying to make the trip easier and faster. Otherwise it would add at least a day to our trip just to avoid injury to the horses and damage to the carriage."

"Wow," Winnie didn't know what else to say. While she wasn't suffering the way Stephanie appeared to be, it was still noticeably rough travel.

"Exactly," the doctor nodded.

"He does a lot of that kind of thing, doesn't he?" Winnie asked thoughtfully. "Working to make things better for everyone."

"Yes, he does," Stephanie nodded again. "He's always thinking of his people. Remarkable really, considering how bad he's treated for the most part. Of course, that's changing now that he's Lord Marshal."

"I'd never noted it," Winnie admitted. "No one at Cove ever treats him poorly."

"They all respect him for enduring the same hardships they do," Stephanie agreed. "And for his skill with a sword I'm sure," she added with a frown. "At the Gap he fought on the front lines with his men, right alongside men who had been freed from prison to join him."

"That I knew," Winnie confirmed. "That was all some of them talked about when they returned from the Gap. My Papa has a lot of respect for him, too. And that's unusual."

The two young women continued to talk to pass the time as the ambulance continued to bounce its way to the Royal City.

-

Colonel Callens reined in his horse, signaling for those behind to do the same as he surveyed the area around them. His group was still five miles from the palace grounds, give or take, and that was close enough for the moment.

"We'll stop here for now," he ordered, dismounting. There was a stable here that was long out of use and they led their horses inside, out of sight. They would remain here until nightfall, at which time they would make their way into the city and to palace. It would be difficult enough to do without the additional burden of daylight to give them away.

"Get some rest," he ordered as they stripped the saddles from their mounts. "Stand watch by squads and stay out of sight. We can't afford to be seen by someone who will wonder why we're here." He watched as his officers posted guards and divided up the responsibilities, then turned to the footman who had accompanied them.

"You're certain you can get us inside unseen?"

"Yes Colonel," the man nodded. "There are ways known only to the family and one of them is known to me, shared by her Ladyship. When we enter the palace, we'll be mere yards from her door."

"Good," Callens nodded. "That will make things significantly more simple."

"What will we do once we have her, Colonel?" the man asked, curious.

"That will be up to her," Callens admitted. "My own plan is to get her safely out of the palace and away, then link up with the regiment and find Prince Therron, wherever he may be. If Her Ladyship knows where he is, that would make our job much easier."

"She may well know, I don't know," the man admitted. He waited for a moment to see if Callens wanted more, then went to his own saddle and removed a blanket. Spreading it on a bed of hay, he was soon asleep, snoring softly in a stall next to his horse.

Callens envied the man his sleep, though not begrudgingly. He wanted to sleep as well. Knew he should be sleeping, storing it against the next few days when sleep would be at a premium. But the excitement and fear of what he was about to attempt kept him wide awake for the moment. He instead spent his time trying to review the plans he'd made so far and attempting to work out where Prince Therron might have been sent.

He hoped Her Ladyship had managed to work that out for him.

-

Sherron McLeod paced in her bed chamber, furious as ever. She had been angry for the last four days, or at least angrier than usual. Her brother had done this, and set that bastard Grey on her! Even now there were two of those bullish women constables in her apartments, watching her every move. Only here in the privacy of her actual bedchamber did she have any respite from their presence, and even then both women were immediately beyond the door.

Two male constables were posted outside her apartment door as well, ensuring that she was truly made prisoner in her own home. It was hard to imagine that she and Therron were both prisoners while the whelp was not only free, but usurping Therron's place as commander of the army.

She had intended to put an end to that, but had been intercepted actually on her way out. She was sure Callens had received the message and was probably even now awaiting her arrival at the meeting place. What would he do when she failed to show? She had arranged for enough supplies for ten days for his regiment, not easy to do with a war on and supplies at a premium, but she was Princess Sherron McLeod and that still carried some weight.

But not enough to get her out her apartments and free. Her loyal staff had likewise been interred, and she had no doubt were being relentlessly questioned about Sherron's activities. She snorted delicately at that thought. None of her retainers, regardless of her level of trust, had been privy to all of her thoughts and plans. Some knew more than others, but no one knew everything and none of them would betray her. At least not yet. She knew that as time wore on some would begin to crack.

Which meant she had to get out while she could. Every day she spent languishing here was another day that Memmnon could use to secure his ascension to the throne and Parno his control over the army. She would never have believed that Therron's loyal followers would have willingly followed Parno into battle, but reports from the front indicated that not only had they done so, they had scored a great victory doing it.

Traitors one and all!, she thought savagely. Not the rank and file, of course. The men loved Therron. Always had. He was practically one of them. But the officers! Following that whelp Parno who should have been drowned at birth. The nerve of them, treating him as well as they might Therron.

Well, there would be time enough to root out who was guilty of treason against her beloved Therron and deal with them once she had set things to right in Nasil and placed Therron upon the throne where he belonged. With that done she would use her influence to punish anyone who had supported Parno, Memmnon or their doddering old fool of a king over Therron's rightful rule.

Her mind turned to the task of ensuring that she had the opportunity to do just that.

-

Parno tensed slightly as yet another wave of Imperial soldiers crashed against his lines. So far the Royal Army was holding, but his men were taking losses while doing so. Heavy losses in some places.

"The artillery is sapping their strength before they get to the line or they would have swamped us by now," Enri noted, sweeping the line with his glass.

"Yes," Parno nodded. "I'm afraid we're going to have to commit the reserve to the battle before long. We've suffered heavy losses and the men on the line are tiring."

"I would suggest doing so by no more than a brigade at the time, then," Enri replied. "Parcel out the reserve as much as possible to keep one division intact so as to respond to a break through if needed. Allow each division to keep one full brigade in position to bolster the line if that kind of breakthrough occurs, as well."

"Doing that will eliminate any chance we have of a counter-attack, too," Parno sighed, accepting the inevitable.

"There was never much hope of that today, milord," Enri pointed out. "We're too heavily outnumbered. Even should we throw them back today, they may well come again tomorrow. We'll need every man for the next attack. We couldn't spare any losses in a counter-attack that would likely not bear any real fruit."

"I know," Parno nodded. "See to the orders, then, Brigadier," he ordered formally. "Bolster the line in the weakest places and give our men what relief we can."

Sir," Enri nodded and set about issuing orders. Parno watched dispassionately as his plans to strike back eroded with the size of his reserve.

-

"We are hurting them, General," an aide said to Wilson as he watched the battle continue.

"Not badly enough," he replied absently. "Our casualties are atrocious and we haven't cracked their lines yet."

"Our artillery has taken a beating, sir, or we would have broken them by now," the aide insisted. "Sir, our artillery could use a chance to refit. Their losses really are heavy."

"I'll let the infantry know how the artillery has suffered, mister," Wilson all but snarled. "Our men are fighting and dying at the end of Soulan swords, pikes and arrows. I think our artillery can do likewise while supporting their attack!"

"Sir, their losses are approaching the point where they aren't any real help," the aide pressed. "Over fifty percent of their equipment has been damaged or disabled completely. Manpower losses are less but still severe."

"And should I call off the attack so that the artillery can rest?" Wilson demanded. "Recall our troops and let the Soulanies have the field?" he shouted.

Behind him two buglers snapped to attention at hearing that shout and brought their horns to their lips. Surprised by the order, they nonetheless began blowing the notes for the recall.

-

General Darrell Thomas had just committed his final brigade to action against a section of the southern line that showed some weakness when the bugle calls began passing up and down the line. His head snapped around as the notes of Recall sounded.

"What the hell!" he exclaimed, looking around at his staff officers as if for confirmation that he was going insane.

"Sir, that's the recall," one aide supplied helpfully.

"No shit?" Thomas shot back with feigned incredulity. "And here I thought it was the bloody charge!" The man's face turned beet red but he made no further comment.

"This has got to be a mistake!" Thomas yelled, but all around him buglers heard the call and picked it up, continuing to sound Recall until it was passing all down the line. Thomas shook his head in disbelief, but. . . .

"We don't have any choice, now!" he called out to his staff. "The whole army will be falling back. Issue orders to grab any of our wounded we can reach and try to fall back in order. Be just our luck the southerners will pick this opportunity to counter-attack."

The Imperial Army was withdrawing for the first time since the war had begun.

-

"What have you done!" Wilson screamed at the two buglers as they abruptly stopped blowing, suddenly fearful of their General's ire.

"What the hell do you think you're doing?" Wilson demanded.

"Sir, begging your pardon, sir, but you said sound Recall and give the southerners the field, sir!" the senior bugler stammered. "We both heard the order and sounded Recall as ordered, sir!" he added.

"I gave no such orders!" Wilson bellowed.

"Sir, you did, sir!" the man managed to hold his ground despite his fear. "Sir, you said 'Recall our troops and let the Soulanies have the field', sir. Your exact words, sir!"

Wilson was on the verge of apoplexy. He looked at the two buglers in wonder, realizing what had happened and wondering how he could possibly have two dumber men assigned to him as buglers.

"Arrest them both!" he bellowed to his escort, who promptly surrounded both men and led the still protesting buglers away.

"Sir, it was an honest mistake I'm sure," his aide offered, but cut off at a glare from Wilson.

"You want to join them?" he screamed in rage. The man wilted and fell silent.

"Jesus, Mother and Joseph," Wilson shook his head. "I am surrounded by morons. Nothing but morons on my payroll, everywhere I look!"

He continued to bemoan the intelligence of his help as his army slowly broke contact and returned to their own lines, still under a withering fire from the southern army. There was nothing he could do to stop their withdrawal now. His army was tired, suffering from heavy losses and no doubt shocked not only by the ferocity of the southern defense but by the abrupt and unexpected Recall order. There would be no marshaling them, or continuing the battle. Not now.

The attack was over for today.

-

"What the hell?" Parno exclaimed as he saw the Nor begin to disengage and pull back. "What are they doing?" he asked aloud.

"They are withdrawing," Enri said, somewhat unnecessarily.

"I can see that," Parno managed not to be sarcastic. "But why? We had hurt them, but they were on the verge of breaking us!"

"I don't think it was that bad, milord," Enri said automatically.

"Why stop?" Parno mused, ignoring Enri's mild protest. "This makes no sense at all!"

"I don't know, sir," Enri shrugged.

"Perhaps it was an error," Cho Feng offered quietly.

"A mistake?" Parno looked incredulous. "That's a big mistake!"

"It does happen," Feng shrugged somewhat philosophically. "There is no surety in war save death and destruction, my Prince. Wars are fought by men, and men make mistakes. Or, their general may simply have lost his nerve. That, too, happens in war."

"Their losses were piling up," Enri agreed. "And their artillery had been battered severely thanks to your man, Lars. Maybe his nerve did break," he shrugged helplessly. He didn't know what had happened any more than Parno did.

"Gather our cavalry at once!" Parno ordered, excitement blooming. "We can order them to attack their retreating army and hound them all the way back to their lines!"

Neither man moved and Parno frowned.

"Did you hear me?"

"Milord," Enri was hesitant. "Milord, our two cavalry divisions that were in reserve were already broken up and moved into line to bolster our defense. The third was on our extreme left, spread to cover our flank from attack. The division from General Raines' army is in the rear areas providing security against raids. I. . .it would take at least an hour, more likely two, to gather the force together, and even then we would need to brief the commanders. Sir, it would be best to call this a victory and be happy with it."

"I concur, My Lord," Cho Feng said carefully. "Your men are tired and our own losses are heavy. There is nothing that says the Nor will not try again tomorrow. For all we know they have a large force in reserve still. For that matter they may try again later today if they have sufficient fresh forces to hand. I would suggest that a more prudent action would be to consolidate our position and give our men a chance to rest while we see to our wounded and dead, my Prince."

Parno's face reddened as he listened, angry at this defiance. But as the words both men spoke sank in, he was forced to admit they were correct. His desire to attack had outweighed his good sense for once. He had seen only a chance to punish the Nor even more, not the risk he would incur while doing so.

"Very well," he said slowly, defeat in his voice and his posture. "See to it, then," he ordered. With that he left the tower and returned to his command tent nearby, leaving the orders and the details to the others.

He could not help but think that he had just missed a golden opportunity. One that might not present itself again.

-

Wilson wanted to curse the heavens. To shake his fist at whatever Fate had struck this blow against him. None of it would help and he knew that but he needed the release and despite the fact that it might make him look ineffectual he knew that he needed it, lest he kill someone in a fit of rage. His staff was smart enough to stay quiet, knowing that they had, in part, failed him in a number of ways.

He wanted to execute those two idiot buglers for starters, but couldn't bring himself to do it. He had spoken the words they had heard. The fault was his for having two men who were so stupid in a position of such great responsibility. He'd had them arrested, and some time later, in a day or two when he wasn't angry anymore, he'd have them busted and assigned to train duty. Or stables. Something where their idiocy couldn't hurt him or the Empire.

But for now he was facing an unmitigated disaster. His army had just suffered tremendous losses and had absolutely nothing to show for it but dazed troops and a field littered with his dead and wounded. He'd be lucky if the Emperor didn't have his head for this. He was sure that Daly was already composing his own report of how Wilson had failed.

Wilson had distanced himself from the others in his party, sitting his horse slightly in the open and watching as his men returned. Many were burned and bleeding, he assumed from whatever hell it was the Southerners had managed to unleash upon them. He could see in their eyes that many were still in shock. He couldn't begin to fathom how afraid they had been when those fireballs had erupted around them, on top of them, and yet they had continued to press their attack.

"I'm proud of you!" he called suddenly, overwhelmed by the feeling and the urge to tell them that. "You faced a terrible enemy and you held your ground despite any fear and you did your duty and I'm proud of you!" he called, riding along the field now, his horse carrying him without guidance from its rider. Several of his men stood straighter as they heard him.

"You did well, men!" Wilson continued, ignoring the scramble of his escort and staff to follow him. "The failure was mine, not yours! You did all that could be done and perhaps more! I'm proud of you all! No Imperial General ever commanded better men than you!"

He repeated this call for nearly half-an-hour, riding the length of his lines, reassuring his soldiers that they had done well. That it was not their fault. It was his.

Wilson would never be able to explain what had prompted this behavior. He would never know why he had done it. But word of his actions spread through the army like a wildfire and soldiers that had been despairing and broken and afraid beyond reason began to stand taller, to straighten their bent backs and raise their lowered heads.

No Imperial General had ever enjoyed the loyalty that this simple act would earn Gerald Wilson in that short half-hour. His broken army began to stitch itself back together right before his eyes.

"Sir, there is a rider approaching with a white flag," his aide mentioned as Wilson finished what would always be remembered as The Ride.

-

"Send a courier with a flag of truce," Parno ordered, looking at the littered field. "Offer the Nor General the opportunity to have his surgeons and litter bearers come and remove their men."

"Sir?" Enri Willard looked confused. "Sir, what about the Black Flag?"

"That's for combat," Parno shook his head. "And besides, we can't have thousands of dead bodies lying here around our lines. We don't have the resources to care for their wounded or bury their dead. Let them come and take them."

"Yes sir," Willard nodded and selected a runner to carry the message. The young man was understandably nervous, but willing. He took the parchment and the white banner and headed for the Nor lines.

-

". . .and so I offer you the opportunity to send parties to remove your dead and wounded from the field unmolested, provided they are litter bearers and surgeons only. Wagons will be permitted on the field as well, but no cavalry forces. Violation of these terms will be seen as a return to hostilities. The terms of this truce will expire at dawn, should you agree to them. Signed, Parno McLeod, Marshal, Royal Army of Soulan." The young Captain finished reading and lowered the roll.

"Parno?" Wilson looked stunned. "Who the hell is Parno?"

"Ah, sir, I believe he is the youngest of the McLeod Dynasty's children, sir," the young Captain offered. "I believe it was also he that commanded the southern forces at the Gap where General Brasher-"

"Yes, yes," Wilson waved off the rest. "I recall that now. So I haven't been facing Therron McLeod after all," he shook his head. "Figures." He looked at the field before him. Many of the figures lying there were moving, though far too many never would again.

"Agree to the terms," he said firmly. "Have parties out immediately retrieving our wounded. Wagons and ambulances only on the field. No more than four men and a driver per wagon. Litter bearers in pairs. Make sure we in no way violate the terms of the cease fire. Save every man we can."

"Yes sir," the Captain literally ran to obey. In the past, Imperial Generals had been notorious for abandoning their dead and wounded wherever they fell. Rumor had it that Brasher had followed that same pattern in his failed attack in the east. Wilson had just added to his stature among the army yet again with an act that should have been a mere formality.

He cared for none of that at the moment. All he could see was the horrible errors of this day, and the terrible costs.

-

"Nor are gathering their people, sir," Enri reported an hour later. "We have men on watch of course. One battalion of each regiment is on line, ready. Our cavalry not earlier engaged are now reassembled and prepared to respond to any violation or attack. Our own wounded have been removed to the tents and we have work parties working to clear the dead and bury them properly."

"Any word on losses?" Parno asked with a sigh. This day had gone better than he'd had any right to hope, really, yet he still viewed it as a failure.

"We're looking at an estimate of twenty percent losses total, sir," Enri reported stoically. "Some unites suffered more of course, and some less. That's an average, and as I said is an estimate. It will likely be tomorrow before we know any kind of exact losses." Parno nodded.

"Have Lars report usable ordnance and status report on all artillery," he ordered. "Have the engineers ready to place new mines once the Imperials have cleared the field. Poll the Hubel archers and see how many arrows they have left, then reissue as far as we can. I don't actually know how many we had to start with," he admitted. Why didn't he know that?

"Sir, if I may?" Willard spoke and Parno looked up at him.

"Milord, do not concern yourself with such minutiae," the Brigadier told him plainly. "It's too much, milord. You are still trying to be a regimental commander. It's impossible for you to do. There's simply too much information. You don't know how many we had to start because you had a hundred other things occupying your mind and your time and because there are staff officers who are detailed to know those things. And we had just over nine thousand of them on hand when the battle started," he added, smiling gently. "More will be brought to the front along with replacement . . . ordnance," he mouthed the strange word carefully, "this afternoon."

"And if I may add, milord, you should get some rest," Willard finished. Parno snorted lightly, a ghost of a smile appearing on his face.

"Are you trying to manage me, Enri?" he asked around that smile.

"That is my job, sir," Enri nodded, returning the smile with a rueful grin of his own. "Sir, you view today as a failure and there is no standard I know of where this was anything but a victory and a sound one at that. Regardless of why they withdrew, the fact is that the Nor did withdraw, leaving us in command of the field. Their losses were much heavier than our own and our lines, while strained, are intact. We did not end up committing our reserve, either, which means we still have four cavalry divisions that are fresh and ready to fight if need be."

"Our artillery losses stand at roughly eight percent, remarkable really considering the fire they took. Being forced to distance them from each other due to the nature of their projectiles has paid an unintended dividend there, as no one attack damaged or destroyed more than one piece."

"Good," Parno nodded again, standing. "And I'll rest tonight, Enri," he set a reassuring hand on the older man's shoulder. "Right now I think I'll ride the front, well back of course," he raised a hand to ward off objections that he knew were coming. "I want to see the men, and they deserve to see me checking on their welfare. I assume you have someone of command rank keeping an eye on the Imperial medical parties?"

"General Davies assigned a particularly capable brigade commander to that duty, sir," Willard nodded. "The same man who commanded the rear guard at Loville in fact," he added.

"Very well, then," Parno nodded. "If you were to need me to look at any. . .minutiae," he grinned much broader this time, "then send a runner after me."

With that Parno took his jacket and put it on as he left the tent. Willard followed him, shaking his head as he went about his own duties of dealing with the minutiae for his Marshal.

-

The day waned. On the field between the two armies, litter and ambulance carried wounded to surgeon's tents while wagons carried the dead to their final resting place. Wary men on both sides watched the other carefully, sure that at any minute their enemy would attack them despite the white flags fluttering everywhere that afternoon.

Parno McLeod rode his lines, much as his counterpart had done, seeing his army and allowing them to see him. He paused along the way to speak with a few he remembered from his first such ride when he took command, noting sadly that many of them were now absent.

His men were in high spirits, having thrown back an army nearly three times their size. Parno did not trouble them with the fact that it had most likely been an error that led to the Imperial Army withdrawing from the field. He didn't know that for a fact, and there was no reason to rob the men of the morale boost it gave them to believe they had beaten the larger army back.

Across the field, Wilson's despondency grew as wagon after ambulance rolled off the field carrying men of his army either to waiting surgeons who were sorely overworked, or to the field set aside to bury their dead. So many lost and all for nothing thanks to a careless error. The losses would have been bad enough in victory. In defeat it was indeed a bitter pill to swallow.

Daly had the good sense not to antagonize him, though he did send a courier with word that he had 'informed the Emperor of the situation'. Wilson knew that meant the little weasel had undoubtedly galloped back to his quarters to dictate a message of how Wilson's ineptitude had cost the Imperial Army so much.

For once, he didn't care. He had failed, after all. He deserved whatever came his way. He had already decided that he would inform the Emperor of his failure and subject himself to whatever punishment he might chose, hoping to save his family from a similar fate if possible.

Oddly enough, his main worry was who would command after he was gone, and how well they would treat his army.

The day could not pass quickly enough for all that the sun moved rapidly across the afternoon sky.

-

"We'll be stopping soon, milady," a voice came through the window, startling Stephanie out of her brief nap. Once the road had smoothed out the gentle rocking had lulled her to sleep. Winnie was curled into a ball across from her, sleeping soundly.

"What time is it?" she asked, rubbing her eyes.

"Perhaps two hours until dark, milady," the man supplied. "We have made good time. We'll be able to exchange horses at the inn, and you'll be able to get a good meal, clean up and rest. If all goes well, we should be in Nasil before dark on the morrow."

"Thank you, Captain," she smiled. "I appreciate it."

"Milady," the man nodded and rode on ahead of the ambulance. Stephanie reached across to gently shake Winne's shoulder. The younger woman was instantly awake, knife in hand as she looked around her.

"Easy, there," Stephanie soothed. "Just wanted you to know we're stopping soon."

"Really?" Winnie put the knife away as she swung her feet off the bench and back to the floor, sitting up straight and stretching. Her blouse strained to contain her ample bosom and Stephanie made a note to get the girl more proper clothing while in the city. Buckskins and cotton were fine for training, but a young lady should have properly concealing clothes.

"Really," she replied. "We've made good time, and the Captain says we'll likely be there before dark tomorrow."

"Good!" Winnie smiled. "I've never been there, you know," she added wistfully. "Is it grand?" she asked.

"It is," Stephanie nodded. "It has its dark and dirty spots of course, as any large city will, but there are grand buildings and wonderful works of art there. Artisans from all over the kingdom come there to display their work and scholars come to study. You'll find people of almost every walk of life and every lifestyle in the Royal City."

"Why is it called the Royal City?" Winnie asked.

"Well, it's where the kingdom began," Stephanie explained. "After the Burning, the Dying Time, Nasil was where Tyree gathered the survivors and started over. The kingdom grew from there out of alliances with other survivors in a few other cities like Lana and Bingham."

"So Tyree was the one who organized all of that?" Winnie asked.

"No, not at first," Stephanie recounted the history she'd been forced to learn as a girl. "He was a warrior, actually. Very young, in fact, not having reached his majority. He led a small group of warriors who were among the most fierce of the survivors. They protected the city and the people who came there, and defended them against attack from outside. Gradually the people came to love him and his men, and as he grew older it was the people who decided that Tyree should be king. History records that he was reluctant to accept such a title, but someone eventually convinced him it was the best thing for the times they lived in."

"I wonder why?" Winnie said aloud.

"Well, when times are dire, people need someone or something to rally around. To protect and to serve, I guess. That was once an old motto among some

I'm told. Having a dynasty to be loyal to is a uniting factor for so diverse a people, too," Stephanie added. "When they can all agree on that one thing, meaning who is good enough to lead them, or wise enough to lead them I suppose, and strong enough to keep them safe, then their other disagreements are less likely to cause division. Essentially, if something is bad for the Crown, it's generally bad for the kingdom, and that means bad for the people of the kingdom."

"That makes sense," Winnie nodded. "Tyree must have made quite an impression."

"That's what the historians say," Stephanie nodded, thinking of another young ruler who made quite the impression.

-

"Impressive, isn't it?" Callens remarked aloud, not really to any one person. He and his chosen men were looking at the palace from perhaps a mile distant as the light began to fade.

"Aye, Colonel," the man nearest him replied in almost a whisper. "Been too long since we looked upon it," he added.

"And likely to be longer before we do again," Callens nodded, turning to face the thirty men he had selected for this mission.

"Our primary objective is to free Her Ladyship," he told them. "Secondary to that is to find the location of Prince Therron. It is possible that she knows where he is already, which will make our lives much simpler. Mister Beals," he indicated the footman, whose name he had only just learned, "will guide us into the palace through a route that will bring us literally to Her Ladyship's door."

"Expect her to be guarded, since we assume she is under house arrest. Understand that we kill only when necessary. These are still our people, misguided though they may be. We kill only to protect ourselves or Her Ladyship. I will kill any man who kills another indiscriminately in the House of Tyree. Is that clear?" Heads nodded agreement.

"Very well," he nodded. "Once we've secured Her Ladyship, providing no alarms have been raised, we will then attempt to gain what intelligence we can. If the alarm has been raised, we will take her and go immediately. All of us are expendable if it means Her Ladyship is freed. That includes me. Are we understood?" Heads nodded again.

"In the event I am killed or captured, your orders are simple; ride to the rendezvous, meet up with the Regiment, and from there Her Ladyship will instruct you on what course of action to take. You will keep her safe and do all in your power to ensure that Prince Therron is freed and returned to his rightful place. Are there any questions?"

There were none.

"Then move out. Groups of five, remember your routes, and meet at our rendezvous as planned."

CHAPTER TWENTY-THREE

-

Beals led Callens directly to a small door that was hidden in a darkened alcove beneath the windows of Sherron McLeod's apartments. They waited just inside as the rest of the group arrived, slipping inside unnoticed. Once they were all present, Callens nodded to Beals who turned and led the way quietly up a set of recessed stairs.

The men moved carefully so as not to create any noise. After two flights of stairs, Beals motioned in the dim light of a single lamp to wait and moved forward to the wall before them. Pressing lightly, he pushed the panel aside revealing a small room with a single chair. Motioning Callens and his men forward, Beals moved to the door, using the small window to ensure that the coast was clear. Satisfied that it was, he turned to Callens and nodded.

The colonel led the way out of the room and to the left, walking directly toward Princess McLeod's rooms, his men following while Beals closed the door and remained to secure their way out. As they rounded the corner before their destination, two men in the garb of Royal Constables stood at attention outside the doorway. The two lawmen turned their attention to the soldiers but showed no undue alarm as they wore the garb of the Royal Family.

"We're here to escort the Princess to see her brother," Callens informed them briskly. "She should be ready to go by now, correct?"

"Sir?" the lead guard showed his surprise. "I have no information about that, sir. No one has been here in the last hour with news."

"She would have been informed before then," Callens shook his head.

"We need to move smartly. The Prince has other business tonight." He moved to the door and knocked as if he had all the authority in the world to be there and do so.

A tall woman in identical uniform to the door guards opened the door, frowning.

"We're here to escort the Princess down," Callens repeated. "Prince Memmnon says she'll be returned once the meeting is over, but did not specify how long that was to be."

"We weren't advised," the woman admitted. "I don't think Her Ladyship is prepared to go anywhere," she added.

"That's her problem," Callens replied gruffly. "No disrespect, but she was told he would see her this evening. That's all I know, but my orders are to escort her down. So ready or not, she goes."

"Understood," the woman nodded. "Wait here and I will go and get her."

"Quickly as you can," Callens nodded. "We're on a schedule." The woman nodded again and moved to allow Callens and two of his men into the sitting chamber while she moved to the Princess' bedchamber.

"My Lady, there is an escort here for you," the woman called. "You are to see your brother, they say."

"Then he can come here!" the muffled reply came through the door. Callens resisted the urge to shake his head. Of course she would complicate things when so far the plan was working. He moved to the door, motioning for the female Constable to wait.

"Princess, our orders are to escort you out," he said forcefully. "That is going to happen, My Lady. How is up to you. Please open the door. Now." *Please open the door you headstrong woman*, he silently plead. His prayer was answered as the door was abruptly yanked open to reveal a red faced Sherron McLeod in all her fury.

"I told you I-" she cut herself off abruptly at seeing Callens. She looked at him, then to the men behind him, then back to him. His eyes begged her not to make a scene. Looking cowed, she nodded jerkily. She turned to gather a small satchel that she had kept prepared for her escape and then threw a coat over her dress.

"Fine," she replied in a sulky tone. "I see that I'm to be treated no better than a common street walker."

"We will not in any way be disrespectful of Her Ladyship, but we will carry out our orders," Callens replied dutifully. "Please let us do this as gently as possible."

"Very well," she sighed dramatically. "Let us go." Callens extended an arm and allowed the Princess to exit the room ahead of him, his two men falling into trail. Three others waited outside while the remainder stayed out of sight around the corner.

Sherron McLeod managed to maintain her routine until they were out of earshot before she turned to Callens and grinned.

"I knew you would not fail me," she said simply, her voice breathy and soft.

"Indeed," Callens replied stoically. "Let us make good our escape while there is no alarm," he added. Sherron shook her head.

"Not yet. I must find out where Therron is being kept. The quickest way I know to do that is to force the information from my father."

"My Lady," Callens fought to conceal his alarm, but Sherron cut him off.

"No. I will not leave without it. We can stumble about looking or we can go to the source. I prefer to go to the source. Let's go." With that she led the way down the hallway to the stairs and Callens had no choice but to follow with his men.

-

Memmnon had been anxious all evening. He of course had many reasons to be anxious with a crisis among his family, a war being waged and a father in ill health. Still those problems had been present for some time.

He decided to walk the walls to see if that would relieve his anxiety. It was something he did often of a morning time. Perhaps it would help this evening as well.

Leaving his offices, he made his way out to the stairway near the main gate and climbed to the top, followed by a single guard and an aide who maintained a respectful distance from the Crown Prince. His walks and moods were well known and his actions surprised no one. The guards nodded to him in passing but otherwise continued their watch. There was a war on, after all.

-

Tammon McLeod let the book he'd been reading fall to his lap, rubbing his eyes. He was feeling better today than he had in some time. Well enough to try and catch up on what was happening. His son had visited earlier in the day when he was still sleeping so he had not had the chance to see Memmnon as yet. Feeling more lively than he had in some time, he decided to send for his son. He pulled the servant cord, and when his footman appeared asked him to summon Memmnon for him.

While he waited he decided to continue his reading but before he could his physician walked in for his nightly visit. Sighing in frustration, Tammon endured Smithe's poking and prodding with a minimum of fuss, hoping that would satisfy the man and get him out that much quicker.

Smithe was all but done when the two heard a commotion outside Tammon's door.

-

The two guards at Tammon McLeod's door had proven capable and Callens regretted their death, but neither had gone easy. One of his own men was also dead and two others injured, one seriously. Sherron McLeod ignored that and barged into the king's apartments without a backward glance.

Smithe had just enough time to open his mouth in shock before the ornately jeweled dagger in her hands pierced his chest, perforating his left lung and striking his heart a glancing blow. In all likelihood the fussy man was dead when he hit the floor. Stepping over him as casually as if he were a log, Sherron entered her father's bedchamber.

-

The footman decided to deliver the message himself. It was almost time for him to retire and a good walk might make it easier for him to sleep. With the king's declining health, the man faced his own imminent retirement as well. He would no longer live in the palace but would be relegated to housing in the city. Not that he would suffer. Tammon McLeod was generous to a fault with his servants, but the man would miss the amenities of the palace. He planned to make use of them as long as he could, especially the kitchen. Perhaps a snack before retiring. Once he'd located the Prince, of course.

It took longer than he'd imagined, going first to Memmnon's offices and then following the directions of the staff to the wall. There he finally managed to catch up to the young ruler and inform him of his father's wishes. That done, he decided he would head to the kitchen. Now that his work was done, he could get a light snack and then retire to his own chambers for the evening. Barring some unforeseen problem, he would not be needed again tonight.

Memmnon took a deep, cleansing breath of the chilled night air and then descended the stairs to attend to his father. There was no sense in putting it off, he figured.

-

"What are you doing here, traitor?" Tammon demanded, some of his old spine showing even as he faced his own daughter with a bloody knife in her hand. "And you Callens," he looked past her to the colonel. "I pegged you for many things, but treason was not among them."

"Should it prosper, none dare call it treason," Sherron answered for them both. "I have a proposition for you father," she said harshly. "If you tell me where Therron is, I will kill you quickly. If you refuse, then I will kill you much more slowly. Now," she advanced slowly;

"Where. Is. My. Brother."

-

Behind her, Callens felt his axis tilt slightly. Killing the king had been no part of his plan. Nor had killing the Crown Prince for that matter. He had assumed that Therron would banish or exile the Crown Prince once he was on the throne, but. . .regicide was not something he'd considered even for a second.

It struck him as he listened to her speak that Sherron McLeod might not be well balanced.

"Kill me then and be damned to you!" Tammon shot back. "I'm dead anyway, you wretched child. My heart simply doesn't recognize that yet. What is it you hope to gain by knowing where your snake of a twin is anyway? He's of no more use to you now."

"On the contrary," Sherron smiled nastily. "I've groomed Therron for years to take your place, old man. To rule from the seat of power the way a true king should rule. With all the power and authority of a true king, not some cowardly doddering old fool! The people will at long last have a king worthy of the name and worthy of following! Now *where is he*!" her voice raised as she spoke until she was almost yelling.

"I'll tell you nothing," Tammon assured her. "Go ahead. Nothing you do to me can be worse than knowing that two of my own children have betrayed their family and their heritage," he added sadly. "To think I ever doted on you, you shrewish wretch!" he all but snarled, showing the fire that he had demonstrated as a younger man. Sherron was momentarily taken aback by that.

"At least I still have two children worthy of the name," Tammon added, wounding his daughter where it mattered most.

"So you value Parno above Therron and I?" Sherron asked, far too calmly for Callens' liking.

"I valued all of you until you proved yourself unworthy of that value," Tammon shot back. "He, at least, is loyal, even when he needn't be. Unlike the two of you he puts the well being of this kingdom above his petty likes and dislikes."

"And Therron will never rule Soulan," Tammon couldn't help but add. "Memmnon will sit upon the throne whether you like it or not and Parno will see to it that he does!"

Sherron had heard enough. Screeching in rage she ran forward and plunged the dagger into Tammon McLeod's chest, a deep and deadly blow though not instantly fatal. As she knelt over him, seething, she could hear his breath rattling in his chest.

"Tell me where he is or I will find Memmnon tonight and kill him before I leave," she threatened, and finally was rewarded with a glimmer of fear in her father's eyes. Not for himself, but for his son.

"You. . .you will do it. . .anyway," he managed to gasp out.

"It's your only chance to save him, though," she told him, eyes flat, absent any emotion. "If you don't tell me, I'll definitely kill him. If you do, maybe I won't. It's your only option."

Tammon realized in his last minutes that his daughter was more than just disturbed, as he'd always thought of her. She was in fact insane. Criminally so, in fact. Perhaps Callens would make her heed her promise, but he didn't count on that. His one comfort as he made his decision was that Parno would make Sherron suffer for this before it was done.

"K. . .Key Ho. . .Horn," he gasped out. "I exile. . .iled him to the Key Horn."

"I should have known," Sherron all but snarled. "Goodbye father," she said, smiling suddenly. "Die knowing that you are a failure. You'll be forgotten, a faceless name on the roster of the dynasty." With that she twisted the knife savagely in her father's chest, tearing into his failing heart muscle.

Tammon died still looking at his traitorous daughter, refusing to look away from her as he breathed his last. In fact, his last thought was that he hoped his image haunted her, if he himself could not return to do it.

And then he was gone.

Sherron was still for a moment as the import of what she'd done sank in. Standing slowly, she pulled her dagger from her father's chest, looking at it. Suddenly, to Callens' horror, she giggled. She whirled to find him and several of the others looking at her in shock.

"How did you expect this to end?" she demanded. "Come, Colonel. We know where Therron is. We mustn't waste any more time." She was almost to the door when it opened, leaving her face to face with her brother and two other men.

-

Nothing could have surprised Memmnon more than to see Sherron standing there. He froze for a second, caught completely by surprise. In that instant Callens' men struck, killing Memmnon's guard and his aide, surrounding the Prince.

"Brother dear," Sherron all but snarled. "I really don't have time to deal with you the way I should, but allow me to tell you that father has, sadly, passed away," she faked a sniffle and wiped an imaginary tear away from one eye. Memmnon stared at her and then to Callens.

"So, you are a traitor, then," he said evenly. "I had refused to believe it until now," he added, and Callens felt that statement to his bones. But it was too late, now.

"He's no traitor, Memmnon," Sherron shot back. "He's the most loyal soldier in the army! He just happens to be loyal to the rightful ruler of this land instead of you! Now I have to go, brother dear. Daddy was good enough to tell me where Therron is to try and save your life, miserable though it may be. I have to go and get him. But I do want to leave you with something," she said, moving around behind him. Memmnon gasped as he felt the blade enter his back, slicing into his left kidney. He could feel the blade being pulled out again as he began to slip to the floor. Sherron bent to whisper to him.

"You will linger for some time, brother," she promised. "But there's no one to come and see to you, is there? No one to care. And even if there is, Smithe is lying on the floor not far from you, dead already. So you see," she stood, having wiped her dagger on Memmnon's jacket, "by the time Therron gets here, the kingdom will be in an upheaval, with the king and Crown Prince both dead and no leader to follow. He will restore order and then ensure that the Nor are driven from our lands, as always. Oh, and Parno will be dealt with as well, I assure you," she added almost as an afterthought.

"Enjoy your failure, brother dear," she called over her shoulder. "I have work to do."

Callens looked down at Memmnon and a shadow crossed his face. Memmnon's look was one of pure contempt despite the pain he had to be in.

"Run, Colonel," he said softly as blood burbled around his lips. "Run quickly and run far, but you cannot hide. Parno will find you. And unlike me, he will kill you and like as not enjoy doing it. She is insane, Callens," he added. "And you have allowed her to lead you to your doom. Outrun it if you can, traitor."

With that Memmnon lost consciousness, leaving a now highly disturbed Callens to follow the Princess out of the palace before any alarm could be raised. His shock had still not worn off by the time they were in the saddle and on their way to the rendezvous. This had gone out of control too quickly for him to follow, and now he and his men were accomplices in the murder of the king and his heir.

-

A guilty conscious is a terrible thing. Tammon McLeod's footman considered himself an honorable and loyal man to his liege. He had served the king well for over thirty years. As he prepared for bed after visiting the kitchen, it gnawed at him that he had not checked in on his charge one last time before retiring for the evening. True, there were guards at the door, but. . .

He shook his head as he pulled his boots back on. A mere soldier would no more know what the king had need of than a horse. It wasn't that they were bad men for they were among the best in the kingdom, but they were fighting men, not personal servants. While warriors might look at men such as he with contempt, serving the king ably was just as important as carrying a sword.

He made his way through the silent hallways toward the king's apartments, taking no notice of the brief bustle of activity on the upper floor. There was always movement about these days, around the clock really with the war on and all. As he rounded the corner to the king's private rooms he drew up sharply.

The guards were prone on the floor, blood running along the marble. And between them, struggling to get to his feet. . . .

"Milord!" the man ran to where Crown Prince Memmnon was trying to move.

"King," Memmnon said weakly. "Sherron killed him I fear. Check the king." With that he fell back, exhausted.

"Alarm!" the man shouted, turning his head that his voice would carry. "To arms! Intruders! To Arms!" Hearing the call picked up he ducked into the King's chambers to see physician Smithe on the floor, clearly dead. Leaping across the still form he entered the king's bed chamber to see his liege lying, eyes still open, blood having soaked the bed clothes about him.

"No!" the man exclaimed as he rushed to the king's side. "My lord!" He shook the king, knowing all the time that it was useless. Nothing.

But the Crown Prince still lived. Taking the blanket from the king's bed he hurried back to the hallway, tearing the fabric as he went. Once back he searched Memmnon's unconscious form, finding the wound and using the first of the strips to try and staunch the flow of blood. He could hear the sound of running feet coming his way now and looked up in time to see two members of the Palace Guard coming down the hall.

"Get a doctor!" he called immediately. "The King and his physician are dead! And Prince Memmnon gravely wounded! He must have help at once!" One of the guards turned and ran back the opposite way while the other continued forward, stopping beside the servant.

"What happened?" he demanded as he knelt to lend assistance.

"The Prince said that Princess Sherron killed the king," the man told him. "I found him and the others like this when I came to check on His Majesty before retiring. I . . . I checked on the king and found the Royal Physician in chambers, dead, and the king murdered in his own bed!" the man's voice was breaking now as the import of the situation began to hit him.

"Dear God," the guard breathed. "Are you saying the king is dead?"

"Yes," the man nodded as he removed a blood soaked cloth and replaced it with a fresh one. "And so is his doctor! We have got to find a doctor and quickly! The Crown Prince must survive! There is treason as foul as any heathen Nor or Godless savage here and it has already cost us the king! We cannot allow the Prince to perish as well!"

-

"Beg pardon milady," Stephanie looked up to see her escort's Captain standing beside her table.

"Yes, Captain?" she asked, setting her journal aside. "What can I do for you?"

"I wanted to inform you, milady, we've replaced the horses for fresh mounts, and . . . it's moon bright, milady and the clouds have cleared. Should you desire to continue on tonight, we can."

"Surely the men are tired, Captain," Stephanie demurred. "They will need rest too."

"My Lady's pardon, ma'am, but we're trained to go for days at a time with little or no sleep," he informed her. "Truth is, it's a good night to ride and allow the men to train in the moonlight. But only if you should desire to do so, ma'am. If we were to continue on in say, an hour, then should all go well, we would arrive in Nasil by noon or soon after tomorrow. At that point I can allow the Palace Guard to assign you an escort for the rest of the day and give the men off to rest."

Stephanie considered that for a moment. Was it worth moving on tonight?

The ambulance was designed to allow sleeping in moderate comfort, so she could rest on the trip of course.

"Is there any other reason you'd prefer to press on, Captain?" she asked suddenly.

"With respect, milady, no one knows you're about yet save our own people. If word travels, you become a target. I've no fear of bandits and the like with forty swords along, half of them Prince's Own. But with the Nor solidly on our ground, milady, and your connection to Himself, the Marshal, you become a target, milady. In Nasil you would be much safer than you are on the road with only us between you and some Nor raiding party."

"Would we not be more likely to encounter such a party at night?" Stephanie asked, eyebrow raised at the Captain's 'connection to Himself' remark.

"If they were to be looking, then yes milady," the Captain nodded. "But they aren't, as yet, since no one knows you're about. But the inn last night, they know you were there. Was they to be hit, they might tell it, either to save themselves and their family or under torture. Then they'd be after us for sure. If we're still moving, be hard to catch us at this point."

She couldn't honestly fault his reasoning, Stephanie decided. And she supposed the fact that she was 'connected' to Marshal McLeod did indeed make her a target. Something she had not even bothered to consider until this very moment.

But Parno had, she thought to herself. *This is the very kind of thing he feared most.*

"Winnie?" she called. In seconds the younger woman was there, still carrying a hunk of lamb the inn manager had offered her.

"Yes, Lady Freeman?"

"How would you feel about continuing on tonight instead of staying over?" Stephanie asked. "It would mean being on the road until around noon tomorrow, and trying to sleep in the ambulance, but-"

"Sure!" Winnie nodded enthusiastically. "Let's go!"

"Well, Captain, that settles that I suppose," Stephanie fought to hide a grin. "How soon would you like us to be ready?"

"An hour will do milady," he assured her. "Just enough to see to feeding the men and then we'll hitch up the fresh team and saddle up. We'll be ready in an hour."

"An hour it is, then," Stephanie agreed, looking at Winnie.

"Gives me time to finish eating," Winnie grinned.

Stephanie shook her head slowly, laughing despite herself.

An hour later they were bumping their way down the trade route in the moonlight.

-

"The battle ended rather abruptly," Tinker reported when he arrived back at the inn that evening. There were no leaves for anyone in camp with the possibility of hostilities resuming in the morning so everyone had the night off so to speak. Bell was sitting on the porch, for all the world looking like a loafer. His sword was within reach, however, hidden by an old blanket.

"Know why?" he asked, whittling as he rocked back and forth idly.

"No, but it was quite the surprise apparently," Tinker replied. "The Nor were pushing hard against the line, then simply withdrew. The Prince offered a truce until morning to allow them to gather their dead and wounded."

"Hm," Bell nodded but said nothing else.

"I believe we will be safe enough to remain, and in any case the army isn't leaving," Tinker told him, rising again. "I believe I will have something to eat, since I skipped lunch today," he smiled.

"Reckon I'll sit here a spell and. . .watch," Bell replied.

"Very good Mister Bell. I expect there will be work aplenty later on tonight and certainly tomorrow for myself, Mister Wysin and the others. I suspect that you and the ladies here will have a slow day tomorrow, however," there was a hint of humor in his voice.

"Imagine so," Bell chuckled. "Enjoy your meal, Mister Tinker."

"Thank you, Mister Bell."

-

"Preliminary reports show our estimate on losses to be holding up fairly well, milord," Enri Willard reported. The staff were gathered together around a makeshift table in Parno's command tent, having a working meal as they tried to make sense of the aftermath of the battle.

"I see," the Marshal nodded. "Did the Nor succeed in retrieving their dead and wounded?" he asked.

"Yes, milord," General Davies nodded. "In good order and very proper about observing the truce as well, sir."

"Good, good," Parno nodded absently.

"What's bothering you?" Karls asked suddenly, watching Parno almost fidget, something he never did.

"I don't know," Parno admitted with a helpless shrug. "I really don't. There's something bothering me, but I can't for the life of me put my hand on it. It's almost like we've left something undone, but I don't think we have. Have we?" this to the table in general.

"No, milord, we haven't," Davies assured him. "Our men have been well cared for, fed and guard posts set. Our wounded are all being attended to and our dead removed from the field and treated respectfully. We are prepared to receive enemy action with little or no notice and our reserve is assembled again and prepared to support the line when and where needed. We are as prepared as we can possibly be."

Parno listened to the list as Davies ran down it and agreed it was sufficient, or should be. So why was he so jumpy? He was not, by nature, a nervous man. Never had been. So, what was wrong with him now?

"There's something wrong," he said aloud finally, halting the talk that had started again around the table. "I don't know what it is, or where, but something is out of kilter, somewhere. If it's not here, then it's somewhere else. Of course, if it is somewhere else, then I won't know about it for days, will I?" he laughed, but there was little humor in it. He noted everyone looking at him and waved a dismissing hand.

"Don't mind me," he told them. "Whatever it is, there's nothing to do about it that we haven't already done. Eat," he told them. "No telling what we'll find tomorrow, right?"

They resumed eating, but would cast surreptitious glances at him from time to time, almost as if studying him to see if anything were wrong. Finally, he'd had enough of it. He rose abruptly and the others struggled to get to their feet as well.

"Oh, stop it!" he exclaimed, waving them back to their seats. "You know I don't cater to that foolishness unless I have to. Keep working and finish your meal. I'm going to stretch my legs is all. I was informed earlier today that I had to distance myself from these minor details and allow my staff to do their jobs. So, do your jobs," he indicated the papers and logs strewn about the table. "I'm sure I'll be fine."

He acknowledged murmurs of farewell as he departed, but stepped out as quickly as he could and took a deep breath of cool night air. He started walking without any real destination in mind, just aimless wandering. He was conscious of a small detail falling in around him but keeping their distance.

Is this what it will be like from now on? He wondered bleakly. No privacy, no being alone with his thoughts. Always someone watching, listening, guarding. He shook his head at the idea.

"What bothers you, my Prince?"

Parno had to force himself not to start as Cho Feng's voice interrupted his train of thought. Feng appeared at his side out of the very night, it seemed, always quiet and deadly.

"I already said I don't know," he reminded the oriental warmaster.

"Something else was bothering you just now," Feng would not be put off.

"I was just thinking about how I have no privacy anymore," he admitted, gesturing to the guard around them. He wondered suddenly if Feng had slipped past them or if they had merely allowed him to pass unchallenged.

"Understandable," Feng nodded. "One surrenders a great deal when he moves into a position of authority and responsibility. The greater the service, the more one loses."

"I can vouch for that," Parno agreed. "Anyway, I don't have that much to complain about, really. Heck, do you know my life is actually better now than at almost any point in my life up *until* now?" he grinned. "How sad a testament is that?"

"Such a discovery can be both illuminating and disheartening," Feng agreed with a low chuckle. "Things have gone rather well, all facts taken together. Today you managed to dodge a more serious blow while dealing one of your own."

"Nothing but luck," Parno scoffed. "Skill and ability had little to do with it."

"Do not discount luck on the battlefield, my Prince," Feng lectured lightly. "While it cannot be planned for or anticipated, the wise leader never discounts it as a worthy ally. Or deadly opponent if it falls for the enemy."

"Guess that's true," Parno decided after a minute. "And I wasn't complaining about luck, either," he stressed. "Just pointing out that it wasn't anything I did that caused the Nor to break off their attack."

"That you know of," Feng reminded him sternly, slipping further into lecture mode. "You took many actions today, and in the days leading up to this battle. Since you have no idea why the enemy withdrew so abruptly, you cannot claim to know that nothing you did played a part in his decision, mistake or no. It could have been Mister Finn's weapons that created the panic in the enemy general and broke his nerve. You are responsible for them, are you not? It could have been the way you marshaled your archers for concentrated fire on the advancing enemy, the bonfires and scouts that gave you warning of the impending attack, the fire that you personally ordered down on the enemy artillery at the risk of allowing the enemy's infantry to approach your lines; all of these are things you did or ordered done or supported in getting done. Any one of them, any combination of them, could have been what caused today's victory." Conscious that his voice had risen, Feng stopped short. After a moment he continued.

"Since we do not know," Feng's voice calmed a bit, "we must not assume. Assumption is the death of all decisions, my prince. It must not enter into your thinking, ever."

"Okay then," Parno decided to simply agree since this was the most animation he'd seen from Cho Feng since he'd known the man. It was obvious that this was a sore topic.

"Tomorrow is a new day," Feng noted, refusing to be drawn into another display of emotion. "Perhaps the enemy will come at us again. Perhaps not. Having won the field today, your men will fight harder tomorrow. Do not rob them of that feeling by second guessing what happened today."

"I'm not," Parno defended himself. "I made sure of that in fact this afternoon. Had that same though," he said triumphantly. "That it was more important that they believe they had won than for me to stress that I hadn't done anything special. Guess your teaching is rubbing off on me after all," he mock jeered.

"It was bound to happen eventually," Feng nodded stoically. "If one flings sufficient manure at the stable wall, some will eventually stick."

Feng was already several steps along his path back to the tents when Parno realized what he had said.

"Hey!"

—

By the time Parno returned to the tent Cho Feng was nowhere to be seen, but Karls Willard was waiting patiently in a camp chair. He pointed to another one for Parno and then handed the prince a beer as he sat.

"Nice," Parno complimented after a long pull on the chilled bottle. "Where'd you get it?" he asked.

"Pair of Urian suttlers make it," Karls replied. "Husband and wife. Pretty good set-up, really. She dresses like a barmaid and him like a tender. I guess they make it at night and sell it by day. Or maybe the other way around," he frowned. "I don't know."

"Well, it's good beer," Parno nodded, taking another draught. "What's on your mind?"

"I'm going to ask Dhalia to marry me," Karls said suddenly, looking Parno in the eye. Parno nodded slowly, having expected it.

"I'll expect you to be good to her," he said simply, eyeing his friend closely. "It would pain me to kill you, Karls."

"I'm sure it would," Karls snorted and Parno had to laugh at the dead-pan delivery. "Seriously, I wanted your blessing. You're the closest thing she has left to family. If you say no, of course, then I'll have to murder you in your sleep," he added.

"Of course you have my blessing," Parno agreed. "But I meant it when I said I expect you to take good care of her. Were I to hear otherwise, Karls, I would be grieved."

"I know," Karls smiled. "But I promise I'll treat her like the treasure she is beneath all that tomboy exterior," he grinned.

"Yes, describing her as a delicate flower might be risky even for you, brother," Parno chuckled. "I assume your visit to her new holding went well, then?"

"It's a nice place," Karls nodded. "There is an older couple living there as caretakers. We spent a good while talking to them, then rode over the grounds. The buildings need some work, but it's a nice place, Parno. A place where a man could raise a family and make a good living if he's allowed to. Dhalia fell in love with it immediately."

"I hoped she would," Parno nodded. "I'll see to the repairs," he said a minute later. "As soon as I can send a rider to Cove, in fact. A detail can escort her down there and she can supervise the work herself if she'd like."

"We can do that, Parno," Karls objected mildly.

"Consider it a wedding present," Parno smiled.

"She'll kill you," Karls warned.

"I'll tell her it was your idea," Parno shot back, laughing.

"What about you?" Karls asked after a minute's pause.

"What about me?"

"You and Lady Freeman," Karls clarified. "What did the two of you work out while we were at Cumberland House?"

"We talked," Parno admitted, fidgeting again. "I hadn't been very fair to her, apparently. In fairness I was trying to be. I didn't think a woman of her quality had any business in the same room with a man such as me. I still don't, to be honest. She informed me, however, that she was able to make those decisions for herself. Rather pointedly I might add," he shrugged.

"I bet," Karls grinned. "And?"

"And we have agreed to do things her way," Parno shrugged helplessly. "As I'm sure she knew we would," he sighed theatrically, shaking his head to Karls delighted laughter.

"I think she'll make you a fine wife, Parno McLeod," Karls told him sincerely, though still chuckling. "Everyone knew it was going to happen sooner or later."

"Is that a fact?" Parno shot back.

"Oh yes," Karls nodded. "There was a pool going among the officer's wives, and another among the NCO wives as well I believe, on when the two of you would stop . . . beating around the bush, I believe was the way it was most often put? Yes, that was it, I'm sure. Apparently, your arguments were the stuff of legend around the camp."

"Well I'm glad we were able to keep folks entertained," Parno said. "And I think she just purely likes to argue, come to think of it."

"She is a woman," Karls agreed sagely. "I still think she'll make you a fine wife, my friend. She's strong that one. Stands up to you nicely, in fact," Karls twisted the knife just a bit.

"Yes, I've seen the way you 'stand up' to Dolly," Parno sneered back, causing Karls a sudden fit of coughing.

"Anyway, I daresay that should I manage to live through the war, the doctor and I might well retire to Cove Canton and raise our own fat babies. You and Dolly can come and visit and we'll return the favor and all just be happy and domestic and live happily ever after," he finished brightly. Karls looked at him for a moment, a faint look of horror dawning in his eyes.

"That's a joke, right?" he asked as Parno rose, setting the empty bottle on the table so that Karls could return it.

"Good night, Karls."

"Hey, seriously Parno!" Karls voice followed him. "You're just joking, right? Parno?"

CHAPTER TWENTY-FOUR

-

"The blade undoubtedly has penetrated the kidney. That is the source of the bleeding here, externally, as well as the internal bleeding that results in his coughing up blood."

"What can be done?" Memmnon's chief adviser and retainer, Henry Govan, was looking at the hastily summoned Army surgeon who had been caring for Memmnon through the night.

"Ideally the kidney would be removed," the surgeon replied. "But that takes a level of skill, training and education that few possess, as well as experience that is in even shorter supply. It is a detailed and precise operation that is not routinely performed. I do not have the knowledge or the skill to do this," he admitted. "I am sorry, truly I am, but. . .I simply do not know how. It is an intensely intricate operation that requires intimate detail of biology and the know how to remove the organ and ensure that doing so does not result in still more damage or blood loss. Lord Smithe would have been able to do this without hesitation, but. . . ." he trailed off, not knowing how to finish. Lord Smithe was dead, as was their king. The surgeon, named Spurgeon oddly enough, Govan thought, had worked through most of the night to try and stop Memmnon's slow and agonizing death, but so far has been unable to do so. Only a large dose of opiates was keeping the Prince from literally screaming in pain.

"Surely there is another doctor that can do something like this!" Govan exclaimed.

"Of course there is," Spurgeon nodded. "Several of them in fact. The problem is that none that I know of are here, now. Doctor Freeman once could have, but his eyesight has faded to the point that he no longer operates. He would not be able to perform so delicate a procedure and would never attempt it. The nearest physician I know of at this very moment would either be at the royal hospital at Bingham, or at the front. The two physicians I personally know that would normally be here in Nasil and could perform this surgery are in the field with the army, assisting with the wounded. They could not be here in less than five days, allowing for time for the messenger to get there and for them to return."

"I can't believe he has five days," Govan shook his head.

"I'd say two at most, and that is most generous," Spurgeon agreed. "I am truly sorry," he said heavily. "It would be the greatest service I could perform for the Crown to be able to save his life and I would do anything, *give* anything that I now or will ever possess to have the skill to perform the surgery, even just this once if never again. But I simply do not." The man looked as if he were going to cry.

"What can you do?" Govan asked.

"I can slow the bleeding, which I have, it's almost stopped in fact, and I can keep him comfortable. Anything more than that is beyond what I am capable of."

"Then do that," Govan ordered. "Try and keep him alive, and I will see if I can find someone who can help him."

"I pray you can," Spurgeon remarked earnestly. Govan left the room, on his way to roust out the off duty members of Tammon McLeod's regiment. They were angry men, to say the least. Angry and looking for someone to hold responsible for the death of their liege lord.

They could channel that need into searching for a physician who could do the miraculous.

-

Sebastian Grey looked at the quartet of constables with something akin to hatred, glaring at them in silence because he did not trust himself to speak. He breathed deeply, trying to calm himself. There was no point in being angry because what was done was done. And, in all fairness, had these four realized what was happening and tried to prevent it, they would merely have been added to the list of dead.

"They were wearing the uniforms of the Royal Family, sir," the senior constable spoke in their defense. "We had no reason to suspect they were not. Technically, if they were a part of Prince Therron's regiment, they were servants of the Royal Family, I suppose."

"Your orders were to prevent Princess McLeod from leaving her apartments without the express authorization of the Crown Prince or the King," Grey ground out between clenched teeth.

"Sir, the Colonel reported to us that it was Prince Memmnon himself who had dispatched them to escort her to his offices," the man nodded. "The Princess was reluctant to even leave her room, but the Colonel told her through the door that she was going, as the Prince had ordered it. Had he not invoked the name of the Prince we would have refused them entry."

And been killed in the process, Grey knew. Again he was reminded that there was nothing that these four could have done besides die. Reports were that the group that had freed Sherron McLeod was at least twenty strong, all seasoned soldiers and among the best trained the army had to offer. Four Constables would have stood no chance at all against even an equal number, let alone so many.

"Get out," he ordered them suddenly. "Speak of this to no one until I tell you, personally, to do otherwise. There is an investigation ongoing. You are excused duty until that is concluded. Report to the barracks and remain there until I release you. Go."

The four left at once, glad to be away from their angry superior. Grey watched them go and then turned to the report from the Tammon McLeod's footman. Had the man not gone to make a final check on the king before retiring, then Prince Memmnon would likely have bled out before anyone found him. Even now the news was not good concerning the Prince. Which reminded him; someone needed to inform Prince Parno of what had happened. He was suddenly the only member of the Royal Family that was capable of taking the reins of the kingdom at the present. Despite how badly he might be needed at the front, the need for him here, in Nasil, was far greater for the moment.

He quickly wrote out a message to the young prince and then headed to the stables to find a courier and a fast horse. The sun was already high above the horizon. The rider should make good time.

-

The search for a trained physician spread through most of the Royal City before noon. The members of Tammon McLeod's personal regiment were not given to politeness that morning in their fury over what had happened. Broken into squads led by young officers, the troopers fanned across the city in search of someone who could save Prince Memmnon, or that knew of someone who could. The city was not quite locked down, as the men to do so simply were not available. Prince Memmnon's Own were supplementing the Palace Guard in the event of another incursion, so it was left to the City Guard, mostly militia that were a bit too old for front line duty, the city constabulary, and Tammon's Guards.

Failure to secure the services of a physician that could perform the lifesaving surgery led to increased tempers as the sun moved ever higher in the sky. Mindful of how time sensitive things were, the soldiers were becoming more angry with each passing hour.

One squad was on the eastern outskirts of the Royal City around noon, combing the older sections for even a retired doctor capable of helping the prince. Their lieutenant saw an ambulance approaching with a heavy escort and moved his men into position to stop it. The Captain leading the escort drew up, halting his small column a short way from the smaller party.

"State your business," the lieutenant demanded in what he fondly imagined was an intimidating voice. Several of the Black Sheep actually snorted at that, but were silenced by a glare from their Captain.

"We're escorting our charge into the city," the Captain replied amiably enough.

"And who might your charge be?" the lieutenant asked.

"I'm afraid I'm not at liberty to say," the Captain responded more slowly, wary now. None of this was normal. "What has happened?"

"I want to know who is in that ambulance, right now!" the lieutenant barked. Behind the Captain of the escort several of the Black Sheep silently drew swords, allowing them to hang along their saddles.

"Lieutenant, I've answered all your questions I intend to," the Captain stated slowly and clearly. "We are members of Prince Parno McLeod's personal regiment, escorting a party at his order. Who that party is being no concern whatsoever of a snot-nose lieutenant who likely shaves no more than three times a week." The Captain spurred his horse forward and the front rank of his men followed.

"Now whatever you and your men are engaged in, feel free to continue in it while we go on our way."

"You aren't passing here until we've inspected that ambulance!" The lieutenant was angry, he was scared, and he was looking for a fight. Unfortunately, he had chosen the worst possible group to pick one with. The remainder of the escort now drew their swords almost in unison. Without a single spoken order, half moved to support the Captain while the other half collapsed on the ambulance, ringing it with steel.

"You won't be inspecting this ambulance, lieutenant," the Captain's voice turned icy. "Any attempt to get inside will result in your painful and immediate death, I assure you."

From inside, Stephanie McLeod looked out, wondering why they were stopped and why the escort suddenly had their swords drawn.

"What's going on?" she demanded.

"Not sure, milady," the man nearest her window replied softly. "Kindly stay out of sight, milady, and keep your voice low until we can sort this out. I'm not caring for this at all."

"There's. . .the road is blocked by soldiers," Winnie reported, having leaned out the window on the other side. "I think they're actually threatening the escort," she added, amused. "That won't go well."

"I can't see the humor in that, Winifred," Stephanie frowned. "Perhaps you should get back inside."

"It's not funny, I agree," Winnie lithely moved back into the carriage.

"But the very idea of ten men challenging this bunch?" she shook her head. "That is just sad. This outfit will essentially walk right over them like they aren't there."

"How are they dressed?" Stephanie asked, trying to see out but refraining from actually hanging from the window as her young friend had done.

"Similar to the Prince's Own, now that you mention it," Winnie looked thoughtful. "I wonder if other personal regiments dress that way."

"Yes, they do," Stephanie nodded. "The colors are the same, as are them emblems. The designs are unique to the regiment, but the black and green of the McLeod dynasty is always the same."

"Then I'd say we're facing a squad of either the King's Own or Prince Memmnon's," Winnie declared. "And they're still about to get their backsides handed to them," she added.

"I need to speak to the Captain," Stephanie ordered the man near her window.

"Not a good time, milady," the man almost whispered. "I don't know what burr is under their saddle, but they're demanding to inspect the carriage. That is not going to happen, milady, no matter what."

"If they're the King's Own then it's stupid for them to fight against us!" Stephanie exclaimed. "Find out what the problem is!"

"We're trying, milady," the soldier assured her.

Up front, the lieutenant had finally realized that he had well and truly poked the bear, but didn't know how to *un*poke it now that he had. He did recognize that bluster wasn't going to work.

"We're in search of a skilled physician," he admitted finally.

"What?" the Captain could not have been more surprised if the younger man had told him they were searching for a unicorn. "Why?"

"There was an attack on the King last night, and several others," the younger man replied after a brief hesitation. "The Crown Prince is severely injured and the Royal Physician is unable to care for him at present. Because of the war, most other trained physicians are away. We desperately need someone who can perform surgery or we. . .we could lose the Prince."

"Why in the hell didn't you say that to start with you imbecile!" the Captain shouted, angrier now than before. "Stand aside or lead us to the palace at once. At once do you hear! We're escorting one of the best doctors in the entire kingdom at Marshal McLeod's orders!"

"What?" it was the lieutenant's turn to be stunned.

"Lead, follow, or get out of the way!" the Captain yelled, then turned around in his saddle.

"Double time, lads! To the palace at once!" As the column started the small unit blocking the road scrambled to get out of the way. The Captain fell back to the carriage where he could speak to his charge.

"Milady, did you hear?" he asked.

"No, what's happening?" Stephanie demanded, resisting the urge to climb out her window as Winnie had once again.

"There was an attack on the palace last night," the Captain said as the column picked up speed. "The King was attacked, as was Prince Memmnon, and the prince is sorely injured. They need someone who can perform surgery on him or we may lose him."

"Get me there at once," Stephanie ordered, no longer the Lady, but the Doctor, now. "If you can get me more information before we arrive, bring it to me." She was already reaching for her bag.

"Guess it's a good thing you always carry that," Winnie remarked. "What can I do to help, Lady Freeman?"

"There's nothing either of us can do until we get there and find out what's happening," Stephanie admitted as she opened her bag and began setting tools aside. "Keep a sharp lookout though," she added. "If the palace was attacked then there may still be Nor in the city. We're a nice target according to the Captain."

She was conscious of Winnie moving about in the carriage, but was so preoccupied with preparing her instruments that she ignored it. When she finally did look up, Winnie had donned her quiver and was uncasing her bow, having already strapped a short sword to her side. Seeing Stephanie's wide eyed look, the younger woman shrugged.

"You care for the Prince and I'll watch your back," she said simply. Stephanie looked at her a moment longer then nodded.

"Very well."

-

Sebastian Grey always kept his cards close to his vest, as the saying went. Very few people yet knew that Prince Memmnon had told the man who found him that it had been his own sister that had killed the king. He was keeping it that way for the present. There was too much that was currently not public knowledge to allow that to get out until Prince Parno could arrive and be ready to take over.

Grey acknowledged that it was a lot to throw on the young man who had only just assumed command of the army, but . . . there was no one else. Prince Memmnon, assuming he lived, would not be up and about for days, perhaps weeks. The kingdom simply could not languish without a head for that length of time. Worse, the situation with the twins had to be dealt with and sooner rather than later. Again, only the Prince could do that. Orders that could only come from the sovereign or regent would have to be issued.

He looked at the courier, one of the King's Own personal couriers. Hard riding professionals, the King's Couriers were the best riders and among the most trusted men in service to the king. He handed the small satchel to the man who took it and tucked it inside his jacket.

"This has to get to Marshal McLeod without delay," Grey stressed. "Kill horses if you have to, man, but get this in his hands as soon as humanly possible.

I can't stress enough how important it is."

"Yes sir," the man nodded and leaped into the saddle. With scarcely a pause he was away and gone, galloping north as fast as his charger would carry him. Grey watched him go, turning his gaze away before the man was out of sight, just in case the old wives' tale was true.

He couldn't afford any bad luck right now.

-

The escort pulled in to the palace grounds just under too fast, startling a still jumpy Palace Guard. They, too, were smarting, since it was technically on their watch that mayhem had occurred. The Captain and four men dismounted at once, tossing reins to others as they formed a cordon around the carriage door. Stephanie stepped out after passing her bag out to one of the men, then securing again in her own hand as Winnie simply jumped to the ground behind her. Several eyes were raised at the sight of the young mountain girl with her bow and sword, but none of the Sheep were among them. They knew how deadly Winifred Huble was.

The Captain led the group inside, passing the guard without offering a comment other than 'move aside'. The man was wearing Dynasty colors and acted like he should be there, so they moved aside, not realizing that this was exactly what had happened the previous evening.

Once inside Stephanie grabbed the first person she saw and demanded to be taken at once to the Prince. The startled maid servant bowed and practically ran to the Prince's apartments, the doctor's group following. There was a strong guard outside the door and they formed a barrier against the group.

"This is Lady Corsin-Freeman," the Captain spoke calmly. "She is the personal physician of Marshal McLeod as well as the teaching physician at the Cove Canton military hospital. We're here because we were told the Prince is in dire need of her services."

"Praise be on High," one of the men murmured as the others stepped aside while he opened the door. "Mister Spurgeon is in with the Prince right now, milady," he offered as Stephanie passed him.

"Thank you," she said absently.

"We'll be here if you need us, milady," the Captain called. Stephanie turned to see the tired soldiers still in the hallway. Beside her stood Winnie.

"That won't be necessary, Captain," she said gently. "You and your men should rest. We don't know what will happen in the next hours or days."

"Yes, milady," he bowed slightly. She disappeared into Memmnon's apartments and the Captain turned to look at his men.

"We'll stand two-hour watches, starting now, with two men on this door at all times." Two of the men stepped forward at once, nodding. "She goes nowhere alone," he told them flatly.

"We're standing a permanent watch here, Captain," the sergeant of the guard detail offered. "She'll be safe here."

"Yes, she will," the Captain nodded, ignoring the man otherwise. "You'll be relieved in two hours," he told his men, then departed with the rest of his men in tow.

The two hard eyed members of Parno's Company took places along the wall opposite the door and settled in to wait.

-

"Freeman?" Spurgeon looked amazed. "My God, are you Doctor Freeman's daughter?"

"I am," Stephanie nodded, frowning at the irrelevancy. "Status on the Prince?"

"Single stab wound that appears to have perforated the left kidney," Spurgeon detailed professionally. "I've managed to stop the bleeding for the most part, and I've kept him sedated against the pain since his squirming was aggravating the wound. I've found no other signs of injury on his person. He is bleeding internally, presumably from the wound or the kidney itself. He's presenting blood that is red and not frothy from the mouth, coughing it up in non-congealed form."

"Opiates would have thinned his blood and made it harder to stop the bleeding," Stephanie noted in disapproval.

"It was that or watch him tear his bandages loose and bleed more heavily from the wound, Lady Freeman," Spurgeon nodded. "It was a poor choice either way, I admit. Not knowing that you might be nearby, I chose to keep him somewhat comfortable and try to minimize the damage. I wanted to give him as much chance as possible."

"You've done well," she agreed. "I'll need you to assist me," she informed him. "Have you a nurse?" she inquired.

"I'd be honored, milady, and yes. Two of them, one a well-trained surgical assistant, though not able to perform the surgery herself of course. The other is a general nurse, but a good one."

"Get them, and get me a gown at once," Stephanie ordered briskly. "We've no time to spare."

Fifteen minutes after she had walked into the room, Stephanie Corsin-Freeman was operating on Prince Memmnon in an attempt to save his life. It did not cross her mind at the time that this surgery was all that stood between Parno and the throne.

-

Govan had heard the news and ran to the Prince's apartments only to be told that the surgery had begun already. He could do nothing but wait with the rest to hear what happened.

Sebastian Grey was relieved to hear that Lady Freeman had arrived, unexpectedly, and was now working with others to try and save the Prince. It still irked him to have had this happen, but he took some comfort in knowing that Tammon McLeod's insistence on how the entire affair had been handled was the root cause of this trouble. That didn't make him like it any better, but it did ease any pangs of guilt at the failure of his own people to prevent what had happened.

Colonel Mason Stang, commander of Tammon McLeod's personal regiment, arrived soon after Grey and joined the other senior men in waiting to hear if the surgery would be successful. In less than ten minutes their number grew again as Colonel Robert Moore, the commander of Memmnon's regiment arrived, followed by the changing of the guard. He frowned at the two men from Parno's regiment, but both ignored him, confident in their place as combat soldiers assigned to Prince Parno's Own. There was very little either of the other commanders could do to them, especially when following orders.

And so the small group filled the hallway, hoping against hope that the talented young 'lady doctor' could indeed save the life of the Crown Prince.

-

Inside, Stephanie worked quickly but skillfully, knowing that time was against her in more ways than one. Memmnon had lost entirely too much blood for her liking and now she was forced to cut him open in order to repair the damage done by the stab wound. As she literally pulled his insides apart in order to get to his kidney, she realized right away what had happened.

"The knife missed the kidney," she told Spurgeon and the others with no small relief. "The blood is coming from a slice in the main vein into the organ, see here?" she allowed Spurgeon to see. "What we must do is collect the blood that has pooled inside his body cavity, while repairing that vein to insure that it stops losing blood. Can you see to cleaning him?" she asked the surgical nurse.

"Yes milady," she nodded firmly. "I've done that work before."

"Excellent," Stephanie nodded. "Have the other nurse assist if necessary. Meanwhile, Doctor Spurgeon would you assist me in caring for the Prince's wound?"

"I'd be honored Lady Freeman," Spurgeon said gently. "And thank you so much for being here," he added.

"I'm glad I was here as well," she assured him.

The two sewed the vein's damaged area closed, with Stephanie adding two additional cross stitches of sterilized cat gut to the work to strengthen it while it healed. As the wound healed, the stitches would slowly dissolve and be absorbed by Memmnon's body, eliminating any need to remove them later. She allowed Spurgeon to place two of the stitches himself under her supervision, and then inspected Memmnon's innards to make sure all the lost blood was cleaned. Using distilled water, they carefully washed his insides, cleaning the residue from the blood as well as any foreign material from the weapon used to stab him.

Finally, she allowed Spurgeon to close Memmnon's wound while she supervised. The man's hands were steady and quick, and his eye sharp. By the time they were finished she was impressed with his ability and said so as they all changed from their bloody smocks.

"Thank you, milady," Spurgeon almost glowed. "I sincerely appreciate that, and the wonderful opportunity to assist you. I've never had such an opportunity before and like as not won't again. Thank you," he repeated.

"Don't thank me, you performed very well and earned whatever opportunity you received here, I promise you." She turned to the nurses.

"I want someone trained with him at all times. The slightest hint of a fever and I want to be informed at once. Likewise, any scent of infection or sign of continued internal bleeding. And well done, both of you," she smiled tiredly. "I appreciate your efforts sincerely. Prince Memmnon is fortunate indeed to have you in his household."

Both women flushed at the praise and bowed slightly before working out a schedule between them to ensure that Memmnon had someone with him all the time.

"I believe you should remain in the palace for the time being, Doctor Spurgeon," she added. "You are quick thinking and well read, obviously. You did well and the Prince could do far worse than have you caring for him. Speaking of which, I have to wonder why my uncle wasn't doing this. Do you know where Physician Smithe is at? Was the king injured as well? I cannot imagine him not coming to the Prince's aid unless. . .what is it?"

-

"Dead?" Stephanie felt her face grow pale as Sebastian Grey explained what had happened to her uncle.

"Yes, milady, I'm afraid so," he nodded. "He was killed the same time the king was, and just before the Prince was injured. Apparently he was checking on the king's health before retiring for the evening. I am so sorry," he added sincerely.

"I. . .I don't know-," she stammered a bit, then asked; "Does my mother know? Have you informed his family?"

"We have not, milady," Grey admitted. "I'm afraid we've all been a bit consumed with finding someone to help the Prince. Please forgive me."

"Of course," she nodded absently, thinking of how her mother would react to this news. She and her brother had been very close, despite their age difference. "The living always take precedence, Constable."

"Thank you," Grey bowed slightly. "Now, if I may, Lady Freeman? You need rest. You look as if you are about done it, and you've done a great deal of work after a long trip and now I've given you quite the shock."

Grey had quite a gift for understatement Stephanie noted. Shock was hardly the right word to find out that one of your mentors had been killed, as had your liege. Even in time of war you expect some places to be safe, and if the Royal Family's apartments on the palace grounds weren't among them. . .she shook her head at the thought.

Parno was right to be fearful, she thought bleakly. *He was right to be fearful and I was wrong, or at least terribly naive, to brush those concerns aside. And he worried about his age,* she shook her head again. He seemed to be more mature than all of them put together.

"Where do we go from here, Lady Freeman?" Winnie asked softly.

"Winnie, for goodness sake call me Stephanie," she managed to smile. "And I have no idea."

"We should be nearby in case the Prince needs you," Winnie pointed out. "You have to be close by until he is out of danger. He. . .he's the king, now."

Stephanie hadn't considered that until this very moment. She nodded absently as she thought about it. An idea hit her of a sudden and despite the gravity of the situation around her the thought brought an almost sinister smile to her face. She schooled her features and grabbed a passing servant.

"Can you direct me to Lord Parno's apartments, please?" she asked sweetly.

-

The new shift for her guard detail had arrived and now all four followed her to Parno's rooms.

"They've not been used much of late, milady, but we dust and what have you on a regular basis," the young woman leading them informed her. "Though I am not certain this is proper," she added hesitantly.

"I assure you it' fine," Stephanie smiled again. "Lord Parno and I. . .that is, I am his. . .what I mean to say is that he and I . . ."

"What she is trying to say is that she and Lord Parno are affianced," Winnie offered with a straight face, ignoring her friend's sputtering. "As she is attending to the Crown Prince while he recovers, it is of vital importance that she be close by. Considering her relationship with the Marshal, this seems the easiest solution to the problem. Under the circumstances I cannot imagine Marshal McLeod or the Crown Prince objecting."

"Very good," the maid's eyes had gone wide at Winnie's initial remark but she now realized there had just been a power shift in the palace.

"It would be the height of impropriety to speak of their betrothal before there has been an official announcement," Winnie added, this time a bit more sternly. The maid's eyes grew wider still as she nodded her understanding. She opened the doors to Parno's rooms, firing a lamp to add more light in the dimming natural light of day.

"Nice," Winnie murmured. She turned to the escort.

"Post outside and no one is to enter without my permission," she ordered. "I'll remain here with Lady Freeman at all times, as well as accompany her when she is about. Once the escort is rested, suggest to the Captain that a four-man detail might be a good idea, considering our situation. I don't want any of you at risk because there are too few," her voice grew gentler at the last sentence and the men nodded. It never occurred to either of them to question her right to issue orders. Winnie turned to the maid.

"Please bring food and have a bath drawn for Lady Freeman," she ordered, though not unkindly. "I assume there is a tub here?"

"Yes milady," the maid nodded.

"Call me Winifred," Winnie smiled. "I am not a lady, nor a peer. Be at ease. Please see to the food and the bath." The maid bowed slightly and almost ran to obey. The two soldiers followed her out, closing the door behind them and posting themselves at the door. Winnie crossed the room and locked the door before turning to face Stephanie.

"You shouldn't have told her that," Stephanie said at once, looking at the floor. "It isn't proper."

"Parno is hardly proper," Winnie reminded her. "And besides, you were doing so well explaining your. . .that is how he and you. . ." she teased gently and was rewarded with a slight smile.

"It's. . .complicated," Stephanie admitted.

"I know," Winnie said gently. "I am sorry about your uncle, Stephanie," she added in the same gentle tone. "It's obvious you cared for him a great deal."

"I did," she sighed heavily. "He was one of my mentors as well as my mother's brother. He was a cantankerous old devil at times, but he was always good to me. He almost had apoplexy at the thought of my 'throwing my career away' by going to Cove. 'We do not answer the summons of an egotistical whelp such as Parno McLeod, Stephanie'," she imitated her uncle's voice quite well. "My mother swore that one of the reasons I went was to show him he couldn't tell me what to do," she laughed softly.

"Imagine that," Winnie murmured, shaking her head. "You two are definitely made for one another," she added and Stephanie blushed, but nodded. She looked around her, studying the apartment for the first time.

It was actually quite nice. It was obviously a man's domicile as the lack of gentleness showed clearly. Had Parno's mother lived the room certainly would have borne her touch, Stephanie was sure. Had Therron McLeod not interfered in Parno's relationship with the Willows, then Edema's hand might have found its way here eventually. She could imagine the graceful duchess clucking her tongue as she went through Parno's things.

The apartment was clean and orderly. A sitting room, two bedrooms, an office and a bath. The rooms were all furnished comfortably, the beds made and the sofas covered with spreads designed to keep them clean. She inspected the closets and found clothing neatly hung or folded, several pairs of boots, three robes, and a selection of weapons ranging from a bow to a very large sword. She snorted lightly. Of course there would be weapons in Parno's closet.

"Nice," Winnie noted the bow and pulled it carefully from the closet and inspected it.

"Like it?" Stephanie asked and Winnie grinned, nodding.

"It's very well made," she said, replacing it. She had made her own from an ash sapling and would never part with it willingly, but the Prince's bow was very nice. Before they could do more the young maid returned with a tray of food and another woman, who moved to the bath and began preparing hot water for a bath.

"Please find the Captain of our escort, or his lieutenant and have our bags brought up," Winnie 'ordered' the maid, who nodded. "And. . .what is your name?" Winnie asked suddenly, changing her subject.

"Amelia, milady," the girl bowed again.

"Amelia, please inform the staff manager that you will be attending to Lady Freeman on a permanent and full time basis as of now. If he or she has a problem with that, refer them to me and I'll deal with it." She walked to the door where four men from the escort now stood guard.

"May I ask one of you to escort Amelia to speak with her boss and ensure that whoever that is understands that she now serves Marshal McLeod's party directly and there should be no issues with that? Once that is over if you could have someone find our bags and bring them up I would sincerely appreciate it. And perhaps inform the Captain that Lady Freeman may require a courier from the escort while she is caring for the Prince? Having a messenger who is so obviously a soldier of the Marshal's Own should serve as both a warning and reminder of who she is." For all that she was still a teen, Winnie had learned well from older women at the Canton and now handled the staff, the soldiers and the issues facing them with apparent ease.

"I'll see to it, milady," one of the soldiers nodded. "Ma'am?" he looked at Amelia, who blushed red at being addressed as 'ma'am' and almost curtsied before following the soldier away.

"Thank you, so much," she told the remaining soldiers, who nodded silently.

"We'll be here," one offered then turned to watch the stairs while the other two stood guard at the door. Satisfied, Winnie closed the door and secured it. She turned to see Stephanie studying her with a raised eyebrow.

"What?" she asked.

"You've taken over quite nicely it seems," Stephanie smiled and Winnie shrugged.

"Just doing what has to be done. You would be doing if not distracted by so many other things. And I will be with you from here on anyway, so I might as well make myself useful."

"What do you mean, with me?" Stephanie asked.

"I mean that I'm not letting you out of my sight until we know this place is safe," Winnie said bluntly, taking a seat and crossing her legs. Stephanie once more had to admire the hard muscles that knotted and relaxed beneath Winnie's breeches. She really did need to start exercising, the doctor decided.

"Winnie that's hardly a job for you," Stephanie objected. "You're an instructor, for goodness sake. They can't spare you from that simply to 'watch' me!"

"Want to bet?" Winnie asked. "There current crop is well enough along that the instructors really don't need me anymore, anyway. The job was never meant to be permanent. And once Lord Parno gets word of all this, I'm sure he'll agree that you need a companion. He has one, after all," she added. "Two if you count Cho Feng."

"What?" Stephanie was surprised by that. "Who is 'watching' Parno?" she asked, curious.

"I wasn't supposed to say that," Winnie winced slightly. "Captain Sprigs is. . .well, let's just say he's not only a secretary," she shrugged, the damage already done. "Cho Feng had trained him to a much higher standard than most of the regiment, and his real job is to safe guard the Marshal. It would be much better for everyone if you didn't tell him that," she eyed Stephanie closely. "I'm not supposed to know, either, but my father helped Sprigs with the bow, and he and Feng are. . .not friends, I guess, but they respect one another."

"Your secret is safe with me," Stephanie promised, glad to know that she was not the only one concerned with Parno's safety, since he himself didn't seem to be.

A knock at the inner door came and the other maid entered.

"The bath is ready, Milady," she informed Stephanie.

"I appreciate that," the physician smiled tiredly. "I promise I'm not normally so lazy," she added. "I'm just really tired."

"You were working on the Prince," the woman nodded. There were no real secrets in a Royal Household. "Thank you," she added softly.

"It was my privilege," Stephanie nodded. "Winnie, when our bags come up will you call me?" she asked over her shoulder. "I will soak I think until then, if you don't mind."

"I'll see to it," the younger woman promised.

"When she is finished I'll draw more hot water for you, milady," the woman offered.

"That's all right," Winnie smiled. "I'm not a lady, either. I'll get my own. I appreciate you taking such good care of her, too," Winnie added. "She has had a very hard day."

"It has been a very hard couple of days," the woman agreed. "Will the Prince. . .I mean, will he. . ."

"He should, so far as I know, but neither she nor the surgeon spoke to me about it," Winnie answered the broken question. "I think, though, if he was still in danger, they would be much more concerned. Let us not borrow trouble if we don't have to," she smiled.

The woman curtsied and departed, leaving Winnie alone with her thoughts, her head spinning at how easily she had fallen into the role she was now playing. Where had she gotten the nerve?

CHAPTER TWENTY-FIVE

-

Memmnon was vaguely aware of floating somewhere. That was odd since he was nowhere near the sea, and he would never swim in the river. In fact, he rarely went into the water at all, even the pool on the palace grounds. He didn't have anything against swimming, he just didn't really care for it himself all that often.

That didn't explain why he felt as if he was floating. He tried to look around him but couldn't, seeing only darkness. Why would he be in a pool in complete darkness. That made no sense of any kind.

How had he gotten here? He tried to track his movement and memories before waking up here and suddenly jerked as the memory of the knife sinking into his back hit him.

"Milord, wake up please," he heard a distant voice saying. The pain was still there, however, and he turned to try and lessen it. Did the witch *leave* the knife there?

"Milord, it's time to wake up," a female voice said this time. He didn't recognize it. Had he brought a woman to his bed? That wasn't like him. To carry on like that. Parno, on the other hand, wouldn't hesitate, but Parno wasn't the Crown-

Memmnon awoke with a start and tried to sit up. Fortunately, strong hands were nearby to hold him steady until he calmed. He saw two women and a man he didn't know, and Howard Govan, his right hand.

"Howard?" Memmnon said, or tried to. His throat and mouth were so dry that all he managed to get out was a horrible sounding croak.

"Take this, milord, and drink," one of the women told him. Pretty thing, he noted in passing as the cup met his lips. As the cool water hit him Memmnon drank greedily, his body crying out for fluids.

"Not too much now," the woman advised. "Ease into it, milord. That's better." Her voice was soothing. He imagined she was a nurse.

"Welcome back, milord," Govan spoke gently.

"Howard," Memmnon managed to get out. "How long?" he asked.

"A day, milord," Govan admitted.

"Summon Brock at once," he ordered and Govan nodded, moving to do just that. "And Grey!" he added to Govan's departing back.

"That will have to wait, milord," the woman told him. "You're going to have-"

"No, there is no waiting," Memmnon shook his head, paying for it with a dizzy spell. "Listen to me, the kingdom is in peril and already a day is lost! I have to speak to Brock and Grey at once!"

"Very well," the woman agreed reluctantly. "But if you show signs of fatigue, then the meeting is over," she told him flatly. Anger flushed Memmnon's face.

"Who is it you think you are?" he demanded.

"I'm the doctor that saved your life," she replied tartly. "I'll thank you to remember that when you address me, too," she added. Understanding dawned on Memmnon as he shook his head ruefully.

"You must be Lady Freeman," he said finally.

"If I must then I am," she nodded. "At your service."

"Thank you," he told her simply. "And I am very sorry about your uncle," he added softly. Her gaze softened for a moment and she nodded slowly.

"I cannot stress enough how important it is that I see those two men," he told her. "I do not in any way exaggerate when I say the kingdom is at risk. And please clear the room," he ordered. "Though you may stay, of course," he added when thunder appeared in her eyes once more. She shooed the rest of the staff out of the room, though she didn't bother to make the attempt with the younger woman holding the bow. He looked pointedly at her but the doctor shook her head.

"I'm afraid I can't get rid of her," Freeman smiled at him and Memmnon was momentarily distracted by the woman's beauty.

"This has to be kept secret for the time being Lady Freeman," Memmnon shook the distraction off. "She has to go."

"I'm not going if she doesn't," Winnie said flatly. "She's a possible target of the people who managed to get in here and attack you, milord. I am her shadow, for now."

"The people who attacked me won't be back," Memmnon assured her. "Not for several days, anyway." Just then the door burst open and Govan returned with Brock and Grey in two.

"Milord, it's good to s-" Brock began but Memmnon cut him off.

"No time for that now," he said. "Sherron killed my father, Physician Smithe, and tried to kill me. Callens and some of his men killed my aide, my guard, and my father's door guard. I don't know how they got in or out, assuming they did," he frowned. "But Sherron took great delight in telling me that she had learned where Therron was from my father and was on her way to free him. She wants to put him on the throne."

"We know she stabbed you," Grey nodded. "And we assumed it was Callens from the description though you are the first one to name him. He had left two men behind, however, and though one isn't talking and the other can't, they are clearly his men."

"They came in through one of the family routes, I assume led by one the Twins' servants that we missed," Grey continued. "We believe they escaped the same way. As I said they left two men behind and we found one of them there, at the room where the route is hidden."

"We have to stop them," Memmnon said firmly. "Brock, we have to assume that Callens' entire regiment is on its way to free Therron. We cannot allow that to happen!"

"The company I have with him won't be able to prevent it," Brock said grimly. "I'll have to gather a force to go after them. Callens is a bastard but his regiment is an elite unit. We'll need a strong force to deal with them."

"Get whatever it takes and make sure that this doesn't happen," Memmnon ordered. "We need to spread the word about this, too," he added grimly. "With my father dead, it won't matter about Therron, and including him in the plot with Sherron will turn most of his followers against him. Have warrants issued for both of them, Callens, and any of his officers you can name. Arrest and question their families as well. I hate to do that but. . .one of them might know something we can use."

"Yes sir," Grey replied as the one who would be responsible for that. "I'll see to it."

"Treat them gently, but let them know that this is because of the treason of their family members and the murder of the King!"

"They will be hard to catch," Brock returned to the more immediate problem. "Especially with a day head start."

"I don't think so," Memmnon shook his head and again was rewarded with a bout of lightheadedness. "My sister is a creature of comfort. She will ride a horse for a while, but it is a long way to Key Horn. She will not ride day after day without a break and Callens will do all he can to please her because he thinks she will. . .reward him," he finished with a surreptitious glance at the two women. Winnie chuckled and Stephanie blushed slightly, but having lived on an Army post most of year or more had remove that sort of squeamishness.

"I see," Brock nodded. "By your leave, then?" he straightened. He had work to do.

"Go," Memmnon nodded. "Has anyone contacted Parno and let him know what's happening?"

"I sent a courier with orders to kill horses if needed to get word to him as quickly as possible. But he's been gone but a day, or just shy of it."

"So at least another day before he even knows," Memmnon sighed. "He'll be in danger if Callens left anyone behind." A delicate snort from Winnie drew his attention.

"You have something to add?" he asked, fighting to be civil.

"Beg your pardon, mil- Your Majesty," she corrected, "but the Marshal is capable of caring for himself quite handily, first of all," Winnie held up a finger. "Second," she added another, "he is surrounded by the most feared fighting regiment on either side of this war, all of whom would give their lives for him in a heartbeat, and three," one more finger, "he has at least two full squads of said soldiers who do nothing but protect him, and two other men inside that bubble who could kill Callens and any ten of his men he wanted to choose, alone," she added one last finger.

"So, you're saying Parno is probably going to be okay, then," Memmnon grinned, and Winnie smiled back at him, nodding.

"I'd say that's a given, sire."

-

Parno watched the sun rising, relieved that the new day and the expiration of the temporary truce had not brought renewed attacks. His men were ready for it, he knew, but they were tired and the fighting had cost them. If the Nor would hold off another attack for two weeks or so, he might have Herrick and

Freeman's Corps up and with the army, at which point things would change.

In his mind he had already made the moves he was going to make. He would send one mounted infantry division to Raines in place of the Cavalry division he had taken from the western forces, along with a militia division of cavalry. Not near the equal of the unit he'd surrendered, Raines would still be able to make use of the horsemen.

He would then form all of his cavalry divisions into a separate force, six in total though some of the divisions would not be full strength, and send them on an end around to hit the Nor right just as the rest of the army stuck from the front. He did not know exactly how many men he would be able to muster for that attack since five of those divisions had suffered losses in the previous fighting. Davies' men in particular had been in contact since the war began and some of his units had suffered heavily. He made a note to try and place them in the reserve, if he had one. They might be able to avoid the worst of the fighting that way. It wasn't rest, really, but it was better than being thrown against an army that had slowly been beating them back all this time.

The cavalry force would number about the same as the frontal assault he figured, allowing for losses in the units so far engaged as well as the men he had stripped from them to form Beaumont's command. Thinking of the hearty brigadier made Parno wonder where he was and what his men had accomplishes so far.

"Sir," Sprigs' voice cut into his thinking and he turned to face him.

"I believe that General Beaumont's forces have returned, milord," Sprigs informed him. "A runner arrived just a moment ago with news of a large group of men approaching the left, with horses, cattle, and a train in tow."

"How about that?" Parno grinned. Once more it was as if thinking about someone had conjured them up. He wished he knew it would always work.

"Let's go and see, shall we?"

-

"That's a lot of tents," Beaumont remarked to Whipple as the two rode side-by-side at the head of their column. Both were dusty and dirty and tired, but happy to be in the relative safety of their own lines for the first time in weeks.

"We may have missed a battle," Whipple nodded as he observed medics running to and fro. "Those tents appear to be housing wounded."

"So they do," Beaumont nodded. "I wonder how long since the battle?"

"No way to tell without asking, I guess," Whipple shrugged. He turned to his second in command.

"Have the horses taken to the wrangler camp and the cattle to the quartermaster. Tell him we require fifty head for our own us to resupply and the rest are his to do with as he pleases. All wagons other than our own are to be left with him as well. After that, move to the rear and select a place for us to make camp. Keep the units together," he added.

"Yes sir," the colonel nodded and started issuing orders of his own. That done, Beaumont and Whipple moved out, seeking information about what they might have missed in their absence. Even as they rode toward the camp, Whipple spotted the Marshal's small group heading their way.

"Look," he elbowed Beaumont. They two pulled up where they were. Seconds later Parno McLeod stopped his charger next to them.

"Welcome back, gentlemen!" he beamed, taking each man's hand. "Looks like you did well for yourselves," he nodded toward the spoils that were moving off.

"Not bad," Beaumont grinned. "Ate good," he added, to which Parno laughed aloud.

"Looks like we missed a brawl, milord," Whipple mentioned, and Parno's smiled dimmed.

"That you did."

-

"Sounds as if it were quite the battle," Beaumont remarked as Parno finished sketching what had happened in their absence.

"It was indeed," Parno nodded. "Don't let me keep you two, though," he ordered suddenly. "I'm sure you're looking to clean up and sack out, so go ahead. Tomorrow is more than soon enough for us to catch up."

"Thank you, milord," the two replied in unison.

"I'll see you for lunch tomorrow, then," Parno ordered and the two bowed slightly and departed. Parno watched them go, pleased with the outcome of their first foray behind the lines. They seemed to have done quite well, so far.

"Milord," Enri Willard's voice broke into his thinking and Parno turned to see his Chief of Staff holding a sheaf of papers.

"Reports?" Parno asked, trying to hide his trepidation.

"Corps and Division level only, for now," Enri nodded. He offered the papers but Parno shook his head. "Just give me the gist, for now," he ordered.

"Five thousand, three hundred and eleven dead, eight thousand five hundred, ninety-two wounded. Seven artillery pieces lost, five more damaged to the point of needing overhaul. Fortifications damaged but nowhere broken."

"Could have been worse," Parno sighed. It could have been, but it was bad enough as it was.

"It could," Enri agreed.

"Who was hurt the worst?" Parno asked.

"1st Infantry, Heavy, milord," Enri replied. "5th Infantry, Standard was right behind. In my opinion, sir, 2nd Corps is approaching being combat ineffective. They have borne the brunt of the Imperial Army since the war began and their losses have been heavy. They are tired, too. They need time to rest, refit, and replenish their losses, sir."

Parno considered that for only a moment before nodding.

"As soon as Herrick arrives, he will move into the line and 2nd Corps will withdraw. We'll attach Herrick's command to 1st Army and Davies will remain in command. Have him select his most able Division commander to replace him, and give him a brevet promotion. If he does well, he can keep it. Tell Davies to select someone able, I don't care who his family might be."

"I'll see to it, milord," Enri made a note to himself.

"Any estimates on Imperial losses?" Parno asked.

"We can only estimate of course, but. . .based on counts of those left on the field and what we could count as the enemy gathered their dead and wounded. . ." Enri trailed off, eyes narrowing. Parno raised an eyebrow.

"That's why you allowed them to collect their dead and wounded," he said suddenly. "So, we could tell how many dead there were, and how many injured."

"Didn't even think about it," Parno said evenly. "Like I said, just didn't want all those bodies lying underfoot. Not healthy."

"Of course," Enri kept a straight face. "Well, our estimates are seventeen thousand dead and at least eleven thousand wounded, though you have to remember that many of their wounded would have been carried away before the truce. Also, their rear ranks, including their own artillery, suffered significant losses as well."

"Good," Parno nodded. "Any sign of activity on their front?"

"None so far," Enri shook his head. "We hurt them, milord," he said firmly. "More than that, we shook their confidence. Again. This is the second time you've bested them and it has to hurt. Beyond their losses, I mean. You wanted them to see the cost of being here, and now they are."

"Costing us, too," Parno mentioned and Enri nodded.

"Yes sir, it is. War is costly. In lives, material, money, the list goes on. That's just how it is."

"I wanted a decisive victory that would leave me in a position to throw the Nor back and then go after them," Parno sighed after a moment of silence. "I failed to achieve that. Losses to 2nd Corps, as you pointed out, are such that continuing to use them could well be ruinous." His fingers thumped the desk for a moment as he thought.

"I want you to begin looking at a force structure that assumes 2nd Corps will be off line, or in a defensive garrison position, for the rest of the summer. Using 1st, 4th, and 5th, Corps, how many troops can we muster against the Imperial army? Assume in that factor that we will release one Mounted Infantry division and one militia cavalry division to Raines, but keep the cavalry division I took from him to supplement our striking power."

"Examine my options," he ordered his Chief of Staff. "What can I make work using what we have available?"

"I'll work on it, milord," Enri nodded, already thinking. "Anything else?"

"Not for now," Parno shook his head. "If the Nor will stay quiet and still, so will we. Our men need rest and refit, and we need to wait for Herrick and Freeman so we can consolidate our strength."

"Yes sir."

-

Royal couriers were tough. Selection was very trying, starting with only the finest horsemen chosen from among men whose trustworthiness was beyond question. Trials were stringent to say the least and any failure would see an applicant washed from the group. It seemed like a great deal of nonsense for a position that left a man basically sitting around for days at a time with nothing to do, save being ready to go at a moment's notice.

Until times like now. Times of war when the messages that courier carried could mean the difference between victory and defeat.

The man selected to carry the all-important message to Parno McLeod from the palace was above average even for the select group he belonged to.

Knowing the importance of what he was carrying, the man had pushed himself and his horses beyond normal. The first horse he had chosen was lathering heavily when he slid to a stop at the first station, where he relieved himself and grabbed a ready made sandwich while his saddle was placed on a fresh mount. He was on the ground less than five minutes before being on his way once more.

Normally at some point another messenger would have taken over for him, but not this time. This particular message was too important. Time too precious. For all the courier knew, Prince Memmnon had perished already and Prince Parno had no idea he was already King Parno.

Leaving lame and useless horses behind him at every stop, the courier stayed in the saddle through the night and into the next day. He knew that he would pay for it afterward, and scarcely be able to walk in the days after this hard ride, but his duty was clear; the Marshal had to know.

And so it was that a completely exhausted courier riding an all but lame charger finally slowed as he approached the pickets along the trail to the army's rear areas. He had been in the saddle for just over two days without stop and was on his last legs. A total of eleven horses had worn his saddle in that time, and two of them would never wear another.

The pickets saw the McLeod seal and immediately brought him to the Marshal, pausing only long enough to place the man on a fresh horse. Staggering from the saddle before the Marshal's tent, the man presented his satchel, saluted, and then nearly collapsed.

-

"-so, we decided that it was time to come in for a few days, to leave our wounded and refit a bit," Beaumont was just completing his report. "All in all, however, we felt like we had done a good job of disrupting their supply chain."

"And killed a good many Nor in doing so," Whipple added in his cultured voice.

"Sounds like it," Parno nodded. "I am most pleased, gentlemen, most pleased indeed. It sounds like you've done far better than I had hoped, to be honest. I knew you'd be able to do damage, but this sounds like you took the idea and made it your own, to great success!"

"Thank you, milord," Beaumont nodded. "I must say that having Horace with me was a stroke of great good fortune. I hope he feels the same, but I believe the two of us have made a good team. What one doesn't see, or think of, the other usually does."

"Agreed," Whipple smiled slightly.

"So when do you-" Parno cut himself off as Harrel Sprigs entered his tent, his face neutral.

"I'm sorry, milord, but there is a courier here for you," he said.

"Just give it to Enri," Parno waved, but Sprigs shook his head.

"A Royal Courier, milord, and it is most urgent," the young man's face fought to stay flat. Parno looked at him for a moment and felt a chill run through him for some reason. He looked again to Beaumont and Whipple.

"You two go and see to your commands," he ordered. "We'll meet again later once you've had a chance to see to your duties."

"Of course, milord," Beaumont nodded, rising. The two departed as Sprigs waved the exhausted courier into the tent. Parno took one look at the man and offered him water from a pitcher he had. The man accepted it gratefully, but did not offer to drink until he handed the folder he carried to the prince. As he drained the cup, Parno broke the seal.

"From Memmnon?" he asked, not looking up. When the man didn't answer, Parno did look up. The courier's face looked pained.

"Milord... better for you to read, milord," he shook his head. "I don't know the details." Parno looked at him another moment before turning to the hastily penned missive. He had stood by the time he was half-way through it, his face reddening. His hand tightened around the letter, crumpling it slightly as he looked at Sprigs.

"Get Beaumont and Whipple back here," he ordered. "Have Karls prepare the regiment to ride and have someone get Davies at once." Sprigs nodded and hurried away, leaving the courier to face Parno.

"How many know about this?" he demanded softly.

"When I left, only a handful, sir," the courier replied. "They were keeping it close until you could be notified and return to Nasil. I... I'm sorry, milord," he added hesitantly. Parno nodded absently for a moment, then looked at the clearly exhausted man.

"Not a word to anyone," he cautioned. "Now go and get food and rest. Remain here until you're recovered and then return to Nasil. Check with General Davies before you leave to see if he has any messages that need to return with you. And thank you," he added, extending his hand. "I can't imagine how rough a ride you've had, getting this here so quickly."

"My privilege to serve, milord," he man replied, accepting the hand but then kneeling.

"Rise," Parno said gently. "Go and see to yourself, with the thanks of your Dynasty." The man rose and departed, leaving Parno alone, but only for a moment as Enri Willard came rushing in.

"What happened?" he asked. Parno handed him the note from Govan in answer and Enri read it quickly.

"My God!"

"Yes," Parno nodded, his eyes distant. "It would seem that my sister is somewhat more unstable than previously thought. And that Colonel Callens is guilty of the most heinous of treason."

"Sir, I. . ." Enri trailed away, nothing coming.

"We'll be leaving as soon as we can," Parno told him. "I've already sent for Davies. Karls should be assembling the Sheep, and I'll be speaking to Beaumont and Whipple shortly. Make sure that all our preparations are made. I'll also have. . .I need to see Mister Parsons," he settled for saying, and Enri nodded.

"I'll find him," he promised.

"Go ahead then," Parno ordered. "I have a note to write."

-

"I need this given directly to the Tinker, Mister Parsons," Parno said evenly. "I'm sure you remember him."

"Oh, I do sir," Parsons nodded, taking the small envelope. "Want me to see to it personally, sir?"

"If you like, of course," Parno nodded absently. "I'll be riding to Nasil within the hour. The men you attached to Beaumont's command will need to stay with him, is that all right?"

"Of course," Parsons nodded. His men were Parno's to command, the prince knew that.

"See if you can figure out what's going on over there," Parno waved a hand in the general direction of the Nor encampment. "I don't want to lose a man to them, mind you, but if you can scope out what they are doing, Davies will find that information useful I'm sure. Be wary of the Tribal warriors," he cautioned. "I was surprised we didn't see them during the battle, looking for payback."

"We'll do what we can, sir," Parsons nodded. "You don't want us with you?" he asked.

"No work for you where I'm going, I'm afraid," Parno shook his head. "I like as not won't need Karls and his men, either. I'm taking them out of an abundance of caution. That's all. Please get that delivered as soon as you can. And good luck," he added.

"Thank you, sir," Parsons nodded and departed, heading to town to find the Tinker himself. Karls Willard entered the tent as Parsons departed, grim looking at best.

"You've heard; I take it?" Parno asked.

"I was going to ask if it was true, but from the look on your face I see it is," Karls nodded.

"Oh, yes," Parno nodded. "We'll be riding within the hour. I don't know what we'll find when we get there, either."

"We'll be ready, whatever we find," Karls promised grimly. "We'll be ready when you are," he added and left without waiting for a dismissal.

Parno leaned back for a moment, formulating what he would tell Davies. This morning things had been so simply. Not easy, by any means, just simple. Straightforward.

That was all done, now.

-

"We'll hold, milord," Davies promised as Parno mounted his horse.

"I have no doubt, general," Parno nodded. "Godspeed," he said simply and turned his horse. Cho Feng and Enril Willard rode behind him with Karls beside him and two squads of troopers ahead as a screen. They would make the trip as quickly as possible. With luck the moon would stay with them, allowing them to ride even after sunset.

Without a word Parno started on the road to the Royal City and the destiny that waited for him there.

CHAPTER TWENTY-SIX

Stephanie made her way toward Memmnon's apartments with Winnie at her side, two soldiers in front and two behind.

"Is this really necessary?" she asked softly.

"Yes," her friend nodded firmly. "If the death of the King has taught us anything, it's that not even this place is safe right now. I will not be the one to have to tell the Marshal that something has happened to you."

"Very well," Stephanie sighed as they reached the new King's apartments. Her escort took station outside, joining the one guarding Memmnon's door, while she and Winnie entered. The King was awake and smiled weakly at them when he saw them coming.

"My two guardian angels," he joked. "Ah, one even has her bow," he winked at Winnie who blushed furiously. "You know," he continued, "I'm not sure I've ever seen you without it."

"I try never to be without it," she nodded, amazed that she could speak so in the presence of the king.

"I can see, in hindsight, where that is a good policy to have," Memmnon said stoically, though he winked again to lighten the tone and Winnie had to choke off a giggle.

"Let us see how you fare today, my liege," Stephanie said, moving to inspect the incision. She probed and prodded, Memmnon wincing once or twice, and finally hissing in pain.

"You already checked there!" he insisted.

"Patience, my King," Stephanie chided and instantly regretted it as she saw Memmnon's face pale.

"I'm sorry, my lord," she said softly. "I didn't mean to make you think of it."

"Just takes some getting used to is all," he admitted, shrugging. "So, will I live, you think?" he asked, grinning again in an attempt to erase the momentary loss of good humor in the room.

"I suspect so," Stephanie nodded, rising. "There's almost no drainage now, and what drainage is present is clear, which is ideal. The stitching is holding nicely, despite your refusal to follow doctor's directions," she frowned at him. "You're going to be sore for a while, and it will take some time before you are able to get around as you like, but. . .yes. Barring some sort of unforeseen complication, you will make a full recovery."

"Parno will be relieved to hear it, I'm sure," Memmnon sighed, resting his head back, missing Stephanie's blush at the comment.

"What do you mean, sire?" she asked, fumbling with her equipment.

"The last thing he wants is to be saddled with a crown," Memmnon chuckled mirthlessly. "He would be certain that I had died just to spite him and make him King."

"Oh, surely not," Stephanie smiled back, now realizing that Memmnon's remark hadn't been directed at her, and her relationship with his brother.

"We had to beg him to take the post of Lord Marshal," Memmnon told her. "Thank God he did it," he said earnestly. "I don't know where we'd be right now without him."

"I see you aren't eating enough," Stephanie inspected his tray, noting the soup that still remained. "You really must eat, your Majesty. You need your strength if you are to recover."

"I'm just not hungry," Memmnon shrugged. "I eat when I'm hungry, though," he added when she frowned.

"You're going to need to eat when you're not, then," she ordered. "You aren't getting enough at this rate to sustain your recovery. I'll have fresh soup sent to you from the kitchen and I expect you to eat it this time."

"Then send me something besides soup!" Memmnon shot back. "I'm sick of the sight of it."

"How about a nice sandwich of beef and some potatoes, then?" Stephanie asked, smiling.

"That's more like it!" Memmnon practically rubbed his hands together.

"Eat your soup today and we'll see about that for tomorrow," Stephanie lowered the boom without pause, and Winnie had to smother a laugh as the look on Memmnon's face fell with the pronouncement.

"That was cruel and entirely uncalled for, Doctor," Memmnon told her with mock solemnity.

"Eat. Your. Soup." Stephanie ordered. "I'll be back to check on you in a bit. I expect to find that you've eaten all of it, this time. Then we can talk about some red meat and bread." She gathered her things and started out, Winnie falling into step beside her.

"Do you ever go anywhere without your shadow?" Memmnon called out to her back.

"No, my liege, I do not!" she called over her shoulder as she went out the door. She informed his servant to see to it that fresh hot soup was fetched for him from the kitchen, then started back for Parno's apartments, which she was already thinking of as 'her' rooms. Winnie was silent until the two of them were back inside, guard posted outside, then laughed.

"I think he's flirting with you."

"What?" Stephanie looked scandalized. "Why would say something like that?"

"Because I can see," Winnie told her, grinning. "I think he likes you."

"That would be completely improper," Stephanie remarked at once. "Especially knowing that hi-" she broke off suddenly, realizing something.

"He doesn't know," she said softly. "No one knows, really. Not outside Cove Canton. Oh, dear," she sat down abruptly. Winnie frowned, now, concerned.

"What is it?" she asked. "I was only teasing, you know," she added.

"So, you don't really think he's flirting?" Stephanie asked, looking hopeful.

"You know, I doubt there's another woman in the kingdom who would look hopeful that Memmnon wasn't flirting with them," Winnie teased again. "But yes, I do think he is. He doesn't know you and Parno are 'affianced'," she laughed. "If he did he would never do such a thing. Perhaps a judicious word from your 'shadow'?" she asked.

"No, not without- I mean, we couldn't possibly say anything like that without Parno's approval, and even then it would be-, well, never you mind about whatever you think you see," Stephanie waved her hand as if shooing a fly. "Besides, he is my patient, which prohibits any such. . .foolishness. Period."

"Hm," Winnie nodded.

-

Winifred Huble was a very smart young woman, but she was not quite as sharp as she fondly imagined. The request that afternoon to speak to the doctor 'privately' was met with trepidation by Stephanie and outright resistance by Winnie, especially knowing her friend's discomfort from earlier, but the bottom line was simple; Memmnon was King of Soulan now. If he wanted privacy, he got it. When the two were finally alone, Memmnon sighed in relief.

"God, I thought she'd never leave!" he exclaimed, then looked at Stephanie.

"Are you nervous, Doctor?" he asked, frowning in concern.

"No, your highness," she lied easily. "What may I do for you?" she smiled, then instantly regretted it.

"I need. . .well, look," he said, trying to put himself to a more comfortable position in the bed. "I wanted to ask you something and... well, this may seem most improper of me, but with all that's happening I have to be cautious." He paused and she nodded her understanding.

"You know I am unwed, of course," he went on after a moment and Stephanie felt the floor fall out from under her. She nodded shakily, hoping her face hadn't lost all its color.

"Just so you know for sure," he nodded, looking into the distance, despite their being cloistered away in his rooms. "The thing is. . .I mean, I had thought of courtship, of course, being the Crown Prince and what not, but I thought I had plenty of time so I hadn't really engaged in any king of serious attempt at it, and now I'm glad I didn't because I've met someone that intrigues me a great deal, only. . ." He paused, obviously frustrated.

"Just say it, sire," Stephanie told him, knowing in her heart this could only end badly.

"I'm trying to," Memmnon almost hissed in aggravation. "Very well, but I'll have your word that this stays between us for now!"

"In so far as it does not violate any previous oath I have taken, you may have it," Stephanie told him after thinking about it for a minute. Apparently satisfied, Memmnon nodded.

"Just so you understand, there's nothing that says I have to marry within the peerage," he began and again she felt awkward. Despite how she was addressed due to her family's influence and standing, Stephanie herself held no title, and the family name would pass to her brother, most likely.

"I see," she managed to keep a neutral face.

"There are many who would expect me too, of course, but I'm of a mind that it doesn't matter what a woman's background is so long as her character is strong," he said seriously. "Any woman who would raise my children would need to be able to handle them firmly. And to be honest, I've yet to meet a woman at court that doesn't make my teeth hurt," Memmnon made a sour face here, and at any other time Stephanie would have laughed. Not today.

"You may of course tell me if I'm out of line here, good doctor, but I felt I did not want to wait any longer before asking; Is Winifred married? Or betrothed in any way? Do you think she might fancy-, now see here, Doctor. I don't think this is a laughing matter at all!"

-

Stephanie was still dabbing at her eyes when she emerged from the King's room, and Winnie was at once on the alert.

"Are you all right?" she asked, fighting to keep her voice neutral. A wrong answer here could see the men of Parno's regiment brawling with those of Memmnon's right here in the palace hallways.

"What? Oh," Stephanie nodded, "yes I'm fine, dear, just fine. A bit worn, but that's all. Let's do go and rest a bit," she said, heading toward Parno's rooms with Winifred hastily trying to catch up as the guard also struggled to surround "Lady Freeman".

"That's it?" Winnie almost hissed as she came even with Stephanie. "You come out after a private audience, having been crying, and you're fine?"

"Crying?" Stephanie looked at her. "I haven't-, oh, I suppose I would look like it," she laughed slightly. "No dear, I was laughing, that's all. Harder than I have in some time, in fact."

"So, he told you a joke?" Winnie glared, which made Stephanie glare yet again.

"Not exactly," Stephanie shook her head as the two reached their rooms. As soon as they arrived, Stephanie corralled Amelia and whispered to her. The girl's eyes widened for a moment and she shot a surreptitious glance at Winnie, then she nodded as Stephanie finished and shooed her on her way out the door.

"What's all that about?" Winnie asked. Stephanie just looked at her for a moment, studying her young friend. She didn't know why she hadn't seen it before. Perhaps she had and had just put it away.

"What?" Winnie demanded, one hand on her hip, the other on her bow.

"Winnie dear," Stephanie savored her words as if they were a rich cup of chocolate on a frosty night. "Winnie, you are not nearly as clever as you think you are."

-

Winnie stood glaring at Stephanie as the tailor measured and clucked and talked to himself. The woman paid no mind to the fact that Winnie was all but naked, or that she was very close to erupting. Another woman was studying her hair, nails and other areas, also clucking her tongue and occasionally shaking her head sadly.

"This is ridiculous," Winnie steamed and Stephanie had to fight a grin.

"Dear I had already planned to do something along these lines anyway, but with things the way they are, I don't think we'll have the opportunity. So, I'm taking advantage of the fact that we're staying in the palace to get it done. And the quality of clothing will be far greater here than anywhere else I'm quite sure."

"Indeed, my lady," the tailor nodded as she finished her notes. "We'll have something up here this afternoon we've altered, and then we'll outfit the other items custom to order, of course."

"That would be fine," Stephanie nodded. "Thank you. And you?" she addressed the cosmetician. The other woman turned to her and curtsied.

"I think about one inch off the ends to care for splitted ends, milady, and of course around her face," the woman detailed. "Eyebrows must be done of course, perhaps something for her lashes as well. Nails are a complete loss I'm afraid, but we can clean and even them up, at least. We'll do the pedi as well, though I doubt she'll need that for now, no sense in putting it off." She thought for a second.

"Perhaps three hours, my lady, all totaled," she said firmly. "The. . .other. . .will take a bit longer, of course," she added.

"That will be fine," Stephanie nodded. "We'll begin after lunch if that's convenient?"

"We serve at your pleasure milady," the woman bowed. "We'll arrive around one?"

"Perfect," Stephanie nodded. "We'll see you then." She walked the woman out as Winnie got dressed, her anger boiling.

"And just what, may I ask, is the 'other'?" she demanded, pulling her leather shirt over her head.

"Winnie dear, I sense that you've had little in the way of female education in your young life," Stephanie replied by way of answer, casting her line out casually. "Would that be accurate?"

"If you mean did I have a woman to teach me what's what and where it is, not exactly," Winnie's face reddened. "A woman that delivers babies in the mountains. . .my pa, he took her a deer he shot, and a cow hide he had tanned, to pay her to explain to me. . .to show me how. . .to talk to me," she settled for saying. "Why?"

"Well, let's just say there are other items that are of import when a girl reaches your age," Stephanie temporized, jiggling the bait ever so slightly.

"I'm not a girl!" Winnie took the bait, sinker and all.

"Exactly my point, dear," Stephanie seized the line and pulled to set the hook. "You're a young woman now, and there are things that young women, young ladies, need to know. Fortunately for you, I'm a doctor, so I can explain them to you in great, medical detail. And, also very fortunate, we have access to the workings of the palace."

"You, my dear, are about to get a royal makeover!"

-

It was a tired and dirty column of men that pulled into the Royal City in the faint light of a dying full moon. The lights of the city, lit at dusk each day and fueled by gases piped throughout the city, lit the way to the palace, where a startled sentry called out the guard in a panic before he'd had time to realize who was approaching.

"Don't worry about it," Parno said tiredly as the man tried to apologize. "It just shows you're on the job. I'd rather you do it every time as miss just once."

He staggered out of the saddle, as did his followers. Men took the reins from them and headed for the Royal stables to leave the horses. Parno waved off his escort.

"Not tonight," he told them. "We'll be fine in my rooms and you need to rest. Have a guard report after breakfast in the morning, and set it so it rotates every four hours I guess," he ordered Berry. "I'll let you decide what's best. Tonight, get some rest." It was a testament to how tired Berry was that he didn't argue.

Parno led Cho Feng, Harrel Sprigs and the brothers Willard into the palace grounds, heading for his brother's rooms. No one had spoken to him yet about what he might find, and he was apprehensive to say the least.

And shocked to find Stephanie Freeman coming from his rooms when he arrived.

"Stephanie?" It was a sign of how tired Parno was that he neglected to refer to her as Lady Freeman.

"Parno!" Stephanie exclaimed and had taken two steps in his direction when decorum caught up with her and she brought herself up short.

"It's good that you've come, milord," she managed not to stammer.

"You can drop that," Karls Willard grinned tiredly. "We're not blind, doctor. Or stupid."

"Quiet," Parno ordered over his shoulder. "How is he?" Parno asked, nodding to Memmnon's door.

"He's quite well, I assure you," she smiled. "He is awake. Come and let me take you to him," she offered her hand.

"You know where my rooms are," Parno told his retinue, then frowned as Stephanie cleared her throat.

"Ah, I'm afraid that Winnie and I have been staying there, while I cared for the king, my lord," she said formally, her face red. Parno hid his surprise at hearing Memmnon referred to as king behind his surprise that she and Winnie had been using his apartments.

"Find a servant, tell them to put us in the dignate's quarters for tonight," he ordered. "It's close by but secluded." Enri nodded and the four of them left. Parno raised an eyebrow at the lovely doctor.

"I sense a story behind your using my apartments," he grinned. "And did you say Winnie? As in Winnie Huble? What is she doing here?" he asked when she nodded.

"Well, it's a long story."

-

"Parno, it's good to see you," Memmnon smiled as he struggled to sit up. His new footman assisted him, then withdrew, leaving the new king sitting up in bed.

"Memmnon," Parno nodded. "You're looking much better than I had imagined when I read Howard Govan's note. I am relieved to see you recovering," he said sincerely.

"No desire to be king, brother?" Memmnon teased, glancing at the doctor.

"If you had died I would have killed you," Parno nodded and Memmnon laughed aloud at that.

"Sit," he ordered, and Parno sat. "Sherron killed father, Parno," Memmnon said at once. "I don't know if Howard included that, but it's true. She thinks she killed me, I'm sure. Likely would have, were it not for your lovely doctor," he nodded to Stephanie who blushed, nodded, but stayed silent.

"What do you want me to do?" Parno asked simply.

"They have to be stopped," Memmnon replied just as simply. "We cannot let them live, Parno. Not after this."

"I didn't intend to," Parno assured him. "I have a unit that will be here tomorrow, or day after at the latest. I'll be sending them after Callens as soon as they've rested their horses and took on supplies as needed. They just spent three weeks or better behind enemy lines," he explained. "They are very good," he added.

"All right," Memmnon nodded. "Brock will have a force ready by then as well. I want them to accompany your men. If they can be arrested, then we should try them. Get this mess into the open and be done with it."

"Are you sure?" Parno looked dubious. "Looks to me like it would be better to just get rid of them and be done with it."

"Short term, yes," Memmnon agreed. "Long term, for the health and strength of the Dynasty, we need to follow the rule of law insofar as we can."

"Insurrection is punishable by death, as is treason," Parno said stiffly. "Leaving aside murder, particularly of the king."

"All true," Memmnon nodded. "I didn't say it was a necessity, Parno. I said if we could. Don't risk the life of a single man to keep them alive. If they have to be killed, then so be it, but make sure they're dead and bring back proof. I want this laid to rest. Forever."

"It will be," Parno nodded. "I swore to father that there would be a Soulan to rule, and that you would rule it. I will fulfill that oath, one way or another."

"You look tired, Parno," Memmnon said suddenly. "Get some rest. Please visit me tomorrow, though."

"I will," Parno promised. "Until then."

-

In the hallway, Parno found himself accompanying Stephanie toward his own rooms. She had told him how Winnie had come to be with her, and how the two of them had come to be here.

"I'm glad you were," Parno nodded. "Without your help, I'd be king now," he shuddered at the thought.

"I doubt anyone else would be so happy at not being king," Stephanie teased.

"They can have it," Parno made a pushing motion on front of him. "Memmnon will make a good king. I am sorry to hear about your uncle," he offered gently. He had despised her uncle with a passion that was mutual, but the pain his death had caused her was reason enough to regret his passing.

"It's hard to believe he's gone," she sighed.

"Does this make you the Royal Doctor now?" he teased and Stephanie looked at him, startled.

"What?"

"Your family has provided the Royal Physician since the time of Tyree," Parno pointed out. "Will you be the next?"

"I think not," she scoffed. "No," she shook her head.

"Someone has to do it," Parno shrugged.

"Yes, but not me," she said firmly. They reached the doorway and she opened it without thinking, and Parno stepped inside with her, also without a thought, since it was his apartment.

"I *hate* this!" an alley cat screeched at them and Parno jerked his eyes away from Stephanie to see-

"Winnie?" his mouth dropped open.

"Don't you say a *word*!" Winnie pointed at him with a painted nail. She was in a beautiful gown of flowing green silks, her red hair complimenting it nicely as did her curves. Curves that her previous clothing had hidden quite well but this dress did not. Could not.

"Winnie, you look-" Parno began.

"Men die in training accidents all the time, Parno McLeod," she growled at him almost like a wolf, causing him to bite off his comment, as well as the laugh he felt coming at her discomfiture.

"I'm sorry, Winnie, I forgot this was still going on," Stephanie stammered apologetically. "Parno, I'm afraid you simply must go," she turned to push him back out the door. "Get some rest and we'll talk tomorrow, I promise," she told him, pushing all the while.

"But I want to kno-"

"Not now!" Stephanie cut him off, then beneath her breath, added, "I worked too hard to get her to do this. Not now!"

"All right, all right," Parno held his hands up in supplication. "But tomorrow I want to know what's happening."

"Yes, of course," she nodded, closing the door literally in his face. "Tomorrow. Now good night!" the door slammed shut, leaving him surrounded by the four guards.

"Well. Put out of my own rooms," he shook his head, then turned to look at the nearest guard.

"That's a first."

-

Parno slept late the next morning, as did most of his retinue. Cho Feng, of course, was up with the roosters, looking and acting disgustingly fresh and rested. The others didn't stir until well after eight o'clock, and even then were reluctant.

"Good morning," Feng welcomed them to the sitting room where the remains of his morning meal were being cleared away.

"Why are you so cheerful all the time?" Karls demanded, then turned to Parno. "Why is he so cheerful? Do we have to put up with that? All that. . .cheerfulness?"

"Someone apparently slept on the wrong side of his bed," Parno grinned back, taking a seat. "Load me up this morning," he told the steward. "I need a power breakfast, Rafe," he smiled.

"I'll see to it, sir," the steward grinned back. "You gents?" he looked to the others who agreed with their leader.

"I'll set a meal and let you gents dig in, then," Rafe nodded.

"So what's on the agenda today?" Enri asked.

"I imagine I'll spend most of it with Memmnon," Parno admitted. "I'd like you two to check over palace security. Enri you worked here with the Guard so you should know it pretty well. Karls, select a few of the men who might be, talented let's call it, and let them look for ways inside. If they find any, block them."

"All right," the brothers nodded in unison.

"And me?" Feng asked.

"You may do the same if you like," Parno shrugged. "Unless you want to spar with Harrel and let him practice some. It's a rare opportunity for the two of you. Might as well take it."

"Very good," Feng nodded as Rafe returned with the food.

"And here's breakfast!"

-

"Beaumont should be here today, tomorrow at the latest," Parno repeated for Brock this time. "Your men will join him, and head south. No matter how they get there, Sherron and Callens will be headed to the Key Horn to get Therron. Stop them. If you can't get there ahead of them, make sure they don't leave."

"Milord," Brock nodded.

"Grey, while he is gone, I want your investigation to continue," Memmnon ordered. "Anyone here in the palace, or in the city for that matter, who aided and abetted them in any way I want in chains."

"We're working on it, sire," Grey nodded.

The two left, their orders in hand, including the arrest warrants for both Sherron and Therron as well as Callens and his officers.

"Well, this will get something going for sure," Parno sighed.

"How are things at the front?" Memmnon asked. Parno shrugged.

"We missed an opportunity by not having Herrick and Freeman up sooner, but we're holding just fine," he reported. "We beat off a major attack less than a week ago, though they broke off for no reason I could see. We had hurt them, but they had hurt us too. I'm going to have to pull 2nd Corps off line and let them rest and refit. Their losses are making them ineffective to be honest."

"Your planned offensive?" Memmnon asked.

"Will have to wait at least until Freeman is in place and we've recovered from what damage we can that we took in this last round," Parno admitted. "I wanted to push against them with our cavalry, but the risks were just too great, in all honesty. Once our strength is concentrated, it will be different."

"Raines?" Memmnon spoke again.

"I'm sending him a mounted infantry division and a division of militia cavalry to replace what I took from him," Parno explained his plan. "That will let him have some leeway and strengthen his defenses. Plus, he will have received Roda's goodies by now and his men will have been instructed in their use. That will be worth a lot, right there."

"I never did get down there to see what it is he does," Memmnon admitted.

"Ask Enri about it later," Parno suggested. "He got a good look."

"I will."

"I need to check on something, so I'll leave you to your lunch. I'll be back before supper."

"Very good, then," Memmnon nodded. "I have something I'd like to discuss with you, then."

-

"I'm sorry, but could you repeat that?"

"Your brother, the King, is somewhat enamored with our Winnie," Stephanie repeated the most important part, not bothering to go over, once more, how Winnie had been so sure that Memmnon had in fact been 'enamored' with Stephanie.

"So that's why the clothes and the cosmetics and what not?" Parno asked.

"Yes," the firm reply.

"And does she know all this?" Parno asked, the hint of a grin forming at the corners of his mouth.

"No!" firmer reply. "And she mustn't know until I'm finished!"

"Finished?" Parno frowned. "She looked fine last night. How much else is there? I almost didn't recognize her."

"There's more to it than a dress and some color," Stephanie informed him primly. "And she will likely resist the idea, anyway, so no teasing!" she ordered.

"All right, I get it," Parno backed down for the present. "But . . . look, I can't just let this go forever," he chuckled. "I'll give you a day or so, but then. . .well, I'll have to say something or bust!"

"You had better bust if it means spoiling all this hard work," Stephanie threatened.

"Don't forget the processional," Parno reminded her. Stephanie's eyes widened as she realized she had done just that.

"When is it?" she asked.

"Memmnon wants to do it day after tomorrow," he replied. "He'll have to be carried there, most likely, but he has to speak, at least a little."

"I don't know if he's strong enough for that," Stephanie frowned.

"He'll have to be, at least for a few hours," Parno shrugged. "He's king now. He's got to be seen and heard. This isn't some state funeral, Stephanie, this is the processional for a dead king and the coronation announcement for a new one."

"Just the announcement?"

"Yes. The actual event will be months in the planning. He's already king, the celebration is. . .well, I call it frippery. I'm not sure that's a real word," he admitted.

"He can probably make it, then," she nodded.

"Be a good place to display your protégé," he grinned.

"Parno, what I wanted to talk to you about-"

"Is it about a girl, because if it is, honestly Memmnon I just don't want to hear it," Parno said with a straight face. Memmnon faltered a bit at that, but nodded, his lips set in a thin line. Parno managed to hold his laughter for less than a half-minute before bursting.

"I'm joking, Memmnon," Parno told him, laughing. "I understand you have an eye on my archery instructor." His brother delighted him just then by blushing slightly.

"I wasn't aware she was an archery instructor," he said with what dignity he could muster.

"She might be one of three best shots in the kingdom," Parno nodded. "Certainly one of the ten, without question. And, she's cute," he grinned.

"I'm surprised you haven't already bedded her," Memmnon said stiffly and Parno's face froze for a second, anger rising until he noticed a glint in his brother's eyes.

"I had that coming," he laughed. "Not funny, but I had it coming."

"I thought it was funny," Memmnon folded his arms across his chest.

"Yeah, but you have no sense of humor," Parno waved the comment away. "And no, just so you know, I haven't. She's a fine young woman, I know that. Her father is a fine man, and he probably is the best shot in the kingdom. Might want to keep that in mind," he grinned.

"Anyway, I have a.. .an arrangement, let's say, with Lady Freeman," he said gently.

"Arrangement?" Memmnon eyebrow shot up. "What the hell does that mean?" he demanded.

"It means if I manage to survive the war, then. . .we'll probably get married," Parno shrugged. "We're a little fuzzy on the details, yet," he admitted.

"Really?" Memmnon's shock was apparent. "Married?"

"Really," his brother assured him. "Of course, I do actually have to survive the war," he reminded him.

"You will," Memmnon sounded sure. "You will."

CHAPTER TWENTY-SEVEN

-

The funeral of a king is a solemn event at any time. For a king murdered in his own bed, in time of war, it's more so.

The people of the city and from the surrounding area turned out in droves to throw rose petals at the wheels of the carriage that conveyed Tammon McLeod down Royal Avenue one last time, carrying him to once more be beside his beloved wife.

Waiting at the tomb were Parno, Memmnon, Stephanie Freeman, Edward and Edema Willows and Dhalia Nidiad accompanied by Karls Willard, a host of other nobles, and Winifred Hubel, whom Memmnon could not seem to take his eyes off of. The girl had been irritated at first, then perhaps a bit flattered. As it began to sink in that the King of Soulan was staring at her the way a grown man stared at a grown woman, she began to be nervous.

Parno ignored that by-play, remaining calm and formal for the occasion. Stephanie was by his side, which would tell all and sundry they the two of them were together in some way. Parno regretted that in some ways, but in others he was glad. Had Memmnon been taken with her rather than Winnie, then he might have actually killed his brother. That would never do, he told himself daily.

The carriage was set up for a team of ten horses, but for this event one was missing. Tammon's favorite horse followed the carriage, unsaddled, reins hooked to the back, following his master on his last ride. It was a heartbreaking sight, and for most it resulted in tears. Parno was not among them. He had not shed a tear over Tammon McLeod in a very long time and would not be a hypocrite by doing so now when it meant nothing. He was stoic, reserved, even sad, but he was not mourning. It just wasn't in him.

Eight members of Tammon's personal guard waited to carry their king to his final resting place, their armor shined so bright it gleamed. The rest of the King's Own stood arrayed in splendor, swords drawn, angled over the final stretch of road where the carriage made its way to the sepulcher.

The service was surprisingly brief, the priest speaking words that he had said countless times over his lifespan, but never like this. One did not bury a king often. Parno was surprised when it was done so quickly.

Memmnon was taken back to the palace, where he had to preside, or at least open the feast that celebrated Tammon's life and rule. He managed to do that but no more as his carefully hoarded strength gave out and he was carried off to bed.

Parno was forced to stay, as the sole remaining member of the McLeod Dynasty that was not dead or guilty of sedition, and play host. He knew nothing of being a host. He did know that Winnie was attracting far too much attention for his liking, but. . .she was rather striking and she was single. There was little he could do without betraying Memmnon's trust. He had tried to get his brother to talk to the girl, but he refused until he was healed or at least back on his feet.

He raised his glass countless times as idiots and buffoons who had scarcely known Tammon McLeod and would never be allowed to sit at his table under other circumstances raised salute after salute to their fallen king. It was tradition, and Parno honored it though he wished to be anywhere else.

And of course they all had to pay their condolences. He lost track of how many times he heard "sorry for your loss" or he replied "thank you" of "that's kind of you". He didn't feel loss, anyway. Not really. His father had never been a real father to him. He wouldn't miss him because he'd never had anything to miss. He wouldn't miss being able to ask his father something because he'd never been able to do it to start with!

As these thoughts raced through his mind, even as he continued to raise his glass and bob his head with useless thanks to useless toasts and eulogies, his anger began to rise. These people were parasites. Many of them lived from the fortunes their ancestors had made, doing nothing for themselves, their families, or the kingdom. Born into wealth by accident of birth, they served no purpose save to occupy a name or a title, and seek for more.

Parno hated them with a passion. His rage grew and grew as each one passed until suddenly his hand dropped to his sword and he decided, idly, that he'd kill the next one who offered false sympathy to him. Just cut their head clean off, right here. As a warning to the others if nothing else.

Just as a hapless potential victim was making his way down the table, Parno caught sight of a flash of black and green that drew his eye. He saw Stephanie Freeman, standing in the doorway, a black dress with green trim hugging her body. She had chosen the colors deliberately, announcing to everyone that she now had a place in the McLeod Dynasty. She walked steadily toward Parno, who stood and took her hand as she arrived by his side, raising it to his lips and kissing it lightly. He then pulled a chair out for her and helped her seat before he returned to his own place, beside her. The talk that had died down at her arrival was slow to start up again and many looked as if they wanted to say something, or at least ask something, but Parno's facial expression made it clear that would not be wise.

So no one asked anything. Or said anything. At all.

The rest of Parno's night went fairly well.

"How are you, dear boy?" Edema Willows asked as the theater came to an end.

"I'm tired," Parno admitted. "I'm glad you both could be here," he added, embracing Edema and taking Edward's hand.

"Anything for you, dear Parno," Edema smiled and Edward nodded his agreement.

"I appreciate that," Parno said, his tone one of true sincerity.

"Edema," Stephanie spoke into the silence, "since you're here, I wondered if I could get your assistance with something?"

"Of course, dear," Edema replied at once. "What can I do?" Stephanie led her away, no doubt discussing Memmnon and Winnie. Parno shook his head, fighting a grin. Wouldn't do to be seen smiling.

"I understand that you were looking after my safety not long ago," Edward said gently. Parno looked at him in puzzlement, then recalled where Edward had been.

"I appreciate that, given our. . .history," Edward continued. "I hope you know how much I regret that foul business, milord."

"Just Parno," the reply came quickly. "For the two of you it's always just Parno. And I do know it. Don't think of it again. Therron and Sherron have been machinating behind our backs for years. I'm sorry you were a victim of their treachery."

"Look, Parno," Edward spoke swiftly, as if trying to get through something. "Not to speak out of turn, but. . .if you need someone to speak to, about anything, I hope you know that I would be honored to help you any way I could. That I would be proud to be someone you believed you could depend upon."

Parno looked at him for a long moment before nodding slowly.

"I appreciate that very much Edward," he said evenly. "Thank you."

"Not at all," Edward looked relieved. "I will mingle a bit, I think, but don't hesitate to call upon me if I can do anything at all." He shook hands with Parno once more and then withdrew. Parno watched the dissipating crowd another few minutes then took the opportunity to slip away to his room. It had been a long day, and tomorrow promised to be more so.

Beaumont and Whipple stood before Parno in Memmnon's office, which he supposed would now be his as Memmnon was now King. The two men looked suitably grim.

It was the day after the funeral and the city was in mourning, though it was muted, as there was a war on. At some point there would be an official period of mourning, probably immediately before the coronation ceremony for Memmnon, but right now the war had to be fought, so essentially it was business as usual.

The matter of the Royal Twins was another one altogether.

"Alive if you can, their heads if you cannot," Parno's voice had been like iron and the two battle-hardened warriors had fought not to wince at its hardness. "This cannot go unchecked. I want every single hint of this foolishness eradicated completely. Not so much as a whimper or whisper of it left. Understand?"

They understood.

"Destroy Callens and his regiment," he ordered ruthlessly. "Take him and as many of his officers prisoner if you can, but don't risk the life of a single trooper to do so. They aren't worth it. If you have to, just kill them where they stand and then burn the bodies. Leave their heads on pikes around the cremation site as a warning to any of their friends."

"Brock's men will join you, but you are in command," Parno stressed. "They are there to lend the authority of the legal process to your actions. If you can arrest Therron and Sherron, do so and return them here in chains. The more humiliating the better, in fact," a tiny hint of hatred peeking through his business like demeanor.

"Take no chances in returning them here," he warned. "They could have help anywhere, and at any level of government. Kill anyone who gets in your way or attempts to stop you. I don't care who they are. We are at war, I am the Lord Marshal, and you are my official representatives. Interfering with your mission is grounds enough for execution and so far as I am concerned should be carried out on the spot. Remember that I want every ember of this sedition to be doused completely so that it can never be kindled again."

"Yes sir," both men replied in unison. They were seeing a new side to their Marshal here. Both men would later agree that they liked what they saw.

"You both enjoy my complete trust," he told them finally, standing. "Do whatever it takes to complete this mission and protect the Crown. Thanks to my sister's actions I was almost King of Soulan, and that alone is reason enough for me to want her dead," he grinned darkly and both men chuckled slightly.

"Take this day to make whatever preparations you need to make and then be gone when the sun rises tomorrow. Brock's men know where you are going and Callens does not. Not exactly. That may give you an edge, though they have a week on you, nearly. You will likely be too late to prevent them from reaching Therron, so hunt them down and destroy them."

"Godspeed, gentlemen." Both men came to attention.

"Thank you, Marshal," Beaumont replied for them both and Whipple nodded. The two departed, already talking out their plan between them.

Parno watched them go, then returned to the chair behind the desk, turning to look out the window behind him. The city was bathed in sunlight, banner streaming at half-mast in honor of Tammon. He could see birds flying around the window and into the courtyard below, peaceful scenes that belied the fact that the kingdom was in a state of turmoil.

So much had happened so fast. It seemed like only days since he had been at Cove, staying away from his family and trying to make a quiet life for himself and a few friends. Trying to build a small legacy for himself other than a reputation as a womanizing, brawling, drinking young prince with a chip on his shoulder. That hadn't seemed like so much work, really. At least not now it didn't.

Now he was commander of the entire army, the present Crown Prince of Soulan. How had it all changed so quickly?

Because of the greed and insanity of his twin siblings. They weren't responsible for the war of course, but they had tried to use it to their advantage there was no doubt. Their actions could have seen the fall of the kingdom to the north. Could still, he admitted reluctantly. There was no promise that he would be able to drive the invaders out, at least not soon. The Nor were proving far more resilient that he'd bothered to give them credit for.

And now all of this. He shook his head as he contemplated all that had happened in just the last two or three weeks, leaving aside the events before that. Sometimes it seemed like a blur when he looked at it in hindsight. He sighed deeply, suddenly very tired.

"Parno?" a feminine voice drew his attention and he turned to see Stephanie Freeman standing in the doorway, looking as lovely as ever. She reminded him that not everything in the last little while had been bad. Some things had been very good indeed, she chief among them.

"Yes?" he smiled, his fatigue draining away a bit.

"Would you like to go for a walk?" she asked, smiling. "It's a beautiful day. We don't have to leave the palace. In fact, I'd prefer not to, considering how volatile things still are, but the grounds are lovely."

"Yes, they are," Parno admitted, standing. He'd never paid much attention to that in the past. He had hated this place with a passion. It reminded him of years of ill treatment and bad memories were the bane of his existence. Perhaps with Stephanie he could make new memories. Good ones.

Lasting memories to keep with him always.

"I'd like that very much, I think," he smiled again, broader this time.

Taking her hand, he walked with her toward the gardens, a quartet of soldier front and back reminding him that his life had changed forever, now.

But not all changes were bad.

One week after the funeral of Tammon McLeod, Memmnon stood before the door to his brother's rooms, now apparently the permanent rooms of Doctor Freeman and one Winifred Huble. The King looked again to his dress, brushing imaginary lint and dust from his jacket and straightening a wrinkle that wasn't there, buying time. The soldiers escorting him were careful to take no note of their king's nervousness.

Finally, realizing he could put it off no longer, Memmnon used the knocker to announce his presence. Almost at once a shy young servant girl opened the door, eyes almost bugging out of her head at the sight of the King.

"M-m-m-milord?" she stammered. "How may I help you, sire?" she recovered quickly.

"I would like to see Miss Huble, please," Memmnon replied amiably. "Would you ask her if she would receive me?"

"Please come in, sire," Amelia backed out of the way, opening the door wider. Memmnon stepped inside and stifled a laugh at how feminine his brother's rooms had become in a few short weeks. Doctor Freeman had reluctantly agreed to stay on as the current Royal Physician, at least until Memmnon was completely recovered and someone suitable to take her place had been found. Parno had urged her to do so as the palace, now, was a very safe place to be. Winnie had stayed as well, though more reluctantly.

And now Memmnon was recovered enough to stand without assistance and walk unaided, save for a cane to steady him when needed. So here he was.

"I'll go and fetch her, sire," Amelia said, closing the door. She hurried away as if afraid Memmnon would chase her. He heard a startled squawk from within and soon Amelia was back, looking apologetic.

"It will be only a moment, sire," she curtsied. "Miss Huble is preparing. Would you care to sit?" she waved to the sofas. "I could summon something to eat or drink, of course."

"I'm fine, thank you," he nodded, moving to take a seat near the window. He forced himself to be patient as he gazed out the window, eyes taking in the city beyond. He had known he'd be king someday, but had thought it would be some time yet. While not unprepared, he was surprised, and was only just now adjusting to it. He missed his father. Unlike Parno, Memmnon had enjoyed a good relationship with Tammon, all in all. He missed his father's steady hand. While he had not been a good father to Parno, he had been to Memmnon, and had been a good king.

"Milord," a soft voice drew him from his thoughts and he turned to see Winifred standing in the doorway, her red hair cascading down a green blouse that was complimented by black trousers and soft leather brown boots. His eyes showed faint merriment at the dagger on her hip. There was only so much compromise she was willing to endure, it seemed.

"Miss Huble," he rose smoothly, though not perhaps as smoothly as he once would have. "You look lovely as ever," he told her, delighting in her blush.

"Thank you," she attempted a curtsy, and managed it barely. More or less.

"I was wondering if you'd care to walk in the garden with me, my lady?" Memmnon asked and her blush deepened.

"I'm no lady, sire," she said softly, though she looked directly at him.

"I beg to differ, Miss Huble," Memmnon replied at once. "You are every inch the lady and I desire your company very much if you would so honor me." He held a hand out to her tentatively. Winnie hesitated only a few seconds before accepting it. Memmnon touched his lips to the back of her hand and motioned to the door.

"Shall we, then?"

Doak Parsons looked down from his vantage point and fought not to swear, since someone might hear him. As it was his lookout was shaking his arm to point toward an approaching outrider. Parsons lifted a hand signifying that he had seen him, but kept looking, raising his glass again.

Banner after banner moved in the wind as the long column of soldiers moved south, snaking along more than one road. He had men watching them all, counting as they went. Lowering the glass once more he frowned at the insistent shaking. Acknowledging that their position was no longer tenable, he pulled back, eliciting a sigh of relief from his companion. The two slipped down the hill to their waiting horses and were soon on their way, galloping to stay well ahead of the scouts behind them.

Near dusk they met with the rest, some miles further south though still behind enemy lines. Using an abandoned barn for shelter, Parsons collected information from the others and compiled it into one report on his map. The news was bad.

At least thirty thousand Imperial troops were marching into the Tinsee Valley, on their way to join the Imperial Army threatening Soulan. At least that many because none of his men had gotten close enough to ensure there weren't more behind them. The Nor were being very careful, scouting far and wide to screen their movements from men just like him.

He examined the map for some time before making his decision. This had to get to the prince.

"We head back in the morning," he ordered. "Set a guard, two-hour watches, no fire. We'll eat good when we get home, but it's hardtack and jerky tonight, boys, or we'll have Nor heathen on us before morning."

No on argued. Parson looked at the map and his notebook once more before putting it away. He hoped his prince had a plan for this.

Because an entire new army headed their way would change everything.

THE END

To be continued in the forthcoming book,
<u>PARNO'S GAMBIT</u>

A MESSAGE FROM AUTHOR
N.C. REED

I hope you enjoyed this short story. If you did, please do me the honor of leaving a review. Reviews are like gold to a writer, and we treasure them!

For more stories, snippets of upcoming works, and exclusive content, visit my publisher's website www.creativetexts.com or visit my own webpage http://badkarma00.wordpress.com/

While you're there, don't forget to follow me on Facebook, and sign up to follow the blog page for updates on upcoming releases and additions to the original content on the blog site.

Happy Reading!

N.C. Reed

THANK YOU FOR READING!

If you enjoyed this book, we would appreciate your customer review on your book seller's website or on Goodreads.

Also, we would like for you to know that you can find more great books like this one at www.CreativeTexts.com

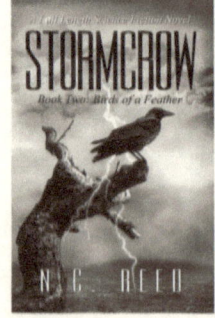

www.ingramcontent.com/pod-product-compliance
Lightning Source LLC
Chambersburg PA
CBHW020658110726
47901CB00001B/240